Sede, Seed of Eden

volume 2

Kathleen Nennemann

Unless otherwise indicated, all Scripture quotations are taken from the KJV Bible. Copyright © 1994 by Zondervan. Used by permission.

Book of Enoch. Translated from the Ethiopian by R.H. Charles, 1906. English E-text edition scanned by Joshua Williams, Northwest Nazarene College, 1995. Edited by Wolf Carnahan, 1997. Resource taken from free internet posting.

Book of Jubilee. Salt Lake City: Published by J.H. Parry & Co., 1887. Resource taken from free internet posting.

Book of Jasher. Salt Lake City: Published by J.H. Parry & Co., 1887. Resource taken from free internet posting.

Book of Cave of Treasures. Salt Lake City: Published by J.H. Parry & Co., 1887. Resource taken from free internet posting.

Book of Bee. Edited and translated by Earnest A. Wallis Budge, M.A. Oxford, the Clarendon Press, 1886. Resource taken from free internet posting.

Sede, Seed of Eden

ISBN: 978-0-692-35628-9

Library of Congress Control Number: 2014910685

Copyright © 2014

Published by Kathleen Nennemann

sedeseedofeden@outlook.com

Prepared for publishing by: Orion Productions, LLC.

PO Box 51194
Colorado Springs, CO 80949

www.orion316.tv

Editor: Daphne Parsekian

I dedicate this book to Jesus, the "Promised One" who fulfilled prophecy.

Contents

Preface

As you open the pages of Sede, Seed of Eden: Volume II, Sede beckons you:
'Come, continue the journey with me'! After reading Volume I, you discovered the world she lived in and came to love the people she loved. You've
seen great changes take place in her world. What is to come? Will Shem
be waiting for her? Is her family still alive? What kind of future awaits the
world that seems to be crumbling around her?

Sede's story began its conception during my first year in Bible College.
The class of 'Old Testament Studies' sparked a fascinating interest in ancient
Biblical history. It seemed the people who lived then, lived by amazing faith.
They overcame in the most perilous of times. History has declared them
to be our forefathers, and examples of those who lived by faith. I found
wonderful resource material on the Internet: the Book of Enoch, Book of
Jubilee, Book of Jasher, Book of Bees, The Book of the Cave of Treasures, and
most importantly: the Holy Bible. All of these ancient manuscripts and books
inspired and ignited my imagination concerning pre-flood history. I began
to ask myself questions about what life would have been like then. What was
the culture of the time? What spiritual understanding did they have? How
did God interact with them? What were the women like who looked to the
heavens for help in time of need? From these questions came the idea of a
young woman named "Sede" who would be of the family of Noah.

Writing on the book continued for the next two years until I graduated.
At that time I set it aside for a year. Looking back, I realize what I had writ-

ten so far needed time to lay dormant. My book had become as its theme…
a seed. It needed time to germinate until new inspiration came. And it came
through my sister and friends. It was my sister Renee and my friends Connie,
Cynthia, and Tom, who watered the seed with their encouragement to finish
the book. And then sunshine came from my publisher, Jenna, and editor,
Daphne, with their rays of professional support that encouraged the seed to
take root. Without the love and support of all these people, the seed of this
book would have never bloomed.

There are several themes I developed within the story. The main theme
is the seed. As you read you will discover it has several meanings. A seed goes
through many stages before it becomes what it is intended to be. Another
theme is the parallel worlds of 'innocence' and 'corruption'. I attempted to
describe both the subtle and overt evil in which mankind had fallen, as well as
the dark powers that directly influenced them. For the more sensitive reader,
I encourage you to keep in mind that the description of the corrupt world and
the behavior of fallen mankind were written to bring you to the conclusion
that the days in which Noah lived were so wicked and corrupt, that God had
to judge the world in order to save mankind. And last of all, is the underly-
ing theme of endearing love. All love is tested, and in the testing, love has a
choice. As you read Volume II, you will see love's choice unfold.

It is my hope you enjoy Volume II of Sede, Seed of Eden. I was both
inspired and blessed to write it; and it is my hope you will be inspired and
blessed as you read it.

Chapter 1

Sede's Comfort

The forest was quiet; not a song of bird or rustle of leaf. All that could be heard was the sound of Sede's breathing and soft footsteps as she walked the path before her. The deer trail wound and turned, leading higher into the mountain wilderness. There she would find the answers her heart yearned for. She clutched Eden's seed to her chest while tears blurred her vision. She stumbled, but pulling herself up, pressed forward. Playtheus was gone and she would never see him again. Oh, to never again hear the sound of his voice or the touch of his hand; never to see the softness in his eyes as they searched hers. Pain pierced her heart at the thought. She longed to smell the scent of his fragrant oil. Inhaling, she could almost smell it, only to stumble on her feet from the hot tears that filled her eyes. Holding her hands to her face she slumped to the ground and wept, emotions of loss overwhelming her.

Her turmoil was unbearable. She had watched Playtheus die before her very eyes from the spear that was intended for her. She had witnessed his body lie lifeless upon the ceremonial altar and sang her people's "Love Song for the Dead". Ba-nea had breathed a prayer in her ear at their parting. Now she was alone in the forest. She knew that she could never return to her village until she found her heart once more, and peace within.

She exhaled and stood, forcing herself to move on. Her head was pounding with grief and she tried to clear her mind. It was getting dark and she knew she must find a place to rest for the night. A twig snapped and she darted a quick glance in its direction. To her relief it wasn't danger. There, not a stone's throw away, was a small cave. 'Yahweh has prepared a place for me,' she thought. She paused and closed her eyes, listening to the forest. All her senses honed in to hear, making the forest sounds come alive. The wind gently swayed the trees above her, calming her in a strange but loving way. The soft sound of a running brook was nearby. The evening call of the turtledove echoed from far away. With an exhale she knew she needed to kindle a fire and began to silently gather wood. Suddenly, she burst into tears once more, pain and sorrow rising again and beating on her tender heart. She cried and cried, crying until the fatigue of weeping drained her. She curled up next to the fire and fell asleep, wrapped safely in Ba-nea's cloak.

The rest that came relieved the exhaustion that had overwhelmed her. When she woke early the next morning she resolved to press higher up the mountain. Something was calling her to go higher and higher. After climbing for several hours, she found a vantage point that overlooked the vast lands in the distance. Far, far below was her village and the river as it ran to the south. Mighty herds that looked like specks of dust moved as they searched for grazing pastures. If only she could see her life from a vantage point like this. Oh, how good that would be.

Searching the forest floor, she found a long, narrow branch of the petra tree. Its wood was smooth as stone and just as hard. She was thankful that when it broke from the tree it had left a sharp point. She now had a hunting weapon.

After spearing a small dworta she prepared a fire. As she watched the flames a pleasure rose within her. She sensed the forest world around her—this world of the hunt, a place she understood. The wind swaying in the trees, water rippling over smooth stones in a brook nearby, the snap and pop of the fire—they all spoke the language she knew. The dworta satisfied and renewed her strength, and lying down once more by her fire, she fell into restful sleep.

For the next two weeks she hunted and rested. And as each day passed, she felt restored in spirit. She allowed herself to remember Playtheus, not fighting the love she felt for him. Their memories together were her comfort as she lay before the fire each night. She could almost hear his voice as she recalled their conversations, in both laughter and tears. She wasn't sure if her mind was playing tricks on her, but she could almost feel his arms around her, holding her. Always her prayers at night were the same: that Yahweh would help her find a resting place in her heart for all that had happened.

She found Playtheus' pearl box she had slipped into her pocket the day she stood at his ceremonial altar. Curiously she also found a secret pocket sewn inside the cloak Ba-nea had given her. Pulling a thread the seam unraveled, revealing a small, folded parchment. On the wrapping was written: 'Do not open until Yahweh bids you so.' She thought of Ba-nea and knew she had purposely given her the cloak with this message inside. As she considered this strange find, she put it back in the cloak, rethreading the seam. Tenderly smiling she spoke to herself: "Yes Ba-nea, I will wait until Yahweh bids me so."

Holding the pearl box to her chest she pondered the love that had made it. Somehow holding it made her feel close to him. Her deepest regret was that she never told Playtheus she loved him while he was alive. It would have meant everything to him. Her only comfort was in knowing he had loved her with a selfless love—a love that was willing to let her go -- and a love that was willing to die for her. Being with her had changed him. But being with him had changed her too. Her father had told her that her heart was capable of greater love than she knew. How true those words had become. By Playtheus' example of selfless abandonment, her heart had grown in its ability to know greater love. She wondered, if they had traded places, could she have let him go? Would she have had the strength of conviction she saw in him?

As she continued to spend quiet days in the forest she found pleasure in new discoveries. When she reached the snow line of the mountain, she found new and strange tracks and hunted game she had never seen before. She mused: 'surely Yahweh is glorious to have so many new and undiscovered creatures in the world.'

She found a cave that had strange yellow rocks. They glistened with brilliant light from her torch as she searched within. Was this the gold that

Playtheus said the slaves of Atlantis mined? If they were here, it would be no work at all to gather the abundant rocks that lie about the cave walls.

One day she came across the delicate gaymett giving birth beneath a sheltered tree. She watched in wonder as new life came forth and marveled as the mother cleaned the newborn with her tongue and then gently nudged it to nurse while standing on wobbly legs. Yahweh had put this nurturing instinct within this creature. She knew that someday she would give birth to her own little one, and this same natural instinct of love and care would be in her.

She made tools of bone and stone, smoothing and softening the leather animal skins from her hunts. They would make a new hunting skin for her. Crushed berket berries made the paint she used to write the symbol of Sethite on the front. The robe she had worn the day of Playtheus' ceremony had worn thin; only the cloak remained as if it were new. It was woven of strange threads and showed no wear. At times she felt it held a power she didn't understand, but always it made her feel safe when she wrapped herself inside.

One night as she slept she dreamed of being on a hunt with Shem. They had circled their prey and she waited for his signal. She crouched in the grass and waited...waiting for what seemed a long time. Then unexpectedly he stood and called to her, "Come to me. Come to me, Sede." In her dream she rose and walked toward him through the waist-high grass. She had no thought for the herd around them, only that she wanted to come to him. When she drew near, a blanket was spread before him on the ground, and a beautiful banquet awaited. Extending his hand, he said, "Come to me. Come to me, Sede." She felt her heart burst with love for him as she took his outstretched hand. They sat together, feasting, and feeling great happiness. Even the docile herd seemed to enjoy their presence, lowing as they grazed nearby.

When she woke in the morning, Shem was her first thought. And from that day on, her thoughts were of him. What had it been like for him while she was gone? His heart was certainly broken in her absence. She had thought of him every night when she had been at Playtheus'. Had he thought of her every night? Was he well? Had he looked for her? Or worse yet, had he been captured and was now a servant or slave?

As the weeks had turned into months, she knew she must return to him. Yahweh would somehow make a way to set her heart right with his. She knew she had to share what had happened. Love's true bond holds no secrets, and she did truly love him. Her dream had an interpretation. It would prove true. He was calling her home—home to him. The feasting would be the good things in life they would experience together. He had been waiting for her... waiting for her to come home!

She smiled as the sun rose in the eastern sky. "This is the day of my return. This is the day I will see the face of my husband!" She turned south, knowing her village was but a day's journey.

When she began her descent, she heard Yahweh on the breeze. "Do not go to the village, child. Follow the hawk!" Just then she heard the call of a hawk overhead. Cupping her hands to her forehead she watched as he circled and flew east. Excitedly, she followed the hawk's lead as he rested in distant branches while she closed the distance between them. Farther and farther through the forest she was led.

And then, to her utter amazement, she saw something in the valley below—a sight she would never have imagined to be in a forest—a gigantic ship! It was magnificent. Nearly finished, the men working on it looked like ants compared to its size. Cautiously, she made her descent, amazed how much bigger it looked close up. As she stepped from behind a tree, she saw him. It was Shem, climbing a rope on a vertical beam.

He caught sight of her and yelled out a thrilling shout. "Sede. Sede!" Sliding down the rope, he came running and stumbling over his feet. When he reached her, he couldn't help himself; he scooped her up in his arms and threw his head back, laughing with great joy as he whirled her around. The others stopped their work and climbed down, running to greet her. The women, too, hearing the excitement, ran to see what was happening. It was joy unspeakable as each took their turn embracing her.

Tolmaka burst into tears as he held her, not wanting to let go. "Oh, my child. You're home at last!" She squealed like a little girl as he whirled her around.

Shoda playfully grabbed her by the back of neck and shook her head. "Where have you been? I've missed you. Don't do that again, okay?"

Sede couldn't help herself. She grabbed her and began to cry. "Oh, Shoda. I'm finally back. Back with my people."

For the rest of the day Shem shared with her what had transpired from the time their village had been burned and she had been taken. Their whole Sethite world had changed, and now only six families held true to Seth's teachings. All the people in Taasa-toka had forsaken Yahweh and were now living a life of corruption as Cainites. She cried in horror for her people. How could this be? Her cousins, friends, the elders, and the children—all those who had survived the raid had forsaken Yahweh? It grieved her to the depth of her soul.

"What is to become of them, Shem?"

"We return to the village once a week and preach to them. We try to convince them to turn from their wickedness and return to the ways of Seth. Each week we come back in mockery, shame, and reproach. Father says they are a stiff-necked people. I agree, for we have pleaded with them over and over, warning them of Yahweh's coming judgment. When elders from other villages visit Taasa-toka, they, too, mock us and say, 'Why are you building a ship in the middle of land? We think you're mad. We no longer want you for our leader. We have our own leaders now. They are the Cainites, our brothers. Our new gods are greater than Yahweh. The Cainite gods give us both pleasure and pain!'"

Sede cried, knowing the elders had said such things, and that Noah had been rejected and mocked. Her father and Gruetat were elders too and worthy of honor and respect, as were Dollo and Noah's sons.

He told her of Sethites raiding each other's villages and robbing those who innocently traveled through their lands. They had intermarried with the

Cainites, corrupting the seed line of Seth so it was no longer pure. The new births at Taasa-toka showed signs of Nephilim inbreeding. Their children had elongated heads and six digits on hand and foot. Few babies survived for they were sacrificed to the gods. They followed the dark knowledge of the "fallen ones." The sacred altar Seth had built was desecrated by the blood of their children. Shem could no longer see a distinction between Sethite and Cainite; they had become one people.

Sede felt so overwhelmed. Their families, their culture, their whole way of life…was gone. It had come to pass as the Watcher had said—'A great evil was coming to their villages'—and now she knew what that evil was. Shem held her, knowing her great disbelief and sorrow for he, too, had found it hard to accept the change that ravaged their kin. Their whole world had been turned upside down by Nersha's raid. Their lives would never be the same.

"What is to become of us? Will they try to corrupt us? Or steal from us?" she asked in fear.

"No, Sede. When people from the village try to come here, they get lost in the forest. Yahweh has put a veil of protection over this place, they cannot see it with the eyes of their flesh. It is just as the Watcher had told us when we were in the Cave of Treasures. Their eyes have a veil over them, and they cannot see what Yahweh is doing here. We are convinced more than ever, that Yahweh's judgment will come, and destroy the world with a flood. This ark will save those who believe Father's message."

The new village they had built was small with only six huts. Life had begun anew.

That evening Ne-el and Adat played their flute and drum, and the air was filled with the sound of celebration. Sede's return had brought joy to all their hearts and a reason to celebrate. The men and women clapped with the drum beat while Sede, Shoda, and Zilla danced the "Dance of the Maidens" although they were maidens no more. Zilla and Dollo had married while Sede had been away, and the only maidens left were playing the instruments. It was a great delight to see the three young brides wear the ceremonial robes, swaying and turning with flowing ribbons in hand. They all felt that somehow they were now complete with Sede's return. The little village settled into the calm of night and each family stopped to bid her good night, rejoicing again that she had returned.

Tolmaka kissed her on her forehead. "My little one is back...I can now sleep in peace." Smiling up at him, she saw his wonderful love for her, and it warmed her heart. She was home....

Shem held her in his arms as they watched the slow-burning flames. All was now calm. He sat quietly, just loving the touch of her skin, the smell of her hair, and the rise and fall of her chest as she breathed. He felt his love for her well up within. "Sede, you're really here. Oh, how I've missed you!"

Squeezing her gently, he lovingly kissed her neck. "Tell me of your time away and all that has happened to you. I long to know how you lived and how you made your way back to me."

Turning to face him, she looked into his eyes, searching them. She saw the same softness she had seen the night of their wedding. That seemed so very long ago. Why trouble the closeness they were both feeling? She knew Yahweh would give her the right time and the right words to share with him. "Oh, Shem, how do I tell you all that has happened? I want to forget for tonight and think only of us and how we will begin again."

Cupping her face in his hands he kissed her tenderly. It was a kiss of a man for a woman. She looked at him in surprise. Through his kiss he had communicated his desire for her and she felt herself respond. Slowly, she stroked his face, looking into his eyes. She leaned forward and warmly kissed him back. He, too, felt himself respond to her. They both looked at each other and said at the same time, "Wow!"

Then a small smile rose from the corner of her mouth. "Yes, we'll begin again," she said. She considered the surrounding huts and the peacefulness of the village. "We'll begin again, just like this place we now call home."

With a broad smile he rose and scooped her up in his strong arms. "Come, Wife. Let me take you home!"

Sede's Comfort

How good those words sounded—their home.

Inside Shem lit a small oil lamp, and the soft yellow glow gave the hut a warm and comfortable feeling. "This is nice," she said as she looked around the room.

"Yes, Sede, I've had this prepared for a long time, anticipating your return."

The glow of the lamp reflected off the soft furs that covered a large cot. She could see where he had lain, the shape of his body still there. Hanging over the bed was their three-stranded cord. Her heart leapt to see it. It was the symbol of their unity. Enoch's scrolls were piled neatly on a low table with two small lamps on each side, and dried folendia hung from a wooden peg by an open window. How had he known they were her favorite flower? She had only mentioned it once when they were coming back from a hunt, yet he had remembered.

Red embers glowed from the hearth at the end of the hut. The bow she had lost the night she was captured hung above the hearth next to his spear. Something was carved into the beam. Stepping closer, she read: "To everything there is a season and a time to every purpose under heaven." Tears filled her eyes as she realized he had spent his nights here thinking of her. Everything in this room was a reflection of her.

He could see the glisten of her tears in the flickering fire light and softly said, "Sede, I knew you would return. Yahweh had given you a promise. It would come to pass in the right time and season. Our lives do have a purpose. The faith of the others believed too that Yahweh would someday bring you back." Leaning forward, he whispered, "And I am so glad He did!" She saw again the tenderness in his eyes, and it brought her loving comfort. She had been alone in the mountains for a long time, at times feeling very lonely. Now she would feel lonely no more.

"Come, Sede, I wish to give you something." Kneeling on the furs, he reached beneath them and presented a beautiful wooden box. It was intricately carved with her name on the lid, and it had many small symbols she recognized that were etched on the sides. She turned the box to read each one: love, joy, peace, patience, faithfulness, goodness, gentleness, meekness, self-control.

"Oh Shem, this is beautiful!"

"I made it during the long wait for your return. As I carved each symbol, I thought of your innocent virtues. You have them all, you know."

She looked at him in surprise. When had he discovered these things about her? He spoke with such loving confidence. He knew who she really was. Playtheus had *sensed* her virtues, but Shem had *known* them. She slowly opened the box and saw the fine fur of the glendak: pale blue, velvety soft, and very rare. As she removed the fur, she slowly unfolded the edges. There in the center of the fur, she saw it: her seed from the Garden of Eden.

"My seed!" Throwing her arms around his neck, she breathed, "Thank you. Oh, thank you. I wondered if you had found it and if I would ever see it again!" She looked down to see it resting in her palm and then brought it to her ear. "Yes…the sound of heaven. I remember!"

Shem watched as she enjoyed her reunion with her precious possession. He savored her every expression: the sparkle in her eyes, the light of surprise on her face, and the deep emotion of thanksgiving. "Sede, you and I are the only two people in the world who know of this seed. It is our treasure!"

She leaned against his chest and sighed, connecting to the love she felt for him, "Yes, Shem, our treasure. Just as this is a seed of promise, I am *your* seed of promise. Together, you and I will bring forth the child that will be in the lineage of the 'Promised One' to come. I look forward to the day when we will look into the eyes of our son and know…he is the one to carry on the promise." They held each other in their special moment created just for them by Yahweh. (For every good and perfect gift comes down from the Father of Lights. And Yahweh had given them this perfect night.)

Sede carefully wrapped the seed in the velvety fur and returned it to the box. As she brushed her fingers across her name, she pondered the beautiful thing he had done for her. This box and all that surrounded her in the hut reflected a quiet yet strong love he had for her. She leaned forward and kissed him warmly; the soft glow from the light reflected the love in her eyes. He stood and extended his hand to help her up. Slowly, he began to untie her skins. She watched his face as they gently fell to the floor. There she stood before him in all her beauty, his eyes reflecting the glory he saw. His warm breath touched her shoulder before his kiss fell upon her skin. A thrill swept through her. She hadn't felt like this since their wedding night.

He kissed her shoulder once more, lifting her hair to kiss her back. And then he saw them—the welted scars. He let out a cry. "Oh, Sede, what happened to you?!" He touched them, not believing what he saw. He bent to kiss them, weeping as his lips touched her skin. She felt his tears on her back, and the sting of tears was in her own eyes remembering how Playtheus had wept over her wounds. "Oh Sede, I was not there for you...to protect you. I was not there for you!"

She could hear his pain, wanting to sooth him. "There, there, Shem," she tenderly said as she turned to face him. She lovingly stroked his head as he wept on her shoulder. "They no longer hurt and are but reminders of the wickedness that exists in this world. In time I will tell you all that has happened to me, but tonight, let us love one another as we did on our wedding night in that beautiful tent Father made for us. Remember?"

She smiled at him, breaking his sorrow. Shyly, she pulled his hand to lie upon the furs. As he held her, she felt the warmth of his body next to hers, and felt his love communicated in his gentle touch. She had thought about their wedding night and their time "set apart" during those many months she had been in the forest, rehearsing in her mind the sweet and precious moments they had shared. Here she was with him again, sharing precious intimacy once more. Now again, she was in the arms of love. She was in the arms of her husband....

That night Sede dreamed. Playtheus had found a peaceful resting place within her heart. He was there, sleeping on the soft grassy ridge that overlooked the "heart of the world" deep within the cave he had shown her.

Beauty surrounded him everywhere. She would always remember him there in that place he had dreamed of.

Then, in her dream, she saw Shem. He was beside her, reclined on the blanket and nestled in the tall grass. A banquet was spread before them just as she had seen in her other dream, when she was in the forest. To her delight, he began to offer her the food that was set before them. He seemed to know just the things she wanted to eat. She knew while she was dreaming that he would always know what she needed and be able to provide it. She had found peace in her heart. She had known the love of two men: one who had died for her…and the other who lived for her. She would begin anew, just as their recovering village had done. She had prayed each night while she had been in the wilderness, and Yahweh had answered her prayer. She had found a peaceful resting place for all she had experienced.

Chapter 2

Atlantis Recovers

Atlantis reeled with the death of Playtheus. The supply of the "innocent" had stopped for only he held the secret knowledge to supply the Renown with the innocence and virtues of mankind. He had developed an intricate system of supply and distribution that ran smoothly and peaceably, but now that system had crumbled, and his knowledge had been lost. Soon the Zodiac year would end, and the Renown would feel the craving to have the innocence from the children renewed within them.

Talimus-qua-tam chose three of his sons to propagate the secret knowledge of the "innocent"; there was no time to groom just one as he had Playtheus. He chose his Renown sons: Croas, Pa-lum and Tra-sus. They were similar to Playtheus: regal, beautiful, and strong. They were born of Ma-get, one of Talimus-qua-tam's concubines. These three did not possess Playtheus' greatness. They were undisciplined in their thirst for the "innocent,'" and their one and only ambition was to be appointed a "Mighty One" as their half-brother had been. They competed against one another with fierce jealousy; each wanting to be recognized as supreme before the face of their father. They behaved admirably when they were in his presence, but away from him, they were arrogant, manipulative, and devious.

Many months passed before any sense of calm was restored to their world. A Nephilim left without his source of innocence is a most dangerous being, and much violence was experienced in Atlantis during this transition time. The attempt to withdraw the innocence of man led to chaos. Many,

many Sethites died as well as Nephilim. They had turned on each other to devour the human innocence held within them. A culture of beauty and peace had been turned into a feverish nightmare of the "thirsty" lusting to be satisfied. Playtheus had experienced this same fevered thirst when he had surrendered his "innocent" to Toleshba, but this was magnified. This was a "race" of Nephilim that crazed to be satisfied.

On one occasion, the Renown of Champion Hall rallied to raid Playtheus' mansion in the country. They had heard where he bred children for their innocence, and descended on them with the intent of withdrawing their innocence. The children died from their ravishing lust for innocence, and even the "innocent" within the womb were destroyed, killing both baby and mother. After this frenzied attack, it was decided among the 200 that Talimus-qua-tam should appoint a successor to Playtheus.

This was when he chose his three sons to possess and guard the dark knowledge of the "innocent." They would supervise the supply and distribution to the Renown. Pa-lum was to oversee the harvesting of the Sethites from their villages and bring them to market. He savored the ability to scout out prospects of interest for himself. On many occasions, he withheld the "innocent" through his own greed and coveted them for himself instead of providing them to his fellow Renown.

Croas was in charge of the smooth operation of the market. He supervised the Renown, providing them with the innocent virtues of their choosing. Croas relished his appointment. He had the first pick of any innocent virtue he fancied and discarded them when he tired of them. Always he looked for the next best virtue.

And Tra-sus—he alone had the room at Champion Hall. Playtheus' name had been removed, and his now glistened in its place. Behind this door, he facilitated the transfer of virtue and innocence to the Renown. He enjoyed the vulnerability that he controlled. At their most vulnerable moment, he could see within their souls, discovering their hidden secrets and weaknesses. Their memories played out before him, revealing everything to his devious gaze. He had this inside knowledge and used it to his own benefit. Playtheus, in his greatness, never passed this line of respect with his fellow Renown. It was this aspect of his character that made him great and why the 200 had wanted him declared a "Mighty One." He had proven himself trustworthy.

Through the course of time, the three sons established a smooth-running system that restored Atlantis' stability and greatness, but Talimus-qua-tam knew his sons would never be appointed "Mighty Ones." He knew their hearts. They were undisciplined, and their jealousy was evident. They had hated Playtheus because he truly *was* a great Renown, and they were not. With his foresight, he knew they would never be the son Playtheus had been. Still, he was their father, and he himself desired recognition among the 200. So he tolerated his sons and tried to mentor them.

Ma-get was thrilled that her sons now had influence. Through mere association with them she would receive glory. She was jealous of Ba-nea and perceived the mysterious power she had over Talimus-qua-tam. They shared a special bond—a bond she did not have with him. She also knew Playtheus was his favored child. With him dead, she saw the promotion of her sons as the opportunity to win his favor and replace Ba-nea as queen. She would become his high companion. Ma-get was a witch indeed, for she practiced the art of manipulation, and this was her opportunity.

Her first manipulation began when she assisted her sons to prosper in their new appointments of rendering the "innocent" to the Renown. She used her power of divination to grant them favor in all they set their hands to. They prospered on every turn and began to receive recognition for their work from the 200. In turn, they shared information with her concerning the Renown: which "innocents" they possessed, how many, and the secrets Tra-sus discovered during their vulnerable moment of transference.

It was at this time that she began to develop a plan. This plan would ex-alt her sons and herself. The New Year was approaching, bringing with it the "Ceremony to the Gods." Each year one "innocent" was sacrificed to honor the 200. This would be the event she would use to see her plan succeed. She had made it her quest to find a worthy and rare "innocent." Through the secrets her sons had discovered, she learned of a rare "innocent" that possessed "Tella-la-no-ah." This "innocent" had been, of all people, the high companion of Playtheus. She had never seen her but heard many accounts of her beauty, the brilliance of her innocence, and the great power she had over Playtheus. To be an "innocent" that possessed power over a Renown would be a rare "innocent" indeed. She had only a few months to try to find her. She set her heart on this one thing: She and her sons would deliver a "Tella-la-no-ah" for this year's sacrifice!

She began her search using Pa-lum to scout the Sethite villages with his intricate network of spies and work force. His generals were organized in the known Sethite regions, having captains that reported to them and each captain having spies that fed them information. Through this network, they learned that this unique Sethite was from a wilderness village in the Estoloph region. The search focused there. Many of the villages had been destroyed by raiding Hagonoths and no longer existed. But they would search even them. Rumors of this Sethite maiden spread abroad, and every spy wanted to be the one to discover her. Pa-lum himself traveled to the wilderness to supervise the search.

One day his generals informed him they had located her village. It was Taasa-toka, and it had been burned by raiders. When he arrived, he found the village rebuilt. The newly appointed elders greeted him, honoring him as a Regal Renown from the famed city of Atlantis, and offered sacrifices in his name on the altar of Seth. At the council meeting, he learned that Sede-quete had indeed come from their village but had been kidnapped by Nersha. She was the mighty warrior who had led the raid on their village. Sede-quete and Nersha had disappeared with Playtheus and a witch. With the witch's magic, they watched them dissolve into mist and fly through the sky. Pa-lum reasoned that Playtheus must have returned to Atlantis with her. With this news, he returned home to inform his mother.

Ma-get then called Tra-sus to Horizon's Gate, where they met at her private mansion. She questioned him for information he might have from his vulnerable Renown's. Where had Sede-quete gone after Playtheus had whisked her away to Atlantis? Tra-sus remembered transferring an "innocent" to Castius and saw his memory of Playtheus' ceremony as a "Mighty One." Sede-quete was there, where she exalted her power by joining it to Playtheus'. Their orb was glorious for all to see. Nersha had murdered Playtheus that night, and Sede-quete had left with Talimus-qua-tam and Ba-nea. After that, Castius knew nothing about her whereabouts. From this information, Ma-get concluded that she was still alive, and Ba-nea knew where she was.

Through her manipulations, Ma-get planned a grand social luncheon for all of Talimus-qua-tam's concubines and the royal queen. This would be the perfect environment to use her craft and glean information from Ba-nea. She would host the event at her private mansion, and began preparations. Exotic food was prepared and musicians summoned. Through her witchcraft, she divined unique gifts for each concubine, discerning what would rapture their hearts. It would be their favor she would win by this manipulation. She knew they all shared a common bond: they had given Talimus-qua-tam Renown sons. Under the disguise of a social gathering, her true motives would not be easily detected. She would learn of Sede-quete's location by catching Ba-nea off guard and waiting for the perfect moment to withdraw the information.

On the set day, the concubines arrived in their finery. Ba-nea looked stunning in her elegant regal gown. Among all of them, her "Tella-la-no-ah" set her apart in beauty and mysterious innocence—innocence the other women no longer possessed. The socializing was pleasant, and Ma-get sensed her moment to approach Ba-nea. "Thank you for coming, Ba-nea. It is refreshing to be in your presence. Your 'Tella-la-no-ah' excites something in me that I've long forgotten. But enough of me, tell me of you. How have you been since the loss of your son?"

Ba-nea cringed with her words. Her son's death was still near her heart, and she wasn't about to discuss it with Ma-get. She knew her manipulative heart and wondered what she really wanted.

And here it came.... "Whatever became of that sweet high companion of his? Was she given to another Renown, or did she retreat to the wilderness, bearing her loss in solitude?"

Ba-nea knew she was fishing for information and wondered why she would be interested in Sede. She would tell her nothing, giving her only vague information. "Yes, his queen left to a forest retreat where she presumably abides in seclusion. I'm unfamiliar with the location. I haven't heard from her since the day she left. And how are your sons doing with their new appointment as guardians of dark knowledge?" she asked as she purposely tried to divert the conversation.

Ma-get was flattered by Ba-nea's inquiry and took the opportunity to boast of her sons. "They're doing magnificently." The tone in her voice reflected the pride she felt as she gloated. "They have received acclaim from the Mighty 200 and have restored Atlantis to its greatness. What would Atlantis do without my sons?"

Ba-nea smiled and flatly said, "Isn't it interesting that it takes three Renown to do the job one had done?" Her remark was like a slap in the face and well deserved. Ma-get cared little that Ba-nea's beloved son was dead but was secretly glad her bumbling sons had gained his position. Ma-get struggled to compose herself.

Knowing she needed to regain supremacy, she clapped her hands for her servants. Quickly, servants appeared, carrying beautifully wrapped gifts on silver trays. Graciously, they made their way through the crowd of women, extending the trays. Each woman knew which gift to choose, for it was Ma-get's magic that drew them to their gift.

When the servant extended the silver tray to Ba-nea, she knew which one to choose. It was small and round and beautifully wrapped. Unfolding the sparkling fabric, she held the object in her hand. There in her palm was a medallion. Tears filled her eyes as she beheld it. It nearly took her breath away for the emotions it evoked. Engraved in the medallion was the emblem for the Sethites. She brought it to her lips while tears fell from her closed eyes. It blessed her and yet it broke her heart, all at the same time. It was though it were a double-edged sword. Oh, to hold something that reminded her of her past, but then to have Ma-get divine that this would mean something to her; it was so intimately intrusive.

Just then Talimus-qua-tam appeared in their midst. A sigh echoed throughout the room as all eyes fell upon his beauty. He glowed with a dazzling blue light that the women eagerly absorbed. Exhaling with pleasure, they themselves began to glow with the satisfaction they felt.

The music changed to a romantic melody that stirred their hearts. As if moved by magic, they formed three circles around him—rings of 10, 20, and 30. Ba-nea took one step forward from the inner circle, apart from the others. The circles began to slowly move in different directions with their graceful dance. Their delicate feet stepped in unison while their shoulders swayed to the waving of their arms and hands. Every concubine moved with synchronized precision to the warm, romantic music. It was magic indeed.

Talimus-qua-tam glowed as he watched. This was the world he had created for himself: beautiful women who adored and worshipped him. Through them, he had gotten the family his rebellious heart had desired. They had given him Renown sons that reflected his glory, as Adam and his children reflected Yahweh's. He had become a god. These women were his and his alone. He had carefully chosen every one of them. As they danced, they released their warm breath and uttered a unanimous "umm." Their growing desire for him was evident.

They began humming the haunting romantic melody and then gave way to singing the words they instantly knew but had never learned. While the circles moved with their dancing, they harmonized with perfection. Talimus-qua-tam stood in their midst and radiated the pleasure of their worship.

We see your beauty, we know your love
You wooed us with your dark power
On that fateful day you captured our hearts
And inhaled our essence as from a flower

We tremble to give you your heart's desire
Draw close to us we pray;
Partake of our sweet essence
And draw until the dark of day

Our innocence is yours, our bodies too
We bore you sons from your seed;
We surrender and worship you
Give us the pleasure of your deed

Ah, ah, give us your pleasure
Give us the pleasure of your deed
Ah, ah, give us your pleasure
Give us the pleasure of your deed

The air was electrified with their desire for him. As he absorbed the energy they were releasing to him, his light intensified and turned from blue to flaming red. He was responding to their desire. The women began to sigh with growing passion and eagerly absorbed his flaming light. Slowly, he began to turn. As he leaned forward, he inhaled, drawing their fevered desire from within them. Similar to what Polisha had done at Champion Hall, he drew their silver strings of desire, forming one single strand that he deeply inhaled. He closed his eyes to savor what he now held within. A deep hum of power began to rhythmically pulsate with the flaming light he was emitting. The women, with heightened eagerness, absorbed more and more of his light. The flame in their eyes reflected their escalating pleasure.

Only Ba-nea had not responded to his light but kept her heart veiled, watching as the women became spellbound by his alluring magic. He stepped toward her and drew her to himself. He sensed her power. She began to glow with brilliant white light while the blue tattoo on her forehead glistened with flecks of light. As his red light intermingled with hers, it formed a pastel pink orb over their heads. The electrified union was felt by everyone in the room. Every woman's envy was what they saw. Drawing but a breath from her lips, he whispered, "Of all the beauty that surrounds me in this place, you alone are the most mysterious in alluring power. It's your innocence that you purposely veil from me." He threw his cape around the both of them, and they exploded with a burst of red light and disappeared.

As the light exploded, he released to his concubines the full impact of his pleasure. This supernatural pleasure far outweighed what any physical experience could give. They collapsed on the floor, their chests rising and falling as their bodies glowed with soft red light. They savored his pleasure and took several minutes to recover. Gradually, they stood to their feet and gained their composure. Ma-get trembled from what she felt. Her heart pounded wildly, wanting more. If only she was with him at this moment. What dark pleasure would she be savoring? He had chosen Ba-nea, but oh, how she wished he'd chosen her. This made her even more determined to find a way to be named his queen.

She focused on her plan once more. Through her conversation with Ba-nea, she had discovered that Sede-quete still lived and that she was somewhere in the wilderness. After much thought, she instructed Pa-lum to appoint sentries at the entrance of all the major cities. Her son had manpower at his disposal, and these soldiers were eager to please him. By her request, he brought his captains to Playtheus' mansion. There, she revealed Sede-quete's likeness from the mural on the corridor wall. They would be able to recognize her and put a face to this woman of mystery. Ma-get knew that she would eventually surface, needing supplies to survive in the wilderness. Her spies would be waiting, and then she would be hers!

Chapter 3

Preparations

When Sede opened her eyes, there he was, just as he had been the morning after their wedding. His eyes were closed in sleep and breathing softly. He looked so handsome and strong. She blushed as she remembered last night. She wondered if there would be a time when she would get used to intimacy. In her heart, she hoped she never would. She loved the newness of what was happening to her and the discovery of this wonderful thing called marriage.

He stirred and a small smile rose on his lips as he opened his eyes. "Good morning, wife." he warmly whispered. He slowly stretched his arms and yawned. Then, as if he had a sudden thought, he playfully grabbed her and rolled them both over, kissing her as they rolled. Then, rolling again, he kissed her once more. "I said, good morning, wife!"

"Good morning, husband," she giggled. They both laughed and kissed again.

He settled back on the furs, pausing to think. "Wow, wasn't last night wonderful?"

"Umm, yes…wonderful," she mused as she settled in his arms. She blushed once more.

As if thinking out loud, he sighed, "I hope it will always be this way between us…fresh and new."

She leaned forward to kiss him and breathed a soft, "I wish this too." The look in his eyes was so warm and soft. (Shem was a strong man and capable in every way, but he, too, possessed an innocent soul. Both of them were "the innocent" on the wonderful journey called "marriage".)

Their quiet was interrupted by the sound of hammer and saw. "The others must be already up and working," he said with a smile. "Let's get dressed. I have so much to show you!"

They searched through the furs looking for their skins, laughing because the bedding had been so messed up. When she stepped from the hut, she was taken aback. There was the ark! Noah and the men were already busy climbing the ropes to reach the scaffolds and seemed dwarfed in comparison to the great side of the vessel. It had been dark when Shem had carried her to their hut, and the ark was no longer visible. Somehow through the night she had forgotten about it being there. But now the reality of its enormous size was right before her. "Wow!" she said in unbelief. "This is amazing, Shem!"

Throughout that day and the days that followed, Shem gradually explained the transition they had made to their new lives in the forest and the building of the ark. Noah had chosen this site because of the type of wood in the area. Yahweh had given him specific instructions concerning what kind of wood to use, its dimensions, and the interior design. It was a tremendous undertaking. The valley seemed huge from the clearing of the trees, creating an open plain around the ark.

At first, they had the help of their kin. This was when they had returned to Taasa-toka after Nersha's raid. The men had rebuilt the village and eagerly helped Noah with the ark. They had believed the word of the Lord. They labored many, many months constructing the framework and then the bulwark. Some had gone a great distance to haul and carve the counterweight stones that would steady the ark from the violent waves that would surely come. It was only when the Cainites began infiltrating their village that the men of Taasa-toka abandoned Noah and the work on the ark. They forsook Yahweh and His ways and chose instead to follow the gods of the Cainites.

But the women helped, bringing pitch, hammers, saws, and ropes. They prepared the food that Shoda hunted and made life for their families…a labor of love. Ham showed great enthusiasm in the building of the ark. It was his delight to work beside his father and brothers. He had recovered from Shoda and Japheth's marriage. It sorrowed him to know he would never share a life with Shoda, but he was honored that they had married to bring up their firstborn as his namesake although they would no longer have to fulfill this pledge. Ham would marry Ne-el when she came of age. He had found great happiness being with his kin once more and told Sede, had it not been for her desire to return to Shem, he would have never seen his father and mother again, as well as his brothers.

Sede soon acclimated into her new life. It was good to be among her kin again. She felt their love, and it brought healing to her soul. She hunted with Shoda, and still loved the thrill of leaving in the early morning and discovering what the day would bring. Their time of fellowship during long hunts, brought a new depth to their friendship. At night, around the light of the fire, they shared their discoveries and wonder of this new thing called marriage. In their innocence, they never imagined the richness of a relationship and the depth of love that Yahweh intended when two hearts became one.

Shoda taught her the songs Yahweh had given her and Japheth, and they sang together in the quiet night. Sede shared her growing understanding of Yahweh and His ways. It had all began the night she heard Him on the breeze—that special night in her room. She shared the insight the Watcher had given her about seeing with the eyes of the spirit and not the flesh and how everything looked and felt different when the veil of the flesh has been removed. Shoda listened in wonder as Sede told of the wondrous trans-formation she had seen in the Nephilim who had held her captive. He had repented, and the evidence of a changed life was demonstrated by his selfless choices. She had seen Yahweh in a whole different way through the mercy He had shown him. It was during these quiet times together that their bond grew and became as Sede had always knew it would…an enduring relationship of friendship and sisterly love.

One night the families were called together around the village campfire. Noah wanted to speak to them. They looked to him, eager to hear his words.

"We've made great progress with our work on the ark, but we need provender for the animals that Yahweh intends to save. He has told me the small compartments will be for animals. It was His desire to save people, but they will not listen. So he intends to save his animal creation. Each compartment will be their individual stall or cubby. He will save them from the flood that will cover the earth. Let us pray to hear what we are to do next."

They joined hands in prayer, lifting their voices high into the starry night and reaching out to the great God in heaven. As they were praying, Sede heard Yahweh whisper His words on the breeze: "Remember the gold, child." She felt a rush of excitement as the memory of finding the gold was brought back in her. She recalled the wonder she had felt when her torch reflected the glistening golden light. She suddenly saw the connection. This gold could be used to buy what was needed.

After Noah finished, he asked, "Did anyone get a word from Yahweh?"

Sede stepped forward with confidence. "Yes, **I** did." She told them about finding a cave of gold in the wilderness and was certain she could find it again. Once they had the gold, they could purchase supplies and fill the ark with what they and the animals would need to survive.

Noah decided that five of them would leave in the morning. Together they would take camels and load them with gold, buy what was needed, and return with the storehouse of supplies. Yahweh had even shown Noah what to buy and where to buy it—the city of Sidon. Shem, Sede, Ham, Dollo, and Zilla would go. Dollo knew of Sidon from his five years of living in Atlantis and helping Playtheus with commerce. He had facilitated supplies for Playtheus' mansions and knew contacts in the city. There he would organize the many tons of provender they would need for the ark. Ham had the knowledge of the route to Sidon, the great city by the sea. While in Castius' room at Champion Hall, Ham had studied his maps of the known world. Yahweh had orchestrated what they had needed: Sede's knowledge of the gold, Zilla's care for the camp and preparing their food, Ham's knowledge to find the city of Sidon, Dollo's contacts in Sidon, and Shem's strong leadership that would keep them united. As each contributed their special skill and knowledge, they would complete this assignment. They would see Yahweh's will come to pass.

Sede knew they would be gone a long time traveling, trading the gold, buying the supplies, and returning. She would be leaving her kin once more, but this time she would have Shem by her side.

She woke the next morning as Shem whispered softly in her ear, "Time to go. All is ready." He had risen early, preparing with the others.

She stirred, collecting her thoughts. 'Yes!' she thought. 'This is the day we'll begin our journey!' She excitedly began to dress and prepared the things she would take. She wore her skins but took a robe, veil, and cloak. When they were in the city, she would have to dress according to the custom of women. She removed her seed necklace from her precious box and felt it once more beneath her skins. When she gathered her bow and quiver, she was ready.

Tolmaka pulled her to himself and kissed her on the top of her head. "Oh, Daughter, my heart goes with you. I love you so."

"I love you too, Father." She hugged him, feeling his love.

"Go with Yahweh, for He goes with you," he whispered.

She felt a prick of sadness to leave him. Even though time had passed, it seemed she had just returned, and now she was leaving again.

They formed a line, and Noah laid his hands on each one, praying for Yahweh's protection and a prosperous journey. He then kissed their foreheads, and after embracing them, they were ready to begin.

Shem led the caravan of camels, while Sede scouted the trail that would lead them to the snow line of the mountain. They traveled two days and arrived where snow covered the ground. Shem, Ham, and Dollo enjoyed learning new tracks and hunting game they had never seen before. And it was Sede's delight to share what she had discovered about their behaviors when she hunted them and learned their ways. The fresh game satisfied them every night as they rested around the fire. Zilla enjoyed the camp's domestic work. She eagerly prepared the meat they brought and attended to the tents. Sede enjoyed her quiet ways and the love she sweetly expressed to Dollo. She discerned they had found great happiness together. They had thanked her for being instrumental in uniting them once more. Both of them knew they never would have seen each other again had it not been for Sede's determination to leave Atlantis and return to her kin.

The next day she found the cave, and they began the process of preparing litters to carry the gold to Sidon. Working until dark they cut wood from the forest, fashioning poles for the framework and secured them with leather straps and animal skins. They now had strong and sturdy litters. Every camel would pull a litter as well as bags over their backs. The region they were in was called Havilah, famous for the fine gold that Atlantis desired. Dollo was amazed they wouldn't have to mine the gold but could simply gather what lay near the walls of the cave. He knew the gold to be of a fine quality and that it would be of greater value than gold from melted ore.

When they had finished gathering the gold, they looked at each other and laughed. All of them were covered with fine gold dust. Zilla laughed, "We're the golden children of God!" She playfully picked up a handful of gold dust and blew it into the air toward Dollo. It sparkled as it fell in his hair, some landing on his eyelashes. As he blinked, the dust sparkled and fell on his cheeks. He laughed and did the same to her. Soon all of them were throwing gold dust at each other, laughing with the joy they felt. As Sede watched, she reflected how precious one moment can be. Here they were, part of a plan that would change the world, and they were sharing the simple pleasure of laughter. How glad she was to recognize life in the moment with the people she loved.

They journeyed from the mountains and came to the great river Pishon. This was one of four mighty rivers that flowed from the Garden of Eden. Dollo was amazed that the river was so low. The last time he'd seen it was years ago, on a hunt, when he lived in his home village of Tagma. At that time it was a raging mighty river. Their crossing would be easy for the camels laden with the heavy burden of gold.

It was on the night of their crossing that Sede and Shem desired to stroll the restful riverbank. In the moonlight, they could see across the river and the far-reaching plains that disappeared in the distance. How beautiful this night was. As they walked hand in hand, they talked of all they had experienced since they had married and how the whole world had changed before their eyes. Their old way of life as children was gone, and their future lay undiscovered.

They stopped to rest on a rock ledge overlooking the great expanse beyond the river; it was though it symbolized the unknown future awaiting them. There they sat in silence, just taking in the peace they felt. The soft sounds of night surrounded them with soothing clarity: the slow-moving water that peacefully swirled over stones in the rocky bed, the faint sound of two crickets answering each other in the dark, and the warm evening breeze gently moving the bulrushes growing along the water's edge; whispering their wind song as it passed through their waving blades.

Filled with the wonder of the moment, he turned to look at her. There she quietly sat, pondering her thoughts. How beautiful she was silhouetted in the soft light of the moon. He was taken aback with a sudden thought: 'She is mine to love.' And oh, how he did love her.

She turned to see him watching her. A lovely smile parted her lips, and she whispered her heart, "I see the softness of your love for me, Shem. It soothes me and makes me feel so safe and cherished." She was struck by a sudden thought and couldn't help but say, "You are an amazing man, capable of so much love and not afraid to show it. What would I have done in life without your love?" She could hardly contain the emotions rising within herself. The clarity of understanding how important he was to her was before her eyes.

She continued, "In this moment, I am so blessed to know who you really are and have the love of your heart."

Her words were like warm, smooth oil flowing over his soul. Oh, how she made him feel complete. What would life had been for him without knowing her love? She leaned into him, wanting to communicate the awe she felt for the man who held her heart in his hands. As her lips touched his, an explosion of feelings went off inside him and he shuddered. He responded with a tender embrace, and he felt the rapture of love. She sensed his emotions and felt herself respond with deeper intensity. It was like a ripple effect—each responding to, and from, the other.

That night they slept beneath the stars on the soft grass near the river. The intimacy they shared only resounded what they had exchanged between their souls. They both knew they were in the arms of the only person that could make them complete, the one and only person who had been ordained for them alone—all by the plan and will of Yahweh. (That night it was Yahweh's blessing to see what two hearts could give each other. They were what He intended when two hearts could say, "We have become one." They were a living example of what the "crowning glory of creation" was to have been like. Not only was it a night of intimacy for them but for Him as well. In them, He saw what He had made, and that it was very good.)

At dawn, when they crossed the river, it was Ham that now led the way; he knew the landmarks of the region from Castius' maps. They passed mighty works of architecture; the gigantic, three-sided stone monuments that Trihedron had boasted of to Sede, calling them pyramids. They looked as though they rose from the ground beneath them and were as high as any mountain. Colossal stone Sphinx were the stone rendition of the combination of man and beast. They, too, made those that passed them seem but specks of dust in comparison. As the days of traveling unfolded, they approached a continual line of stone statues along the caravan route. They were the images of the 200, pointing the way before them. The statues were as tall as a tree and stood erect with one arm stretched before them, their finger pointing the direction of the city ahead. Ham had seen these replicated on the great map in Castius' room. He could only guess that they were the work of the same

Nephilim that had created the pyramids and Sphinx. Who but a Renown could have the knowledge to build such things.

The next night they camped outside the great city. Dollo wanted to scout the marketplace and see if he could make contacts with anyone he might know. Ham left with him. They approached the city late at night. The stars were so beautiful from the plains; somehow the sky always seemed bigger away from the forest trees. They felt such freedom walking under the vast openness of the night. The closer they came to the city, the more amazed they became. It was not lit by torch or flame of candle. Everywhere were crystals that illuminated from within. These crystals were the city's source of light.

Dollo whispered to Ham, "I've heard of this city, but never would I have believed such wonder. This must be the 'City of Lights.' The great statues we saw on the caravan route were pointing to this place. Atlantis was built for the Renown, but this city was built for the 200."

It was though the city never slumbered or slept. Everywhere people were doing business and walking about the streets. They saw marvels that they didn't understand. This mysterious power in the crystals moved huge wheeled carts pulling cargo and people. It was amazing to see something moving that wasn't pulled by animals but rather moved of its own power. They looked up to see a chariot gliding through the air without horses. The two people inside looked below and threw flower petals that gracefully fell on those beneath.

Dollo looked at Ham in astonishment. "The wonders of this city are not of this earth. This must be the result of the dark knowledge of the 200!"

They were able to spot the fallen angels by the brilliant blue glow radiating from their bodies and their glistening red tattoos on their forehead. Humans gave them homage as they passed them in the streets. Some kissed their feet in adoration, thrilled to be in their presence. Other desired only to touch but the hem of their robes. If they did manage to get close enough to touch them, they groaned with pleasure from something imparted to them. There was a compelling aura about them. Both Dollo and Ham felt the urge to worship them and struggled in resistance.

They made their way to the market, where Dollo searched for business contacts. There seemed to be no end to the market; it stretched down a huge boulevard as far as the eye could see. They spent several hours walking, taking in the spectacular size and grandeur of what the people of this city would call a common place. Everything imaginable was sold from the merchant booths: strange and exotic animals, regal garments of fine needlework, and forged silver swords the like of which they had never seen. As the merchant wielded the sword through the air, fire blazed from the blade. Dollo wondered if these were the same swords used by the great heroes of legend, the "Warrior Renown."

There were women displayed for purchase, beautiful beyond description, having an air of magic about them. Their bodies glistened with light; the light that surrounded them traveled through the air and descended on Dollo and Ham, touching and embracing their bodies. They were astonished and looked at each other. They both felt the alluring power seducing them and gripping their minds. "Let's be going, Ham, else we be snared by their powers!"

Ham shook himself as though he had awoken from a trance. "Yes, we need to move on!"

They continued and saw a grand platform with Sethite "innocents" lined up for sale. Dollo whispered, "Just like Atlantis, but these must be for the 200 to purchase."

They watched as a brilliant angel stepped forward and took the hand of a beautiful maiden. Her face shone with an innocence that came from within. He led her from the platform to a gazebo beneath a willow tree. Untying her robe, it fell at her feet. As she stood before him in her innocence, he circled her, taking in her beauty. He seemed to gain power from the vulnerability she felt. He took her hand and kissed her palm as the tattoo on his forehead burned red hot. The glistening blue light that he was emitting intensified, now sending flecks of red light sparking around him. Suddenly he clasped her face in his hands. Barely touching his lips to hers, he inhaled, drawing light from her body. It flowed from her legs and arms, circling in her chest, and then was pulled from her mouth into his. In an explosion of light, he disappeared, the maiden disappearing with him. All that remained was her robe, lying on the ground. They were speechless. Dollo grabbed Ham by the arm and said, "We need to go!" They continued their search, feeling both fear and awe.

Meanwhile, Zilla had fallen asleep next to the fire, and Sede and Shem sat nearby. "Will you walk with me, Shem?" Holding hands, they slowly walked the path along the stream outside their camp. They, too, noticed the beautiful night sky. The moon reflected off the water, and the gentle rippling sound soothed them. "This is lovely, is it not?" she said.

He stopped and turned to face her. "Yes, you are lovely," he said, looking at her in the moonlight.

She smiled at his loving comment and rested her head on his chest, enjoying the strength she felt from his body. "It's so comforting being with you, Shem. I sense the time has come to tell you about my captivity and those long months we were parted."

They climbed a large rock and sat together. From this vantage point they could see the moonlit plain and the distant lights of the city. A sense of peace and wellbeing seemed to surround them. "Shem, I have prayed for Yahweh to help me find a place in my heart for all I experienced while I was gone from you. He has given me that place of rest."

She paused briefly and then began. "When I was taken by the raiders in the forest, the female Nephilim we saw recognized who I was. Her name was Nersha; she had been given to Playtheus as his companion. Through her jealousy, she was enraged that his heart was set on me and not her. Playtheus had told her that he not only wanted my innocence but also my heart's affection. Out of consuming jealousy, she set out to find and kill me. She seized me in the forest, taking me to her camp where our Sethite kin were being held. She humiliated me, stripping me of my skins and parading me naked before them."

Shem began to weep for the great horror of what she must have felt—to be humbled in such a way; alone; not having anyone to help her. Hot tears fell from his eyes.

"When she paraded me before our elders, they covered their eyes in shame for me. Erud prayed with a great voice that Yahweh would cover me with the robe of righteousness. At that very moment I felt the power of Yahweh come upon me. No longer did I feel the shame of nakedness before the eyes of man. Nersha saw my courage, and it enraged her. In her hot anger, she ran a sword through Erud. When Zara watched her father murdered, she stood and threw her boomerang, trying to kill her. Nersha caught it midair and laughed. Launching her spear, she threw it at Zara. She died on the ground, beside her father. She then tied me to a post and beat me with her whip. The pain was unbelievable. I could see the ground turn red beneath me. Greater than the pain from the whipping was the pain I felt seeing Erud and Zara die before my eyes."

Tears fell from her eyes as she recalled the scene of their death. Shem continued to weep as he touched her back and gently stroked her.

"Nersha then turned her attention to our kin, hoping to inflict pain to my heart. Throwing my skins back at me, she ordered me to put them on. She held me with my hands behind my back and forced me to watch as her captain hung the oldest of our elder women up by their hands from trees. As they helplessly hung there, her soldiers used them for spear practice. Their screams filled the air, and I closed my eyes, wondering if I would endure what was happening. She knew the emotional pain I was feeling was greater than the beating I endured. She laughed as brutal Nephilim tied ropes to the arms and legs of our brave Sethite hunter/warriors. As if it were sporting competition, they 'hind and quartered' them, pulling them apart and seeing which hunter would last the longest before their bodies were pulled apart. They then ate them in front of the whole village. It was barbaric beyond belief—a horror of torture, pain, and brutality and an evil unlike any known! This is but one of the evil 'imagination of the heart' that has grieved

Yahweh and why He is justified in judging the wicked. Their day of terror will know an end."

"After this, I collapsed. When I regained consciousness, I realized she had chained me by the neck and bound my hands. She led me by the neck behind her horse. If I stumbled and fell, the horse drug me until I regained my footing. Nersha arrogantly boasted, 'I am the victor and *you*...the conquered. What kind of queen are you now, Sede-quete?' Her laugh was wicked and full of hate. She spit on me and kicked me with her foot, causing the horse to drag me once more. I was emotionally exhausted and faint from losing blood. I knew I didn't have long to live."

"Just then, and with no warning, a witch appeared with Playtheus. Nersha's horse reared for their appearing surprised us all. Playtheus humbled Nersha, who knelt in silence before him. He freed me from my chains and ordered the raiding Nephilim to return our kin to Taasa-toka. The witch then used her sorcery and we flew through the sky. We were but mist floating through the air. When we touched the ground, our bodies became solid once more. Playtheus dealt harshly with Nersha, humbling her before our eyes. He turned her over to the witch, who became her master."

"He then carried me to his mansion and cleaned my wounds. I saw in him a great change and transformation from the lustful Nephilim who had held me prisoner before. He showed me kindness and generosity. I was suspicious of his behavior for I knew how devious and hungry he had been for power. But what I saw made me so very sorry for him. He had never felt the feelings of the human part of himself, and because of what he saw in me, it changed him. He saw the life of Yahweh in me, and it turned his heart. He came to know repentance. Being with him was like being with someone new."

"As I slowly healed, I felt peace in his presence. I was thankful that I still lived and had hope of someday seeing you again. He had helped me, and I will always be grateful for the kindness he showed me. As the days turned into months and I finally began to heal, I could see my heart was changing toward him. I began to have a conflict within myself. My love for you was being challenged by the love he was showing me. I knew I had to leave. I could never hurt the love you and I have for each other. I told him I had to leave and return to you. In selfless abandonment, he made arrangements to return me."

"His father interfered and brought us to a ceremony to declare Playtheus a 'Mighty One.' During the ceremony, Nersha threw a javelin at me, wanting to kill me. Playtheus turned me around, knowing he would die in my place. He died in my arms."

"My heart was broken. I had resisted his love while I was with him, but in his death, I realized I did love him. I don't know how I could love both you and him, but I did."

Shem was silent. He began to tremble; he felt his world tear. A sudden panic gripped him as he realized she had loved someone else; his beloved had loved someone else. His face went pale, and he felt as though he had been kicked in the stomach. He couldn't breathe.

She could see the change in him and knew he was devastated. It broke her heart to know what she had told him had caused such pain. She could feel his panic and his pain. But in her wisdom, she knew she couldn't help him with what she had shared; only Yahweh could speak to him and heal the breech this had caused. The silence was so loud it could be felt. She knew this would test the very foundation of his love for her. However he handled this sudden news would affect both of them for the rest of their lives.

As she gathered her strength, she leaned into him and whispered tenderly, "I have put all things in Yahweh's hands and trust Him to help you with this truth. I love you, Shem, with such a great love. I could never live my whole life and not tell you my heart. I want nothing, and will let nothing be, between us. I have known the love of two men: one who died for me and the other who lives for me."

As she spoke these words, Shem burst into tears, and his emotions released within him. He wept as a strange but loving power swept through his heart. "Oh, Sede, I love you. You are life to me. I feel the release from my pain of heart. I'm free. Free to see the truth. I see the truth in your love for me. I do live to love you and will always live to love you. You are my Sede, my own!"

He bent down and kissed her. With her hands, she softly touched his face, which was wet with tears. Her eyes searched his, speaking louder than her words ever could. "Never will I keep anything from you, Shem, for you are 'love' to me. Together we make one soul—yours and mine together. I sorrowed for Playtheus in his death, but I rejoice in life by loving you."

They held each other in silence, letting what had just happened settle within them. She had been given her moment to tell him all her heart. Now he knew the depths of her soul. The way had been made for them to be truly one, with nothing hidden between them. It was a mystery to him that he could know this about her and not have it destroy his love for her. It had the opposite effect. Rather than destroying their love, it made it stronger, richer, and more secure. Only Yahweh could give this kind of grace and assurance.

It was almost dawn when Dollo and Ham returned, excited to report the wonders they had seen in the city. They hadn't found the contacts they had hoped to make, but they were amazed by the sights they had seen. They continued their journey toward Sidon, and as they walked with the caravan, Sede and Shem held hands. Something had grown stronger between because she had opened her deepest secret to him. Love's true bond would hold no secrets. She had waited for Yahweh's perfect timing, and now their love could only grow deeper.

As they approached the city of Sidon, Dollo instructed them in its customs. There was certain protocol that had to be followed as well as appropriate attire. Sidon was an ancient city, built as a namesake to Sidon, a descendant of Cain. Although Cainites were a vile people, the city of Sidon reflected the influence of Atlantis. Many Renown did business in this great city, and where the Renown went in the world, always they brought the influence of their culture with them.

They camped outside the city to keep their cargo of gold safe. Shem decided that he, Ham, and Zilla would stay and guard the camp. Dollo and Sede would enter the city. Disguised as a couple, they would look less conspicuous than two men doing business. Shem knew that out of them all, Dollo and Sede knew best the way of the Nephilim. Dollo knew its business world, and Sede knew the Renown culture. It was hard to let her go without him, and he struggled with his decision. She had been lost to him twice.

That night as he walked beneath the stars, he lifted his troubled heart to Yahweh. "How can I let her go and not be there to protect her? The thought of her scarred back is a torment to me. I was not there for her when she needed me most."

Just as he felt anxiety rise within him, Yahweh came to him on the gentle breeze. His loving words came sure and true, calming his anxious heart. "Shem, your 'beloved' will be in the safest place in the universe. She will be in *My* hands!"

Tears filled his eyes as he held to every word. They were filled with such love and compassion. He felt as though the arms of God enfolded him. This was the comfort and assurance his heart needed. Yahweh would be with her when he couldn't. What safer place was there but in the hands of God?

Chapter 4

The Sacrifice

Dollo and Sede changed their clothes in preparation to enter Sidon. Instead of their hunting skins, they donned attire of the city's custom. Sede wore a robe that covered her arms and hung to the ground. Her cloak was wrapped at her shoulders. A beautiful veil allowed only her eyes to be seen. Dollo wore a distinguished robe, and a gold band circled his forehead. As they readied to leave their camp, Dollo kissed Zilla farewell. Holding her, he spoke his words of comfort in her ear, "We were parted once but never again. I will come back to you. You my beloved, are the joy I live for."

After Shem had kissed Sede, he held her face in his hands. Tenderly, he looked into her eyes, searching them. "It's so hard to let you go. But I let you go knowing this: 'You will be in the safest place in the universe. You will be in the hands of God.'" His words reflected his faith, and she couldn't help but be reassured. She was thankful for his example of trust, for she had felt anxious about leaving without him. She threw her arms around his neck and wept. "I love you so much, Shem—so very, very much!"

When they entered the city, Dollo led the way to the market he knew so well. As was the custom, she walked two steps behind him. "This is very different from the last time you and I went through a city!" she whispered.

"This time we won't have to sneak through the streets!" Dollo smiled, remembering the night they had fled Atlantis. They arrived at the market where Dollo began to do business with different merchants. He would negotiate for grain, hay, seeds, nuts, and dried meats. Sede stood nearby, as if she were his wife. She spoke to no one, for in their custom, women were not allowed to speak unless their husbands gave them permission.

As the day progressed, Dollo was lost in the world of dealing and bargaining. Occasionally he looked over to check on Sede. At one point he noticed a Renown watching her. Lifting his hand, he stopped the merchant in mid-sentence. The Renown approached her, trying to engage in conversation, but she stood mute before him, not responding to his questions.

Dollo flew to her side and aggressively confronted the Renown. "Why are you speaking to my wife? You know she's forbidden to answer you!" The tone of his voice was furious.

"She is wearing the cloak of royalty," the Renown answered, shaken by Dollo's sudden reach for the hilt of his sword. "I only wished to honor her."

Sede began to tremble. She realized she had unintentionally put them at risk by wearing the cloak Ba-nea had given her.

"That cloak was given to her by a friend; that is all!" Dollo retorted. "Don't speak to my wife again!" The Renown bowed and dismissed himself.

Dollo saw her shaking fear and patted her hand, reassuring her. "It'll be okay, Sede. When we finish our business, we'll leave."

Sede stayed even closer to him. She began to feel the same anxiety she had felt when she had been captured and sent to Atlantis. Dollo worked throughout the day, ordering from the list Noah had made. He made arrangements for the purchase of more camels, oxen, and carts. They would need them to haul the many tons of cargo. He also employed the service of servants. This great journey would require more than just themselves to see its end. In three days everything would be brought to their camp and the exchange of gold would take place.

As they passed through the gate archway to leave the city they were suddenly surrounded by six guards. Their abrupt movements startled both of them. Tall spears formed X's around them, pinning them tight.

"You will come with us!" the captain ordered.

"What is the meaning of this?" Dollo challenged. "By whose authority do you confront me?"

"By the authority of Croas, I make this demand!" he bellowed. "Now come with us!" The guards lifted their spears and pressed in close, forming a tight circle around them with the armored bodies. Marching, they were escorted to a large pavilion. Dollo felt Sede's trembling hand grab his and nervously squeeze it. How could this be happening?

They entered through a side door and saw a Regal Renown sitting on a throne, elevated on a high platform. Servants stood at attention on each step that ascended to the throne. Before him stood a line of people waiting to be seen.

"This Renown must have a political position," Dollo whispered. "All these people must be here to settle disputes."

When Croas saw his guards enter with captives, he had the room cleared of everyone, even his servants. The guards ushered them to stand below him and Croas extended his scepter toward Dollo.

Having been given permission to speak, Dollo let his anger fly. "What is the meaning of this," he demanded, maintaining an aggressive façade. "We're in this city to conduct business, and we've been treated with great disrespect. Have the customs of this city changed?"

Sede was glad he had such confidence and that he knew how handle the situation.

"*I* will do the talking," Croas thundered with authority. "*You* will listen!" Dollo trembled but set his chin in defiance. "I've received a report from one of my spies that your woman is wearing the cloak of royalty. She will remove her veil before me."

"No she will not!" Dollo hotly retorted. He struggled in the guard's grip, trying to break free. The guard standing next to Sede ripped the veil from her face and Croas' mouthed dropped open. He knew who she was; Ma-get had shown him her likeness from Playtheus' mural. She had made sure her sons weren't looking for a faceless "innocent" but would be able to recognize her when they saw her. And he recognized her. "This is the one we've been looking for!" he boomed with a loud voice. "Take him away and bring her to me."

They led Dollo away as he screamed, "We'll come for you, Sede. We'll find you!" They led him from the room and released him in the streets, throwing him with a force that made him fly through the air and roll when he hit the ground.

Sede stood alone and bewildered. What was happening? Was she being taken yet again? She was in shock and couldn't move. Where had they taken Dollo, and how would she ever let Shem know where she was?

Croas approached her. Slowly, he circled her, looking at what stood before him. As he drew near her neck and inhaled, the hair on the back of her neck stood on end. She felt his evil discerning her. "So you were Playtheus' high companion? It was said that you have power over a Renown. Do you have power over me?" He waited for her to respond but then laughed as she remained mute. He ran his finger slowly down her arm, feeling the softness of her skin. "Umm, I sense what Playtheus saw in you," he groaned lustfully. She felt panic rise within her, and her heart began to pound wildly. What was he going to do?

Croas whirled around in sudden excitement, thundering his command to the guards: "We leave for Atlantis at once!" His words echoed coldly through the great hall, settling within her. She was to see Atlantis yet again....

Taking Sede by the arm, he pulled her close, whispering in her ear, "You're coming with me. There'll be no hiding in barrels this time!" She looked at him in shock, wondering how he knew such specific details about her past escape. He led her to the dock where they set sail.

She couldn't eat and spent a sleepless night of worry while guards stood next to her bed. Croas had said they'd been looking for her. What could he gain by capturing her? Why would he take her to Atlantis? Was she to become his high companion? Sailing all night, they arrived in Atlantis the next morning. There before her was the familiar stone archway she and Dollo had found refuge in the night of their escape.

The Sacrifice

A dread filled her as they passed under the looming arch to a waiting chariot. There, a servant stood ready for Croas. They moved through the city and up a winding road to Croas' hillside mansion. Ma-get waited anxiously, having gotten word that her son had found her. She was beside herself with excitement.

Grabbing Sede's arm, he ushered her forward. "Here she is, Mother. My spies were most effective. We'll now have what we both want."

"Yes, Son. What we both want." Sede felt her evil, and it made her tremble. 'Oh, Playtheus, if only you were here to help me,' she thought. She hadn't thought of him since the night she spoke of him to Shem. Her love for Playtheus had found a sweet resting place within her heart. It was only soothing memories she now had of him—no more tears, no more sorrow. Somehow she knew he was all right, wherever he was. But oh, how she wished he was here to help her now. He knew this world of Atlantis and would have set things right.

Ma-get barked her commands to her servants: "The ceremony is tomorrow. We must prepare her tonight. I will supervise everything so there are no mistakes and no escapes!" Eager servants stepped forward and ushered Sede while Ma-get followed. They led her to a pool and removed her clothes, helping her into the water. It brought Ma-get pleasure to see Sede's scars. She felt a devious delight that her beauty had been marred. Jealousy rose within her as she discerned her "Tella-la-no-ah" innocence, for she wished she possessed such purity and glory. She had felt the same jealousy when she was in Ba-nea's presence and discerned her "Tella-la-no-ah."

Sede saw her seed necklace resting on top of her clothes. As the servant bent to take them away, she cried out, "I must have my necklace. It gives me power to magnify my innocence in the presence of a Renown!" Ma-get's eyes widened. "Ah. So this is your power." Sede continued her plea. "Yes, and it works only for me and none other. It was made just for me and gave me great power over Playtheus." She concluded that Ma-get knew that she had been his high companion and needed some reason to keep it; otherwise it would be lost forever.

"By all means, give her the necklace. We want her to have a brilliant innocence when she stands before the Mighty 200."

Sede trembled. Now she knew why she was there. Playtheus had told her about the yearly sacrifice of an innocent. *She* was the sacrifice!

* * *

Dollo breathlessly ran from the city to the camp. He was beside himself when he saw Shem. "They've taken Sede, and we must go back and find her!" he gasped.

Shem screamed in unbelief, "What? NO! Not again. Not again!" He crumbled to the ground, grabbing handfuls of dirt and throwing it in the air, the dirt falling like a cloud on his head. He buried his face between his knees and cried out in agony, "Sede. Sede. SEDE!"

Dollo, Ham and Zilla knelt around him; they bent their heads forward, touching his back. "Oh, my brother, my friend," said Dollo. Ham moaned in sorrow, weeping. Zilla, too, began to cry. But then Dollo had a thought. "Grab some gold. We'll pay to find out where she is!"

Leaving Ham with Zilla, Shem and Dollo went back to the city and found an eager guard that was glad to exchange information for gold. They learned that she had sailed to Atlantis just that day. The guard had heard she had been chosen as this year's sacrifice to the gods. Shem was beside himself with fear—his Sede, a hostage *and* a sacrifice!

As they rushed to the pier, Shem heard Yahweh speak to his heart. He felt his whole body respond, and he slowed to a stop and listened. Dollo abruptly halted and turned back, wondering why he'd stopped. It was then the glory cloud fell and Yahweh's words rang crystal clear in strength and love.

"No, my son, don't search for her. Put your trust in me. I will bring her to you. When you bid her farewell, you told her she was in the safest place in the universe. She still is. She is *still* in my hands. Go back to the camp and wait, for she will surely come back to you!"

The Sacrifice

Shem staggered on his feet from the powerful glory that now surrounded him. The air seemed to be alive and charged with energy, love, and power. His being was flooded with the presence of the Lord, and he could hardly stand. Dollo was standing at his side when the glory fell and had collapsed. He, too, was filled with Yahweh's presence and power. He struggled to stand, amazed at what Yahweh had just said and done.

Shem stammered in amazement, "Dollo, you heard Him too?"

"Yes, Shem, every word!"

They were to do nothing. Yahweh would bring her back to him once more. He would again have to trust in Him, but this time it wouldn't be hard. Yahweh had spoken to him, and she was safe in the hands of Almighty God. They returned to camp, walking side by side, their arms around each other's shoulders, filled with wonder and glory!

* * *

Sede had another sleepless night knowing the terror that awaited her in the morning. She heard the muffled voices of Ma-get and her son as they made their plans.

"Croas, what a wonder that we actually found her the night before the sacrifice. This is unfolding just as I had planned. All my hard work is paying off. I'm going to send for your brothers to meet us at the sacrifice altar. We'll stand before the whole assembly and receive recognition for providing a 'Tella-la-no-ah' to the gods. Your father will see my supremacy to Ba-nea and forsake her. It will be me he will choose for his new queen, and you, my son, will replace Playtheus as favored son. This will be your reward for finding her. I will see to Ba-nea's death myself."

"But Mother, Father is able to see 'within.' He'll discern it, and I fear... he'll destroy us!"

"No my son, I've gained the knowledge of how to veil his sight. I paid a great price to get this dark knowledge from another witch. I surrendered all the 'innocents' I possessed as payment." She held her arms out for him to see. Her arms were bare, having no tattoos. "We won't be in danger but will receive the glory both you and I deserve!"

On and on they went throughout the night. Sede turned a deaf ear to their endless prattle. What would happen in the morning? How would she ever escape the fire that would surely burn her? She clasped her seed, thinking of Shem and the promises Yahweh had given her. Trying to encourage her heart, she thought, 'Surely Yahweh will save me. I will live and see the deliverance of the Lord.'

In the morning, Ma-get dressed her personally, making sure she had her necklace and the cloak that implied royalty. Sede did look magnificent. There was no equal to her. Something about her "Tella-la-no-ah" electrified the air. The roar coming from the arena filled the air and the closer their chariot came, the louder the noise. Ma-get would usher her personally to the sacrifice platform, and her three sons would stand by her side. They would know the glory of having the 200's acclaim. They would be forever known as providing the first "Tella-la-no-ah". The most worthy sacrifice ever made to the gods.

The Mighty 200 had taken their seats around the magnificent altar, unparalleled to any on earth. Its size was exceedingly great. Made of gold, it reflected the light of the rising sun. The wood was arranged below the altar, allowing the "innocent" to be above for all to see. As she led Sede to the long, broad steps of the altar, Ma-get was giddy with excitement. All her manipulations had paid off and she would get Talimus-qua-tam for her own. She would get the glory she deserved. The crowd hushed as drums began to beat their mystic rhythm. Sede took her first step, trembling in fear, while Ma-get held her arm to steady her. Those seated next to the steps gasped in wonder as she passed. A soft, radiant light glowed around her, and her forehead glistened with the marking of "Tella-la-no-ah." The whole stadium seemed enchanted by what they saw in her. An "ah" could be heard from those she passed.

Ba-nea spotted her before Talimus-qua-tam did. "Look, it is our Sede-quete. Oh, we can't allow this! We have to stop them. She was the one our son set his love upon!"

Talimus-qua-tam rumbled with power. "Yes, we *will* allow this. This is the day for all the gods to receive power and glory from the yearly sacrifice. She is a "Tella-la-no-ah," making this sacrifice rare indeed. I want, and will have, the power she will give me through her death!"

Ba-nea trembled. His words reverberated with power. She knew she couldn't challenge him and win. She left her seat and made her way up the steps.

When Sede reached the platform, Ma-get led her to the center of the sacrifice altar. The crowd erupted in a wild frenzy, roaring with exalted praise: "Great are the Mighty 200! Great are the gods! Great are the Mighty 200! Great are the gods! Great are the Mighty 200! Great are the gods!" Over and over the chanting echoed throughout the stadium; the sound was deafening. The 200 glowed with light, their eyes aflame, hungrily anticipating the power and glory they would receive from her death. Ma-get joined her proud sons, leaving Sede to stand alone. She looked so small on such a large altar.

Just as Ba-nea reached the top step, the fire exploded from below the wood. It had been ignited from the extended torches of Ma-get and her sons. The flames shot upward into the sky, forming a ring of fire around the altar. As the flames exploded, Ba-nea was blown backward and staggered on her feet. Sede stood in terror. She clutched her seed necklace and cried with a great voice, "Yahweh! I am *Yours...forever!*"

Suddenly the altar began to shake and rumble, startling the wild crowd; it felt as though the earth was moving beneath them. A ring of magnificent angelic beings began to materialize and circle the altar. They were radiant in glory and brilliant in splendor; the sound of heaven filled the air. The whole atmosphere shifted from wild frenzy to the awe of holiness. And there, in the middle of them all, was Playtheus! He glowed with a brilliance that matched the angels.

When Sede saw him, she could hardly believe her eyes. "Playtheus, it's you!"

He stepped forward, holding his arms out to her. She ran into his embrace, joy flooding her soul. With a voice that amplified the beauty within him, he spoke. "Sede, I was sent with Yahweh's angels. You are a 'Tella-la-no-ah' indeed and Yahweh's chosen seed in this generation. It is my great honor to have known you and loved you. Because of you, I forsook the evil within me and embraced Yahweh. I will now rest in his love forever!" His words crescendoed, the whole stadium hearing his reverberating praise, filling them with wonder and awe. With loving kindness, he looked into her eyes and gently said, "This has happened because of you, my dear Sede—because of you."

Tears of joy filled her eyes, streaming down her cheeks. Her heart burst in great happiness, knowing he would be with Yahweh forever.

Playtheus raised his head from Sede's loving embrace and spoke. "Come, Mother, for you, too, desire to forsake evil and will find life in Yahweh!"

With a look of glory on her face, Ba-nea stepped forward through the fire, the flames incinerating her body. Her glistening spirit passed through the fire and stood in radiance beside her son. Leaning forward, she tenderly clasped Sede's face and kissed her cheek. "Thank you, my child. Through your influence and testimony, we have been saved by the Great Yahweh, the God I never forgot and who never forgot me!"

She took her son's hand, and they smiled at each other, joy radiating from their faces. The angels that surrounded the altar began to sing "Heaven's Song of Salvation." One who was lost to heaven had found her way home. As they sang, Ba-nea stepped forward and lifted her hands toward heaven, her face shining like the sun. This song was being sung for her!

I have sinned against heaven and in your sight
I have wandered far from my home
I am not worthy to be called by your name
A child of the "Father of Light."

The Sacrifice

Bring forth the best robe, new shoes, and a ring
My child was dead, but now lives
My heart is her home, my arms her rest
Her love song, forever I'll sing...

After the angels had sung the last note, Playtheus, Ba-nea, and the angels began to disappear and became but sparkling mist. Sede now felt the flames growing closer, but then Ba-nea reappeared before her. She spoke with calm assurance: "Wrap yourself in your cloak, Sede. Yahweh will use it to shield you from the flames and take you where you want to go." She then disappeared, leaving Sede alone.

This majestic display of power made the 200 quake in fear. They were in the presence of the very angels they had once worshipped with before the throne of the "Most High." Just being near the glory they once knew brought great fear and dread upon them. They knew they were forever doomed, and Yahweh would eventually execute judgment on them. The brilliant blue light that emitted from them was now darkened, and they covered their face with their hands. The reality of their great shame in the light of holiness was something they couldn't deny. In their self-deception, they thought themselves glorious, but in the presence of true glory, their sin had been reflected. (In the light of TRUTH, all is laid bare and open.)

Sede was stunned by what had just happened. But now the angels, Playtheus, and Ba-nea were gone. She felt the waves of heat as the fire grew closer; she put her arm against her face, attempting to shield herself from the blasting heat. Suddenly remembering Ba-nea's words, she thought, 'Oh, the cloak!' She threw it around herself and disappeared before them all, just as the flames engulfed the altar.

The 200 began to shine once more, their brilliant blue light streaming from them. A great roar erupted from the crowd. The 200 had seemingly accepted their sacrifice. After Sede's disappearance, Talimus-qua-tam seethed in rage by Ba-nea's betrayal. How could she embrace Yahweh and abandon him! And his son—his great son—lost to him forever. He would be with the "Most High," the one he once served and now despised. He had lost them both.

He angrily rose to his feet and joined Ma-get on the platform. They clasped hands, raising their arms in the air as if in victory. The stadium roared in wild praise. He would claim her as his new high companion and receive recognition among the 200 for the sacrifice she had brought them for they all thought that Sede had been consumed by the flames. The sacrificial power they felt was only their deceptive light returning to their beings after being vanquished by the holiness of the Lord's angels. And Ma-get? Ma-get had gotten what she wanted. She had gotten Talimus-qua-tam. She had manipulated all things well.

When Sede opened her cloak, she was now standing outside Sidon's walls. Shem's camp could be seen in the distance. The power of Yahweh had transported her, and the cloak had shielded her from the flames just as Ba-nea had said. Joy exploded within her, and she threw her head back laughing and rejoicing, spinning in great delight as her cloak whirled in a magnificent circle. She was free. Free! Yahweh had delivered her. She began running toward the camp, adrenaline pumping through her veins.

Shem raised his hand to cup his forehead. Who was that running toward them from the distance? What? He let out a shout. "SEDE!" He started running to meet her. Yahweh had brought her back to him. The joy they felt burst when they met! 'Oh, to feel her in my arms once more.' 'Oh, to have him hold me, and feel safe.' When the others saw them embrace, they came running. Sede had returned!

That night as she lay in Shem's arms, she rehearsed the terrifying yet glorious events that had taken place. She shared her terror of the fire and how Yahweh had sent magnificent angels to deliver her. Playtheus had been with them, and his mother, Ba-nea, had stepped through the flames and was received into glory. The angels had sung her salvation song and Yahweh's power had transported her to the camp.

The Sacrifice

Shem held her, listening in wonder and awe. Oh, how his heart rejoiced to know the supernatural power of Yahweh. The same God that had made heaven and earth had intervened in their lives, saving the one he loved. As he reflected, he realized that Yahweh *was* all powerful. He would see that His will come to pass no matter what. The amazing thing was, of all the people in the world, they had been chosen to be part of that will. He could not put it to words, but that night his faith grew from a mustard seed to a mountain. He had been part of something so supernatural that words could not explain the impact it made on his life. What would the future hold for them? He considered the coming judgment of the world and the preparation for the living. They had been a part of building the ark, finding a way to buy the great storehouse of provisions, journeying to this city, and now the planned return. He sensed there was more to come. A deep confidence settled within his spirit that night. He knew that whatever the future held for them, they would not be alone. If Yahweh was for them, who could be against them.

Chapter 5

Caravan

All was ready. The exchange of gold and merchandise had taken place. Never had Sidon seen such a caravan depart their city. It was though the orchestra of heaven played in great pomp as a continual stream of camels, oxen, and carts trailed from the city to the open plain before them. The air itself seemed charged with life as they moved forward in power and might. The first night they camped, Shem, Ham, and Dollo built an altar to offer a sacrifice of thanksgiving—thanksgiving for bringing Sede back and making their way prosperous. Shem searched the flock for a perfect white, spotless lamb; then they sang the "Song of Thanksgiving," the song they knew from their youth. With hands and faces lifted to heaven, the five sang in beautiful harmony.

> *Our hearts we lift to you,*
> *In thanksgiving and in praise*
> *You've made your face to shine on us*
> *You've brought the light of day!*
>
> *From the rising of the sun,*
> *Until the setting of the same*
> *We will honor what you have done,*
> *We give thanks unto your Holy Name*

Fire came down from heaven, and Yahweh spoke on the breeze. His word came loving and sure. "Fear not, Shem. I will cloak you with my glory. The eyes of the flesh shall not see you as you journey back to your father. I go before you to prepare the way." The others rejoiced, for they too, heard the spoken words.

Many days they journeyed and saw other caravans. None seemed to see them, though they passed but a stone's throw away. Once a troop of Nephilim, moving their captives, came alongside their caravan. As Dollo brought his camel to a halt, a giant passed right in front of him. He hadn't seen them. Yahweh's hand *was* upon them.

Every night they camped the servants attended the animals: feeding, watering, and unloading their burdens. Every morning they again packed them for another day's journey. These men knew that once the cargo was delivered, they would be able to return with the livestock as payment for their service. Dollo, again, had been a shrewd business man. With this added manpower, the days seemed to flow one after another, and a sense of ease and peace rested on Shem and his company.

At night, when they lay beneath the stars, Shem and Sede talked of what lay ahead for them. What would this great judgment be like? It was hard to imagine all this open land would someday be covered with water—the mountains too.

Shem pondered the heathen and their ways. He knew in his heart that the mercy of Yahweh must have been exhausted to decide to destroy the earth. For above all things, he knew Yahweh was a God of mercy and love. He thought of Taasa-toka and how he and the others had tried to plead with them to turn from evil and return once more to Yahweh. It grieved him deeply to see their wickedness, but he knew that Yahweh was grieved even more.

Noah had told him Yahweh's word: 'I have seen that the wickedness of man is great on the earth. Every imagination of his heart is only evil continually, and I regret that I have made mankind. Every living creature that I have made will I destroy from off the face of the earth.' Although Shem hated to see this beautiful world come to an end, he knew that the corruption of man would not end but only get worse. The threats on his wife were evidence of that. Evil had tried to destroy her three times. Yahweh had to make a judgment on evil but there was hope. He had promised Sede that their descendants would fill the earth. As he reflected, he knew he needed to look to the future and let the past die along with the corruption of the world. His comfort was that Yahweh would begin again with mankind.

As the caravan approached the great river Pishon, Shem knew they were but days from their village and the ark. He needed to secure a tow line across the river to facilitate the transfer of their cargo by barge. The river had swollen past its banks since they last crossed and was now swift and treacherous. He would have to swim the tow line to the other side.

Tying a rope to himself, he entered the water. The current pulled him downstream, over rocks and white rapids, sucking him under the surface just to push him up again. He finally reached the other side, and although he was weakened by battling to keep afloat, he pulled himself up the muddy bank and collapsed. After regaining his strength, he stood and waved to the others that he'd made it.

Securing the line, Ham crossed next. Hanging above the raging waters he inched his way along the rope. Far across the river, the others watched in nervous anticipation. When he swung from the rope to the bank, Shem in great relief embraced him. He had made it across safely. He then sent him to bring their father and the other men. They would need their help to transport what they'd brought from Sidon.

When the families arrived at the river, they rejoiced for they had returned, and now the ark would be filled. Everyone would be a part of the work. The women set up camp and the men began the planning of transport. They built a large barge and secured strong tow lines. Many, many times the barge went back and forth as tons of grain and supplies were transferred from one bank to the other.

Finally, the day came that they had one last load of grain to pull across the river and they would be finished. At camp that night, they celebrated to see the work coming to an end. They had worked together to accomplish a great feat. As the camp settled for the evening, Tolmaka walked the quiet path by the river. His gaze was drawn to the night sky, and wonder filled his heart. He had helped to bring Yahweh's will to pass. His daughter was settled in her life with Shem, and he knew she would have a good life with him. As he walked, a Watcher suddenly appeared beside him. Startled, he froze! But then peace settled his heart. It was the same Watcher who had led him to the Cave of Treasures. He felt great pleasure being in his presence once more.

As they walked together, the Watcher spoke. "Tolmaka, I have been sent to tell you…it is time."

Tolmaka was silent. He knew this day would come. He had wondered how he would feel when he was told the time had come to leave this world. He searched his heart to know what he felt. It was both sadness and excite-ment—sadness because he would be leaving his beloved Sede but excitement remembering the great joy he had felt in Yahweh's presence when he was in the cave.

"You must bid you daughter goodbye and prepare her heart for your death. She will greatly mourn your passing. You must leave her with your words of love to help her accept her loss." As they continued to walk, the Watcher told him of the great glories of heaven, making Tolmaka's heart swell with longing. He would be with his beloved Lettah again, his father and mother, and his kin of old. His heart began to yearn to be in their presence.

When Tolmaka returned to camp, he found Sede and Shem sitting near the fire. "Sede, would you walk with me?"

She happily rose to her feet, kissing Shem sweetly as she left with her father. They began to walk the same quiet path he had just walked. In silence, they listened to the night sounds: the water washing over the rocks, the turtle doves call, and the sound of their own feet upon the soft earth. The warm, soft breeze seemed to embrace them while they walked side by side, creating an atmosphere of peace. It brought a resting comfort to her heart spending this quiet time with him.

He took her hand and brought it to his lips, kissing her fingers sweetly. "I love you, my daughter. You have been the joy of my life. My delight has been seeing you grow into the beautiful woman who now walks beside me. I have every confidence that you and Shem will have a blessed life together."

She gave him a tender kiss on his cheek. "Thank you, Father. I do feel the blessing of Yahweh when I'm with Shem. I remember when you told me that my heart would know greater love when I became his wife. I now know that greater love. You have been such a good father to me. You will always be Abba, even though I'm grown." She hugged him sweetly around the waist, and they continued their walk along the path, sharing their hearts.

When he walked her back to camp, Shem was already asleep. "I have something for you, Sede. It's a gift." Tolmaka opened his hand to reveal an engraved smooth stone. She recognized the names on it. It was his and her mother's. "Your mother gave me this the night of our wedding. I have saved it these many years for the day I would give it to you."

Tears misted in her eyes as she felt the great love he had held for her mother. She knew this stone was most dear to him. "I wish I had known her, Father."

"You will someday, Sede, when your days are fulfilled. She and I will be there, waiting for you." He held her by the camp fire one last time, loving the life he felt in his arms. "I will love you always, my precious daughter, always."

"And I will love you, Father, always."

As he turned to leave, tears filled his eyes. Oh, how he loved her. He knew the words he had given her would be the last she would hear. It would be as he had said; he would be there in heaven, waiting for her.

As she watched him disappear in the dark, she felt her heart swell with love for him. Oh, how she loved him.

The next morning the men prepared the last load to ferry across the river. Shem and Tolmaka would take it across. With the bags of grain secured, Tolmaka began to pull on the tow line. Shem used his pole to push against the riverbed and turn them when they needed to adjust against the pull of the current.

Ahead of them, they could see that fallen trees were approaching, rolling in the current, turning and slamming into each other. They felt a sudden bang. They'd been hit. As their cargo shifted, they began to tilt. Tolmaka grabbed the tow line, trying to straighten the barge. Shem pushed his pole against the river bottom to slow them only to have it snap in his hands. Neither attempt worked; the barge started to pull against the rope, which was beginning to fray from the tension. "We must lighten the load!" yelled Tolmaka. "Quick, throw the bags into the river!" Both of them began to toss bags over the side.

Those on the riverbank saw their distress. They shouted to them, but they couldn't hear; the roar of the river was too loud. All of a sudden, the rope snapped, and the barge began to race down the river, bumping and banging against rocks and fallen trees. Shem felt panic as he clung to the rail of the barge and shouted, "Tolmaka, what should we do?"

"Jump in the river, Son, for I fear the rocks ahead!" He pointed to the fast approaching boulders.

Shem leapt into the river and was pulled downstream. His head could be seen bobbing occasionally to the surface and his arms flailing wildly. Just head were rapids. The huge boulders made the water run swift and then drop, falling into roaring white water. Tolmaka looked to the river's edge and saw Sede screaming to him. His heart ached for her; he knew she would see him die. He raised his hand in sad farewell as the barge blasted into a large boulder. He was thrown from the barge, and pulled beneath the surface between two rocks.

Shem saw what happened and tried to swim against the current, but it was no use; the water was too swift. He knew he couldn't save him. "Tolmaka! Father!" His voice roared above the thundering water. He yelled out in great agony for he knew he was gone.

As Shem grabbed a tree branch overhanging the bank, the water pulled at him, trying to wash him downstream. Sede and Noah raced to the water's edge and reached for his hand. As they pulled him to higher ground, he gasped for breath. Sede was frantic; she had seen everything. She started to step into the water to rescue her father.

"No!" said Noah, pulling her as they both fell back. "You can't save him, Sede. He's gone!"

"No! No! Let me go; I have to save him!" She was wild with panic as Noah held her, and she screamed above the roaring water, "Fa...ther! Fa...ther!"

They saw the rest of the barge crash into a thousand pieces as it hit the rapids; small pieces swirled to the surface and were swept downstream. She anxiously watched the water. When would she see him? Where was he? She stood there watching for a long time.

The others knew Tolmaka was gone. They would never see him again. One by one they came and silently touched her arm or gave her a loving hug. When Dosta stood before her, she touched Sede's face and looked lovingly into her eyes. Her pain was so deep she couldn't speak but kissed her sweetly on the cheek. Ne-el gently wrapped her arm around her waist as little Adat grabbed her leg. Gruetat and Mersta, with great tenderness, put their arms around her. And Shoda...Shoda softly touched her forehead to hers. Sede could hear her sobs as she tried to control herself. Dollo and Zilla embraced her, holding her as they felt her pain, and Noah and Ezmere surrounded her with their arms, holding her in their embrace. Japheth and Ham touched her shoulder and breathed their words. "Took-la-say-a-lay-nah' Tolmaka. 'Took-la-say-a-lay-nah...'"

As the sun was beginning to set, Shem held her in silence. She continued to look to the water with her head resting on his shoulder. He would stay with her until she was ready—ready to say goodbye. Finally, she burst into painful tears. "Why did he have to die? Why couldn't we save him? Why? I don't even have a body to bury!" She wept as he held her, and he began to weep too, his own heart breaking for the woman he loved and for the father he lost.

Sede didn't sleep that night but felt anxious. What was she going to do without her Abba? He had been her whole life. He had always known what was best for her, and his words of wisdom had helped her to accept her new life with Shem. How could she bear not hearing the sound of his voice or not feeling the warmth of his arms around her, or his heartbeat that made her feel so safe? How was she going to live without him?

As they began carrying the cargo over the mountain to the ark, she remained numb with grief. She didn't talk but worked silently with the others. When she did hunt, she was thankful for the time alone. Somehow she could connect with her heart in the quiet of the forest. The others knew her heart was broken and they ached for her. Shem held her in his arms every night while she lay silent in grief. With all his heart, he wished he could help her and lift this pain from her.

Shoda saw her by the fire one night. She looked so sad, sitting there alone. She came softly and sat beside her, saying nothing. After a while, she began to hum a soothing melody of heaven that rose from her heart and then softly began to sing the words. It was though an angel was singing, for Sede felt the presence of the Lord.

> *My song takes wings into the night*
> *For a friend great with grief*
> *Her sorrow is near, and tears held back*
> *Her freedom won't take flight*
>
> *How can you let your loved one go*
> *The father you knew so well*
> *Who was both life and breath*
> *Whose wisdom you came to know*

Caravan

Comfort will come, you'll find its embrace
For the heartbeat you knew so well
Waves of love will call and welcome you
Nestled warm beneath the wings of grace

Tears rolled down Sede's face as she listened; this gift of song had ministered love and comfort to her. The peace of Yahweh descended gently on them as they sat together looking into the fire. Shoda was silent as Shem came for Sede. He gently bent down, lifted her, and carried her to their tent. She would fall asleep in silence once more. She couldn't find the words to speak her pain. It ran too deep...too strong....

As they made their last trip over the mountain, she saw the cave she had found the day after Playtheus' death, and she had the strongest desire to stay. She approached Shem. "If you could give me anything in my sorrow, what would it be?"

As he looked into her eyes, he saw her vulnerable soul. "If I could give you anything, Sede, it would be peace."

She hesitated, searching for the right words. "I once found peace when I stayed in this forest. I found my heart once more. I want to stay here alone. Would you let me go? Would you let me find my heart in Yahweh?"

He could see her pain once more, and it moved him so. He would do anything for her, anything. "Sede, where would you stay?"

"There's a cave not far from here. I wish to stay there."

He touched his forehead to hers. "Oh, my love, I can see how you still grieve for your father. I will trust Yahweh once more with your life. Go with Yahweh for He goes with you."

She began to cry as she felt his love and compassion for her. She held him close and wept in his arms. "You will tell the others for me?"

"Yes, Sede, they know your heart is broken." He kissed her with a love that came from the depth of his heart.

"Thank you, my husband."

He watched her step into the trees and disappear in the shadows. Closing his eyes, he stood still and listened. The forest was speaking to him. As the breeze whispered in the height of the trees, his ears strained to hear the sound. He, too, knew its language. He exhaled in acceptance. She would find her heart once more, and when she did, he would be waiting for her.

Chapter 6

Taasa-toka

Shem thought of Sede every day. He knew she would find what she sought. She would come back to him with a healed heart. He worked beside his father and the others as they labored day after day, feeling a satisfaction and pride in what they had set their hands to. For truly their work had been supernaturally blessed. As he worked atop the great ark, he looked often to the forest path below. It had been two weeks and he longed to see her coming to him. She would be home, and his heart would know the peace she'd found.

As the sun began to set behind the forest, it cast a growing shadow in the valley below. Then he saw her! She stepped from the shadows and walked the path toward their village. Gratefulness filled his heart as he lowered himself with a rope. She was back...

When she saw him walking toward her, she began to run and fell into his arms. Oh, just to feel her in his arms once more. He cupped her face with his callused hands and kissed her. "You're back!" "I'm back!" they said at the same time. The comfort of just holding her filled his heart, and he sighed, "You're home!"

That night as he held her in their quiet hut, she told him of her time in the forest. She had cried much and struggled with anger about the way her father had died. "Yahweh was so gracious to me. His gentle words came to me on the breeze. 'You long for your father to come to you, Sede, but he will not come to you; you will go to him.' A great peace filled my soul as sorrow gave way to hope. Father had told me the night before he died that when my days were fulfilled, he and mother would be there waiting for me."

He felt a sudden prick of loss. He knew she would die someday, but the reality of her really dying was suddenly made real to him. She would go, leaving him. What would he ever do without her? He pulled her to himself, holding her tight, not wanting to let go. He didn't want to accept it. But deep in his heart, he knew; there *would* come a day when she would leave and not return down a forest path.

A quiet rested on their little village that night. All was well once more. As Noah slept, he dreamed. He saw the people of their little village return once more to Taasa-toka. They preached to their kin of old, pleading with them to repent and turn from evil. Then, on the horizon, he saw a great cloud of dust. Something was coming. As the dust began to clear, he saw them—a multitude of animals—coming to him. They came from all directions, multitudes of them: beasts, fowl, and creeping things. As they passed before him, those who bowed at his feet were chosen to enter the ark. They would be the ones that would live to see the "new world." When all the chosen had entered, two mighty angels closed and sealed the ark. He felt great wonder in all he saw. It felt like power, glory, and love all intermingled into one glorious feeling. When he woke, he shared his dream with the others. As he spoke, their hearts leapt that they would have this one last chance to turn the hearts of the people they had once loved.

With excitement, they held hands by couples, walking the forest path toward the village. As they moved through the quiet trees, Shoda began to sing a song as it rose spontaneously from her heart. While she sang, the others listened, their hearts warmed by the love they felt.

> *We walk the path to our past once more*
> *To Taasa-toka of old*
> *The village of our childhood*
> *Where precious memories unfold*

Taasa-toka

It was there we joyfully lived
And fellowshipped with our kin
Life was simple and full of love
Until a dark root grew, revealing sin

Their hearts are deceived now
Lost is the purity of light
Our hope's desire is the veil will lift
Restoring the gift of sight

Just then a dove flew from above. They watched it glide over the path before them. She continued...

With excitement in our hearts
We follow the way of the dove
To see repentance born in them
And witness the miracle of love

When they had reached the end of the path, the clearing opened to the village below. The excitement and love they felt gave way to shock. What they saw was unbelievable. It could only be described as confusion and utter chaos! There was no sense of control or order. The noise in the air was a jumbled combination of mumbling people aimlessly roaming about, and others loudly cursing as they argued. Dust hung like a cloud from the confused traffic of a multitude. People wore bazaar clothing while others were but scantily clad. Cainite symbols were everywhere. Suddenly a brawl brought out. Two elders were drunk and fighting in a furious rage. The violence was so great that one crushed the head of the other with a stone.

Even as this was happening, a large group of Sethites had gathered around an animal being butchered and began fighting and wildly grabbing at the flesh, eating it raw. With trembling hand Sede gripped Shem's arm trying to grasp what was happening around them. The atmosphere was so charged with evil that it pressed upon her and became hard to breathe.

When Noah and the others walked through their midst, the people hushed and descended upon them, touching them and chanting strange words. Shem and Sede looked at each other, and without saying a word, they both knew this was just like Zadanim. His face filled with horror, pulling her close to his side. There was nothing about this place that resembled the Taasa-toka they had loved and known. It was now a spiritually dark and dangerous place.

Noah led them to the council platform. As the small group stood hand in hand, they looked strangely different from the crazed people surrounding them. Their innocent faces glowed with radiant light that the crowd eagerly absorbed.

Noah stepped forward and spoke with a loud voice. "We have come to warn you this one last time. Yahweh's great judgment is about to be unleashed upon the earth. People of Taasa-toka, save yourselves and your families. Turn from the evil that surrounds you and repent. With Yahweh, 'mercy rejoices over judgment.' Do you not remember our ancestors teaching 'I, Yahweh, have no pleasure in the death of the wicked but that the wicked turn from his way and live'? Turn, turn from your evil ways, my brothers and sisters. Repent, and come with us to the ark. Your lives will be spared!" He held his arms out to them in a pleading gesture.

Ma-la, Te-mar, and Ro-nad stood below the platform, laughing and mocking him as they extended their arms in pleading gesture. Sede's eyes filled with painful tears as Te-mar and Ro-nad grabbed Ma-la and began caressing her in an unseemly manner. She laughed, watching Sede's reaction. They knew they had the power to grieve her innocence and took delight in purposely doing it. Their evil was not so much in the acts they were doing, but in the emotional pain they desired to inflict upon her innocent heart. (This is the dark evil that the Cainites had taught the Sethities: pursue and corrupt the innocent of heart and relish in its wounding).

Ro-nad taunted her, saying, "We saw your beauty, Sede, when Nersha stripped you before all our eyes. We saw your pale body and the blood that flowed when she beat you. The memory of your body and blood excites me. I desire to know you, and cut you that I might taste your blood."

Sede buried her face in Shem's chest. She could bear no more. She had loved these young hunters and now to see what they had become! Gruetat held Adat and Ne-el to his chest, covering their ears. The others lowered their heads, appalled by the evil spewing from this young man.

Spouting one after the other, as if to take turns, the elders began to taunt Noah. "Who are you to be a judge before us, Noah?"

"All the Sethite villages know you are crazy. Build a boat in the middle of land...hah!"

"The other elders have heard of your folly. They want nothing to do with your boat or your judgments!"

They all began to laugh at him, jeering and throwing food at him. "Go back to your boat and leave us!"

"We no longer care for the ways of Seth!"

"Enoch's teachings are but childhood fables. What is Yahweh's mercy to us?"

"We serve the great gods of the Cainites!"

"Yes. They give us pleasure *and* pain. *Both* are our delight!"

"We live for the pain inflicted upon us. It burns deep within our souls, giving us rumbling, dark pleasure!"

"Yahweh never gave us this kind of pleasure!"

The elders began to chant as the crowd calmed and listened. Drums began their rhythm. Their strange pounding grew louder and louder as they continued to chant. The atmosphere became charged with expectation and then, with a great single boom on the drum, there was a sudden stop! A dark hush overshadowed the great crowd as demons began to rise from the ground. An excited trill rose as the women vibrated their tongues in eager expectation. Rejoicing to see them, the people ripped their robes open and began to cut and beat themselves with knives and whips. Like magnets, the demons were drawn to their blood. All the people, young and old, eagerly welcomed them. The blood flowed, turning the people and the ground red. People began to drink each other's blood, holding a bowl beneath the flow. They laughed with shrieking pleasure as they lifted their bowls to the sky and praised the Cainite gods. It was utter mayhem.

On the platform, the "innocent" were sickened by what they saw. It was the darkest of evil: sadistic perversion; depravity; and utter corruption. The demons only added to the confusion. They were hideous in appearance and exuded only evil. (This is why the people summoned them. They knew they were evil and wanted to embrace the darkness of their sin.)

Noah shouted once more, "People of Taasa-toka, turn from this great wickedness. Save yourselves!"

Several elders yelled out, "Come down, Noah, and bring your family. We wish to know your innocence."

"We will savor defiling you and your family!" Shouts were heard throughout the crowd as they called to them to come down to them. Sede quaked as she clung to Shem, and terror filled her heart. Noah lifted his hands toward the crowd and shouted, **"STOP! You wicked and perverse generation! Yahweh REBUKE YOU ALL!"** The power of his words shook the ground, and the people weaved and staggered, struggling to stand. Terror filled their hearts. The power of Noah's rebuke brought a sudden halt to their plans.

Just as the ground had calmed from Noah's command, a low rumble began to shake the ground. A great hush fell over the crowd and the demons instantly disappeared. Bewildered, the bloodied people looked to the horizon. A cloud of dust was approaching from the distance. Noah and his family looked at each other, breathing a sigh of relief. It was as Noah dreamed.

But as the cloud of dust drew closer, their joy turned to panic. It wasn't the animals for the ark but mighty Nephilim raiders. Screams of terror filled the air from the frightened crowd. They were about to be raided! Noah led his family from the platform, but the village elders surrounded them, not letting them pass. One of the elders approached Noah and sneered. "Where is your Yahweh now? Your fate will be the same as ours." He drew back and struck a blow to Noah's jaw, knocking him to the ground. Shem drew his knife and stood before his father as a warrior, while Japheth and Ham knelt to help him stand. Drawing their blades, Sede, Shoda, Dollo and Gruetat formed a circle around their families. The elders backed away in fear of them.

Just then, like swift water flowing over rocks, the huge army rushed over the crumbling village walls that had been destroyed by Nersha's raid. It was easy to encircle the terrified people, who cowered on the knoll before the council platform. The giants shouted in rage, stomping and pounding their feet up and down as they moved in a clockwise motion around the people. The earth rumbled with the sound of their pounding feet, adding to the panic. Sede's hair stood on end, and fear gripped Shem's heart as he pulled her to his chest. He knew there would be no escape. While the Nephilim squeezed the multitude into a tight circle, frantic screams rose in the air. No longer was pleasure their heart's desire but life itself. Some of them cursed Yahweh, lifting their fists to the sky. Others screamed out for mercy from their Cainite gods. As they frantically grabbed at each other, Sede was pulled from Shem's arms. Terror filled her heart as she struggled to catch sight of him. The giants pressed the circle of captives tighter and tighter, compacting their bodies and leaving no space to move.

Then suddenly a horn sounded. In unison the giants took five steps back and drew back their spears and released them. They threw their spears, and more spears, and more spears. When they had none left to throw, they pulled bow and arrows from their arsenal. Arrows darkened the sky as they flew without number. As the last arrow was released, all was still. The whole village lay in a mound of bodies. Death hovered over the mangled and twisted that collapsed where they fell. As if released from a spell, the circle of giants silently dispersed, regrouping around their leader.

It was then the order was given to torch the huts and gather the grain and supplies from the storehouse. Animals were herded together, and they rallied to leave. They began pulling spears from the dead, saving them for their next raid, and as they retrieved the spears, they stepped through the dead, mashing them and cracking bone beneath their feet. Choosing the fattest bodies, they stuffed them in their nets, slinging them over their shoulders.

They would eat well tonight. This raid was a victory, and the feasting of the dead would be their celebration. It had been executed with surprise, speed, and no resistance. They had gotten what they came for: to pillage and destroy.

As they thundered off in the distance, an eerie silence fell over the charred and smoldering village. The only sound was the lonely whispering of wind through the tall pines beyond the crumbled walls. The devastation was complete. The massacred lie dead, nearly too numerous to count. It had happened so fast, and now it was over. But then an unexpected thing happened.

A hand moved from beneath a body. Slowly, a heavy body rolled out of the way, and Shem gasped for air. He struggled to sit up. Not far away, he saw his mother push a body off herself. Trembling, she drew herself to her knees and then stood, slowly weaving back and forth from shock. Looking around, she held her hand over her mouth, not believing what she saw. What had just happened? When Shem saw her, he stumbled and tripped over the dead in a frantic attempt to reach her. She saw him and cried out in horror. When they met, he pulled her tightly to his chest, releasing the only sound he could: "Ahee! Ahee!"

Farther away, Noah pushed himself from beneath two bodies. After he stood, he slowly turned in a circle, holding his hands to his temples. The emotional trauma of seeing all this death was almost more than he could bear. "Ahh!" he cried.

Shem and Ezmere scrambled over the dead to get to him. They huddled together, dazed and overwhelmed. As Shem's thoughts began to clear, he felt deep panic and dread. Where was Sede? As he quickly scanned over the multitude of dead, he looked for any sign of movement. How would he ever find her in this sea of death?

Splitting up, they began to find the living: Shoda, Ham, Japheth, and then Ne-el. Shem was overwhelmed. Where was Sede? He searched through the dead, crying as he turned over the people he once knew and loved, people who shared his memories. Grief bore hard upon him; evil had corrupted and consumed them. He could hardly see for the hot tears in his eyes. But then…he saw a bloody hand with a bracelet—a bracelet he recognized. It was hers! She was under Lebna, the elder who had announced their Sethite games. He rolled him out of the way and grabbed her limp body. Was she still alive? He lowered his ear, pressing it to her chest. He heard it…her heartbeat! He burst into tears, rocking her body in his arms. "You're alive…alive!"

Slowly, she opened her eyes, and from pale lips she whispered weakly, "Sh…em."

He burst into tears and drew her to his chest. "Oh Sede, Sede…"

The eight survivors gathered and sat in a daze. What had happened? Everyone was dead. Their loved ones were gone too, cruelly murdered. What were they to do about all this? It was so overwhelming. Noah opened his arms and beckoned his trembling sons to himself. As they pressed their heads into his chest, they wept. With his strong arms, he embraced them and then tenderly kissed them on their foreheads. When the time was right to speak, he gave his comfort and counsel. "We live, my sons, and it's nothing less than the supernatural hand of Yahweh that has preserved us. Our lives have a purpose that is not yet fulfilled. We will live and declare the glory of the Lord. I see what we must do in the face of this horror that surrounds us. We will find our family and friends and honor them in death. We'll bury them here in Taasa-toka, the place they once called home. Then we'll show our kin this kindness…we'll burn their bodies with fire instead of leaving them to rot and decay under the open sky. Let us draw strength now from one another to do what we must." His words brought them comfort, and by doing this act of kindness, they revealed the life of Yahweh that burned strong within them. They were still Sethites.

The men found their loved ones: Dosta, Gruetat, Mersta, little Adat, Dollo, and Zilla. With great care, they laid them gently in their graves. Shoda and Ne-el wanted Adat buried in her mother's arms and Mersta in the arms of Gruetat. They were beautiful as they lay in each other's arms. Sede wanted Dollo and Zilla buried together as well. As they were together in life, they would be together in death. Wild flowers were placed on the soft earth that now covered the ones they loved.

Sede knelt at Dosta's grave as her wet tears darkened the earth as they touched the ground. Her beloved aunt was gone. Dosta's happy heart had been so dear to her, her hugs so comforting. She thought of her wedding day and how joyful Dosta had been. The first thing Dosta had said to her that day was, 'Good morning, young bride.' She had answered, 'Good morning, mother of my heart.'

She knelt at Dollo and Zilla's grave, and a deep gratitude rose within her. Dollo had been such a wonderful friend. He had become the brother she never had. It was his kindness that had strengthened her when she was trapped in Atlantis. She would have never escaped without his help. And beautiful Zilla...she loved Dollo in such a quiet, yet strong, way. All those nights she had prepared their meals as they traveled to and from Sidon. Dollo loved her so. He said with endearment that she was the joy he lived for.

And Mersta, Gruetat, and Adat. They were like family. Mersta had been as a comforting mother, and Gruetat often called her daughter. Adat had been her little shadow. She could still see her sweet face lifted to Yahweh while they stood side by side at the altar that day so very long ago. It was the last time their village had celebrated the yearly festival. It would never be celebrated like that again. But poor Shoda and Ne-el; they not only lost their father but their mother and sister as well.

Noah and Ezmere joined them at the graves. One by one, Noah prayed over each mound of earth, weeping as Ezmere stroked his back. He lingered at Gruetat's grave. He had lost not only a friend but the last link to his own past. Tolmaka's death was deeply grieving for him for he was his dearest friend, but Gruetat's death signaled finality. He was truly now the only elder left to carry on the ways of Seth. At that moment he felt so very alone.

Shem saw how he struggled and drew near his side. Touching his father's forehead with his own, he said, "Come, Father. Let us honor them with the 'Love Song of the Dead.'" With tears in their eyes and a heart that struggled to sing, they held hands and sang together. Though only eight voices lifted the song, it was beautiful by the love in which it was sung. Harmonizing, they sang...

> *Cruel death has challenged love*
> *Your arrows pierce my heart*
> *Where once was life and light*
> *Now only hollow dark*
>
> *Bitter grief with burning tears*
> *Fall hot upon my face*
> *All is still within me*
> *Of breath, there is no trace*
>
> *Time stands still, as if it waited*
> *For my days to know their end*
> *When then your face I see*
> *Our love will triumph then*
>
> *This sacrifice I offer you*
> *My heart within my hand*
> *With open palms I lift it up*
> *Sent to you, in heaven's distant land*

They raised their palms to the heavens, sending their love skyward. The music soothed them, and they felt a blessing. The Sethite way of life was still among them. But as they pondered, somehow they knew; their lives would never be the same. This marked a change for them all.

Numb with grief, Sede told Shem she wanted to walk the path among the trees. He offered to go with her, but it was her desire to walk alone. As she walked in solitude she pondered.... When she woke that morning, little did she know it would be the last day she would spend with those who had died. How precious is the gift of just one day. No one knows when their days will come to an end and be fulfilled, as her father had said.

As she slowly walked, she saw Shoda at a distance. When she drew near, she held her, and they both cried in each other's arms. "Come sit, Shoda." Sede gestured to a rock next to the path. "Can you bear my words?"

Shoda nodded yes, unable to speak. Sede began to soothingly speak, "When we received word that you had been trampled and killed in the stampede, your mother told me such a wonderful thing. She said she had a living hope. She knew she would see you again in paradise. I felt your mother's faith and strength. Her words soothed my sorrow when I thought I'd lost you. I hope her words will now sooth your heart, Shoda." Sede was silent for a while and then remembered Shem's comforting words he had given her about her death. "The night Shem told me you had died in the stampede, he spoke these words concerning you: 'Shoda was loved. And may her life be like an arrow that shoots straight to the heart of Yahweh, finding its place of rest.' Shoda, you will see your family again. They have found a place of rest in the heart of God."

Shoda burst into tears, sobbing on Sede's shoulder. "Thank you, Sede, for your words of comfort. You and my mother are right. We, the people of Seth, have a living hope. I *will* see them again!" She sat in silence as Sede's words of comfort settled in her heart. Sede then walked farther by herself.

She saw Ne-el crying by herself and drew near, sitting beside her. She pulled her to her chest, holding her tenderly. "Oh, Ne-el, my heart is with you. I love you, little sister." When the moment was right, Sede spoke again. "My father told me something so precious the night before he died. I told

him that I wished I had known my mother. Comforting me, he told me that
when my days were fulfilled, they would be there waiting for me. I would
see her. Ne-el, your family—they're in the arms of Yahweh. They are there
waiting for you. When your days are fulfilled, you, too, will join them."

Ne-el looked through her tears into Sede's eyes. "Yes, I will see them
again. That day my heart will rejoice for we will be together again!"

Sede kissed her forehead and rested her cheek against her head. "The
grief you now feel, Ne-el, will find a place of rest within you. I found that
place for my father. Ezmere will now be your mother, and I will always be
your sister. You and Shoda will find strength and comfort from each other."
Sede led her to Ezmere, who held her to her chest.

"Come, child, you will live with me and your father, Noah. You will
someday be my daughter through marriage to Ham, but for now, you are the
daughter of my love." Ne-el began to weep, feeling Ezmere's love. She would
be all right.

When Sede joined the others, Noah had gathered them together.
"There is no way to bury the whole village, but we will honor them still."
They gathered wood for nearly two days, piling it high and covering the dead.
Lighting the fire, the flames rose in the sky. Bowing their heads in reverence,
they honored the people they once called kin. Slowly, they made their way
through the forest and back to their small village. The comforting presence
of Yahweh was close to each heart, and as they began their descent into the
valley, they saw it—the ark! It was though it welcomed them. Encouragement
filled them, and they felt renewed in some strange but comforting way.

Months passed as they continued the work on the ark; it seemed but
days for the great pleasure they felt as they labored. Sede and Shoda continued to hunt for the village while the men remained steadfast in finishing the
work. Ne-el had been joined in marriage to Ham and delighted in doing the
domestic work with Ezmere. She truly loved Ezmere, who had become her
mother and had loved her in her deepest sorrow. Noah continued to travel to
the remaining Sethite villages, preaching his message of repentance and the

judgment to come. It was love that compelled him to go, even though they continued to reject his pleadings.

The day finally came when the ark was at last finished. All the grain and hay had been stored and sealed within their cargo holds long ago. It was well preserved. The wooden tanks of water were full and could hold no more. As they stood before the open door, Noah felt a deep yearning within him to return to Taasa-toka. He couldn't shake the memory of seeing the ash and bones of his people open to the sky and not covered. If he could do one last thing before the flood, he wished to honor them and the lives they once lived as Yahweh's people. "Let us return" he said, "and do them this honor."

Gladly, they walked the path they knew so well. When they arrived, they began to cover the sun-bleached bones with the foundation stones of the huts that had been destroyed long ago by fire. Sede found the foundation of what remained of her father's hut, and a pang of loss pricked her heart. This was where her life had begun, where she had grown up and knew loving times with her family.

Shem saw her struggling and knew her heart. "Here, let me help you, Sede." He put several stones in his leather sling and said, "Let's put these as a marker for Dosta's grave."

A loving smile rose on her face, and she felt sweet comfort. "Thank you, Shem. This would be a kindness to use our stones in such a way."

They spent nearly all day covering the bones of the dead. Returning to the graves of their beloved dead, Sede saw that Shoda and Japheth had done the same for her family. They had put the stones from Gruetat's hut as markers for their grave. Ham had used the stones from Dollo's hut to mark theirs. Standing hand in hand, Noah prayed, "Yahweh, we honor our loved ones, and our hearts yearn to see them again." Shoda and Ne-el began to weep. "We know we will in Paradise. We look to that day as a day of reunion and joy!"

Sede felt compelled to comfort Shoda and Ne-el. As she hugged both of them she whispered, "Dosta and my father wait with them. When our days are fulfilled, we'll join them." Tears filled her eyes as she spoke for she, too, missed her father and Dosta. As they started down the path to their village, they heard a rumble; the earth vibrated with the sound of a multitude. There on the horizon was a cloud of dust. Fear gripped their hearts. Were the Nephilim returning to raid once more? As the cloud began to clear, they saw them—the animals that Yahweh had called. They were coming...coming from all directions. It was beyond belief. As they watched, a holy reverence filled their hearts. They realized the days of preparation were over. This was the beginning of the end!

Chapter 7

The Cave of Treasures

As the animals approached, there was a heavy peace in the air. They seemed to be in harmony with one another, and showed no fear or aggression, for they had followed the call of their Creator. Noah turned to Shem, overwhelmed by what he saw. "The hand of Yahweh is upon them. This is no more than, a great and wondrous thing we see!"

Shem was filled with awe too, hardly believing what he saw. "Father, Yahweh has revealed His mighty hand by calling these creatures from all over the world. I can only wonder how far, and how long, they have traveled to be here at just the right time and just the right place." Both of them were captivated watching them come. It was so profound; they were beholding a miracle!

The animals gathered in the plain surrounding Taasa-toka and rested from their journey. Some drank at the village stream, while others bedded in the meadow pastures. Noah and the others wandered around and through the animals, admiring the peace that rested upon them. They saw animals they had never seen before and praised Yahweh for such creatures. Some were strange, and others were exquisite in beauty.

Then Sede saw them as they came trotting toward her. It was Fallon and Mora. "Oh, Shem, come and see! I know these horses. They belonged to Playtheus. I've ridden the female. Oh, look at them!"

Shem marveled at their majesty; their manes and tails feathered in the breeze as they drew near. Fallon nudged Shem's chest with his head, whinnying softly as Shem stroked his muscular neck. His head rose and fell in nods, as if approving Shem's touch. Overwhelmed by what he felt, Shem responded, "Oh, I hope they're chosen; truly, they are magnificent." He saw other horses too that had gathered. Many of the same kinds of animals had come, but only the animals that bowed before Noah would enter the ark. By this act of humble submission, they were acknowledging Noah as their guardian, just as he had dreamed.

That night they camped near the animals and slept beneath the stars. It had been a day like no other. Their eyes had seen the finished ark, they had returned to Taasa-toka and honored the dead, and then there had been the miraculous appearing of the animals. A sense of awe stirred within them as they realized that Yahweh's plan was unfolding before their very eyes.

It was that night Shem had a dream. He and Sede were in the Cave of Treasures, standing once more before the golden table were Adam rested. The Watcher spoke to him in the dream and said, "It is time, Shem. You must bring him to the ark. He and his treasures will be saved from the waters that will cover the earth." When Shem woke in the morning, he shared his dream with Sede and his father. Enthusiastically, Noah responded, "Yes, you must go. Take Sede, and do all the Watcher has said. Great wonders continue to unfold before us, Son!"

While Sede prepared her things, she urged him to take Fallon and Mora. They would be the help they needed to bring Adam's body back. As they began their trek, it was Shem's delight to ride on Fallon's back for he, like Sede in Atlantis, had never ridden before. The world seemed so different atop a running animal. And oh, how he loved it when Fallon ran. It was a freedom he had never known before and a wonderful pleasure to feel the wind in his face. The long distance to the cave was not tiresome but a journey of ease. As they traveled, Shem remembered the landmarks through the mountains. When they stopped to camp, they both felt energized by this strange adventure they were on. Their conversations were filled with the wonder of what they were feeling.

The Cave of Treasures

When they arrived at the cave, the horses were left below; they took only the litter, ropes, and leather bags with them. Slowly they made their ascent, climbing the face of the mountain. The entrance of the cave was dark, and had they not known any different, it seemed like any ordinary cave. They crouched at the entrance and settled back, leaning against the rock wall. But after hours had passed, they wondered why the Watcher hadn't appeared.

"What should we do, Shem? The Watcher delays."

He stood and peered into the cave, wondering what they should do. He sat next to her again and was deep in thought. After a few minutes he answered, "I believe we need to walk by faith and not by sight."

She gave him a puzzled look. "What do you mean?"

"Father told me: 'When there is something we are asked to do by Yahweh, but something hinders us, and we don't know what to do next, this is when we should trust Yahweh and do what we know He wants us to do. We should not consider what we see with our eyes. As we take the first step toward obedience, it is then Yahweh brings the answer.' This is what Father calls 'taking a step of faith.' He experienced this when he received the word from Yahweh to build the ark. As he began to do what seemed impossible, was when Yahweh helped him, and the work on the ark seemed to supernaturally get done. In the same way, I believe we should obey what the Watcher told me to do. We should step into the cave, believing Yahweh will show us the way."

She stood and smiled, extending her hand. "I'm ready, Husband!" He returned a smile and took her hand as she pulled him to his feet.

Hand in hand, they took their first step into the cave, and the darkness suddenly exploded with light! The same iridescent glow they had seen the last time again lit the stone walls, ceiling, and floor. Both were surprised and gave a startled "Oh!" Instantly, their spiritual eyes had been opened. "Shem, you were right about taking a step of faith. Yahweh has shown us the way!"

Clasping each other's hands, they entered the small chamber in the back of the cave. The golden table glowed with light. Nothing had changed. It was as they had left it. The loving presence of Yahweh enveloped them, and they could feel His wonderful peace.

Shem took her hands, and they faced each other, looking into each another's eyes. This was an experience that Yahweh intended for them to have together. "This is really happening, Sede. We are going to bring Adam with us! Are you ready to move him?" She inhaled and nodded in excitement. Slowly, they lifted Adam's body and gently placed it on the litter. As soon as they touched him, the smell of frankincense burst forth, filling the room. The fragrance was heady, and they deeply inhaled. They felt a strengthening power rise within them and looked at each other, the "Light of Life" dancing in their eyes.

Shem secured Adam to the litter and gestured toward the table. "We must take his treasures also. Here are the leather bags, Sede." Carefully, she wrapped the stone vases of frankincense, myrrh, and gold that were leaning against the table. Holding a jeweled covered box she paused to ponder. Carefully, she opened the lid. As she did, the fragrance from the leaves and spices filled the air. She knew there must be a reason Adam had saved them. It was a mystery she wished she knew. She pondered still…. Adam and Eve had lived their lives, making memories, just as she and Shem had. She wished she had known them, had heard their stories, and had seen the love they shared.

Shem looked intently at the golden table. He had an inner knowing that if he lifted the lid, he would find more of Adam's treasures. "Here, Sede, help me lift the lid." As they gently raised the golden lid, their eyes beheld what Adam held dear: an emerald rod, two sets of lamb skin aprons, and a beautiful leather parchment scroll. Both of them instantly knew what they were. The emerald rod was given to Adam by Yahweh to till the soil when he and Eve left Eden. The two lamb skins covered their nakedness after they had sinned. And the parchment scroll…it was father Enoch's. The Sethites had copies, but this was Enoch's very own, handwritten by him. He had wished it buried with Adam.

The Cave of Treasures

Shem held the precious scroll to his chest. He closed his eyes and kissed the cover. His chest rose and fell in deep emotion, and he began to softly weep. All that the Sethites had been taught had come from these writings. Shem loved his people so. As Sede watched, she was deeply moved by his love and reverence. She knew that someday he would lead the Sethites after Noah was gone. Her heart filled with thanksgiving, knowing that he would be her leader too. How wonderful that Yahweh chose such a man!

There was something else—something that was hidden beneath a beautiful blanket of fur. As they brushed the fur back, they saw her. It was Eve! She was not wrapped as Adam but sealed within a jeweled coffin. A lid of clear, transparent stone covered her. They could see her clearly. "Oh!" they gasped at the same time. She was breathtaking and looked as though she peaceably slept. Eve had been Adam's most precious possession. Even in death, he was her covering, for she lay safely beneath him. They marveled that she looked so young, for they knew from the elders' teachings that she had lived as long as Adam—930 years. Sede pondered… 'Perhaps Yahweh restores our youth like the eagles when we die. In Yahweh's eyes, we are forever young.' As she marveled at Eve's beauty and youth, she wished she could see Adam's likeness. He was Yahweh's crowning glory, made in his likeness. What would that image look like?

A thick cloud of sparkling light descended on Sede, and she began to prophecy. "I am the daughter of Eve and carry her seed within me. I am her promise, prophesied by Yahweh himself. My seed will continue the lineage for the 'Promised One' to come. The serpent will bruise his **heel**, but He will crush his **head**!" She staggered on her feet as Shem steadied her. A profound hush settled around them as if heaven had been stilled. And then, angelic music filled the chamber with the sound of heaven. Oh, the beauty of the angelic voices, singing the song of heaven! One voice in particular stood out among the heavenly choir. It was Yahweh, singing his love song to Eve. His voice was crystal clear, pure, and full of love. As they listened, they gazed upon the "mother of all living."

Sede, Seed of Eden

Adam was my crown and glory, until I gazed within his heart
And saw an empty, needing place that was not whole, but part
It was not good he be alone, creation had their mate
From his side I took you, in dreaming sleep, he would wait

You were the first of your kind, one never heard or seen before
You were glory upon glory, a gift given, most precious for evermore
We walked together through the trees, when I led you by your hand
To wake your husband from his dreaming sleep, and before him in glory stand

His eyes did fall upon you, when I woke him from his sleep
In awe and wonder he beheld, as I placed your hand in his to keep
In beauty did I wrap your flesh, with gentle grace and glory
For into his life I've handwritten you on each page of his story

Never had he seen such wonder, in all my hands had made
For in you he saw a part of him that would be forever laid
Once he was but one, and then with you made twain
The best of him I put in you; so he'd never be lonely again

When all was quiet once more, Shem looked into Sede's eyes and with whispered wonder said, "You are my treasure, Sede, as Eve was his. I am your covering, as Adam was hers. They were the first of their kind. After the flood, all will become new. We have been chosen to be the first of our kind in the 'new world.' We, too, will fill the earth with our seed as they did with theirs. With all my heart, I want to be a man of God. Being in Adam's presence has caused me to know this. I will lead our family in righteousness and truth. I make this covenant with you, Sede, before Yahweh right now; I will lead our family in righteousness and truth!" She trembled as he spoke for she felt the power of Yahweh on him and the importance of what he was saying. As he held her in his arms, she felt as though she was in the safest place in the universe. For as he held her, his arms felt as though they were the arms of

God. She was in the arms of love.

They carefully lowered Adam and Eve to the waiting horses below. The glory that still rested on them now fell upon the horses. They whinnied softly and bowed before Adam and Eve, kneeling on one foreleg and bending their heads low. Shem and Sede watched in awe. They, too, knelt and bowed their heads. This honor and respect they would give to the first of creation.

Slowly they began their return in solemn silence. They would never forget what they saw, what they heard, and what they felt. Their eyes had beheld the crowning glory of Yahweh's creation: the father and mother of mankind.

Chapter 8

Chosen for the Ark

When Shem and Sede returned to the ark, they discerned what they had experienced in the cave was to be kept a secret. It had been a gift given to them alone. As they stepped into the ark, they stopped as the reality of Yahweh's judgment seemed to fall upon them. This ark would save their lives. This ark would be their home. This ark would see a "new world!" They listened for a sound, but there was none. The stillness nearly took their breath away.

By dim lamplight, they brought Adam and his treasures to the secret place. It was directly beneath Noah and Ezmere's nook. Noah and Shem had built it knowing it was to remain secret. Yahweh had instructed them that they were the only three to know. (For Yahweh knew the hearts of man. A future generation might see their bodies, as well as their treasures, and covet them or, worse yet, worship them!) Opening the hatch door, they gently lowered Eve's body in place. In the same order they had found them, they set them to rest. Surrounding Eve's casket with fur coverings, they rested the treasures on top of the lid. Adam was then gently laid on top of them. Folding the furs, they padded his body. When the ark shifted and rocked, he would rest secure. Someday he and his treasures would find a resting place in a new world.

"Come, Sede, walk with me. I want to experience the quiet and anticipation that awaits this place." A soft glow reflected from the lamps mounted against the walls, giving light to the long corridors. Everything was ready. All the food and water was in place, and every stall had a bed of straw with its door propped open. The air had the lovely smell of sweet hay from the mangers. She looked at Shem and smiled. He, too, felt the pleasure of his senses. He led her down the quiet corridor to their living space and smiled as she noticed their names carved over the wooden doorpost. Lifting the woven curtain, he led her inside. There, a small but cozy room surrounded them. A bed had been built into the framework, and a small table with two stools rested against the wall.

She leaned her head on his shoulder and softly said, "In this quiet place, we'll find comfort and consolation."

He smiled and kissed the top of her head sweetly. He knew it would be so.

They continued to walk through the decks, seeing their brothers' sleeping nooks. They had carved their names over their doors just as he had. In the middle of the second deck was Noah and Ezmere's dwelling place. This would be where they would gather for all their meals. Their living space was understandably much larger than their sons'. An area had been constructed for meal preparations. A pit with sand and stones was built into the floor's framework. This is where they would build their small fire and prepare their food. Part of the storehouse of food reserved for them included grain for grinding into flour, vegetables, fruits, nuts, cheese, and an abundance of dried meats. They knew too that cows and goats would provide milk.

The ark's interior design was amazing. There were three decks. The first was for large animals, the second for smaller ones, and the third for birds and creeping things. Each deck was similar but yet different. They were similar in that each deck had stalls that lined the great outer walls and a row of stalls in the middle. Every level had their own storage of both food and water. But each deck was constructed somewhat differently in order to accommodate the size and types of animals that would live in them. Because the first deck housed the huge and tall animals, it had a single story of stalls that went from floor to ceiling. The second deck had two stories of stalls. A catwalk serviced the second story with a simple staircase connecting the two levels. On the third deck, there were three stories of many small compartments for birds and creeping things. Three catwalks created access to these levels. There was rafter after rafter of perches for birds and domestic fowl.

In the center of this third deck was a wondrous sight. Built into the framework of the ark was a great kolopus tree. It had been cut to half its trunk's height and secured into the ark's flooring. Though great in size and with many branches, the kolopus wood is fibrous and doesn't have the weight as other trees do. This great tree would give primates and birds a place to exercise with freedom. The tree towered over a rocky area beneath. Here, creatures who nest and make their home in the ground could obey their natural instincts to be in seclusion. Lava rock was chosen for its light weight, and sand filled the space around them. Here, the ground dwellers could make their holes and nests. Yahweh was a master architect. He had designed the universe—how much easier to design an ark to accommodate man and animals.

From his dream, Noah knew where to put each animal in the ark. He knew to group them for the sake of compatibility and ease of feeding. He was to choose a male and female pair of each species of unclean animals and seven pairs of clean animals. This distinction between clean and unclean animals was made by Yahweh himself, though Noah had never considered there to be a difference. This was special knowledge and understanding given to him to discern the intrinsic differences between species and types.

Through this whole selection process, Noah and his sons perceived the heart of Yahweh. What an intricate world He had created, from the largest animals to the very smallest. He not only loved and wished to preserve mankind but these wondrous creatures as well. The more Noah learned about the animals, the more he realized what they didn't know. Why would Yahweh create clean and unclean animals? Why not just create clean ones? How did these animals know when to sleep and when to mate? What causes a bird to take flight and soar? Why did some animals sleep during the season of hibernation? The more he knew, the more questions he had. Truly, Yahweh was amazing.

As Shem and Sede were leaving the ark, she stopped at the great door. "Wait," she said. "I want to do something!" Turning to face the open door, she lifted her palms toward heaven. Looking upward, she whispered, "Thank you, Yahweh, for choosing to save us from the coming judgment and that you have prepared this place of safety. I give you my praise!" And then, with the greatest of tenderness, she breathed, "And I give you my love!"

Shem watched as she spoke from the deepest place in her heart. He was seeing, for the first time, her intimate love for Yahweh. Her heart was so soft and tender. He knew the love he had in his own heart for Yahweh, but for this split second, he was seeing hers. A heavenly peace enfolded him, and his spiritual eyes were able to see more. She seemed so full of life. He sensed her divine purpose, her value, and her importance to Yahweh. All this was open before him. And here he was, seeing her love Him from the most intimate place in her heart. The revelation then dawned on him: 'Every heart that loves Yahweh has this secret place of love for Him.' Oh, how beautiful hers was and that he had been given the privilege to see it.

She turned and saw that he was caught in wonder of what she had given Yahweh. She blushed. She momentarily felt vulnerable that someone had seen her intimacy with God, but trust instantly replaced vulnerability. She knew she could trust him even to see this secret place. She knew that Yahweh was trusting him too by opening his eyes to see it.

"You're amazing, Sede," he whispered in awe. "I'm so glad I know you and that you have such great love for Him. You are so very precious!" He closed his eyes to savor the moment. When he opened them she saw his innocence.

She whispered, "Oh, Shem, you've seen my love for Yahweh. It is a great wonder to me that He would allow anyone to see this secret place and behold worship intended only for Him!'

Shem then had a glorious thought. "Let us join together and love him as you just did—together as one—opening our secret places to Him."

Smiling, she nodded. They held hands and lifted their faces to heaven. Closing their eyes and with purity of heart, they spoke their words of love to the God of their love. They took turns as they spoke.

"Yahweh, I love you from the depth of who I am."

"My love for you far surpasses what I could give to anyone else."

"I am your creation giving back to you, the Creator, the love I hold only for you!"

'Could anything be more glorious?' Shem thought. The atmosphere around them was charged with life, and the fragrance of Yahweh permeated the air. They inhaled deeply, taking in heaven's aroma.

It was then they saw two large angels materialize. With giant wings extended, they slowly and gently enfolded them. There Sede and Shem stood in the middle of the embrace of angel wings. They heard the angel's voices, and even though they were speaking in the language of heaven, they knew they were words of love to *their* God. They, too, had a secret place of love that was now open for others to see. The music of heaven filled the air, only adding to the glory they felt. A song they had never heard before, but instantly knew, arose from their hearts, and the four of them sang these words to the God they worshipped:

> *Yahweh, you are the Glorious One!*
> *Unlike any that was or ever will be!*
> *From our secret place we worship you...*
> *It is you alone we see...*
>
> *"Living love" is exchanged...*
> *It rises and flows between you and our hearts.*
> *Love is released only to be held again*
> *As divine worship imparts.*

When the worship had ended and the music of heaven stilled, the angels slowly disappeared, and silence stilled their hearts. They didn't speak, but both of them knew: Heaven had touched earth.

When the beauty of the moment was satisfied, he softly asked, "Shall we go?"

She smiled with the love of God still shining in her eyes. She felt prophetic words rise within her and spoke, "This is only the beginning for us, Shem. We will live to see more glory when the world is renewed and clean. The end of our days will tell of us that we *were* the people of God!" Her profound words testified to both of them.

As they walked back to Taasa-toka, they held hands in silence, musing within themselves what they had just experienced. A lovely satisfaction filled them. They had just laid Adam and Eve to rest and worshiped with the angels. Sede began to wonder, did Adam and Eve share this same kind of worship they had just experienced? Did the angels fold their wings around them in loving embrace? When they were in Eden, they walked with Yahweh in the cool of the day. Was that when they spoke their love to him from the secret place within them? As she considered the secret place of worship, she realized intimacy with God was a mysterious thing—invisible, but so very real. What a wonder this supernatural God was, that could fill her heart with so much love that she couldn't help but love and thank Him in return!

When they arrived at Taasa-toka, they saw the multitude of animals resting in the plain surrounding the village. They seemed to be waiting for something. As night turned to dawn, the small family knew it would be a day like no other. It was now time; the day of glory had come. The animals stirred and began to line up. No one roused or herded them. They just seemed to know what to do.

Noah called his family to himself. "This work we are about to do is far beyond our knowledge and experience, just as was the building of the ark. We need the supernatural power of Yahweh to see this done." Lifting his hands and face to the sky, he prayed with a loud voice, "Yahweh, Creator of heaven and earth, give us an understanding heart to be guardians of your creatures. Give us knowledge to care for them and know their needs. You alone have made them and know all their ways."

A cloud of glory descended upon them, much like the one they knew from their sacrifices. It glistened and sparkled as it touched their joy-filled faces. They all felt a special knowledge and understanding imparted to them and looked at each other in surprise. The women joyfully grabbed each other and hugged, their faces aglow with wonder. The men, too, hugged, amazed at what they now possessed. They knew that they had received what Noah had asked for. They would be able to care for the animals, understanding their needs and able to meet them.

Noah led the way to the ark, and the animals followed in a line. In the valley around the ark, the animals patiently waited as each pair, male and female, passed before Noah. He and Ezmere kept a record of the sets of pairs according to Yahweh's command for clean and unclean animals. As the chosen bowed, they were ushered into the ark by Noah's sons. Sede, Shoda, and Ne-el stood by the open door as each animal paused to enter. They waited to be acknowledged by the women. Gladly, they petted and stroked them while the animals sniffed their hands, accepting their scent. Each woman seemed to have a special interest in the different kinds of animals. Sede felt akin to the larger animals, while Shoda was drawn to the smaller ones. Ne-el loved the birds that rested on her shoulders while they waited to be ushered inside.

Shem, Ham, and Japheth felt overjoyed by their new abilities to work with the animals. They had an immediate knowing. They didn't have to wonder how to care for them; they just knew. They, too, sensed a special interest in the different kinds of animals, as had their wives. Some male and female pairs were but cubs or young. It mattered not that they were full grown. Their only conditions to boarding the ark were to be a male and female pair and to bow in subjection to Noah.

The large and great creatures came, and Noah marveled at their approach. The ground shook with each step they took. They were the great and mighty beasts of the earth. He knew they were too large to enter, but still they came. When the long-necked behemoths approached, he and his mate bowed and opened their mouths, revealing two large eggs. They gently laid them at his feet. They had carried them from their dwelling place to offer them before Noah. Noah and Ezmere began to weep when they realized the sacrifice these creatures were making. They knew they couldn't enter, but their offspring could. Many more of these gigantic beasts came with their eggs, laying them at his feet. He marveled that Yahweh had found a way to keep these giant creatures alive to see the "new world." All day they came: large and small animals, birds, and creeping things. It was a day of glory, as they had sensed it would be.

For three days they came and passed before Noah. Truly, Yahweh had a sense of humor. Some of the animals were quite amusing. Some had unusual shapes, while others were strange in color and plumage. A tall creature with four long legs and a very long neck approached. Noah had never seen the like. The pair struggled to bow but were able to slightly bend one knee and lower their heads. Small furry creatures with curled tail chattered as they hung from nearby trees, swinging from branch to branch. Strange-colored apes leapt as they approached; their faces matched the coloring of their rumps. They were most amusing in sight and behavior.

The great stork and eagle were familiar to Noah, but some of the birds were not. One kind of large bird had two long legs with a great round body. It was much taller than a man and held its huge head high by a long, thin neck. Feathers fanned to form its tail in colorful plumage. Creeping creatures waddled before him, having scales and long tails. Their mouths were nearly half the length of their bodies and were filled with long, sharp teeth. Noah was pleased that Yahweh had put His peace upon them. For like this animal, some were fierce in appearance.

When the horses began to pass before Noah, Sede held her breath. Several pairs passed but hadn't bowed. Then she saw Fallon and Mora approach, prancing as they came. At the same time, they bent one foreleg and lowered their heads. They whinnied softly as they did obeisance. Noah responded and said, "Rise and enter, for you have been chosen!" They rejoiced by rearing before him on their hind legs, while their front legs pawed the air. It was a magnificent display of praise! Sede began to joyfully cry. They *had* been chosen! As they approached the ramp, they trotted toward her and nuzzled her softly with their foreheads. She gladly patted them while Shem came alongside her.

"Oh, Sede, they *were* chosen. I'm so pleased. They're so magnificent." He ushered them into the ark with tears in his eyes.

Sede contemplated as she saw them follow him, 'Playtheus would have been so pleased. He had loved them, and now they will survive. If only they could tell of their journey from Atlantis.' It occurred to her that perhaps the Watchers were involved in making a way for all these animals to arrive at just the right place and just the right time.

At the end of the third day all the stalls had been filled; there were no other creatures waiting in line. Shem led the last of the animals that had not been chosen back to Taasa-toka. There, the animals from the previous days lingered: the great and mighty behemoths as well as small deer, lions, birds, and a multitude of others. Here they peaceably waited, as if they knew something else was to happen. He returned and told the others what he had seen. Everything about the last three days had been hard to believe. Who but Yahweh could have the power to orchestrate such an endeavor?

Noah and his family walked the aisles of the ark as wonder filled their hearts. All the stalls were full. The large tree branches were filled with birds and happy primates. The rocky areas beneath them were now homes for the ground dwellers. All the animals were together in one place. They were now safe and settled in the ark of refuge.

Chapter 9

Last Farewell

The day had come. All the work of building, traveling for provender, moving the many tons of cargo from the river, sealing the grain and hay in the ark's chambers, filling the water reservoirs, and the animal selection was now complete. None of them needed to say anything to the others. They seemed to know; the time they had prepared for had come. A seriousness settled on them as they gathered at Noah and Ezmere's hut. He looked tenderly at his sons and daughters, knowing they were uncertain of what was to come next. They all felt it. "All is finished, my children. You must go to your huts and gather what you wish to save. Take them to the ark. It is time!"

Shem and Sede entered their quiet hut. It seemed to welcome them. In the time that had passed, sweet memories had been made as they shared their lives within these walls. She had grown into a graceful, mature woman, and just as her father said, wisdom had embraced her innocence, becoming a thing of beauty, full and mature. This place had known her transformation, and this place had known their love. Shem gathered his copy of Enoch's parchments, and Sede collected their hunting weapons. They lived simple lives, and there wasn't much to take with them. She took the box Shem had made for Eden's seed and their three-stranded wedding cord. From the shelf, she took the stone her father had given her, Playtheus' box, Ba-nea's cloak, and a new scroll. They piled everything on their bed coverings, rolling them together in a bundle. With leather ropes, Shem tied them off, and they were ready to leave. They paused at the door. Looking over their shoulders, each felt a pang of loss in their heart. They would never see this place again. "Come, Sede, I want to do something."

Setting the bundles at the door, he took her hand and led her to the hearth. As they stood there, she slowly ran her fingers over the words he had carved into the wood. She mouthed them to herself: "To everything there is a season and a time to every purpose under heaven." Shem watched her as she pondered the words. Then, looking up, she realized he was honoring her moment of reflection. She smiled and sweetly thought, 'How kind of him to give me the privacy of my own thoughts.'

"Sede, let's say our goodbye with a prayer here in this place we both loved."

She stroked his cheek and said, "I would like that."

He took her hands and closed his eyes. Lifting his head, he spoke the words of his heart. "Thank you, Yahweh, for this place we called home. With love I prepared it for my wife and our life together. You know the many nights I spent here, when she was held captive, thinking of her and trusting that you would bring her back to me. You did, and how glad I am for the life we now have as man and wife. I believe the words on this hearth, that you have a purpose for us. Everything about our future will have a time and a season. Help us to bend like a reed in the wind to the many changes that lie ahead of us. Give us courage, strength, and love to see the end of our days. I give you my glory!" He could hardly end his words for the deep emotion that now swept over him. He wept softly as he pulled Sede's hand to his chest. The presence of Yahweh surrounded them as if loving arms held them, and they felt the warmth of His love flowing to the very depths of their souls. Sede, too, began to weep.

She waited until her heart was ready and then began her prayer. "Yahweh, life was so simple in this world I've known. I loved the season of my life with Father, our village, and the adventure of the hunt. I love this season I now have with my husband, knowing the love of a woman for a man. You gave me the promise of the seed of Eden, and we have a purpose to fulfill. Thank you for saving our lives so we can. You hold our future in your hands, and in your hands we rest. My heart rises to say to you, Yahweh… I love you…I love you!" She began to weep once more as she felt a comforting wave of love move through her.

Shem lowered his head to touch her forehead and softly whispered, "Took-la-say-a-la-nay," for it was farewell. They walked to the entrance, and this time they didn't look back but only at each other. They saw in each other's eyes the acceptance they now possessed. They were ready to step into their future, for they had said good-bye to their past.

When they entered the ark, the others came in behind them. They, too, had their things bundled. Sede could see on Shoda's face the tracks of tears where she had cried from leaving the home Japheth had made for her. Ham and Ne-el came, helping Noah shoulder his bundles for Ezmere, who had all their cooking utensils, pans, and bowls. Each couple moved silently to their dwelling places.

Sede and Shem settled in their small nook they would now call home. It smelled of fresh straw. Beneath their feet was strewn a thin layer of straw, making a nice covering for the floor. He set their bundle on the bed and untied the rope binding. He gently set Enoch's scrolls on the table while Sede took the lamps from the bundle and positioned them on each side of the table. In a small way, she wanted things to be as they had been in their hut. She placed the rest of their things on the shelf above their bed. After she had smoothed the furs, she smiled. "We'll dream of the 'new world' on this bed."

"Yes, Sede, together we'll dream of a future that is yet to be discovered."

Standing by the door, they looked around. What they saw was simple but cozy. It was theirs to call home.

They returned to Noah and Ezmere and found the others were already gathered and seated around the small fire pit. They took their place, and Noah settled next to Ezmere, gently patting her knee and giving her a reassuring smile.

"I need to tell you what Yahweh has spoken to me, children." They eagerly hung on his every word. "In seven days the judgment begins. As we begin our lives here in the ark, there will probably be times you'll feel great fear, and other times, you will feel great relief for being spared. This is the one thing we will need to remember: Yahweh intends that we live and not die as well as the animals in our care. What is about to happen has a purpose."

Sede and Shem looked at each other when he said "purpose." They smiled and squeezed each other's hands.

"He is going to cleanse the world of all the corruption of both man and fallen angels. There will be nothing left alive that draws a breath, be it man, animal, or Nephilim. We have never seen rain, but we will. Yahweh intends to open the windows of heaven and the fountains of the deep. For forty days and forty nights it will rain. The whole earth will be covered with water. As we wait within the safety of the ark, the days will pass. They will be filled with caring for the animals and preparing our hearts for the 'new world.' We will draw strength to endure, both from Yahweh and each other. He has determined that each of you, my sons, will care for the animals on the level of your dwellings. My daughters, you will help them. We will gather to eat, just as we did in our little village." He again patted Ezmere's knee and gave her a warm and loving smile. "It will be here that I will gradually share the plans for the 'new world' that Yahweh has shown me. During this time, too, I must impart the wisdom of the elders. We no longer have a culture that can provide this for you. The ceremonies no longer exist that would have ushered you into this knowledge and understanding. It will be the eight of us who will lay the foundation for generations to come."

"Now, concerning the work at hand. In a dream, Yahweh has shown me that many of the animals will sleep the sleep of hibernation. These are the carnivores. It is a great mystery and wonder how this can be, but with Yahweh, all things are possible. The eggs that the great beasts brought before me will be kept beneath the warmth of furs and rotated daily. We will exercise the large animals down the long corridors that stretch the length of the ark.

Yahweh has revealed to me that they have surrendered to us their very lives. They will not resist our efforts in any way. Our numerous storehouses of grain, hay, and water will be opened as more is needed. I'll help each of you, giving you a day of rest from your labor, and rotate from son to son. Ezmere will prepare our meals and see to the filling of the oil lamps in the corridors and your rooms. Ask her, my daughters, for any help you need. Together we will fulfill the will of Yahweh."

They looked at each other as he finished his instructions, feeling strength rise within them. It was though they had received a commission from the Lord.

"And now I have a gift for each of you, my sons. I made them myself." From a leather bag, he withdrew four horns. They were like the hunting horn Tolmaka had carried for their pack. "We will use these to signal each other for this ark is great in size. Strap these to your belt and carry them with you at all times." He paused and then tearfully said, "I love you, my children. I give Yahweh thanks that you have been spared and will live to see a new day!" After the men had secured their horns to their belts, Noah rose and said, "Now, come to the door of the ark, and bid your last farewell to the world we once knew. Yahweh intends to seal the door."

Holding each other's hands, they stood at the entrance. Before them was the cleared valley where mighty trees once grew, cut long ago to build the ark they now stood in. The forest trail beyond led to the old village of Taasa-toka. Their huts stood silent, never again to know laughter or the warmth of their presence. Each of them felt a multitude of memories rise within them. The life they had lived as children, the happiness of their families, the festivals, the hunts, joyous times as they lived their days as Sethites—all had come to an end. They had known the best of this world, but Yahweh had seen its worst. Although they felt a deep sadness to see the end of all things, they knew, too, its evil. They had personally witnessed the indiscriminate slaughter at Taasa-toka and knew this was but one of hundreds of Sethite villages that had known the same fate.

Sede and Ham had seen the evil of Atlantis and the corruption of the fallen angels. The evil was also in the unseen things that had been ravished: their whole way of life that had been stolen, and the irreversible travesty that future generations would never have a connection with the ancient world. Now the only thing that remained of their heritage was what they carried in their hearts. Each one of them knew Yahweh was just and right to condemn and destroy the evil that had corrupted His creation. Out of love for mankind, he had spared the eight that stood at the door and would begin again with a "people after his own heart."

Noah felt impressed to extend his palms and hold them before him. As he did, a drop of water fell on each palm. He began to softly weep for he knew what they were. He knew from Enoch's writings what Yahweh had told Himself after He had finished His creation: 'And I saw everything that I have made, and behold, it was very good.' But now the heart of the Creator was broken: 'And I see that the wickedness of man is great on the earth, and that every imagination of the thoughts of their heart is only evil continually. I deeply regret that I have made man, and it grieves me at the heart.' What lie in Noah's palms were the tears of God... The Creator found no pleasure in destroying something that was once so very beautiful. "Reach forth your hands, children, and bid this world farewell," Noah said with sadness in his voice.

The "eight" raised their hands toward the outside world. In unison, they tearfully whispered, "Took-la-say-a-la-nay."

At that moment their spiritual eyes were opened, and they saw two magnificent angels standing on each side of the great door of the ark. It was just as Noah had dreamed. They were there to close and seal the door. Stepping back, Noah and his family watched as the huge door slowly closed and the last light of the outside world disappeared. They heard the breath of the angels as they blew upon the pitch surrounding the door; it began to melt into the cracks where the door fit into the groove of the frame. They looked at each other, scarcely believing what they saw and heard. The breath of the angels had sealed the door!

Last Farewell

"Come, children, let us begin our work." Each son walked with their wife down the long corridor of their level. Shem and Sede had the lowest level that housed the large animals; Japheth and Shoda had the middle, with the small animals; and Ham and Ne-el had the top level, with the birds, primates, and ground dwellers. It was on this third level that the beasts' eggs rested in warm furs. As the three couples walked hand in hand, a great peace settled on them. Today marked the beginning of the end.

Chapter 10

Ruin of Atlantis

The birth pangs of the world were now in full motion. For the righteous, it was the building of the ark; for the wicked, it was the death of Playtheus. His death marked the end of an era of glory, and the hour was soon approaching that would be the present world's last. Yahweh, in His wisdom, had told Noah to fill the ark with provision. It was the "set time" to do so. For, right after this, the world of commerce began to crumble. No longer was there a steady supply of grain, meat, oil, and spices coming from the frontier. The frontier wilderness had been destroyed by raiding Nephilim. The great abundance from the Sethite villages was scarce to nonexistent. Only the fields outside Atlantis now supplied what the city needed, and the raiding Nephilim began to be in wont. They set their eye upon the glut that existed in Atlantis.

At Zadanim, the Hagonoth giants gathered to organize and unite their troops. Captains over small bands united with other bands that joined with other bands, forming one great army. If there was no more food from the wilderness, they would find it in Atlantis.

Grog was hailed as leader. He was a veteran of many battles and had proven himself to be mighty in their midst. It was he who had fought alongside "Nersha the Great." He would be the one to form a strategy of attack on Atlantis. The "Golden Bird" continued to sail every seven days, and he used this sailing schedule to move his troops near the "City of the Sons"; they waited at their outpost, a remote camp outside the city. For months he moved his army in place, waiting for the right time.

Under his orders, they secretly raided Atlantis' unprotected fields and storehouses. They left paraphernalia of the Cainites to divert suspicion from themselves; the Cainites were blamed, and valiant Renown Warriors were sent to destroy the Cainite villages. Zadanim itself had been attacked and crippled by the onslaught of these mighty warriors. The world had become a crazy world of wars—a world where the violent were taking the violent by force. Things were now in motion for the birth of judgment's destruction.

Atlantis, in the meantime, was oblivious to what was really happening in the world. Life continued as it always had. The Regal Renown socialized at Champion Hall, the business district buzzed with trading, and Sethites could still be bought at the market. Everywhere in the city was beauty, music, and luxury. It was in this atmosphere of ease that the city prepared for the Champion Games.

After the yearly sacrifice to their gods, this sporting event brought the Mighty 200, their sons, and the citizens out of their mansions and homes to the coliseum for a week of revelry and competition. These games were spectacular in displaying the "best of the best" Renown Warriors. Their abilities dazzled the crowd, who also enjoyed the side benefits of their combat. They were able to drink the "drink of the victorious," and it was the people's belief that they received power from the blood of the slain, energizing them with the life that the dead once lived. They mingled blood with wine to make their drink of victory. By the end of the games the whole stadium would be drunk with wine and blood.

The 200 were filled with pride watching their Warrior sons in combat. They refused to acknowledge the Hagonoths as sons but proudly boasted of their progeny: the Renown Warriors. It was magnificent to see the arena decked with the brilliant blue of glowing angels, their breathtaking wives, the Renown sons with their beautiful companions, and the celebrating and enthusiastic people of the city. The air was electrified with the thrill of what was in store for the beholder.

Satsum-kedesh and his son, Apogee, hadn't gone to the games but had spent the day at Champion Hall. There, they had meticulously gone over and over their findings. His room remained the same as it had been when Playtheus had shown it to Sede except now his parchments, maps, and charts were strewn about from their feverish searching. Apogee had become alarmed with his readings for the Renown when he kept reading **death** with each reading. This was very perplexing, and he began to dig deeper into the alignments. Then he found it! The signs revealed there *would* be death to the Nephilim—death by a worldwide flood! He only needed his father's confirmation of what he had discovered was really true.

All day father and son had studied—and restudied—the alignments. With a heavy exhale, Satsum-kedesh finally said, "Enough, my son. We both see it!"

Apogee felt panic and a looming dread. There was no denying it. It *would* happen. They looked at each other, knowing they had to make their discovery known. "My son, we must tell the 200. They need to know. We'll leave at once for the coliseum and call the 200 to assembly!"

At the coliseum, the Games had been underway all day. Both Hagonoths and mighty Renown Warriors had sported. The giants had fought each other in hand to hand combat: one against one, two against one, five against two, and ten against four. These groupings showed the skills of teamwork, strategy, and use of different weapons. When one victor remained from each fighting group, the survivors then fought each other until only one remained. This victorious champion would be honored to fight a Renown Warrior, who wielded the famous silver sword that blazed fire. In arrogance and pride, the champion Hagonoth believed himself to be superior. But always the Renown Warrior was victorious due to their supreme intelligence, skill, and magnificence. After the sun would set, the Warrior Renown would then fight each other. In the dark of night, with only arena torches giving light, the people would watch as silver swords flashed with flames, igniting bursts of lightning when warrior blades clashed. Throughout the day the slain were drained of their blood, which was mixed with wine and given to any citizen who desired to drink the "drink of the victorious."

The sun was just beginning to set when Satsum-kedesh and his son transported to the coliseum in a burst of light. They now stood on the sacrifice altar. Blue light pulsated from the angel as the dazzled crowd beheld his glory. It was the same altar Sede had stood upon. By this time the ground was saturated with blood—sticky and glistening deep red. The smell permeated the air. Every cell in Apogee's body ignited as he inhaled. He had appeared next to a mighty Renown Warrior who had on one hand thrust to the sky with his flaming sword and with the other, held a goblet filled to the brim with the blood of his kill. He sheathed his sword and bowed to one knee in respect of Apogee. Bowing his head, he raised the goblet with both hands, offering it to him. The warrior knew a Regal Renown was worthy of greater honor than a Renown Warrior; Regals possessed the knowledge of their fathers, while Warriors did not.

Apogee gave a nod of his head and gripped the goblet, his bloodlust rising within. With trembling hands, he tipped the cup and slowly savored the warm liquid, energizing every cell in his body. A low rumble exuded from his being.

"Yes, my son," Satsum-kedesh smiled knowingly. "Take your fill. Drink deeply."

Lust for blood was something they both shared. He understood the power they received from it and knew his son would need its life force for what lay ahead. Among all of his sons, Apogee was his praise among the 200. He was as Regal as Castius, Diatus, and Playtheus. And like them, he held no restraint on his lusts. As Playtheus' lust had been for the "innocent," Apogee's was for blood. Just as the meaning of his name, his desires were continually drawn upward to the heights of heaven. But it was the life in the blood that connected his emotions to the earth. The blood linked his heavenly being to his earthly being. It quenched his deepest passions, far surpassing the pleasure of a woman, even though he did have a high companion. What made her attractive to him was her own thirst for blood. Apart from the innocence from the children, blood satisfied Apogee's deepest needs and accelerated his power, making him a glorious Renown.

Satsum-kedesh then turned his attention to the purpose at hand and spoke with the strength of his power, thundering his words. "Hear me, you Great and Mighty 200. We must assemble immediately. Make no delay, for **the Day of Days, has come!"**

The earth shook with his words, rumbling the ground beneath their feet and shaking them as they sat, sending an echo reverberating through the arena. Everyone felt his magnificent power and strength as he spoke. The 200 looked at each other in a panic; they knew what he meant. There *would* be a day when Yahweh would pronounce his judgment on them and their offspring. And now, here it was!

Fear and dread filled them, and the glistening blue light that had radiated from their beings now darkened. After ordering their Renown sons to return to their mansions, they wrapped their cloaks around themselves and their wives and disappeared, leaving the crowd in a state of awe. The people ignited in praise, thinking the 200 had favored them with this mighty display of power. The sons quickly left, and the Games continued into the night.

As the night wore on, the crowd staggered and fell over each other, drunk with the wine and blood of the dead. Grog watched from the arena entrance and realized this was the opportunity he'd been waiting for: the city gathered together in one place and the Mighty 200 gone. He knew he couldn't attack with them present; they would have destroyed him and his army. But now they had disappeared, and the time was ripe to strike. Sending his messengers, he summoned his troops. They would descend on the drunken people and destroy them with little effort. He knew they could overpower the Renown Warriors in spite of their skill and majesty. They would be no match against the great number of his host. Numbers outweighed ability!

Messengers soon came with word that his army awaited his command. He pulled his horn from his belt and blew three long blasts. The crowd roared, thinking a new combat was to begin. It was a new combat but not the kind they expected. The Hagonoths marched double time into the arena. Row after row lined up. They looked fierce standing in position, wearing suits of armor, with legs planted apart and razor-sharp swords clutched across the chest in salute. When the last giant was in place, Grog blew one long blast from his horn. Then the slaughter began. The giants roared in excitement at the ease with which they killed the "drunken." The Warrior Renown fought fierce and long, but in the end they, too, were overpowered by Grog's great numbers. Soon the arena was still, and the dead lie in mangled heaps. There was no place that wasn't covered with blood.

The 200 were in a state of shock. They had just begun their assembly when they received word about the attack on the coliseum. This news could not have come at a worse time. Their priority would not be exacting revenge on the Hagonoths but instead devising a plan to salvage what they could of the world they had created for themselves and their sons.

Satsum-kedesh stepped forward to address the distressed. **"The Day of Days has come.** My son has seen it in the stars, and I confirm his findings. In seven days the world we have created for ourselves will be destroyed by a flood!" The groan of 200 voices filled the air, moaning in great despair; for the mighty beings they were, they now trembled in fear. He continued, "We must make plans to save ourselves, our sons, and the knowledge we possess." For the next hour, different ideas were presented and debated. They knew they would have to be in agreement. Only with their combined power and knowledge could they survive. Finally it was decided. A great cave would be chosen to use as a refuge. Once inside, it would be sealed, preserving them and their sons. There they would wait for Yahweh's judgment to pass. They chose a vast cavern in the land of Arnon, a region not far from Horizon's Gate.

During the days that followed, the cavern was transformed through their joint angelic powers under the expert guidance of Kalibar-buk and his son, Trihedron, the architect. The rocky interior soon became sculpted rooms within huge palaces. All the dwellings faced a glorious courtyard at the center of this new underground kingdom, and a separate chamber was selected to store their knowledge. They would record their dark knowledge on parchment scrolls and save the statues of their great sons that lined the marble steps of the Pavilion. The many fetishes for divination and sorcery would be gathered as well as their great works of art. All their treasures would be sealed in this separate chamber within their underground kingdom.

It was also decided that young Sethite maidens, from both the Atlantis market and their own market at the City of Lights would be brought. A great storehouse of supplies was reserved, and servants were assigned to attend the maidens. Here, the maidens would be kept alive to bare new offspring after the judgment had passed. They would rebuild their world once more, as when they first rebelled against the "Most High." (The pride and arrogance of their hearts would not allow them to see the futility of their plan but moved forward with ambition and great pride!)

Renewed now in strength and determination, they set themselves to secure their future. They made the decision to abandon their high companions. When they began again, they would choose new queens from among the maidens. They knew all too well the jealousy and interference their queens were capable of. When they chose new wives to breed for them, they would be innocent and not possess the knowledge their queens had, making them easier to manipulate. They would also abandon their concubines, leaving them at Horizons' Gate, so as not to arouse suspicion.

Each of the 200 decided to save their most Regal son—the one who possessed their knowledge. Talimus-qua-tam chose Tra-sus. He possessed the knowledge of "the innocent," whereas Croas and Pa-lum merely assisted in his work. He knew their mishandling of the innocent and how they exploited them, caring little for their fellow Renown. He had no regrets about forsaking Ma-get. She was no Ba-nea. Her manipulations were tiresome; her position as his high companion was merely for show. His heart yearned to have another son like Playtheus and a great queen like Ba-nea.

During the next seven days great thunder and lightning filled the heavens above them. Yahweh was sending His warning like contractions before delivery; it wouldn't be a child birthed but judgment. The 200 quaked at the sights and sounds of heaven's display. With urgency, they gathered what they hoped to save from the world they had created for themselves, and by the seventh day, all was in place and the mouth of the cave sealed. Yahweh might flood the earth, but they would be safe beneath it.

Within the glorious cavern were the 200, their mighty sons, their servants, and the maidens who would bare them more "impious ones." These Sethite maidens were not in fear, for they had forsaken Yahweh as well as their Sethite ways. They saw the loathsome deeds of their elders and family members and had desired to participate. They more than likely would have, but they were captured first. They longed to cut themselves and know how it felt to have demons desire their blood. The only virtue that remained within them was their virginity, which they cared little for. They knew it was the only thing that would get them what they wanted. Their hearts burned for, and eagerly anticipated, the dark knowledge of the angels. They wanted to know the depths of their evil. They were Sethites in name only for very little innocence remained in them.

Atlantis wondered at the great signs from heaven. The most Regal of the Renowns had disappeared from the city as well as the Mighty 200 from Horizon's Gate. The high companions were told that they, the queens, were going to be ushered to a new place of preeminence. A ceremony was being planned in their honor. They would wait in Atlantis, at their sons' mansions, until all the plans were finalized. At this ceremony, they would each be given more secrets of dark knowledge. This was thrilling. When told the news, their forehead tattoos pulsated with sparkling green light. Each had their own secret desires for more knowledge. They had lived for centuries and had come to know what would bring the greatest satisfaction to their hearts.

Toleshba anticipated heightened glory with her lust for more companions that she hoped to defile. Polisha had whet her appetite, and Nersha... well, she was her dream come true. With this new knowledge promised to her, she would possess the choicest maiden. It was her dream to possess a

"Tella-la-no-ah" like Playtheus queen, and delight in the adventure of defil-ing the "purest of the pure." To experience the power to defile innocence brought her the deepest pleasure. She trembled with the thought of it.

And Ma-get. She thought only of how she and Talimus-qua-tam would become the supreme couple among the Mighty 200. She was so enraptured with the thoughts of her own grandeur that the air around her vibrated with power. "Ba-nea will be but a shadow in my greatness and majesty," she told herself. "This will be my greatest glory—to be the envy of all the high companions!"

All the queens knew there was great power in the knowledge that the 200 had granted them. And to have more—well, its value could not be compared to anything: not to gold, eternal beauty, or possessing the in-nocence of man. With this hope burning within them, they eagerly awaited their great ceremony. They were told that each of the 200 would take one of their Regal sons and begin the arrangements. The thunder and lightning from heaven was the Mighty 200's majestic foretaste of the new secrets that would soon be theirs. This knowledge would be to them as the power of the lightning they were witnessing. All this the 200 told them to keep them from hindering their plans. For they knew they did have power and would hinder them if they knew they were being betrayed and abandoned.

After Grog had gotten his great victory in the arena, the Hagonoths ate their fill of the dead; they had come to prefer the flesh of man over the flesh of beasts. They feasted late into the night then slept on the blood soaked ground until dawn. When he woke, Grog blew his horn. Giving the order, they each threw two corpses over their shoulders and returned to their camp. They sacked the winery storehouse and drank for the rest of the week, drunkenly celebrating their great victory.

It took the remaining servants of Atlantis three days to clear the coliseum of the dead. They piled the bodies on the sacrifice altar and burned them; the stench was horrific. Bowls of incense were placed at every street corner and lit, helping to alleviate the smell.

Their world had been turned upside down. Two thirds of the city was dead. The 200 were gone, along with their Regal sons, and the ominous noise of the thunder and lightning filled the sky. The only hopeful in the city were the high companions, anticipating the glory they would soon receive.

As the eighth day dawned, a sudden silence fell. The thunder and lightning that had crashed for seven days stopped, and the rising sun was obscured by dark rolling clouds that filled the sky. Nothing made a sound: no breeze, sound of bird, or rustle of curtain. The air felt dead. An eerie feeling settled in, as if the whole world had suddenly inhaled. It was so deeply felt that the Renown woke from their sleep with a start. Their mothers, too, instantly sat up in bed. Leaving their chambers, they joined their sons on the verandas and looked to the city below. They knew something was about to happen.

And then it came…a low, powerful rumble from deep within the earth. Suddenly, a great splitting sound broke the silence as the earth cracked open, and a great rush of air blasted upward as pressure was released from deep below. Their feet slipped and slid as the mansions shifted on their foundations. They gripped the railing as terror filled their hearts from the violent shaking beneath them. Buildings began to crumble as roofs caved in on houses and amphitheaters. With a great crashing noise, Champion Hall slid down the cliff. Bodies of servants and Castius' creatures could be seen falling through the air. The Pavilion columns collapsed, and the whole building folded in on itself while the great arch at the pier fell with a mighty crash. It sent a great cloud of dust rising in the air. The city they had seen but a minute before no longer existed.

They clung to the railing, falling to their knees in fear.

"What is happening, Mother?" yelled Croas as his body shook with the vibrations of the quake. "I don't understand. Father was going to usher you into greater power; I see only destruction before us!"

Ma-get suddenly knew. It now made sense. Talimus-qua-tam had disappeared with his favored son, as had all the other Mighty 200. She had wondered why statues had disappeared from the Pavilion and why some of the great art that was openly displayed had suddenly vanished. They knew what was coming and had taken what they wanted, abandoning everyone else to this fate. A marble statue had been of greater value than a queen! She rumbled in anger, knowing she had been betrayed and deceived.

"Hurry, Croas, your mansion is unsafe on this mountain ledge. It will be safer away from buildings." They hurried to the trees higher up the mountain.

Toleshba had realized too that Masta-lovid had abandoned her. She hurriedly took Polisha and her other servants, fleeing to higher ground. The Renown's mansions, built overlooking Atlantis, were now sliding down the cliffs. As they were in life greater than the citizens below them, so they had lived high above them. But now it mattered not. As the Renown and their mothers fled, they gathered together. Soon a crowd of frightened royalty were clinging to trees as the earth continued to rumble and shake. They watched as Atlantis came to ruin. Everything had been destroyed. The voices from the angry queens rose in the sky, cursing the 200. They knew they had been abandoned, as had their sons.

The earth stilled, and a strange quiet now hung in the air. They looked at each other, for this stillness could be felt. It was then they saw the strangest sight. The water on the beach began to recede out to sea. They looked in wonder, not believing what they saw. "This is a great omen!" shrieked Toleshba. "We must find somewhere to hide." They saw a cave higher up the mountain and scrambled to climb to it. As they stood in the entrance, they saw it. It was coming from the horizon, fast approaching.

Far out to sea, a great wall of water grew in height, raging toward the city, as high as any mountain. The water from the shoreline was now distant to the great approaching wave. What remained on the naked, wet sand was sunken ship wreckage that had been mangled and scattered about. The roaring wave came, carrying the weight of tons and tons of water, hurling forward with tremendous speed and sound. The roar was deafening as the wave fell on the city like a mighty slapping hand! The powerful speed and force of the water burst against the canyon, sending a violent wind up the cliff. The queens and their sons braced themselves to stand, clinging to the cave walls to keep from falling. Their screams of terror were dwarfed by the sound of crashing water and crushing buildings.

They watched as tons of water and debris slammed against the cliff that once held Champion Hall. It circled the canyon wall, moving and crushing everything in its wake. When the wave arrived at the cave, it lapped at their feet. Had they been any lower, they, too, would have perished. It was there that the waters stopped, backwashing and leveling off, high over the submerged city. On the surface floated the debris of buildings, chariots, animals, and bodies. It was a swirling mass, banging and crashing against each other. All who stood in the cave fell to their knees as the reality of what had happened hit them harder than any wave ever could. The city had been destroyed along with their whole world!

Chapter 11

Judgment Day

The end of the first day had come. Noah and his family had said goodbye to the old world, and the great door had been sealed by the angels. It was now a reality. This would be their life until the judgment was over. Shem and Sede left the gathering place, saying their goodnight to father and mother, sister and brother. They would now spend their first night in the little room they now called home. Hand in hand, they walked the long, quiet corridor. Lamps hung along the way, casting shadows before them. Some of the animals lowed as they passed, and a sense of peace filled the air. Shem slid the curtain to the side and grabbed one of the small lamps from the table. Taking it to the corridor lamp, he borrowed the flame and then returned to light the other. A soft, warm glow now welcomed them.

Sede looked around at their familiar things. It brought a small measure of comfort to have something familiar to see and touch. As she ran her fingers over her brow, Shem came behind her and gave her a gentle hug and kissed her neck. "Are you all right, Sede?"

"Uh huh. Just feeling the newness of change." She paused then said, "This is really happening, isn't it? The world *is* going to be destroyed."

He pressed his cheek next to hers. "Yes, but we are safe within the ark. Yahweh found a way to save us."

She felt herself receive comfort from his words. She hadn't realized until that moment how vulnerable she felt about everything that had taken place that day. They had prepared a very long time for this day, and now the day had come. "How glad I am that you're with me, Shem, and that I'm not alone."

"Yes, Sede, we have each other, and the others too."

Resting her head on his chest, she listened to his heartbeat. It was so comforting, just as her father's had been. Sliding her arms around him, she gave him a warm embrace. "I love you, Shem."

He welcomed her words, stirring a warm and tender feeling within him. "Your words are so good to hear. I feel so loved when you say them, Sede."

She smiled, knowing she could give him something he needed: her love. She recalled what her father had told her that day long ago when they rested in the grass on their last hunt: 'the love you give your husband will make him complete, just as Eve made Adam complete.' She closed her eyes thinking about her father's words, and how they still counseled and comforted her. How good it was to remember them.

"May I sit with you as you read, Shem?"

"Of course, Sede." It had been Shem's custom to read Enoch's parchments every night. She reached to the shelf and began unwrapping a scroll he had never seen before. "Oh, Sede, what do you have?"

"A scroll Ne-el helped me make. She has an interest in such things. I'm amazed how she can make things. Mersta had taught her how to make parchments long ago, and for several months she has patiently helped me make this one. I made it to record my days here on the ark. Someday we'll tell our children of this time, when Yahweh judged the world and we were spared. This will be a testimony for them that it really did happen and that we lived each day believing we would see a 'new world.'"

He smiled. She had thought of their children and was already preparing to love and guide them. He knew she would be a wonderful mother. As he read, she wrote. It pleased him that they would have this time together each night.

When they finished, both leaned back on the soft furs of their bed. "Doesn't this feel wonderful?" she said as they nestled in the warmth.

"Yes, but you feel *more* wonderful," he playfully teased.

She giggled and tickled his ribs. They wrestled a little while and then relaxed in each other's arms.

"Sede, as the days unfold, I realize how special it is that we're together. I often think of the times when you were captured. It could have turned out so different. I cherish each day I have with you. I count them as a gift."

She let his words settle within her. Pondering, her thoughts carried her away to when she had been held captive. "Yes, Shem, I feel the same about you. When I was captured and taken to Atlantis, I thought of you every night. And when I was at Playtheus' the second time, I stood every night at the balcony of my room. In the quiet night, I looked up and considered the greatness of what I saw. The warm night breeze always welcomed me, and as I gazed in wonder at the stars, I thought of you. I realized you were seeing the same night sky. I had a deep 'knowing' that you were thinking of me too."

"I was, Sede, every night. Through the open window of our hut, I could see the stars, and my thoughts would turn to you."

She rested her head on his chest and whispered, "We were meant to be together. It was in the heart of Yahweh to make it so."

He gave her a loving hug. How wonderful it was to fall asleep in each other's arms.

Great thunder and lightning began on the second day and continued for seven days. Even within the sheltered walls, the noise was deafening. The great crashing of thunder sent tremors throughout the ark. At times the lightning made Sede jump! The animals were startled by the sound too. The only thing that calmed them was the gentle singing of the women. They walked slowly along the corridors, singing the songs they had learned in childhood, the songs of their kin. As they listened to their sister singing above or below them, they joined in and sang along. There were times their voices harmonized so beautifully that it brought tears to Noah's eyes, for he and Ezmere could hear them too. The calming, sweet sound of their voices restored peace.

On the eighth day, it began to rain, just as Noah had said. The sky began to release the water that had been stored within its chambers; all was happening as Enoch had foretold and recorded centuries before. There were times when Sede felt so frightened she clung to Shem.

As he held her, he felt her whole body tremble in fear. "Sede, the great rain that is pounding and beating on the roof is Enoch's description of the great storehouse of water that surrounds the earth. This is what Father meant when he said Yahweh will open the windows of heaven, and it will rain for forty days and forty nights. Though you're afraid right now, I see the glory in what is happening. Yahweh watches over his Word to perform it. He said this would happen, and it did!" He held her in his strong arms, gently rocking her and reassuring her with his calm and confident understanding. He was there for her, and she knew he would take care of her.

The pelting rain didn't lessen in intensity but instead increased as it fiercely battered the ark. Amidst all the great noise of thunder, lightning, and pounding rain, they worked, caring for the animals and each other. As they gathered every night to eat, Noah spoke words of comfort. He knew his children were frightened by all that they heard and felt, but he seemed to know what to say to each of them. Some days Sede felt strong and full of faith and other days, so very afraid. She clung to what Yahweh had promised: In forty days there would be an end to the pounding rain.

On the fourteenth day the earth shook violently. They had felt the earth tremble before when they were on their hunts but nothing like this. This was like nothing they had known. The earth cracked open and the sound of splitting rock could be heard. Water that had been sealed under pressure beneath the earth was suddenly released. Geysers exploded from the ground, sending water shooting high into the sky. It sent a rumble throughout the ark, and the great construction beams that supported the ark on the ground shifted. The sound of blasting water was deafening, and the shrieks and cries of the animals filled the ark with jumbled and confused noise.

Judgment Day

Then a sudden, crashing wave blasted against the side of the ark! Jolted by the great force, the ark shifted on the construction beams. More and more great waves beat against the side, and the sound of splitting and cracking wood echoed throughout the ark as the braces that held the ark in place fell apart and washed clear. With a great groan, the ark slowly rocked back and forth and began to float. They could feel a sense of buoyancy. It was terrifying as they shifted from side to side. Everything that had not been secured by ropes or nets now flew off shelves or toppled over, all sliding and moving to one side of the ark and then the other. The animals shifted within their stalls. Fear gripped them, and all four men sounded their horns, almost at the same time. They ran with their wives to Noah and Ezmere, panic evident on their faces!

"Come, children. Come to my embrace!" Noah held his arms out to them, and they hurriedly ran to him. Ezmere and Noah encircled them as they huddled together, planting their feet apart to keep from falling to one side or the other. Sede, Shoda, and Ne-el all began to cry in terror. Ezmere, with her arms around them, kissed their heads. "There, there, my precious daughters. We will not die but live and declare the glory of the Lord!"

All three daughters felt the power of her prophetic words. Their cries were soothed to soft whimpers as they clung to each other. The sense of capsizing from the pounding waves, along with the rain, thunder, and lightning, was terrifying. For nearly a day the ark wildly rocked. They didn't leave Noah and Ezmere's side but huddled together. The animals howled and trumpeted their cries of fear. If they were experiencing this kind of terror, what were the perishing experiencing? If this was refuge and safety, what was judgment?! The "eight" could only imagine what the world was like outside the ark.

* * *

And what the world outside the ark was experiencing, was panic and terror. When the queens were watching the destruction of Atlantis, the Cainites grappled to survive. The same great ocean wave that hit Atlantis nearly destroyed Zadanim. The sea level was rising, and the city was beginning to flood. They would seek the higher ground of distant mountains. They fled inland with their supplies and animals, meeting up with other Cainite villages that were preparing to do the same. As they moved east, their band grew. Remaining Sethite villages pooled their resources and joined them. Through the pounding rain, they traveled over slippery ground, forging rivers that had never existed before. In the distance, they could see great water spouts shooting geysers in the air. The earth continued to crack open, releasing more water held under pressure from below the ground. It was a terrifying sight. They thought it a bad omen and fearfully continued their quest to the mountains.

Each night they sought refuge among the trees. But even beneath the great trees, there was no relief from the rain. On the fifth night of the rains they built crude shelters and started campfires. Daagus still ruled as leader and called for a council meeting with the elders from the combined villages. A plan needed to be made. How were they to survive?

During their meeting, several Sethite elders remembered a rumor about a great ship being built outside of Taasa-toka. Their old leader, Noah, along with his sons, had spent years working on it. They suddenly remembered his attempts to warn them. They thought he was crazy to build a ship in the middle of land. Every time he had come to their villages, they had mocked his preaching, but now they had the gnawing feeling that he'd been right. Reasoning among themselves, they concluded that only in the shelter of a ship would they be free from this pounding rain and saved from the rising flood of water.

When they finished their council meeting, they longed for the comfort and pleasure of the demons they loved so much. They called for their drums and began to pound their mystic rhythms. Over and over they played, but not one demon appeared. They cut themselves, and the blood flowed. Maidens began to feverishly dance with all their might—twirling, spinning, and stomping their feet in perfect unison. Still no demons. They were wild to find satisfaction from pain and to feel the pleasure they feverishly desired. Over and over they beat their drums and continued to dance. When they realized the demons were not pleased, they sacrificed a maiden in the fire. Her screams rose in the pouring rain as the fire consumed her. Their offering was only met with silence.

With the deep pounding of the drums they began to breathe heavily, their wild eyes looking upon one another. They became crazed with desire, and they flew into each other, grabbing and slashing with their knives to spill blood. They grabbed who was nearest them, be a man, beast, or relative. They were all overcome with the uncontrollable desire for pleasure and pain. By the time the drums were silent, all lay exhausted and bleeding on the wet ground beneath their shelters. Humanity had fallen to its lowest: a cesspool of degenerates. There remained nothing that resembled the human beings Yahweh had intentioned. Nothing remained of any sense of decency, purity, or restraint. There was no society, no order, nothing that spoke of the boundaries of conscience. All had followed the "imagination of their own hearts." This was the kind of evil that had filled the earth—the kind of evil Yahweh had seen for centuries—and had spread and been welcomed by every human being except for Noah and his family.

Weak from their bloodletting, they rested for a day. The next day marked the seventh day since the rains had begun. They gathered their things and pressed to the higher ground of Taasa-toka. When they arrived at the village, they saw only charred huts and crumbled village walls that had long ago been destroyed by the raiding cloud of Nersha's Hagonoths. They saw the huge pile of stones that covered the bones of the dead and three small graves with neatly placed stones around them.

It was Daagus who devised a plan. He ordered the three graves dug up; he discerned the power that these dead had in life. He would perform the rite that would use their bones to divine his future. He needed this information to manipulate and control this great multitude of refugees. He had used this power many times before and knew the edge it would give him. The arrangement of the bones had to be in a confused but exact order, and the words of enchantment had to be spoken with the right enunciation. He gave the order for the Sethites' elders to dig. 'Let them desecrate their own dead,' he thought. 'This act of defilement will only add to the power of evil I intend to evoke.'

The corrupted Sethites began to dig, feeling hatred in their hearts for those who were buried beneath. They somehow sensed the purity of their lives, and it enraged them. They knew they were once like them, but it was darkness they now desired, not the light of innocence. Deeper and deeper they dug, but they couldn't find their bones. And in truth, they would never find them. Little did they know that Yahweh would never allow His beloved ones to be defiled by evil, even in death. Frustrated, Daagus realized their bones were gone. It was then his men came with an alarming report.

There were strange animals in the meadows nearby; they surrounded the whole area. Following his soldiers, he was led to the village stream. There he could see their shadowy shapes through the pouring rain. They weren't moving or grazing but were looming in the mist. He could faintly hear their strange noises as they howled and bayed, growled and trumpeted. Daagus thought it a bad omen and gave the order to leave. The others agreed, feeling a growing fear just being near them. The Sethite elders knew of a wilderness trail that led over the hills and showed Daagus the way. Surely the ship would be there. And so began the long precession of drenched Cainites and Sethites, slipping and sliding in the mud as they struggled to climb the trail through the pounding rain.

When they crested the top of the trail, they saw it—the ark! The women trilled in relief, their tongues vibrating off the roof of their mouths. The men gave mighty shouts. But just as they began their descent into the valley, the earth began to violently shake. They shifted on their feet, sliding every which way. In a panic, they grabbed for stumps, bushes, and each other. People, along with their supplies and animals, began sliding down the long path, banging against the side of the great ship and its braces. They screamed in terror as they slid down the long slippery mud slide, knowing they would be slammed against the ark.

Judgment Day

A great quake suddenly shook the ground, and a terrible sound of splitting rock could be heard. And then they saw it! Released from the opened earth were the same great water spouts they had seen crossing the wilderness. The water shot vertically in the air; with a mighty force and blew high into the sky.

Daagus shouted to the village elders, "Surely the valley will soon fill with water and the ship will float and drift away. We must enter the ship now!"

The elders led the multitude forward. As the ground continued to shake, more geysers sprayed in the air. They slipped and slid down the path, banging into the ark as the others had. Struggling to stand in the water, they pounded against the great bulkhead of the ark. In their terror and fright, their fists began to bleed from their violent pounding. "Let us in! Let us in!" they shouted.

The Sethite elders screamed with loud voices, "We believe you, Noah! We believe you! Let us in; let us in!" Little did they know Noah and his family could never have heard their shouts and plea. The sound of the cracking earth, gushing water, and pounding rain along with the animals howling and bellowing made it impossible to hear anything.

Seeing their pleas were useless, Daagus gave the order to bring the axes and cut a battering ram. Through the pouring rain, they felled a tree. Fifty men quickly trimmed the branches and shouldered the log. They stood waiting Daagus' signal. Shouting to the men, he gave the order, "Break the door! Inside we'll find safety, food, and pleasure with the 'innocent,' who will be ours for the taking! On men…Break it down!" He knew the repeated force of ramming the door would give them entry.

Just as they took their first step, a herd of stampeding animals came leaping over the crest of the trail! They were the animals that had been waiting in the meadow. Huge beasts, small beasts, creeping things, even great birds of prey descended on them. As they charged, they, too, slipped and slid down the trail, goring and mashing the vile and the profane against the ark. Screams of horror and panic filled the air as they trampled and mangled the wicked. They stomped them with their great feet, and struck them with a flick of their powerful tails. Great birds of prey ripped them with their talons and beaks. Terrified, they desperately tried to escape up the slippery slopes only to slide back down to the waiting animals.

Daagus scrambled to flee. Groping and grabbing at people ahead of him, he pulled and pushed them out the way, working his way up the slippery ground. Reaching nearly the top of the trail, another Cainite kicked him out of the way. Sliding down, he screamed as he tumbled and rolled, building up speed as he flew down the mud. The full thrust of his speed slammed him into a rhinoceros at the bottom of the trail. With his great head, the beast raised Daagus' gored body in the air.

Soon the valley filled with water, and a multitude of people sloshed and banged against each other, their screams of terror filling the air. Just then, the beams that held the ark began to crack and break. A great wave blasted against its side. With a heavy heave and groan, the beams gave way, and the ark began to float. It rocked back and forth among the ungodly dead and the glorious animals that had given their last breath to guard the righteous.

Chapter 12

Queens' Revenge

As the shaken queens stood at the mouth of the cave overlooking the submerged city, a strange and unpredictable thing happened. It began to rain.
They had never seen rain. How could water fall from the sky? And not just a
gradual falling, but it was though the sky had been opened and water gushed
out, making it almost impossible to see to any distance. "What is this strange
magic?" they screamed, looking at each other in panic.

With a loud and terrified voice, Toleshba shouted, "This is the Queen's
Bane. We must find safety!" Ma-get seethed with anger. She knew what was
happening. It was not magic but the sentence of judgment. She became an
instant believer of what she'd been told as a Sethite child: that Yahweh would
pronounce judgment on the 200 and destroy them. Her cold, defiant heart
would not let her repent and cry out for mercy, but rather she hardened her
heart even more.

She saw it all now. Talimus-qua-tam and the other 200 knew of this
coming doom and saved themselves, leaving them to their own fate. How
dare Talimus-qua-tam deceive her? She had deceived him, but how dare he
deceive her? Her foolish heart was so corrupt she could not see the irony. She
knew what she would and must do. She would use her skills of manipulation
and rally the other wives to do her bidding, helping her take revenge on her
betraying husband and son. She looked higher up the mountain and saw that
one mansion still stood. "We must go to that mansion!" she shouted above the
pouring rain. "It is there we'll recover from this horror and make our plans!"

They all began to climb higher through the trees and pouring rain, slipping and sliding on the muddy slope. They approached the mansion and realized it was abandoned. It was Playtheus' mansion. Ba-nea had dismissed his servants and had it closed, not bearing that any should live in it. Ma-get broke the seal on the great doors and pushed them open.

The wet and shaken survivors settled in. The few servants they had brought with them found the storehouse where there still remained dried fruit and meat as well as wine in the cellar. They prepared food for the drenched queens and their sons and later led them to the bathing pools that were fed by warm mineral springs.

As Ma-get soothed herself in the warm water, she looked around. This had been Ba-nea's son's mansion. She still felt the heat of jealousy she had toward her. Playtheus had proved himself to be a great Regal, but she hated him too much to acknowledge the truth. As she was returning to join the others, she passed the corridor that displayed the mural of Regals. She recognized them, having seen them at social events. She stopped before Playtheus' painting, squinting with narrow eyes. She remembered seeing this before when she discovered it searching for her perfect sacrifice for the gods. She brought her lamp closer. "Yes, it's you," she whispered as she recognized Sede. A smirk rose from her lips as she rehearsed Sede's death in her mind. "Perhaps this is the greatest revenge I've had yet: to know I killed the queen of Ba-nea's son!" Her wicked cackle echoed in the abandoned corridor, as she left to join the others.

After she settled in their midst, she searched their bewildered faces and then spoke with authority. "We must unite our powers and devise a plan. We have all been betrayed and abandoned. We are not some simpletons who can be dismissed…we are queens!" She now had their attention. She was setting up her manipulating strategy.

Toleshba stepped forward. "I will stand with you!" One by one the women began to unite. Only ten queens and their Renown sons remained from the destruction that swept through Atlantis. The others had perished when their sons' mansions slid down the canyon wall during the earthquake. "We must use our powers to discover where they've gone. It is there we will confront them!"

"I know how to find them," Toleshba said confidently. "I have the ability to see in the flames." The women's eyes widened, wishing they had the dark knowledge to do such a thing.

They gathered around the fireplace, and Toleshba prepared to see within the flames. She wished to guard her secret knowledge, so she used her incantation for secrecy. With her spell, she would be able to sing her melody of magic, but they wouldn't be able to hear her. Thus, she would preserve the dark knowledge of her craft. After whispering her spell, she began to sing. The other women saw her mouth moving, but they didn't hear a sound. As she sang, she slowly moved her arms through the flames. The others watched with great interest as her arms sizzled from the fire, but they saw neither burns nor sign of pain.

Slowly, the images began to appear in the flames. They saw the cavern in Arnon. It was spectacular in its design and construction. Several queens breathed an "ah" to see such beauty. Ma-get thought, 'Yes, they dwell in palaces while we are confined to an abandoned mansion!' She felt her anger rise to nearly boiling.

As the image changed, it focused on a conversation of Talimus-qua-tam with Masta lovid and Satsum-kedesh. "We will endure the 'Most High's' judgment and begin again. We'll choose new queens among the virgin maidens. This is something we can do while we wait for this judgment to pass. I yearn to know their innocence and partake of their essence!" He visibly shuddered but then continued, "Not only will they bring us great pleasure, but they will give us sons as well. We'll share even darker secrets of our knowledge with our new sons, the knowledge we purposely withheld from our queens. Our new sons will rise to be even greater than our Regal sons that we have spared."

Ma-get trembled with rage. He would be willing to share the darker secrets with a new son but withhold them from her? How dare he?

Then the scene changed to Tra-sus speaking to Diatus Shoal, Apogee, and Trihedron. "When we are released from these confines, each of us will be a 'prince' among the new sons born to our fathers. We will all be declared 'Mighty Ones' in the earth. We were chosen to survive because we are the most Regal, 'the best of the best' Renown." They clashed their goblets together, toasting to their greatness. Of course, Apogee had blood in his chal-lis. Croas, Fathom, and the other Renown sons shook with anger. A rumbling vibration went out from their bodies, making even their mothers look at them with fear.

As Ma-get saw these different scenes, she knew she could use anger and revenge as leverage to motivate them. When the images disappeared, the flames resumed to being but fire. "We have seen all that we will see," said Toleshba as she looked at Ma-get. "What we've seen is enough. We know the 200's plan and what our Regal sons also think. They are in league with their fathers. They care little for the mothers who bore them or the brothers they have left behind." She paused and searched their faces. Doubling her fist and with seething anger, she shouted, "I want revenge! Do you?!"

All the women and their sons roared with one angry voice, "YES!"

Ma-get then continued, "My question is, how will we get to the cavern and confront them without being destroyed by their power?"

Satsum-kedesh's queen spoke up. Falmeth was most fair. All who looked into her eyes were held spellbound. When she spoke, her words wooed them, "I'm sure we can get there, but we need help restraining our sons while we deal with our husbands. I suggest we employ the Hagonoths who overpow-ered the Champion Games. We can persuade them by our magic. They will eagerly provide the muscle power we need to overpower our sons. We won't transport in our husband's midst but outside the cavern. There, the giants will use their brute strength to clear the boulders from the entrance. By lying in secret, we can pick our moment to strike."

Devious smiles rose on their faces. "Yes, that's excellent," said Ma-get.

"I know how to do this," Falmeth continued with her wooing words.

"We'll promise the Hagonoths a night with us if they will do this one service. I know they won't refuse, for our beauty and powers are most seductive, and they are so base that they won't be able to resist us. Even they know about the alluring prowess of queens. We'll transport to their camp and then transport them to Arnon. When they have uncovered the entrance, we'll wait for our moment to confront the 200 using our united powers. Together we will be mighty. And combined with the might of the Hagonoths, we stand a chance to humble them. I personally want to kill every maiden they have secretly coveted. It will be my delight to run them through with a sword, as well as my betraying son Apogee!" The women blinked in amazement at such powerful vengeance coming from such a gentle, beautiful woman. "Now what incantations will we use when we confront them? We must decide and be united before we go."

Several queens offered their counsel. The knowledge of "Unified Power" was suggested from a little known queen named Salom. She was new to the craft and was given this knowledge from the fallen angel that had recently possessed her. It was her prize for submitting to him. The queens would be very powerful under this incantation and have the great strength needed to humble their husbands. So it was agreed, and they practiced the ritual. The words were spoken with perfect enunciation and in unison. The air became electrified, and small bolts of lightning flashed around them as they spoke their words. It surprised even the most seasoned witch. They felt power rise within them, and a low rumble reverberated from their bodies.

"We must remember," warned Salom "that in order for this magic to be at its greatest potential, we must be united, not having our own individual agenda. We must all agree to this before we even go." Each pledged and vowed a vow that could not be broken. Then, with the combined power of several witches, they transported to the Hagonoth outpost camp, leaving their sons at the mansion.

The giants were startled at their appearing but melted at their alluring beauty. Through Adrena's sorcery the air was filled with the most seductive music; she was Diatus' mother. The Nephilim immediately began to tremble in wont for them. Beads of sweat formed on their foreheads, and their palms were clammy. It was Falmeth that would do all the speaking. Ma-get discerned her persuasive powers. She would wait for her moment and then step in and take over.

"Grog, we queens have a proposition for you and your great army," Falmeth crooned.

Grog was beside himself to be in her presence. She held him spellbound by her eyes...he couldn't pull his gaze from them. "Speak on, fair one; I wish to hear your words. They fall so beautifully from your lips."

She smiled, knowing the power of her own abilities. "I will be yours tonight, and my lovely companions will be your soldiers', if you will do me this one service."

He began to breathe heavily with the thought of having her. And to think she was offering herself freely was beyond belief. The women he was accustomed to, were from his raids. They resisted his advances, screaming when he had his way with them. "Oh, fair one, whatever service I could do for you would not be enough to have but one night with you. I agree." The other giants began to howl with their deep voices and stomp their feet in eager anticipation. The fire within their eyes was the fire to consume.

Falmeth stepped forward and caressed Grog's cheek, who trembled at her touch. She drew close and whispered in his ear, "Grog, tonight you will know the pleasure of having a queen. I will give you delights you have never known and that you'll never forget."

He couldn't stand it. It was too much! He stood and howled, throwing his head back, arching his spine and beating his chest. His deep, great voice bellowed into the air. Falmeth smiled knowingly. The other women returned a pleased smirk. She knew what she was doing.

All this had taken place the day after the destruction of Atlantis and the beginning of the great rains. And as both Hagonoths and queens gathered under Grog's great tent, Falmeth explained the service the women would be requiring of them. They would restrain the Renown while the queens overpowered their husbands. In their arrogance and pride, the giants thought to defy their angelic fathers. They had never received recognition from them, and jealousy ran deep against their "princely" brothers. Not only would they see their fathers humbled and their royal brothers killed, but they were promised a night with their queens. What better way to reap revenge.

Falmeth breathed as but a whisper, "This one kindness you will show me, Grog, *and* the other queens: You will allow us to kill our own sons. And, if you are willing, you will secure the maidens that we may kill them as well!"

His eyes twinkled in delight, for he could relate to her lust for blood. It was just as he had seen when he served Nersha the Great. She had this same lust for blood. This made him even more willing to please her.

Toleshba and several other witches used their power to transport the queens, along with Grog and his army, to the cave entrance that held the 200 and their sons. The huge giants easily flung boulders right and left. Gradually, they made an opening to the cavern. They could faintly hear the sound of flutes and harps, along with gaiety and laughter.

Before they entered the passageway, Falmeth reminded Grog and the queens, "You will all wait for my signal before we strike. Agreed?" Both the queens and Grog nodded. They quietly crept through the passageway that led to the great courtyard just ahead.

Before the queens even made their plans, the 200 had already given the command to prepare the maidens for their choosing. They would begin the game they loved to play so well: the game of transforming innocence. They were eager to see what these maidens would become once they had surrendered themselves to them and received the dark knowledge they would bargain for. Within nine months many of them would give birth to their new sons.

The maidens were paraded before them. One by one they stood on the platform with their symbol painted on their forehead, just as it had been done with Sede. There would be no exchange of money for these maidens but bargained favors instead. If two or three angels desired the same maiden, they would deal favors among themselves until an agreement was made. Some of these favors involved the sharing of their dark knowledge, surrendering their offspring from the maiden, or sharing a night with their own, newly appointed queen. Many deals and compromises could be made. The air was electrified at having this many maidens gathered together in one place. Their innocence was manifesting and seemed to multiply and grow in strength. The angels visibly trembled with eager hunger, anticipating what they were about to experience. As the sons watched, they, too, felt the compelling desire to ravish the maidens. Eventually, the 200 chose two to five maidens apiece. They would bare them children, and from these maidens, they would choose their new queen.

Talimus-qua-tam chose four maidens in whom he saw great potential. He sensed their virtues, as was his ability, and anticipated withdrawing their sweet essence. When he did partake of their essence, it was to his great disappointment. He realized they were more interested in his evil than in pleasing him with their virtues. Something had changed among the innocent Sethites. They were no longer as they had once been: pure in spirit and truly innocent. They did not bare the sweet essence he was accustomed to receiving from them.

His countenance grew dark and he brooded. His thoughts turned to Ba-nea, whom he had chosen centuries ago. He had waited for her to mature; he saw her great virtues even as a child. She was a "Tella-la-no-ah" and very rare among humans. She had been such a mystery for she kept many secrets from him. Oh how he wished he still possessed her. These maidens weren't worthy to stand in her shadow. And Tra-sus, he would kill him in a heartbeat if he could but have Playtheus back. The whole cavern and its seeming glory bored him, and he decided to leave. He knew if he disappeared and remained cloaked within an object, he could stay hidden until this great judgment had passed. It would only take the words of a human to release him. With his powerful influence over mankind, he knew he wouldn't have long to wait.

He sought out Masta-lovid and Satsum-kedesh. They both had had similar experiences. Their maidens were a great disappointment, and they wished they still had the queens they had abandoned, but it was too late. They decided to do as Talimus-qua-tam would do. They both sensed if the judgment of the flood lasted any great length of time, life within the great cavern would eventually become riotous among their sons. As they discussed their plans, they thought to approach Castius. Of all the Regal sons, he would be the most valuable after the judgment had passed and could help them as they began to rebuild a kingdom for themselves.

Castius was most agreeable. They promised him the title of "Mighty One" immediately following the judgment, when they began to rebuild their world. He realized he had gotten all he would ever get from his father, and that was his dark knowledge. He also saw what was beginning to happen among the Renown. He knew eventually they would turn on each other. The "innocents" they had possessed had been destroyed in Atlantis, and each burned within to be satisfied with a new "innocent." It would be just as it had been when Playtheus died: a race of ravening Nephilim.

And so, the four of them disappeared using their dark knowledge to cloak themselves. Castius they hid within his statue. A soft light glowed, swirling and turning within his statue's stony chest. The fallen angels hid themselves in a great leather-bound parchment lying in the supreme place on a golden pedestal. Shafts of light streamed in all directions, and a low hum could be heard vibrating from the parchment. All four were safe within the small chamber that they had sealed from the inside. None of the other 200 knew of their plans or that they had even left. They were too busy with their new maidens and the pleasure they pursued.

Their sons, on the other hand, were beginning to feel the absence of their lost "innocents," just as Castius had suspected. They had the gnawing sensation that Playtheus had felt when he had surrendered his "innocent" to Toleshba. They remembered the panic they felt after Playtheus' death, when no one knew how to draw the innocence from mankind. This was just the first day of refuge, and they were already feeling confined and claustrophobic. Fights broke out as their aggression grew. The 200 had to settle the riot with a mighty show of power, binding them all with their words, which were like ropes made of light. They swirled around each of the Regals, rendering them helpless and mute.

It was at this tumultuous moment that a great host of holy angels appeared in their midst! The fallen angels exploded with anger at the sight of them. They released their sons, who scattered in fright. The 200 knew that their kingdom was now threatened by this sudden appearing. They would fight to the death to defy Yahweh's attempt to judge them. Who was Yahweh to defy *them*?!

The brilliance of the appearing holy angels was magnificent. Still radiating glory from leaving the throne room of God, they stepped forward, clad in shining armor and glowing helmets. In one hand, they held high a blazing sword, and in the other, a spiritual chain. Their captain proclaimed with authority and might: **"This is the Day of Days! Yahweh has passed His judgment upon you. Because you did not keep your first estate but left your habitation, Yahweh has reserved for you everlasting chains under darkness! There you will remain until the judgment of the Great Day. He, the Almighty, the 'Most High,' the Ancient of Days has spoken!"**

With fierce defiance, the fallen angels withdrew their own spiritual swords, and a great battle ensued.

Their Regal sons recoiled, as well as the maidens and servants, and found a place to hide. In the darkest recesses of the cavern, they cowered in fear. Being in the presence of the holy angels left them drained of power and weak. The noise was horrific as the mighty shouts of battle echoed. Lightning flashed from their swords as they clashed, bursting with great power. It was as the flaming swords of the Renown Warriors. They fiercely fought! It was a battle of good against evil, light dispelling darkness and Yahweh exercising justice and judgment over rebellion!

The sound of battle echoed throughout the cavern and into the passageway where the queens and their army approached. They stopped just short of the opening to the courtyard. What they saw brought terror to their hearts, and they backed up in fear. Mighty holy angels were fighting the 200! The brilliance from the holy angels was blinding with white light; it radiated from their bodies in glorious streams, while their swords burst with power.

In the passageway, the cowering queens watched the husbands they had feared succumb to those *they* feared. They witnessed the wicked *weaken* and the holy *overcome*. The spiritual chains the angels had brought were transparent yet solid. Light glowed within each chain link like the light of fire—red and yellow, orange and hot white—all swirling within each link. They bound the fallen angels around their shoulders, chest, arms, and thighs—all the way to the ankles. They instantly became weak and powerless. When the last one had been fettered, they disappeared in explosive light.

A dead silence settled in the cavern; the shock of what just happened still whispered in the air. Slowly, the Regal sons and the maidens, along with the cowering servants, began climbing out of corners and holes. Disbelief was on their faces as they gathered at the great courtyard that was left in shambles by the angelic fight. They stumbled over broken furniture and statues, urns, and plants, wandering around in a daze. Where had their fathers gone? Would the mighty angels be coming for them? What were they to do without their glorious fathers? They knew nothing of this judgment, only that their fathers had prepared for their survival and that they would be staying here until the worst was over.

This is when Falmeth saw her opportunity. Whispering to Grog and a few queens standing next to her, she relayed her orders, "This will be our moment of revenge on our betraying sons. We'll spring on them while they are dazed and bewildered."

Grog smiled and passed the order down to his captain, who relayed it to the other soldiers. Passing out swords to the queens, Grog waited for Falmeth's nod. With a nod, she shouted, "Now!" They flew forward from the passageway, their sons startled at their appearing! They put up little resistance, for they had no weapons and were still weakened by the power of the holy ones.

"What are you wishes, my queen?" Grog asked Falmeth.

"Line up and secure our sons." Only a few Regals had their mothers present. The other mothers had died when the earthquake destroyed Atlantis. But the few mothers now stood with hungry sword in hand. Pleading looks were evident on their sons' faces, and a few began crying out for mercy. The reality of having betrayed their own mothers was something they couldn't deny. Their shame was evident. They *had* betrayed them. They struggled in the grasp of the giant who held their hands behind their backs, while their mothers stood cold and callus before them.

With fierceness and might, Falmeth declared with a loud voice, "We were betrayed and abandoned by both husband and son. Our husbands are in the hands of the holy ones, and you, our sons, are in ours! For your treachery and deceit we now take vengeance upon you. Say your last words, queens!"

One by one each mother began to address their son. In the expertise of the dark knowledge their fathers had given them, their mothers mocked them. Falmeth looked Apogee straight in his eyes. His eyes were held by her power. "You used blood to connect your heavenly gaze to your earthly life. Blood was your passion and gave you great power. As you thirsted for blood in life, you shall taste your own in death." She pulled her sword across his throat.

Trihedron stood trembling before Sahad-oden. In silence, she stood before him. Her rage grew as she looked on the one who had despised her life to save his own. A low rumble reverberated from within her, and she uttered her words: "I once saw you as great, my son. Great as the buildings and monuments you built. But as a building crumbles and is destroyed, so now your life. For treachery and betrayal, I now bring you to ruin." She ran her sword through his heart as he slumped forward. Stepping back to see him in death, a small smile rose from the corner of her mouth. This is what he deserved. In the moment he chose not to plead for her life before his father, he had deemed his life greater than hers.

Adrena set her eyes upon Diatus' pleading face. She asked Grog for his dagger, who placed it in her small hand. "Your gift was music and song, and you used its power. Hear now the power of my song. It will be the last sound you hear." She sang it with great control and purity of voice:

What is this pleading face I see
Ah, you wish that I would set you free

Death is but a moment away
For your betrayal you shall pay

You had the knowledge of the song
But what good, when life is gone

Your power was to play the note
But now, my son, I slit your throat.

Tra-sus, who stood beside Diatus, screamed out. "No, you can't do this to us." Adrena smiled at him and said with great control and power, "Oh... but I can!" And with a quick swipe, Diatus was dead.

Ma-get looked fiercely at Tra-sus, who had just witnessed Adrena murder her son. He was terrified! With rumbling anger, she began, "You withdrew the innocence of mankind, Tra-sus, and now I withdraw yours." With her finger, she began to touch each of the new tattoos he had recently acquired from the innocent Sethite maidens in the cavern. They one by one disappeared and materialized on her arms. His face darkened with the loss of them, and his appearance became dark and drawn. He weakened with their absence and buckled at the knees. The giant standing behind him pulled him up. Ma-get, on the other hand, glistened with enhanced beauty. She exhaled with a sigh. "Yes...I, too, delight to know the 'innocent!' Tra-sus, you betrayed the wrong person. Just as I had the power to give you life, I have power to take it. You possess the 'innocent' no more." And with her sword, she took his life.

Shoal trembled before Toleshba. His knees kept buckling, and the giant behind him had to continually pull him to his feet. She got but inches from his face, staring in his eyes with hatred. Her chest rose and fell with her angry breathing; he could feel the heat of her breath in his face. "As we rightly named you, my son, you are shallow waters—shallow in your love and honor of me. I will now, in return, be of shallow love toward you." With a wicked smile on her face, her sword pierced his body and he slumped forward.

After the other queens had killed their sons, Falmeth motioned for Grog to come near. "Your men may slay the rest of the Regals. Take your sport with them." He smiled as he ordered his men to give the remaining Regals a sword. The Regals knew nothing of battle, and it was pathetic as they tried to defend themselves. They were utterly destroyed by their gruesome brothers. With their deaths came an end to their fathers' hopes and glory. They had wanted families of their own and had boasted themselves to be as the "Most High." In the end, they knew only the consequences of rebellion. The judgment on them and their sons was set and had been executed.

While Grog's men were slaying their princely brothers, Ma-get drew Falmeth to the side. "We should reconsider killing the maidens. Being with a Hagonoth would be worse than death. Let's give the maidens to them. While they are filled with wine and pleasure, we can escape."

Falmeth smiled. "Yes, the maidens would be worse off in the hands of the giants rather than a swift death from us!"

The queens gathered and heard the plan. Falmeth gestured to Grog. Pleased that she had given him attention, he drew near. "Grog, my dear. I wish to give you a foretaste of the pleasure you will soon be having with us. Instead of killing the maidens, we queens wish to give them to you and your men. They will whet your appetite for us."

"No, my queen, it is you I want! You will fulfill your word."

She realized that she had failed at tricking him, but she instantly knew what to do. "One moment, Grog, while I tell the others of your wishes. I will surrender to you in but a moment." She stroked his hand, and he trembled with want.

As they gathered together, the witches agreed with the plan that Salom had presented to them earlier. They began to chant in unity and with perfect enunciation. The air around them began to tingle, and small bolts of lightning could be seen in the air. Salom stepped forward and cast granules of light from her hand, as if casting seeds into the wind, but instead of seeds, she cast small grains of light that fell on each Hagonoth, maiden, and servant, freezing them where they stood. They could hear and see, but they could not speak or move. The other witches were stunned at what she had done.

"We will be able to do what we want. We can even move them if we please. They will be frozen until I release them," she calmly said.

Blinking in amazement, they all smiled. Falmeth stepped forward and said, "Take two maidens and bind them to each Hagonoth. When we release them from this spell, they'll have their maidens, and we'll be gone."

With great delight, the witches grabbed the frozen but compliant maidens and tied their hands to the giants' ankles. The witches worked in silence. Falmeth tied four maidens to Grog's feet, feeling especially generous. She delighted in his beastly swooning over her. He had been the mouse, she the cat!

When they had finished, she stood on a broken urn, face to face with Grog. His large eyes followed her every move while his face remained frozen. As she stood before him, she drew near, and with her warm breath, breathed into his ear, barely touching his ear with her lips. He groaned with muffled voice, "umm."

"I will not leave you without pleasure, Grog. You have known the breath of a queen, and now take your liberty with these maidens. We give them to you."

As the queens were becoming but mists, Salom released all of them from her spell. They disappeared from sight and transported back to their Renown sons waiting at the abandoned mansion. Their revenge had been sated. The holy angels had forever bond their husbands, and their betraying sons were dead. The world had come to its lowest, where son would betray mother and mother would slay son. It was just as the Watcher had told Sede the day on the veranda at the country mansion. 'The evil you have seen today will only grow. All that is good in the world will be corrupted.' Even the natural loving bond between mother and child had now been held in contempt. The last of the living were drinking the dregs of the cup of judgment.

Chapter 13

Life on the Ark

The rains continued to beat upon the ark. Day after day and night after night it rained. It never let up. For Sede, the hardest thing was the absence of daylight. She longed to see the sunshine once more. It had been so long since she had seen the blue sky and felt the warmth of the sun. She decided it would be the first thing she would give thanks for when the ark was opened. What would the world look like when Yahweh had dried up the waters that now covered the earth? Would it be strange or similar to the world she once knew? Where would the ark take them? She didn't know how big the world was, but the driving winds could blow the ark anywhere. She did know that everything on the earth was being destroyed, and there'd be no going back to Taasa-toka or the little village they had created for themselves. They would have to begin again.

Each night she wrote in her scroll the events of what transpired that day: something amusing about the animals or what someone had said or done that made an impression on her. She found that she truly loved their nights when the families gathered for the evening meal and Noah shared his thoughts about the "new world."

One night he shared about the knowledge that only the elders of their village had known. He called it "Sacred Knowledge." It was this knowledge that she particularly wanted to record. When a man of a Sethite village came of age, they were accepted as an elder. It was then they were given this knowledge. Now it was time for Noah's sons to know, but Yahweh wished for his daughter's to know as well for they would be the mothers of mankind.

Noah recited what he had been told when his father brought him before the elders of Taasa-toka. Each of the old elders had a part in telling what they knew. It was a great honor for them to pass this knowledge on for they knew that someday this new elder would pass on what he was now being told.

And so it had turned full circle. It was now time for Noah to pass this knowledge to the next generation of elders. "My sons—and you my daughters—it is a great honor to tell you what I was trusted to know about our people. You are now being trusted with 'Sacred Knowledge.' Enoch began this custom among us, and it continues with you."

"The foundation of our Sethite society is simple. We are **Royalty**, **Priests**, and **Prophets**. In royalty, you have <u>identity</u>. As priests you have <u>purpose</u>, and as prophets, <u>you give guidance and counsel</u>. These are like hidden treasures that only the wise can possess."

"As Royalty, we are the people of God. It is a matter of identity. We are His offspring created in His own image. He is royal, so we are royal. Because we live simply and make no great name for ourselves changes nothing. We are what we were created to be: royal. The fallen angels showed great jealousy toward the offspring of God. They knew the splendor that was given to Adam. He was magnificent—a mirror image of the 'Most High.' If you looked at Adam, you could see Yahweh reflected. The angels were created by the spoken word of Yahweh, but we were fashioned by His own hands. We even share the same breath of Yahweh for He breathed His own breath into Adam, sharing the 'nesh-aw-maw' (breath) of God. We are not noble or regal in our own making but are created as royal beings, being the offspring of Adam."

"As Priests, we the Sethite people do not wear elaborate robes, or burn incense, or chant as do the Cainites. As Sethite priests we have purpose: to live a life of simplicity and truth. The greatest events in our lives are all within the family unit: marriage, having children, observing their talents and gifting's, and mentoring their innocence and seeing them come to full bloom.

It is at this point that we release them to start the process all over again with the next generation. As priests, you are to not only rule and oversee your own family but watch out for other families of the village. If you see a family that is struggling within their unit, and they don't seek your counsel, wait for Yahweh to send you to them—for He will. It is your sacred duty to pray for them and give them the help they need. The Cainite elders did not care for their people, and their society came to ruin. If we do not care for our society, it, too, will come to ruin. It only takes one generation to fail at being a priest in your own home or village, and all that was laid as a foundation will crumble. This is serious to consider for we saw this with our own eyes when Cainites infiltrated Taasa-toka, and the new generation was lost because the elders did not stop the corruption."

"As Prophet, Yahweh interacts with the elders, speaking to them His counsel and will. Once you have His words, it is then your responsibility to give those words to the ones who are to have them—be it your family or someone else in the village. This is a most wondrous gift from Yahweh, to be a prophet. It is like the connector between two chain links, joining them and making them one. One chain link is Yahweh's word; the other link is the person who needs the word; and you are the one to bring them together. I have seen the office of 'prophet' beginning in your lives, my sons, as you minister to your wives, giving them counsel and guidance. It pleases me greatly. And you, my daughters, you will see this begin to happen when you raise your children. The 'word of the Lord' will come to you, and you will be able to help your children in all their needs. All of this is 'Sacred Knowledge,' considered foolish by the Cainites but priceless to the Sethites. When we begin our lives in the 'new world,' this will be our foundation and where we begin."

Night after night Noah shared wisdom that had been given him, passed down from generation to generation, all the way from Adam.

Sede wondered if Eve had given 'Sacred Knowledge' to the elder women. When she asked Noah, he turned to Ezmere and smiled. Patting her on the knee he said, "Yes, there is knowledge from Eve, and I will let one of her daughters tell you. Unlike the knowledge that was shared from the Sethite elders, this knowledge is for the ears of women only."

Ezmere smiled at her sons and said, "You are not allowed to hear these words, but you will surely enjoy the fruit of them!" She chuckled as she dismissed her sons and husband. As they graciously left, Sede, Shoda, and Ne-el sat wide-eyed in wonder. Could there be anything more wonderful than what they had heard about the elder's knowledge?

"Tell us, Mother, of the mysteries Eve knew," questioned Shoda, the others nodding in agreement.

Ezmere chuckled softly, remembering her own curiosity when it was time for her to know Eve's secrets. "Yes, Eve was a wonder. Not created like Adam had been, but from Adam she was created—from his very side—and fashioned into a wo-man." The women looked at her with puzzled expressions. Ezmere chuckled once more and continued, "When Yahweh had made Adam, he possessed all that mankind was—both male and female essence. It was only when Yahweh created Eve that He withdrew the soft female essence from Adam. He wrapped it in flesh and called her **wo**-man, for she was taken from man."

"Can you imagine Adam's wonder when he woke and saw her standing before him? He saw himself in another person, much like Yahweh could see himself in Adam after He created him. To touch her hand for the first time, one could only imagine what that must have felt like. To look into her eyes and have her look back at him in wonder? It has been passed down that her first words to him were, 'My husband, my lord,' and his first words to her were, 'Bone of my bone, and flesh of my flesh.' What did it feel like for them to embrace for the first time?"

Ezmere had their full attention. Their mouths were open, hanging on her every word. "Adam and Eve were purely innocent, knowing nothing of the things you and I know of married life. They did not have the benefit of growing in knowledge from infancy but were created with full knowledge as adults yet lacking in experiencing this knowledge."

"The words of Eve that have been passed down to us through the elder women are few but powerful. Adam could never be complete without her, for a piece of who he was, was in her. 'The two shall be one flesh.' When they did come together in union for the first time, it was a reconnection of what had been parted before she was taken from his side. That is why it is so glorious in the sacred union of man and wife. It is all in Yahweh's design that we women experience this. It is our sacred purpose to make our husbands complete but also to feel for ourselves this satisfaction of being complete. It is not to say we are less than them, for this is far from being true. Even though Eve had called him 'lord,' it was not in worship of him but rather an expression of honor and respect. It is Yahweh's heart that we fulfill each other."

Sede smiled with a deep knowing for she had felt this very thing. She knew when she was in intimacy with Shem that a part of herself was truly satisfied, and somehow she felt whole.

Ezmere continued, "What greater purpose in life than to know you were created to complete someone else? Not out of duty or drudgery but in love and selfless abandonment; knowing that as you give yourself, you are actually receiving at the same time. When Noah spoke of Royalty being our identity, it is the same with being your husband's wife. Both of your identities are completed by each other. Together as a couple, you make this 'one' person, as if Adam had been reunited before Eve was taken from his side."

When Ezmere had finished, Sede felt a contentment settle within her. Her own spirit witnessed to what Ezmere had shared. Although she had already experienced some of what Ezmere had explained, she looked forward to discovering more, and knew she had the rest of her life to learn.

Chapter 14

The Last to Die

When Grog and his soldiers were released from Salom's powerful enchantment, the giants immediately howled in displeasure. They had their hearts set on having the queens. Grog grumbled to himself that he had been tricked, but then he smiled. He had been tricked by witches before, and Falmeth, well…she was so lovely. He sighed and then dismissed his disappointment. He turned his attention to the four maidens tied to his ankles. As he untied them, he laughed robustly in his deep voice, "Huh, huh, huh. This is the first time I've had maidens falling at my feet!"

He laughed again at the joke he'd made. He and his army then set themselves to enjoy the spoils of war. They ravished the maidens and feasted on the great storehouse of supplies the Renown had reserved for themselves. After two weeks the storehouse was depleted for the great army's voracious appetite knew no end. This is when they set their eyes to eat the servants. The maidens lived in terror knowing they would probably have the same fate. These Hagonoths were the offspring of the fallen ones: abominations that knew only destroying, devastation, and devouring those around them. They were being true to the nature of who they were.

Grog knew he could no longer stay in the cavern, for the waters were rising on Arnon's mountains. If he sealed the cave from the inside, he knew eventually they would run out of food, even if they ate the maidens. He gave the order to build rafts. He would tow his army on the rising waters. With their great strength, they would row, and he would navigate. Together they would pillage those who fled to the mountains for refuge. The helpless would be there, waiting for them to arrive.

They fell trees in the pouring rain and worked day and night. After several days, the rafts were finished, built strong by the mighty giants. Taking their maidens, they set to sea, rowing under Grog's command. Every day they rowed in the pounding rain, searching for the stranded. When they found them, they consumed their supplies of food and animals then ate them. Day after day they wandered on the turbulent sea, rowing to distant mountain tops and capturing easy prey.

On one particular raid, they snuck up on Cainites in the middle of night. They had seen their flickering fire from the water and heard the distant sound of their drums. Quietly, Grog led the way, rowing to the tree-lined beach that surrounded the campsite. Hiding their rafts along the water line, they crept through the shadows. In the firelight, they saw the Cainites under their shelters, pounding wildly on their drums to summon their demons. They watched as the demons rose from the ground and descended on the humans, who welcomed them with trilling and shouts, ripping their robes open and cutting themselves.

While they watched from the trees, Grog whispered to his captains, "You and the others surround the camp and wait for my signal. You see that fat leader there? He's mine, as well as the maiden with him. They're my booty from this raid. I'll eat him and have me a fresh maiden."

The raiders took their positions, surrounding the wild camp. They watched as the Cainites displayed unspeakable evil, which only stirred their desire to join them.

Waiting for the right moment, Grog pulled his horn from his belt. With a long blast, the giants descended on the unsuspecting Cainites, who were wild in their bloody frenzy and too absorbed in their pleasure and pain. They heard the horn and saw looming giants stepping out of the dark trees. Surprised by the sudden attack, the demons disappeared, while the Cainites fumbled and fell over each other, trying to defend themselves. Weakened from their bloodletting, they were no match for the seasoned marauders.

They were slaughtered, along with all their animals, and only by the bidding of Grog were the choicest maidens saved.

After their gluttony and wild plundering of the new maidens, Grog allowed his army to rest for several days. Beneath the shelters, they savored their full bellies and found relief from the relentless rain. They had longed to stretch their legs for they were no sailors and were not used to being at sea. It was raiding and killing they understood.

It was their quest for more food that drove them back to the sea. Day after day they toiled. But one day Grog saw something that made his heart leap. A ship was spotted in the distance. He was confident his army could capture it and then abandon their rafts. It would be a relief to be under the shelter of a ship and out of the pounding rain. He gave the order, and his strong soldiers put their backs and strong arms into rowing against the wind.

The rain beat against them as they labored to close in. Grog recognized the ship. It was the "Golden Bird!" Its sails were full, blowing in his direction. As they drew closer, they heard screams from below the ship's deck. The passengers could see the approaching giants through the port holes.

They were the queens with their sons!

They had returned to the abandoned mansion after leaving Grog and his army in the cavern of Arnon. From Playtheus' veranda, they saw the "Golden Bird" far below, washed up against the cliff that once was the site of Champion Hall. They were beside themselves with joy. They would not perish from the rising water but would sail to a Renown city on higher ground. Surely some had survived.

Their sons and servants gathered supplies and set sail. Only one among them had the knowledge of the sea and became their navigator. It was Fathom, Masta-lovid's abandoned twin son. He had been passed over for Shoal. It was good he had survived for no one else had the knowledge to navigate a ship let alone the seas. They had been at sea for days, sailing wherever the wind blew them. At first they had been thankful to have shelter from the rain, but after days of sailing, they became discouraged, depressed, and hopeless.

When Fathom spotted the giants on their rafts, he gave the order to change course. Slowly, the ship began to turn away from the approaching giants. In hot anger, Grog blew his horn and lift his fist in the air. "We'll meet again!" he bellowed, his great voice echoing over the water. "And when we do, your witchcraft will do you no good. You've gotten away from me twice, but you will be mine, and I'll have your ship too!"

The frightened queens breathed a sigh of relief as they sailed away, leaving Grog rowing in the distance.

For many days the queens sailed and saw only floating debris. The rising water had brought everything from the land to the surface and tossed it about by the squalls. It was distressing to endure the pounding rain and the beating waves that slammed the debris against their ship. It never let up but continued day after day.

Finally, Toleshba said, "I must look within the flames and see what remains of the world. We need to find more supplies and some relief from this endless rain."

The seasick queens gathered around the fire, and she began her sorcery. They peered into the flames and saw a city, shining bright, like a beacon in the night. It was far to the north. She looked at the queens in relief and exhaled, "It's the city of the gods, the City of Lights! Our husbands' great city is still untouched by the flood waters. There we'll find supplies and relief within our royal palaces. We must sail north. We can't transport to the city, leaving this ship on the sea. The Hagonoths will use it to raid us. We must endure until we reach the port."

The queens' eyes brightened with the thought of being off the raging sea and finding comfort in their palaces. It would be their right to possess them. After all, they were the queens of the Mighty 200, and the people of the city knew it!

Fathom sailed north for two days. As they approached land, they saw the great plateau and the city built high above. Even through the pounding rain, it was glorious to see the bright lights that beamed from the crystal stones. It was like a beacon set on a hill in the darkest of night! When the ship arrived at the base of the cliff, the watchtower blew the signal horn. The guards realized it was the priceless queens, and the whole city greeted them with great pomp, lavishing their service on them. They were led to their husbands' luxurious palaces, still in pristine condition. The pounding rain on their palaces would be the only discomfort they would now have to tolerate.

As they bathed in the warm, scented pools and changed into their beautiful gowns, they settled into the comfort they were accustomed to. (Sin has a way of blinding the heart. And although these queens had once been Sethites and knew the warning of Enoch, they were blind to the judgment that was happening around them. Only Ma-get had made the connection that this was the great judgment.) The pampered queens thought the rains would pass and life would resume as usual, living as royalty and delighting in the life they were meant to live.

One day turned into ten that turned into thirty. They soon forgot their woes at sea and dismissed the memory of the great angelic battle in the cavern and killing their own sons. They were safe from the pounding rain, and that was all that mattered. Music filled their palaces, and they entertained one another in lavish extravagance. Their Renown sons assimilated to their new environment, finding new companions. But the queens were most content to live each day pampered, warm, and well fed, enjoying what they were entitled to.

It was on the thirtieth day after their arrival when the great watchtower's horn blew. Messengers came to each palace with frantic word that the great sea had risen. The waters were now over the plateau, and the city was beginning to flood. The queens flew into a panic. The life they hoped to live in the city had come to an end. As the city prepared to evacuate and move to higher ground, the queens knew the futility of escaping on land. The waters would only continue to rise and eventually drown everyone. They would have to go back to the ship. They called Fathom, who agreed with their reasoning, for he too, saw the futility of higher ground.

Ordering their servants, they stocked the ship with supplies. They summoned their sons, but they refused to leave. They had found their companions so pleasing they wanted to evacuate with them, believing they would be safer in the mountains than on a raging sea. The queens forsook them to their foolishness.

Aboard once more, the ship was blown out to sea. Sorrow filled their hearts as they saw the great City of Lights disappear. Only a faint glow from the crystal lights could be seen beneath the murky waters. No longer would their concern be luxury, but survival. For a week they were tossed about by the wind and waves. A feeling of hopelessness began to settle within them, and they despaired of life. They wept and cried with great mourning, sensing they would perish on this dark and ominous sea.

Grog, on the other hand, was in endless pursuit of more food. The mountains were beginning to disappear beneath the rising water, and they found fewer and fewer stranded survivors. Their maidens had dwindled to but a few, and those that remained longed for death. By a whim, the few who remained, were passed around for pleasure among Grog's troops. It had been the maidens' desire to know the depth of evil in the fallen angels. But now they just knew the depth *of* evil. Ma-get had been right; being with a Hagonoth was far worse than death. A swift death would have been mercy....

* * *

Meanwhile, in the safety of the ark, Noah's family faithfully cared for the animals and each other. Days turned to weeks, and week's months. As time passed, apart from the demands of daily routine, Sede found time to spend with Shoda and Ne-el, enjoying what they had learned about the animals in their care. There were so many. They became very close in friendship and love during this time, more so than when they were younger. Now they were women with husbands. The maturity that had developed from being married had brought a richer depth to the way they saw life, enhancing their insight and perceptions. Shoda had grown in a deep sensitivity since she had married Japheth. Her heart was wholly upon the Lord. She wrote songs and taught them to her sisters, who delighted in their melody and words. She carried a sense of reverence for the Lord that spoke to them all. Truly Shoda was a woman of God.

Since marrying Ham, Ne-el seemed settled and content. She was so very patient in conversation, intently listening and offering her insights that proved to be right time after time. Sede could see Mersta's ways in her. It was in her perception about how she saw things and even the subtle tone of her voice and the way she folded her hands. In all of these expressions, Sede saw Mersta reflected.

There were times too that they had unexpected fun. Sede loved to slip away from her chores and join her sisters on the third level. They enjoyed playing with the primates that swung from the branches of the kolopus tree. One day they climbed the tree and rested against the branches while the monkeys nuzzled in their laps. There was something precious in how they eagerly accepted attention and affection as they held them in their arms like children, rocking them and speaking to them softly. When the energetic creatures tired of being held, they happily scampered across their arms and shoulders and over their backs, shrieking playfully. The women laughed and giggled when the monkeys set themselves to meticulously groom them, picking small seeds and straw from their long hair.

It was during one of these playful times that Shem, Ham, and Japheth came looking for their wives. There they found them, hanging upside down by the knees over a limb, swaying the monkeys from their hands. The sound of their laughter and the animals' playful shrieks filled the air. What fun, seeing their wives playing like children and hanging upside down from a tree! They couldn't help themselves; they climbed the tree to join the fun. This is just what they had needed to break the weeks of confinement.

There were other times too of joy and laughter, when a horn would blow and they'd come running. It wasn't for wont of danger but the perfect timing of birth. The brothers and sisters wanted to share the birth of the animals in their care. These times bonded them in a wondrous way; they felt the joy of new life and the promise of a day when they and the animals would discover the promised new world.

As well as bonding with her sisters, Sede had grown to love Ezmere. She had known her all her life as Aunt, but now she had become Mother. She was a gracious woman who found great delight in mentoring her, for someday Sede would be the mother of their people as she had been. She had been matriarch since Edena, Lamech's wife, had fulfilled her days. Sede sensed she knew things—things that seemed to be a mystery. Some of these mysteries were discovered when she taught the daughters about the "Sacred Knowledge" of Eve. But there were other things—things that only the mother of their people could know.

One day as Ezmere was filling the lamps in the corridor, she found Sede leaning against Mora's side as she rested in the stall. With hands behind her head, she was lost in thought. Ezmere smiled to see her daughter in such peace and contentment.

When Sede saw her at the stall gate, she beckoned her to join her. There they lay, side by side, enjoying the quiet, smelling the sweet scent of hay, and feeling the rise and fall of Mora's breathing. It was if they were in their own world. Their conversation turned to the future, and Sede desired to know what it had been like for her as mother of their people. This led Ezmere to share what she knew to be: imparted wisdom from Yahweh. It had helped her serve Yahweh, Noah, and their people and kept her life in balance. This wisdom she described as "The Three Priorities of Love and Devotion."

The first priority of love was to be given to Yahweh. For if He did not own her heart, then her life would be out of balance. Peace would never find its dwelling place within. The second priority of love was to be to Shem. For first she was a child of God, and then she was a wife to her husband. The third priority was to love and bless her children. Although this wisdom was very simple, it was in keeping these priorities that one becomes a great mother to her people.

Ezmere counseled: "Leading is not something extra you learn or do but rather…an overflow of the life you are already living before Yahweh. All eyes of the Sethite people will fall upon your family unit. If the godly order of priorities is not in place, this will directly affect the people, setting an unseen standard for them to follow. But above all, and even more important, the blessing of the Lord cannot flow in strength and power."

She explained that this knowledge was part of recognizing and understanding the ways of the Lord. To love your children over the love you should give your husband would be like putting the cart before the ox. "You will need unity with Shem in order to guide and nurture your children—and the same with Shem. Your love for Yahweh will have to come first, or you would be putting Shem before God in reverence and love, making him your god instead of Yahweh."

Ezmere could discern that Sede already had the right order in her life. Tolmaka had guided her well. She was thankful for her son's sake; leading their people would flow from him unhindered by having this foundation of priorities already in place within his wife. He would not have to mentor her, but she would flow with him, strengthening what he could do for their people. Ezmere's love and counsel brought a deepened awareness that great days were ahead—days when she would not just *know* about being a mother to her people but actually *live* it.

As the weeks continued to pass, Sede especially looked forward to the day of rest that Noah gave his sons. He took turns giving them a respite from their duties. It was on these days that she and Shem spent time together in their small nook, cuddled in their furs. They dreamed about their future in the "new world," wondering what it would be like having children. What legacy would they leave? What would it be like when their days were fulfilled? They would see their loved ones who had died: Sede's father, the mother she never knew, and Shem's grandfather who spent time with him when he was a boy. It was his grandfather, Lamech, who had inspired his interest and love for Enoch's parchments. This was a time of renewing for them. For whether they knew it or not, the confinement of the closed space of the ark and not seeing the light of day or breathing the fresh, open air had an emotional impact on them. This day of rest helped them look ahead.

Sede had faithfully written in her scroll every night. When she felt discouraged, she read what she had written when one of her sisters or Ezmere had encouraged her. She wrote about the fear she felt with the great noises coming from outside the ark as well as the great shrieking from the animals when they were frightened. As the days were counting down for the rains to end, she had wondered what it would be like to hear nothing but silence. She recorded the teachings from Noah and Ezmere about the Sethite ways and Noah's plans for the future when they left the ark. And it brought her great pleasure to write about the love she felt for Shem and his comfort when she needed it most.

She remembered how Ne-el had helped her make the scroll and was so very thankful she had. It had been in her heart to record her experiences for their children's sake, but she found that she was encouraged and blessed to read her own words. Just this night's entry was how she longed to see the sun once more and the beauty of a clear blue sky and to smell the fresh air and feel the wind in her face—simple things that she now realized she had innocently taken for granted.

It was with those longings that Sede pondered and fell asleep the night before the rains were to end. Tomorrow would be the fortieth day. And as she slept, she dreamed. The clouds rolled back, and the sun broke through; she saw the grey give way to clear, blue skies. The wind blew on her face, and she inhaled the smell of fresh air—like the smell of sweet clover off a green meadow. She saw Fallon and Mora running over an open grassy slope, theirs mane and tails flying in the wind as their powerful muscles flexed from their speed and strength. She saw young boys and girls chasing them, laughing and carefree. In her dream, she felt Shem at her side. When she turned to look in his eyes, she saw his love reflected. The beauty of "life" was looking at her. Such a beautiful dream she dreamed, sleeping next to her husband on their small bed, safe within the ark...

* * *

It was now the fortieth day since the rains had begun. Grog and his army were exhausted by their relentless rowing in search for more food. The mountain tops had all disappeared, and the whole earth was covered with water. If they didn't find something to eat soon, he feared his soldiers would begin to turn on each other. The maidens had been devoured, and they hadn't eaten in a four days. It was on this day they saw a strange ship. It wasn't the "Golden Bird"; this ship was much bigger. As they rowed next to the gigantic side, they saw no entry or port holes. The great side door was sealed, and they had no way of opening it. They circled the ship through the rise and fall of the waves, the rafts banging and smashing against its great side. There, high above, they noticed a hatch door near the roof. How would any of his soldiers climb through such a small opening? As he was debating the idea, he heard a horn. It was one of the rafts signaling. The "Golden Bird" was approaching from the horizon.

Grog smiled, knowing he would get what he wanted: the ship and the women. The queens had exhausted their supplies and knew there was no land left on the earth; Toleshba had seen within the flames. The only place of refuge was a strange ship, shrouded in mystery. She tried to see within the ship but couldn't. It was veiled from her intrusive eyes. She tried to transport them to the ship but couldn't. Some strange magic was overpowering her sorcery. They had exhausted their combined magic, and it was only Fathom's skill that navigated them to their last hope and refuge on earth. When they saw Grog and his rafts, they knew they would have to join league with him in order to survive. The queens believed that dealing with Grog would be as it was before: easy manipulation through their witchcraft.

As Fathom drew them near, he lowered the sails and brought the ship next to Grog's raft. Falmeth stood beneath the shelter of the great awning on deck. Poised on the bow, she looked breathtaking in her royal robes with her well-groomed appearance. Ma-get was at her side, and the rest of the queens stood in anticipation behind them. The tattoos on their foreheads glowed with brilliant green light.

"Ah. So we meet again, fair one," Grog crooned, taken aback by the sight of Falmeth's beautiful eyes.

She smiled with enchantment, letting her words fall like honey. "Hello, Grog. It is most pleasant to see you again. I was troubled to leave you in the cavern, but I had most pressing business to attend to. It drew me away from you. Did you enjoy the maidens I left for you?"

"Yes, I enjoyed them—for pleasure and for food!" Laughing at the joke he had just made, the other giants chimed in with laughter, too.

Falmeth swallowed hard. Struggling to regain composure, she continued, "Oh, I'm so pleased I could give their service to you. Let us join forces and enter this ship. We'll share the booty, and there will be no pressing business to take me away from you this time. I'm longing to breathe in your ear once more."

A dreamy smile rose on his face, and he groaned, remembering what her warm breath had felt like. But then he recalled the outcome of her manipulations. "I hear your words, but you deceived me once before. Will you vow to me your pledge?" Grog knew something about witches. He had heard stories from Nersha, who knew their ways. He waited for her response.

She looked at Ma-get with fear in her eyes. A vow was like a spell, binding them to their words. It could not be broken.

But Ma-get knew they would have to vow—they all would—or they wouldn't survive. Whispering to Falmeth, she groaned in dismay, "We must agree. It's our only hope. We will all have to give our vow to be theirs." Ma-get gathered the queens. After the woeful exchange among them, they agreed to surrender their pledge to the giants. They were at the mercy of their plight. It would be the only way to survive.

It had come to this…from the palace to the pigpen was the depth the queens had fallen. Their dark knowledge of witchcraft and power had proved to be worthless and hollow. Their palaces and status as royalty now meant nothing. The majesty and splendor of their beauty was but spent, and their very souls…forever lost. In the end, their fate would be no less than the maidens they had turned over to Grog.

The queens nodded to Falmeth, and she addressed Grog. "It is our vow to unite with you and be your queens. We give you our pledge. We are yours!"

Grog howled as he lifted his head in the rain, and his voice echoed to the clouds above. The rest of the army joined in, their rafts rocking with excitement as they stomped their feet. "There remains but one problem, fair one—getting into that small door up there." He pointed upward with his huge finger. "We are too large to fit through that hatch door, and it's the only way in. One of you will have to be lifted there and climb through the door. The witch can then use her magic to open the larger door from the inside."

Ma-get saw her opportunity. She had been waiting to step in and take over, and now she saw her moment. Her quick mind had a plan already mapped out. When she got inside, she would be safe, leaving the rest of them to this watery fate of judgment. "I'll go through the hatch!" she spoke up. "It would be my honor to serve you, Grog."

This pleased him greatly. His new royals were submitting to him already. Turning to his soldiers, he gave the order. "Prepare a rope sling to lift her up!"

As his men scrambled to make the sling, he pulled back with his mighty arm and threw his grappling hook, catching the edge of the roof. From the hook hung a ring with a rope to act as a pulley. The queen weighed little, so it would no effort to pull her up the height of the tall ship. Soon he and his men would have food and their women.

She sat in the rope chair, as he hoisted her higher and higher. She laughed to herself as she looked down. Little did they know she had no intention of letting them in; once inside, she'd bar the trap door and never see them again.

* * *

Meanwhile, Noah and his family had kept track of the days of rain. They knew according to Yahweh's command that the rains would cease on the fortieth day—today! They were all relieved that the sound of pounding rain and beating waves would finally stop. Sede remembered the dream she had the night before. It was so wonderful… filled with sunshine, green meadows, horses, and children. Oh, to think of something other than the sound of rain! She went about her daily routine of feeding, watering, and cleaning the stalls, when she had a sudden thought. 'We won't be able to see the sky until the great door is opened. It might be a long time before the waters dry up. Oh, how I long to see the blue sky and feel the sun on my face!'

As she worked, she thought of nothing else. Her mind drifted to her days of hunting in the green, open spaces, seeing the sun rise and set, and smelling the fresh air of morning when they left the village to hunt. Her longing grew as she thought on these lovely memories. Then she had an idea. She remembered the small hatch door beneath the roof. They used it to dispose of dung from the stalls. When the rains stopped, she would be able to see the sun and blue sky.

When she finished her work, she climbed the stairs to the third deck. There was the hatch door, way up there, right beneath the rafters. As she climbed the narrow ladder, her excitement grew. She could still hear the pounding rain on the roof, but she hoped to see the first glimpse of breaking clouds and sunshine. Climbing higher and higher, she made her way up. The door was secured from the inside with a small latch that she lifted. The door cracked open, spraying rain on her face. Smiling, she shook her head, but as she opened the door, instead of seeing parting clouds, she saw the wet face of a woman. It was Ma-get—the very woman who had tried to kill her!

The Last to Die

Horror swept through her and she froze. She was speechless. How could she be here, on this great sea, and this high up on the ark? How had she found her? Had she been looking for her, or was this some strange happening that didn't make sense? She felt her knees weaken, and she wondered if she going to fall from the ladder. She tightened her grip on the rung.

Ma-get, too, was unbelievably shocked! She had the most amazed look on her face. She spluttered her words, rainwater spitting from her lips, "How can you be alive? I saw you sacrificed. You died in the flames!" As the reality of seeing Sede settled in her mind, she gritted her teeth in fury. She was still alive. Ma-get raised her hand to grab Sede by the throat, hate filling her heart. Sede drew back, still too shocked to speak. But this was nothing to what happened next.

The rain suddenly stopped, and the sea instantly calmed. It was as if someone had flipped a switch and all went silent and still. One second there was pounding rain with wild, sloshing waves, the next, utter silence and placid sea. The air felt dead calm. Sede gasped. She could now see far below. There was the "Golden Bird," motionless in the water, surrounded by a multitude of rafts—rafts that held Grog's army! This was the same leader that had raided Taasa-toka with Nersha. Memories of his army brutalizing her kin flashed through her mind. Fear filled her as she wondered what their plans were for the ark and her family. Her attention was then drawn to the high companions on the deck of the ship. They had the look of utter bewilderment. The giants, too, had the same dumbfounded look to why the rains had suddenly stopped. And why this eerie calm? Even Ma-get looked at Sede with the questioning expression…'What *is* this?'

Just as soon as the supernatural calm had brought a hush, a bolt of lightning flashed from heaven. A host of mighty angels, each twenty cubits tall, now stood on the water! The glory of holiness radiated from their beings as they began to walk on the water and encircle the ship and rafts. Grog's army cowered, trembling from the waves of power radiating from these mighty angels. Grog's mouth dropped open, and he buckled at the knees.

The grappling hook that held Ma-get's rope broke free from the roof. Sede saw her fall, almost in slow motion; her hands clawing at the air as her scream became fainter. When she landed, it was in Grog's outstretched arms. Regaining her senses, Ma-get opened her eyes. To her horror, she realized Grog's face was but a few inches from hers. She could feel his hot breath.

"There'll be one last thing I'll be taking from you before I die," he whispered dreamily. "And that will be to kiss a queen!" His huge lips touched hers, and she felt his beastly passion. She felt sickened and struggled to free herself. He held her even tighter, savoring his last minute of life. As a raider, death was always a threat, and he accepted it. For him, this was a glorious way to die!

The dead silence was suddenly broken with piercing screams coming from the queens. The reality of what was happening dawned on them. From their throats came noises they couldn't control! In traumatized fear and dread, they began to pull the hair from their heads; handfuls came out in their hands. They knew! The veil that had covered their eyes was lifted. They knew this was the judgment of Yahweh on the wicked. All the stories they had heard as Sethite children were now present in their minds. They had, with full knowledge, purposely chosen to embrace the Darkness over the Light, the Lie rather than the Truth, and now they would be judged for it. Their hearts hardened in bitter hatred. In a final act of rebellion, they joined hands and cursed Yahweh, blaspheming his name in the secret language of their witchcraft. This was not to have been their end!

Sede watched the angels step closer. They said nothing but slowly raised their hands, palms up. As they did, the water below the "Golden Bird" and the rafts began to sink. As the ship and rafts descended into the sea, it was as though they were sinking down a water shaft, the watery sides held back as if they were walls. Out of desperation, the giants groped at the water walls trying to break their fall only to get handfuls of water. Their terrified screams grew fainter and fainter as Sede watched them disappear out of sight!

Slowly, the angels lowered their palms, and the sea closed over the open shaft and became smooth as glass. There remained no trace of them, not even floating debris. Nothing! It was as though the sea had swallowed even the memory of them.

There standing in the midst of the mighty angels was the Watcher she knew, the one she had first seen at Eden's wall. He lovingly smiled at her and raised his head and hands toward heaven, his face aglow with brilliant glory. Speaking with a mighty voice, he declared, **"Great is the Lord...and greatly to be praised! He is mighty to save! Yahweh's judgment has known its end!"** And just as they had suddenly appeared, they disappeared. All that now remained was a calm, smooth sea as far as the eye could see.

Just then, the clouds began to part, and the sun sent streams of light piercing through the dark billows. Sede burst into tears, joy filling her heart with thanksgiving and praise. At the top of her lungs, she shouted, "Great *are* you, Lord, and *greatly* to be praised! You *are* mighty to save!"

Sunlight fell on her face, and the warmth she had longed for penetrated to the very depths of her soul. She felt Shem climbing up behind her. Joyfully, she slid her arm around his waist, and together they watched the clouds continue to part and a beautiful blue sky break open. Both of them smiled with pleasure and inhaled as a soft breeze began to blow. With a thrill, she nearly shouted, "Do you smell it?"

"Smell what, Sede?"

"The air. It's so fresh. Just like I knew it would be!"

He pressed his cheek against her head. "It's the 'new world,' Sede, washed clean. We're the first to see it!" As her hair feathered back from the breeze, she closed her eyes, inhaling once more. They faintly heard the others coming; their laughter and joy echoed from below. Sede and Shem climbed down so each could see the sun and sky. Shouts of joy came from above as they beheld the end of judgment and the dawn of a new world!

Chapter 15

A Timely Message

That night as everyone gathered around the home fire, Sede told them what she had seen when she first opened the hatch door. Instead of clouds and rain, she saw the wet face of a woman she knew from Atlantis. They could hardly believe anyone could find the ark on such turbulent seas and survive the pounding rains let alone climb the height of the ark. And what about those queens? Who were they and the strange Nephilim army floating on rafts? What wonders brought about the great host of angels that had the power to open the sea with their hands and cover the wicked in the hollowed shaft within the deep?

All their questions brought up other questions, and they began to ask her about the strange world they came from. It had been Sede's hope that all the horrible memories she had experienced would be as Dollo had said: "memories to forget." But with what had just happened, she knew that out of innocence, they wanted to know. So during the weeks that followed, at their gathering times, both she and Ham shared their captivity stories. Shem had been the only one who knew her whole story, and Shoda had heard bits and pieces when they had hunted together while the ark was being finished.

Sede and Ham took turns retelling the story of how they were kidnapped and taken to the city of Atlantis. It all began that ill-fated night in the burning grass of Zadanim. As Sede's story unfolded, she painted a picture of the beauty and wonder of a far off place that only masked the evil beneath it. The world of Atlantis was one of refined culture, music, art, and grandeur, but it only existed and thrived by what they stole from their people. The Sethite "innocence" was the life blood of their society. Through the market, Sethites were purchased, and at country mansions, children were bred. Through the dark knowledge of fallen angels, their "innocence" was withdrawn and given to their sons, the Renown Nephilim, to enhance them and give them something they didn't possess themselves. It was the mystery that enabled their greatness.

Her greatest sorrow was the corruption she had witnessed in Ka-sta. Bought the same day, Ka-sta had been as any Sethite maiden: pure and innocent. But once she surrendered her innocence, she became a completely different person, corrupt and vile. As Sede described her transformation, Noah listened with a troubled heart. He thought of his own sister who had been stolen long ago. Had she become as this Ka-sta? While Sede was describing the change she had seen in her, she discerned Noah's distress. His countenance was troubled, and tears filled his eyes. She felt compassion rise within her for the grief he bore. This was the same sorrow she saw in her father when he spoke of her mother never getting over the loss of Marah, her sister.

She described the loneliness and how she felt suffocated by the evil that surrounded her. Oh, how she longed for her family and people. With tenderness, she reminisced that all she had was Yahweh. He was her only comfort as she stood on that lonely veranda under the stars. As she spoke, Shem's eyes filled with tears, knowing that even though he was not there to comfort her, Yahweh had been.

The one joy she recognized, from all she had experienced, was meeting Dollo. He had told her about his own captivity and how his innocent virtue of "Loyalty" was stolen from him. She gave testimony to the power of Yahweh setting him free and restoring his soul after she had earnestly prayed for him. Dollo had been instrumental in their escape. And through his help and influence, he made it possible to fill the ark with provisions. Tears filled her eyes as she spoke of him being a true Sethite indeed—an elder to be remembered and honored. She began to weep remembering how peaceful he and Zilla looked when they rested in their grave. They were so beautiful in each other's arms.

Ham's captivity had been different than Sede's. His innocence had been taken from him. To his humiliation, he was named Bromos. He had been bought by a Regal Nephilim who had the dark knowledge to combine the seeds of creation. With tear-filled eyes, he told of the horror he felt when he was shown how their people were used to breed and become monsters. He had seen them birthed—grotesque and deformed. Some actually lived and resembled the blended seeds of creation. More often than not, the Sethite maiden that birthed them died. He wept, saying he could still hear their screams in his sleep. He had seen the caverns where the dead were discarded and piled.

There had been one particular creature that he felt compassion for: a centaur. All but Sede had puzzled looks on their faces. He explained what kind of creature they were: half human, half horse. This particular centaur was half woman, half horse. Her name was Fal-lea, and she spoke with a soft, sad voice. She had lived for many years in the dungeons beneath Champion Hall. Through their many conversations, she described the horrors she had witnessed that far surpassed what he had seen. It was only on rare occasions she was released to run the open hills of Atlantis. She confessed that it was the only time she felt freedom—running with the wind in her face while her hooves sped over the hills. He described her torment: to have the wild nature of an animal living within her human heart, and always striving with inner turmoil, not having a moment of peace. His best efforts to comfort her were futile for she had no deliverance from the evil done to her. The life she could have lived as a human had been stolen from her when she became a creature pleasing to a Nephilim. Her own birth had killed her Sethite mother.

When Ham had finished talking, they all wept with their faces in their hands. A great moan and wail rose. They knew there were countless other Sethites that had suffered the same fate, having the seed of life altered to please a race of evil beings.

Turning the mood, Ham expressed his joy that Sede and Dollo had discovered him and that Yahweh had made a way for them to escape. When he heard the conoka signal that night on the pier, he knew his deliverance had come. It was his greatest joy to return to his family and know Yahweh would judge the great evil he had seen. Ne-el had become his sweet consolation in life. Being married to her had soothed his soul and brought solace to his longing heart. As he expressed his words of love for Ne-el, her eyes filled with tears, and she sweetly kissed his cheek. Everyone felt the sweetness of their love. But although her love comforted him, Ham had been marred by his experience with a wound he himself did not see. It would only be later in his life that those ugly scars would surface.

Because of their great sadness over Ham's story, Sede waited several days to speak about her second capture: that horrible night she was taken in the forest. She had been led by a rope through the forest to the Nephilim camp. There she helplessly witnessed their kin from Taasa-toka brutalized and murdered. Those who survived were held with captives from other villages. The young maidens were whisked away and sold in Atlantis. She told Ham and Japheth how she watched Zara die: speared by a ruthless Nephilim warrior named Nersha. Their eyes filled with tears remembering the brave young hunter they had come to love. Her spirit and zeal for life was still with them.

It was after being brutally beaten that Sede was delivered by Playtheus, the same Renown who had held her captive the first time. She held Shem's hand while she spoke of her rescue and how helpless she felt knowing she was at his mercy. Many months passed as her back healed while she spent her days in rest and peace. It was there she met Fallon and Mora and rode a horse for the very first time. As her story unfolded, she told of the miraculous change she had seen in Playtheus. He was transformed by his desire to know the God she loved. Rehearsing his prayer, she repeated the words that had come from his heart. As they listened, they sensed the reality of a life that had been changed. Through kindness and compassion, he tried to return her to Shem and her kin. He died doing that very thing.

A Timely Message

The same female warrior who had tried to beat her to death tried to spear her, only to kill Playtheus instead. Ba-nea, his mother, had comforted her, and it was during that conversation with her that she realized some of those in captivity still longed for their Sethite life, just as Dollo had. At the ceremony for the dead, Ba-nea had sung with her the Sethite "Song of the Dead" to honor Playtheus. To fulfill a promise Playtheus' father had made, he transported her to the hill overlooking their village.

During her time in the forest, she found comfort for her wounded soul. Yahweh came to her on the breeze, speaking words of comfort, and gave her a dream of Shem. As she spoke, she squeezed his hand and said, "Shem called to me and told me to come home to him. Yahweh led me through the forest by a hawk and brought me back to him and you, the people I love." As she spoke her words, she touched each person with a soft hand of affection and said, "It has been all of you that I've returned to. For you are my beloved family." A wonderful sense of love and unity filled them as she expressed her love.

When she began her story of how she was abducted in Sidon and taken to Atlantis but for a third time, they were appalled that she was to be offered as a human sacrifice. They knew of animal sacrifices from their own festivals, but never would they have dreamed a human would be offered on an altar. Noah was especially pleased to hear how Yahweh gave mercy to Ba-nea when her heart was turned to trust in Yahweh. He saw a different aspect of Yahweh's love by receiving her repentance and embracing her. He realized that mercy and justice are balanced in the holy hands of God.

Sede sang the song she heard the angels sing for Ba-nea: "The Song of Salvation." Her sweet voice echoed through the ark, and it brought a holy hush as her family listened to a song that was sung for a repentant heart. Shoda closed her eyes and absorbed the music and words. This would be a song she would remember and add to those Yahweh had given her. As they listened, they knew this song could just as easily been sung for them. (For they all knew from Enoch's writings that all have sinned and fallen short of the glory of God. Only by humbly confessing the wrong that one has committed and believing in the heart that Yahweh truly is Lord can anyone know life-changing salvation. All their sacrificial ceremonies and festivals pointed to this truth.) As Sede sang the song one more time, Shoda joined her, harmonizing with her lovely voice. Oh, the beauty that filled them. The presence of the Lord was so tender and close!

> *I have sinned against heaven and in your sight*
> *I have wandered far from my home*
> *I am not worthy to be called by your name*
> *A child of the "Father of Light."*
>
> *Bring forth the best robe, new shoes and a ring*
> *My child was dead and now lives*
> *My heart is your home, my arms your rest*
> *Your song, forever I'll sing*

Tears rolled down Noah's face as he listened. The love of Yahweh was so near. What a great God to receive the humble in heart and to forgive those who sin. He realized that though sins were different among the people groups, it was all sin: the Cainites with their lust for pleasure and pain or the Sethites forsaking the true and living God. He knew that Yahweh saw no big sin or little sin, but that all people were lost to the sin Adam had opened to humanity. Every individual person needed the "Promised One" to be their sacrifice. They could be forgiven and cleansed from their sin, just as Yahweh was doing with the world by the flood. The world had been washed clean, and people's hearts could be too. It all pivoted on a broken and contrite heart and receiving Yahweh's love and forgiveness.

That night Sede couldn't sleep and decided to walk the long corridors. She slipped from their small room and slowly walked in the warm glow of her lamp. She heard the soft breathing of the sleeping animals, and it brought a smile. She had come to know them all. While she continued in the quiet, she heard a still, small voice. She stopped. It was Yahweh! "It is time, Sede." She strained to hear more. "Time to read Ba-nea's message." Her mind was awhirl. She had forgotten all about the folded parchment she had found in the cloak that Ba-nea had given her. She had discovered it while she was in the forest recovering from Playtheus' death and had re-sown the seam.

She walked back to her room and carefully removed the cape from the shelf over their bed. She heard Shem's soft breathing. Smiling, she paused to listen. He looked so peaceful sleeping beneath the furs.... Taking the cloak into the corridor, she held it to the lamp and slowly unthreaded the seam of the small pocket. There it was, like a secret waiting to be told. On the outside of the folded parchment, she saw again the writing that said, "Do not open until Yahweh bids you so."

As she unfolded the parchment, she saw that there were two parchments: one with her name on it and one with Noah's name on it. She wondered why Ba-nea would write a note to Noah. Sede had only mentioned that he was their village leader. Holding the parchment closer to the lamp, she began to read.

"Dearest Sede, I am writing this to you and will conceal it within my cloak. I fear being discovered by Talimus-qua-tam and jeopardizing your release. When we sat on the bed in Playtheus' room, I asked you of your parents and desired to know who led your people. Because you are now reading this, I know that Yahweh's timing is perfect and there is a reason for your eyes to fall upon my words. Sede...I am, and will always be, a Sethite in my heart of hearts. It was my joy to recognize you when Playtheus introduced you at the Pavilion the night you were declared his high companion. You are my dear sister Letta's child. I am your aunt, Marah." Sede gasped. This was amazing—wonderful beyond belief! She continued to read... "I watched from afar as you escaped from Atlantis and found our people once more. And then, for some reason, you appeared in our lives again. I knew then that Yahweh had a purpose in all of it. Perhaps he was going to find a way for me to finally be free from this world that has held me hostage and help my son in some supernatural way. I saw a transformation in him that I never dreamed possible. He had been so corrupted by his father's influence; I didn't know if there was any hope for him. But there was. I saw him learn to love. And not just love, but love with a selfless love, the kind of love our people understand. I knew then that Yahweh had not forsaken me or my son. Thank you, Sede, for all that you brought into our lives. Though my son has died, I have hope that he is with Yahweh. I also have hope for myself. You had mentioned that you never knew your mother. I see her reflected in you, and I sorrow that you never knew her. She was so precious in all her ways. It has blessed me, Sede, to have known you, if only briefly. 'May Yahweh richly bless you all the days of your life, and may He hold you in the palm of His hand.' With enduring love…Marah."

Sede began to softly weep as she held the parchment to her heart. Oh, how dear these words were. Ba-nea was her aunt. And Playtheus…he was her cousin. Her heart was flooded with love as she pondered how Ba-nea had reached out to her, even in her captivity, to comfort and love her. Then it occurred to her that Ba-nea didn't know she would see Sede again that day she was to be offered as a sacrifice to the gods. She now understood how Yahweh had orchestrated that whole day of the sacrifice. He had drawn Ba-nea to himself by the appearing of Playtheus and offered her mercy, inviting her to turn her back on the world of Atlantis and embrace the God she once knew. Her letter was so comforting. She had just retold her stories of captivity, and it had troubled her heart to remember all the distress she felt and saw, but now…this happy news!

She then considered Noah. She knew he had grief in his heart from the comment he made about his own sister being taken and concern that she had been corrupted. Not only was this perfect timing for her but for him as well. She climbed the steps to the second floor, and to her surprise, she saw Noah sitting by the embers that still glowed from their evening fire. When he saw her, he motioned for her to come and join him.

As she sat next to him, she retold the story of finding a parchment sewn inside her cape the day she was returned to the forest. Tenderly, she read her note to Noah. He began to weep, realizing it was his beloved sister who passed through the fire to be forever with Yahweh. That beautiful song the angels had sang was for Marah. Sede graciously handed Noah the parchment with his name on it. With trembling hands, he held it, just looking at it. His sister had given him a gift…words to a brother she never forgot. Sede kissed him sweetly on the cheek and bid him good-night. She knew he needed to be alone. As she stood to leave, he said, "Thank you, Daughter, for this wonderful gift. The love of Yahweh never ceases to amaze me. We have both been blessed by this gesture of love."

She smiled and returned to her sleeping husband.

Noah slowly unfolded the parchment and pondered the kindness of Yahweh in comforting him in such a way. He *had* grieved for his sister when Sede told of her time in captivity. It made him wonder of Marah's own story. It pained him to think she had probably become as Ka-sta—corrupted. He hoped against hope that somehow she had kept her heart from such evil. As the last fold opened, revealing her words, he realized the last time it had been folded was by her own hands.

Through tears, he began to read. "My dearest brother, it is so good to think of you as I write these words. I never forgot you or our people. Even though I was held captive in this evil world, I always hoped to be delivered and return to our village. I still hold to that hope. But if you're reading this, it means that Yahweh has executed His judgment upon the world just as Enoch had written. I am glad this corrupted world will know an end. I have seen your strength of spirit and the great love you have for our people. I know you will lead them well. I wish I could have been by your side to see all this unfold. Know that my heart is with you, my brother, and that I love you dearly…Your beloved sister, Marah."

Like Sede, he drew the letter to his heart and began to weep. It was though she were there; he sensed her gentle presence with him. And had Noah's spiritual eyes been opened, he would have seen her as her glowing spirit stood beside him. She bent forward and tenderly kissed his forehead while her hand lightly touched his shoulder. As his tears flowed, he rejoiced; Marah was not lost but with the Lord.

After several days of letting the letters sink into their hearts, Sede and Noah read them to the others at the evening meal. Ba-nea and Playtheus were their kin. How wonderful to celebrate the deliverance they had experienced from the corrupt world that had bound them. Marah's courage and faith spoke to all of them: that though she endured hard times, her faith was always in Yahweh to see a better day. They realized that being in the ark had made them feel confined, and they were each wondering if they *would* see a "new day." It was the right time to be encouraged by someone's hope and faith.

Their days continued in predictable routine. In the morning, they fed and watered the animals, and in the afternoon, they cleaned their stalls. While Sede was working beside Shem one day, she had a startling thought. "Shem, it just occurred to me that we "eight" are the only people on this earth. That thought makes me very fearful in a way. I'm glad that I still live, but to be so few is unsettling! The world is such a big place, and we are so small and few."

He smiled, having had the same thought but a couple days before. "It is a fearful thing, Sede—fearful and awesome at the same time. It will be as it was with Adam and Eve. We will be the first of our kind. They only had each other, while we have both father and mother and brothers and sisters. We will be fine."

She listened as he spoke, receiving the comfort from his words. Although the fear of what lay ahead was beating on her heart so was the comfort of family and the promise of a future that Yahweh had planned.

Chapter 16

Shem and Sede's Joy

Weeks turned into months while the ark floated gently on the waters that covered the earth. It was as Sede had said; only eight souls drew breath upon the earth. If anyone could have seen this speck of an ark on a world covered with water, they would have wondered at such vulnerability. The world had been utterly destroyed. But, within that speck of an ark, life continued.

By now Noah and his sons were well familiar with the animals they cared for. Their every need had been their focus. After their daily chores, Sede and Shem's favorite pastime was lying in the sweet hay with Fallon and Mora. While Sede reclined against Mora, she sighed, "I feel such peace when I'm around the smells of animals. It reminds me of the hunt."

Mora snorted softly, making Sede smile. Patting Mora's warm belly, Sede pondered, "I hope when we become established in the 'new world,' I'll be able to still hunt or be a teacher of young hunters."

"I think you'll get your wish, Sede. Some of the old Sethite customs we'll keep, but there's room for adjustments with some of them. The responsibility of teaching our young will rest solely upon us. We'll be the only ones to pass on what we know and have learned about the Sethite way of life. I'm so thankful we have Enoch's written word to help instruct them concerning the 'Knowledge of the Lord.'"

She squeezed his hand. He was going to make a wonderful leader for the next generation.

"How many children do you think we'll have, Shem?"

With a coy smile, he said, "Hundreds and hundreds!"

She giggled and threw a handful of straw at him. He laughed, grabbing her and rolling them both in the soft bedding. As they lay covered head to toe with straw, he affectionately kissed her. "I love you, Sede."

She responded with a warm kiss. "I love you back, Shem."

In the loving embrace of each other's arms, they knew intimacy's sweet touch. They fell asleep in the soft straw, warm against Mora and Fallon's side, enjoying the place that felt like home.

As more months passed within the ark, Sede began to feel sick when she woke each morning. This strange sickness seemed to leave by midday, but every morning it persisted, and her monthly cycle had mysteriously ceased. She remembered the instructions of the elder women during her time of preparation. She wasn't positive about these symptoms, so she decided to seek Ezmere's counsel.

Sweetly smiling, Ezmere simply replied, "It's the way of life. You're with child, my dear!"

Sede's face flushed pink. She and Shem were going to have a baby! A multitude of feelings flooded her. A baby! Her life with Shem was about to unfold in a new way. She would fulfill the will of Yahweh and bear the seed that would continue the lineage for the "Promised One" to come. This baby was their future.

Wrapping her arms around Sede, Ezmere gave her a big hug. "My first grandchild. I'm so happy!"

Sede felt stunned. It was almost too much to take in. She would have to choose the right time to tell Shem.

That night as they lay in each other's arms, she held her seed from Eden. Pondering the Watcher's words, she remembered "seeds within a seed." As she drew it to her heart with affection, she realized these words could mean so many different things. It could mean she would have many children from the seeds of creation within her, or it could be the multitude of generations that would come from them, or it could be something that she still didn't understand about Yahweh's will. The Watcher did say that she would come to know the meaning as Yahweh revealed it to her.

Shem sensed her thoughts had taken her far away. "What are you thinking, Sede? Your thoughts have taken you away, and I want to join you there." He smiled and laughed softly.

"I was thinking of my gift from Yahweh—the seed of Eden." She opened her hand, and they both gazed at it resting in her palm. They faintly heard the song of heaven. Its lovely melody filled their hearts with wondrous awe. "The Watcher said it was 'seeds within a seed.' I was contemplating what that might mean."

He drew her close. "Your gift is a mystery. You, Sede, are like the seed of Eden: a gift and a mystery to me!"

She smiled and looked into his loving eyes. She knew her moment had come to tell him.

"Shem, the seed of creation within me has been touched by your seed. I have the life of our love, in my womb. We're going to have a baby."

Shem gasped in surprise. "Oh, Sede!" He was instantly filled with joy, elation, and the thrill of the moment. He began to laugh and then cry with happiness, a multitude of feelings exploding within him. She watched his face, wanting to capture his every expression of happiness. He shined with joy, and his eyes danced with life. He began to kiss her forehead, her cheek, her neck, and then, ever so sweetly, he kissed her belly. "I love our child already," he tearfully whispered.

Her eyes misted, realizing her news had brought this great happiness he now felt. "We are stepping into a new chapter of our lives, Shem. With this new life, we'll truly be a family."

Shem cupped his hands around hers. As they both held the seed of Eden, he softly said, "Seeds within a seed. The seed of life truly is a mystery, Sede."

The next night, while the family's gathered for their meal, Shem proudly shared the news. Shoda and Ne-el's faces shined with joy for their sister. One day they, too, would be giving their own announcement of new life on the way.

Noah beamed as he called them to stand before him. "Children, I wish to pray for you." Having Shem place his hand on Sede's stomach, Noah then rested his hand on Shem's and prayed, "Yahweh, we rejoice in the discovery of new life among us. As this child is safe within the womb of Sede, it reminds me that we are safe within the womb of your ark. What a mystery that two seeds can become one life!" Sede and Shem smiled when he made reference to the seeds within them. It was the secret they shared about Eden's seed. "When we enter the new world, this child will not have known the darkness of a world gone wrong but rather the light of righteousness, peace, and joy. May your blessing be upon these young parents as they begin their family; give them wisdom, understanding, and knowledge to guide this child, protecting its innocence until wisdom grows full bloom. We give thanks for this life."

They hugged each other after Noah's prayer, thinking, 'What a wonderful way to start a family, with the blessing of the Lord.' While the others gathered around to wish them their own blessing, it was Ham who struggled with what was happening. Deep in his heart, he had wished to be the first son to have a child. It occurred to him that his brother had preeminence in not just birth order or being the future leader but the first to bare children as well. It grieved him that he struggled in his heart with such envy, for he really *did* love his brother, and he knew he should have been happy for him. Playtheus had seen this in his heart when he looked within his soul. He had seen this envy and the struggle it caused him. Playtheus also knew that once this conflict had been resolved, it brought a purity to the innocence of the soul. (Oh, that Ham would have prayed for such resolve.)

It was a few months later that Noah had a dream. In his dream, Yahweh spoke concerning the end of his judgment. "All life is destroyed that was upon the face of the earth: man, Nephilim, cattle, creeping things, and the fowl of heaven. They have all perished, except for you and your family along with the animals I have chosen. The waters have prevailed for many months, but I have not forgotten you. I will make a wind to pass over the earth, and the waters will be assuaged. I have stopped the fountains of the deep and the windows of heaven. The ark will rest upon land, and the waters will decrease continually until the tops of the mountains can be seen. Release a bird to fly to and fro to bring back a sign that the waters have abated and life has returned to the earth. When the time is right, I will open the great door of the ark. You and your family will begin your life in a world washed clean by the waters of My Judgment."

The next morning he was thrilled that he and his family would soon see the light of day on dry land. He opened the small hatch door and released a raven, but it never returned in the evening or any day after that. He then released a dove, but she found no rest the sole of her foot and returned that evening to the small door. Noah gently drew her in, clasping her fluttering wings his hands. After seven days he released her once more, and she returned that evening with an olive leaf in her beak. This was the sign he'd been waiting for. He waited another seven days and released her once more, but she never returned. He knew then that she had found a place to rest and so would they.

With the help of his sons, Noah released the counterweights that had stabilized the ark in the violent waves. These great stones, weighing tons, were released, and immediately they felt a difference in the buoyancy of the ark. For several days, the sensation of buoyancy gently rocked them. Then one day they heard, and felt, the ark hit dry land. No one had to tell them what had happened; they all knew. The ark had come to rest! It sent a thrill through all their hearts.

The next morning Noah blew his horn to gather his family at the great door of the ark. The sound of his horn rang clear and true through the corridors. All who heard it knew. It was time! With joyful anticipation they looked at each other. The day had finally come! Although the ark had been their home for nearly a year and saved their lives, they had earnestly longed for this day. Suddenly they heard a great creaking and splitting. The pitch that sealed the door had cracked, and the great door slowly creaked open. The mighty angels who had closed the door nearly a year ago now lowered it to the ground by their hands. The light was blinding as it streamed on the eight small figures standing in the open doorway. Cheers erupted as they shouted for joy! The light was so beautiful; the air was so fresh; the blue of the sky so brilliant; and the green of the earth so vivid with trees, meadows, and flowing streams. Shem and Sede burst into tears. The sight brought so much joy, they couldn't contain themselves. *This* was the "new world!"

Then Yahweh spoke for all to hear: "Go forth from the ark, Noah; you and your wife and your sons and their wives. Bring with you every living creature that I have preserved within the ark that they may breed abundantly in the earth and be fruitful and multiply."

With excitement and joy, Shem, Ham, and Japheth, along with their wives, began to release the animals. It was as if the animals, too, sensed that their time had come. They leapt, waddled, galloped, and took flight as they flowed from the great ark. The large eggs of the Behemoth had hatched several months before, and the weight of their steps swayed and creaked the door of the ark that had become the ramp. Ne-el patted their backs as they passed her. She had come to love them. They responded with pleasing roars. The birds, great and small, took flight, soaring high and sending their call into the open sky. It was a sight to behold: a steady stream of animals joyfully leaving their refuge and welcoming their newfound freedom.

After all the animals had been released, Noah and his family stood on the ramp taking in the panoramic view before them: animals moving over rich green hills, the air filled with soaring birds, and everywhere sunshine and the sense of freedom.

Joyfully, Noah said, "We will offer a sacrifice to our Great God!"

His sons, sharing the same joy, helped him gather smooth stones to build the altar. Choosing from the clean beasts and fowl, Noah offered them upon the altar.

Yahweh's beautiful voice resounded for all to hear: "I smell a sweet savor. No more will I curse the ground for man's sake. For the imagination of man's heart is evil from his youth. Neither will I again smite every living thing as

Shem and Sede's Joy

I have done. While the earth remains, seedtime and harvest, cold and heat, summer and winter, day and night will not cease. I now bless you, Noah an Ezmere, and your sons and their wives. Be fruitful and multiply; replenish the earth. The fear of you and the dread of you shall be on every beast of the earth, and every fowl of the air, and upon all that move upon the earth, as well as the fish of the sea. Into your hands they are delivered. Every moving thing that lives shall be meat for you, even as the green herb. But the life blood of the flesh you shall not eat. If any shall take a life, surely the blood of him, will I require. Whosoever will shed man's blood, by man shall his blood be shed; for in the image of God I made 'Adam', and every soul that has come from his seed. I now make a covenant with you, and with your seed after you, and every living creature that is with you. I will never again destroy all flesh by the waters of a flood. Neither shall I make another flood to destroy the earth. I now give you a sign of the covenant that I make between me and you and every living creature for endless generations. I set my bow in the cloud. And when I see it, I will remember the everlasting covenant that I now make between me and you and every living creature."

Just then they saw a multicolored rainbow appear in the sky! It stretched and arched across the horizon in magnificent display. Through the sparkling dew, the colors were vivid in yellow, orange, red, green, and lavender. Shafts of light from the sun pierced through the surrounding clouds, and the song of heaven was heard as angels sang Yahweh's praise. It brought an "ah" from all their lips. As Yahweh had supernaturally saved them, He now gave them a supernatural sign of His promise. They would never forget what they saw and heard that day. Yahweh himself had made a covenant with mankind and this sign they would see every time it rained. This would be their constant reminder of His love and promise to them.

As evening drew near, each couple returned to their small rooms to sleep. It seemed strange to walk the long corridors and not hear the sounds they knew so well. As Sede and Shem lay still, they whispered in the quiet. "Wasn't this an amazing day? To see the light of day once more <u>and</u> dry land!"

"Yes, and to see the animals so happy to be free. And the glory of hearing Yahweh speak to us, giving us His everlasting promise. That rainbow was so beautiful!" They talked late into the night and then drifted into restful sleep.

When morning dawned, they were surprised to see daylight streaming down the corridors and passing through the weaving of their curtain. They had become accustomed to the soft shadow of lamplight. How brilliant was the sun's light!

Sede and Shem hurriedly dressed and joined the others at the gathering place. Everyone seemed excited.

"Today we will begin the plans for our first village," Noah announced. "All that we discussed during our times of planning for the future will now begin. Until we have located a place to build our village, we will continue to use the ark as shelter and a place to prepare our meals." He sent his sons to scout the surrounding land and to choose a village site. His daughters would remain with him and Ezmere, tending the domestic animals that remained with them.

The brothers returned a few days later, excited about what they had found. Not far away, beneath the southern slope of a plateau, an open and great valley stretched to the horizon. They would build their new village there. The abundant pastureland would be ideal for the domestic animals, and a slow moving river ran nearby, with great trees shadowing the banks. This would be the place of their beginning.

While the men labored daily, building their huts, Sede and Shem's excitement grew for the birth of their child. At night, as they lay on their furs, Sede would take his hand to feel the baby move within her now well-rounded belly. In the glow of candlelight, she could see the glisten of a tear as he sweetly kissed her stomach. They had never known such wonder—the wonder of their love becoming a child.

It was on a moonlit night that her pains began. She thought the pain might be just from lifting too much that day; she had helped Shem carry firewood to stack next to their hut. But the pains were persistent and growing in severity. She finally realized that it was time.

Shem and Sede's Joy

With excitement, she woke Shem and said, "It's time, Shem. Call Mother and our sisters. An excited panic filled him as he ran to each of the huts, waking the sleeping couples. While Ezmere coached Sede with her contractions, Shoda and Ne-el stood over her shoulder to help and watch. Ezmere explained that the "water" would break first, and then the baby would come, followed by the afterbirth. She also instructed them how to turn a baby if it were breach.

Shem waited with the men by the fire he had made in front of their hut. He jumped to his feet several times when he heard Sede's cry of pain, alarm and concern evident on his face. He wanted to run inside and hold her. Noah patted him softly on the shoulder and said, "Son, the pain she is now experiencing will soon be forgotten when she holds your child in her arms. This is what Yahweh had spoken to Eve: 'In sorrow you shall bring forth children.' This sorrow is the birth pains."

They heard the slapping of a hand against the baby's bottom, and a small cry rang out in the night. Jumping to his feet, he knew their child had come. Ezmere appeared at the door with a small bundle in her arms. Beaming with a great smile, she happily announced, "My son...you have a son!"

With open arms, Shem welcomed his tiny son. Small newborn cries greeted his father's loving face. With joy, Shem threw his head back, laughing, and then he began to cry while great emotion swept through him. He was a father! This tiny life in his arms was his son!

The men began to clap and sing, moving their feet in dance. Shem joined in, dancing with his father and brothers while he cradled his son. It had been a long time since any of them had sung the Sethite "Song of New Life":

> Creation has birthed new life!
> We Sethites rejoice in song
> Welcomed is this new son,
> To carry Yahweh's light!

Sede, Seed of Eden

Gifts and talents have been given this son
His innocence will grow full bloom
He'll learn to love and live
And rejoice in the days to come

Over and over they sang, laughter and joy filling their hearts. As they moved to the lively song around the fire, their shadows danced across the door of his hut. Even the shadows seemed to be rejoicing. Ezmere smiled as she watched her men's reactions, but just then Shoda called out, "Come back, Mother, Sede needs you!" With concern on her face see returned to the hut.

Within seconds, the men heard another slap of skin and yet another cry. Unbelievable joy flooded Shem. They had twins!

Ezmere stepped from the doorway again, bringing another small bundle. "Son, you *are* truly blessed, just as Yahweh had said when we left the ark: 'Be fruitful and multiply.' And you have."

They began to clap and sing once more, their deep, rich voices rising in the night. And from heaven above, the only light upon the whole earth that night came from this lone campfire, there on the open plateau under the stars. Heaven looked down on mankind's new beginning and smiled.

Sede listened from inside, relieved that the pain had stopped and that she and Shem now had not one son but two. Shem desired with all his heart to hold her and waited for Ezmere to give consent to enter. With their sons in his arms, he carefully knelt beside her. Placing a baby in each of her arms, he then drew near to kiss her.

"Oh, Sede, you are so wonderful. You were so brave to endure the pain. I love you so much." He began to weep as he touched his forehead to hers.

She smiled at the love he was pouring out to her. She was weak and worn out from labor, and his words brought comfort and soothed her. Wonder filled her voice as she weakly spoke her words, "Shem...see what our love has made? Aren't they perfect?" She kissed the fuzzy heads of each little bundle as the babies began to make the sounds of new life. With happiness, both Sede and Shem began to laugh and then cry. In almost a whisper, she breathed, "Shem...they're 'seeds within a seed.'"

He blinked in wonder at how her seed from Eden had found its place here at the birth of their sons. Then, with a beauty in his face that reflected his precious innocence, he said, "When we were married, I couldn't imagine anything more wonderful than knowing sweet intimacy between us. But now I see that Yahweh has given us more to treasure and hold precious within our hearts. You have made me the happiest man, Sede. How can anything be more wonderful than this moment with you?"

She felt his great love and gazed upon the miracle of life in her arms, pondering what he had said. She, too, wondered, 'Could anything compare with this?'

This glorious night marked the first of their children. As the new families of the earth became established, they would experience more nights just like this one...full of joy and love. Japheth and Shoda, Ham and Ne-el, and even Noah and Ezmere were blessed with children. The birth of Sede and Shem's twins marked the beginning of Yahweh's commandment: "Be fruitful and multiply, and fill the earth!"

Chapter 17

The New World

They could barely see through the tall grass. There, through the waving golden curtain, was the plain before them. A small herd of dworta grazed, unaware that they were the hunted. Sede heard the excited breath of young Shoda and Ne-el as they crouched beside her, holding their small spears. "Why are we positioned here, Shoda?"

"Because we need to be downwind of our game."

"That's right. Ne-el, which way is the wind blowing?"

With her small hand Ne-el grabbed a handful of dry grass beneath her and crumbled it, tossing it in the air to blow like chaff. "The wind is blowing the grass toward us, Mommy."

"That's right. That means we're downwind."

Both girls smiled at each other. They were hunters too, just like their mother.

To their left, not a stone's throw away, Shem and Arphaxad crawled forward. Shem whispered, "When we rise, choose your dworta. Make your mark for the head."

Arphaxad nodded.

Sede whispered in a hush, "Steady, girls; steady. We wait for your father's signal." Seeing them rise she knew it was time.

"Ha-la-ah!" shouted Shem.

"Go!" shouted Sede. As the beating of drums, their hearts pounded, getting louder and louder as their legs swiftly cut through the grass. The thrill of adrenaline pumped through their veins, making their senses heightened and alive. Their pack was hunting!

All five raced forward as the startled herd began to stampede. Sede's arrow pierced the heart of her mark, and it fell instantly. Shoda and Ne-el threw their small spears but fell short of the dworta they aimed for. Arphaxad released the stone from his sling only to have it ricochet off the back of a snorting beast.

Breathless, Sede and her girls knelt at her felled dworta. She pulled the arrow from its limp body and looked up to see Arphaxad fall behind his father's full run. Knowing what Shem was about to do, she said, "Look, girls. Watch this!" and gestured in his direction. Both girls raised their heads to watch their father racing with the herd. At full speed, he bent and scooped a dworta under his arm; it wiggled and squealed in his strong grip. With broad smiles, Shem and Arphaxad strode through the grass toward them. They had gotten their game.

Shem knelt with the wiggling beast and watched his son draw his knife from its small sheath. "Set your mark. Now, son; through the heart!"

Arphaxad's blade came down swift and true. The dworta now lay still in Shem's hands. "Good, children. This was a good hunt. We never let the hunted suffer." He smiled at his son with pride and continued, "Always pierce the heart."

"Ne-el, you make the knots this time," Sede instructed.

Ne-el's little hands pulled the leather rope from her belt, and began to tie the dworta's legs together.

"That's right, over and under and around to knot the rope." Shem smiled as he watched her coach their little hunter. They gathered their things and walked through the waving grass for home, the children trailing like ducks in a row. As Shem shouldered the dwortas, Sede smiled and leaned into his side, kissing him sweetly on the cheek. Little Ne-el giggled. It made her feel good to see the love between her mother and father. They all felt the satisfaction and the pleasure of being a family.

The New World

While Shem and Arphaxad dressed the game, Sede and the girls prepared the fire. They would roast the dwortas and share them with the village. Every day there was something new to teach their little ones. Both of them delighted in passing on what they had once learned. Now they were the elders of their family, and they would set the standards for what their children knew and believed. This knowledge would become the traditions these new Sethites would live by as well as passing it to the generations to come. Life in this "new world" was a fresh beginning for mankind, and Shem and Sede believed, as Yahweh had said, 'Their generations would fill the earth.' In everything they taught, they tried to show the heart of Yahweh. For if they could leave their children anything, it would be to love Yahweh will all their heart, soul, and strength.

Shem and Sede never got used to the rain. Before the flood, there was no rain. A mist had risen from the earth every night and brought the moisture the plants needed. But now, since the flood, the rains came regularly, and Shem began to recognize there were seasons with much rain and then very little. After a rain, he would bring his family to the door of their hut and show them the bow in the sky. Each time, he had his children take turns repeating the covenant Yahweh had made with them.

On one of these rainy days, Shem gathered his family before him and stood in the doorsill. As they gazed heavenward, beholding the rainbow, he asked little Ne-el to repeat the covenant of Yahweh. In her small voice, she began: "And Yahweh said: 'No more will I bring a flood of waters to destroy the earth, or curse the ground. While the earth remains…" She hesitated, not remembering what followed.

"That's right, Ne-el; 'While the earth remains, seedtime and harvest.'"

Her eyes lit up, remembering, and she continued with her father. "Cold and heat, summer and winter, day and night will not cease."

Shem looked down on her sweet face, pride beaming from his. "That was good, Ne-el. You're memorizing the covenant well!" He bent on one knee and kissed her sweetly on the cheek while her little arms circled his neck.

"I love you, Abba," she whispered in his ear.

"I love you back, little cricket."

Sede heard their whispered exchange and smiled. Her heart warmed, remembering her own loving words to her Abba.

It was on these rainy days that Shem and Sede taught their children the language and writing of the Sethites. They didn't have parchment like they used when they were young, but they used a stick to make the marks for each letter in the dirt. It was easily erased to try again. On this particular day, their children sat cross-legged using their sticks, and practicing the Sethite alphabet. The rain poured outside the hut, and the fire gave warmth within as they practiced. Shoda patiently helped Ne-el, who was having trouble making the curve of her letter. Sede watched as Shoda mentored the younger. She turned and winked at Shem, who was also watching. They exchanged a smile of pride. Their children were learning the ways of their people. This was their family, and they loved investing themselves in their children.

They also taught their children the songs of the ancients: the songs for sacrifice, feasts, weddings, birth, and death. In these times, they asked their Aunt Shoda to tutor them. Shem and Sede wanted them to have skill in both song and music. Shoda gladly helped them make their own instruments, and soon they were making pleasant sounds that harmonized as they played together.

In the evenings around the hearth, Shem told his children the stories of their village of long ago. They eagerly listened to their hunting adventures with grandfather Tolmaka, the leader of their pack, and how they battled a towering giant that cornered them in a cave. The stories of their ancestors, Adam and Eve, Cain and Abel, Seth and Enoch, filled them with awe, and, of course, they had many questions. They especially loved the stories about the ark with Grandfather Noah and the animals. With each new child they had, new and wonder-filled hearts delighted in the stories of their people, the Sethites.

Sede and Shem's firstborn were their twin sons, Elem and Assur. They were the first children to be born in the "new world." Now young men, they no longer hunted with them but had chosen to work with Ham and his herds. Their interest was in shepherding and breeding the animals. It was as it had been in Taasa-toka. Children were given the choice to decide what interests they wished to pursue.

Arphaxad was born two years after the flood. It was at his birth that Yahweh spoke to them concerning the lineage for the "Promised One" to come. They were surprised that it would not be their firstborn, Elem, for this was the custom of their people. But Yahweh gave them His wisdom: "Mans wisdom is not my wisdom. I alone know the heart of my creation. It is by my design that the seed be through Arphaxad." When he was born, they gazed into his tiny face and both knew, yes, he was the one. Shoda, their daughter, followed in birth and then Ne-el. It was both Shem and Sede's desire to honor their sisters by naming their own daughters as their namesakes.

The four families had built their huts, forming their new Sethite village. Their children would grow and learn together the ways of Seth. Once a year, at the summer solstice, Noah observed a new feast—the "Feast of First Fruits"—celebrating their thanksgiving for the bounty of the new season. At this feast, they offered the first of what was produced, either by animals, crops, fruits and vegetables, or skill of hand. This they offered to Yahweh as a sacrifice, rejoicing that He had saved them from the great flood and now blessed them with life and prosperity. These feasts united the four families in celebration and song.

Noah continued to observe the yearly sacrifice of the spotless white lamb in the winter solstice. With both sacrifices, Yahweh was faithful to receive their offering with fire from heaven. The same glory cloud that descended on them when they were children now descended on their children. This new generation had the seed of promise planted within them. The same promise: that someday Yahweh would send the sinless, spotless lamb that would take away the sin of the world, and also restore the hearts of people as it had once been in the Garden of Eden.

Each family had come to recognize their special contribution to the village. Noah had become a husbandman of the earth, growing fruits and vegetables from the rich soil. He continued to be the patriarch of the families, giving them the word of Yahweh and helping them to observe His ways. Ezmere, the matriarch, helped the young mothers with their children's care and delivered each new grandchild. She alone had the knowledge of her ancestors from before the flood. She patiently taught her daughters the knowledge of midwifery and knew they would someday do the same for their daughters. It was also her delight to work with Noah in his interest with agriculture. She found ways to dry the fruits and vegetables he grew as well as the right seasons to harvest nuts and berries. This was a valuable source of food when the hunters remained in the village during the days of deep snow.

Shem and Sede were the village hunters. This was their contribution to their kin, and they never tired of leaving for the hunt. Both found great delight teaching the young to read animal tracks and sharpening their skills with their weapon of choice. They also found great satisfaction in watching them mature in their understanding and respect for Yahweh's great creation. They often pointed out the animals they had once cared for in the ark, seeing them on occasion while they hunted. The children especially delighted in sliding down the long necks of the giant behemoths, their legs as round and tall as tree trucks. These gentle giants loved the children's attention while they joyfully played on their backs.

Ham bred animals, which supplied the village with milk and cheese as well as wool and leather from their hides. Ne-el was an expert in weaving from looms; her cloth was used to make robes and coverings for the tents of those who followed the grazing herds. She taught those who desired to learn the beautiful artistry of design and embroidery. Although Sede and Shem preferred to wear their skins, they did enjoy their fine robes Ne-el had made them and wore them for special times of celebration.

Japheth grew and harvested grains for the village. His wheat made the finest bread. He taught his sons about the seasons: when to plant and when to harvest. He never tired of sharing the mystery of the seed, each growing after its own kind. And Shoda—she loved the music of Yahweh. After the flood she no longer desired to hunt but turned her heart to worship Yahweh in song. She taught the village sons and daughters to make and play instruments for their times of worship. Their abilities were amazing, making celebrations truly festive and beautiful with song.

Just like Taasa-toka, the new elders wished to give the village children the freedom to choose the skills they desired to learn. Both the sons of Adam and the daughters of Eve would be trained according to their interest and abilities. The traditions of the Sethites were being passed down to this new and upcoming generation. The village had become a place of peace and prosperity: "heaven on earth"!

When another year had produced its first season crop, it was again time for the celebration of the "Feast of First Fruits," bringing much excitement and joy for everyone. The women had prepared for days so they that could sit and enjoy their time with their kin and not be cumbered with preparing each meal. For three days the families would feast and enjoy the blessings of the "new world."

They brought the best for a sacrifice offering. Japheth brought the finest ground wheat, barley, and oats; Ham, the choicest fat lamb, calf, and goat; and Shem brought the purest honey he found in the wild as well as a prize gazelle and gamet. And Noah, he poured out the finest wine he had made from the grapes he cultivated. All of them offered their best. Because this was a new celebration Noah was instituting for his people, he asked Shoda to create a song to sing to Yahweh, a song that would forever be associated with the "Feast of First Fruits." She sang the song before them, her voice crystal clear and angelic. The others soon learned the words and joined in with her as they offered praise to Yahweh…

We give thanks to you, Yahweh
We give thanks…

Sede, Seed of Eden

We give thanks to you, Yahweh
We give thanks…

With hearts and hands lifted high to you
The best we offer, the best is due
The choicest, the purest we bring
For the "First Fruits" sacrifice we sing

The first of our flocks, the bounty of the land
The finest and the best work of our hands
We honor you for what you have given
We lift our song to you, great God in heaven

We give thanks to you, Yahweh
We give thanks…
We give thanks to you, Yahweh
We give thanks…

Their voices rose in beautiful harmony while lovely accompaniment rose from the instruments the children played in the background. A heavy peace rested on them when they finished. Fire flashed from heaven and consumed their sacrifices. What they had offered had been accepted! And then the glory cloud fell. Yahweh's presence was among them… With uplift faces and hands, they welcomed the sparkling, loving presence of the God who loved them.

On the second night around the council fire, Shem rose to tell the story he had heard many times when he was a child in the old village of Taasa-toka. It was the story of Adam and Eve. The families delighted in his antics, for he, like Tolmaka, enjoyed drawing the children into the story. Their little hands feverishly grabbed to catch the falling apples from Eden's tree that he tossed from his robe into the air. Sede watched him, remembering her father. It brought bittersweet recollection. She missed him and the times they had shared at festivals, but she was so very proud of Shem and how he had stepped into his place of leadership.

Ham, too, stood at a distance and watched his brother pace before the fire, retelling the story from their youth. He saw the look of admiration in the faces of his kin: a look of respect and honor. Shem had the confidence and charisma he himself lacked, and Ham envied him. If only he had been firstborn, it would have been him telling the story and not Shem. He was beginning to realize he would never have the desire of his heart: to be honored and revered as leader. His old jealousies still haunted him.

Night settled on the sleepy listeners, and each family settled next to the warm fire, sleeping under the open sky instead of their huts.

Sede began to wonder where little Ne-el had gone. She hadn't seen her since Shem's story. Looking out over the sea of sleeping kin, she spotted her lying on a pile of soft firs, hands behind her head, gazing at the stars. A half-eaten apple lay in her lap.

"What are you doing, little cricket?"

"I'm watching the sparks rise in the air and become stars in the sky."

Sede smiled and knelt to lie beside her. Ne-el scooted to her mother, resting in her arms. In wonder, both mother and daughter quietly gazed at the beautiful stars. It *was* breathtaking. They watched as the sparks rose high and then seemed to disappear. It did look like they became stars.

"Who made the stars, mommy?"

Sede was quiet for a while and then answered: "The great Yahweh did… long, long ago."

Ne-el pondered her mother's words and said, "I love all the sparkling lights of heaven. They're like candles in the sky."

Sede loved her innocent perspective. "Yes, Ne-el, they *are* like candles."

"Why did Yahweh make the stars?"

Sede smiled, knowing her little one loved to ask endless questions that usually took a good deal of explaining to answer. "He made the starry night so we would always remember...that when the stars came out, it was time for little 'crickets' to go to sleep!" She tickled Ne-el, making her wiggle and squeal a playful giggle. "Come, little one. Time for sleep." Standing to her feet, Sede lifted her sleepy child.

Lying next to Shem, she held Ne-el in her arms. Shoda slept next to Arphaxad, who still had his sling in his hand. The twins were near, sleeping by the fire. She loved being a mother and seeing what her and Shem's love had made. She often thought of what her father had told her long ago as they waited beneath the grove of trees on their last hunt. 'Your love with Shem will create a life.' And she loved the lives their love had created. She lovingly nuzzled Ne-el's head, feeling the love of a mother for her child. That night, for the first time since the flood, she felt a sense of community. They were Sethites again, and she loved her kin.

On the third day of the festival, the children challenged themselves with games of skill: the bow, the spear, and the sling. Races on foot, as well as horseback, made for an exciting time for both child and parent. Shem and Sede had kept Fallon and Mora, not turning them loose in the world as they had the other animals. Ham bred them many times, and Shem and Sede had learned to use them for the hunt. They found that riding their horses brought them in the middle of the herd where they could spear the choicest game. They still taught the children to hunt from the ground but also from atop their own horses. Today at the festival, the children would prove their skill on horseback.

Shem and Sede's children had become expert riders, able to mount their horses as they ran full speed beside them. Each hunter had a part in their horse's training as well as their care. Japheth's two youngest sons, Riphath and Togarmah, loved to ride, as well as Ham's oldest son, Cush. The riders were to run their horses at full speed past a target on a pole, spearing it. The closest to the center mark would be the winner.

The boys made the run first. So far, each had missed the target. As Shoda mounted her horse, little Ne-el shouted out, "Set your mark, Shoda, right through the heart!" Shoda ran past her mark at full speed, throwing her spear. It struck the target but not in the center. An "ooh" of disappointment echoed through the crowd.

Then it was little Ne-el's turn. She stood atop her horse, her hands in the air, and shouted, "It is *my* spear that will make the mark!" All laughed at her youthful boast. She was the youngest in the village to hunt, and everyone delighted in her sweet ways.

Running beside her horse, she built up speed then mounted, swinging herself up to sit on his back. Pressing her horse faster and faster, she sped toward the pole. She threw her spear, and it landed in the bull's eye! Everyone stood to their feet to cheer. Shoda caught Sede's eye and said, "I think we have another Sede on our hands." Sede beamed, delighting with pride in her little hunter.

When Ne-el passed the roaring crowd, she turned to take another run past them. When she got close enough, she shouted, "Watch me, Abba, I want to show you something!" Running full speed, she slowly stood on the back of the running horse, lifting her hands in the air as they galloped. The wind blew against her small body, making her braids fly behind her. Tilting her head back and closing her eyes, she moved her arms slowly up and down, looking as though she were flying. It was magnificent! The crowd cheered her on.

It was when her horse started his return that she began to wobble. Opening her eyes, she tried to steady herself. Shem bolted from where he was sitting, and Sede screamed, "Ne-el!" She flew from the horse, falling and rolling on the ground. The dust filled the air from the horse's sudden stop and her rolling body. Everyone gasped in horror while the men raced toward her, not believing what had just happened.

When Shem and Sede reached her, she was on her side. Shem carefully rolled her over. Lifting her, she lay limp in his arms. Sede was at his side, kissing her still face and holding her small hand. She searched Shem's white face and saw horror and panic. It made her heart sink for she knew it was worse than she thought.

He carried her to their hut and gently laid her on their bedding furs. "Does she still breathe, Shem?!" she said in a panic.

He lowered his head to listen for a heartbeat. Slowly standing, he faced her searching look. With eyes full of pain, he said, "No, Sede, she's gone...."

"What? No!" she cried. "No! Nooo!" She fell to the floor, collapsing in a heap, crying with her head on Ne-el's small chest. Shem just stood there, looking down at his beautiful little girl. How could she be gone? She was so full of joy and life. His little girl—gone? He began to sob, his shoulder moving up and down.

Their children stood hesitantly at the door. They were in a state of shock from what had just happened. They couldn't believe it. Shem saw their bewildered looks; he opened his arm and they ran to him, huddling against their father's chest, hot tears falling from their eyes. Sede rose, tears blurring her vision. Shem opened his arms to her, and she fell into them. There he stood, holding his family in utter loss....

Noah and Ezmere came to their hut and embraced them. They began to cry, for the pain was in their hearts too. Their grandchild was dead. The "new world" had lost its first child. After they could cry no more, Ezmere took Sede by the hand and said, "Come with me, Daughter."

Tears so filled her eyes that she stumbled as Ezmere led her from the hut. She was in shock. Everything seemed like a foggy dream, with muffled voices and people moving in slow motion. She didn't even know where Ezmere was taking her. She felt numb and dead inside. Not since her father's death had she felt such shock.

During the following days, all the families sorrowed for Shem and Sede's loss. With the greatest love and skill, Ne-el made black banners with three white tiers. Cush helped her to hang them at the entrance of each hut, a memorial of the precious life that had lived among them. They observed three days of mourning and then celebrated three days. She had truly been everyone's little joy.

Elam and Assur wanted to express comfort and love to their mother.

Unsure of what they could do or say, they brought her a handful of florendia. They knew it was her favorite. With tears in their eyes, they kissed her on the cheek at the same time. In loving acceptance, she hugged them and wept.

Arphaxad, too, saw his mother's grief. On the last day of the three days of celebration, he brought her something Ne-el had made for him. He wanted to bless her. "Ne-el made this little flute with the help of Aunt Shoda and gave it me as a gift. I wish to give it to you, Mother. Maybe you can learn to play her flute, and it will comfort your heart."

Sede began to cry once more. She felt the love her son was giving and held him tight. "Oh, Son, you are such a wonderful boy. I love you so much. Thank you for your gift."

He began to cry once more for he could feel his mother's pain. They held each other for a long time, and then he left quietly.

That evening young Shoda came to her mother's side. "Mother, may I comb you hair?"

"That would be nice, dear." Shoda gently combed Sede's hair as she hummed the "Love Song for the Dead." Tears rolled down Sede's cheek as she listened. What she heard was the love a child for her mother. She pulled Shoda into her arms and held her. "Oh, Shoda, you are so very special. I love you, my precious daughter!" Shoda cried softly as they held each other.

For some reason, Sede couldn't talk to Shem. Her heart seemed frozen. She could only speak but to say yes or no when he asked her about her feelings. She knew she needed to find peace for her loss. And though she loved Shem with all her heart, she knew no one could find this for her, not even her beloved husband.

Three months had passed, and still her pain was near. She cried every day for she saw reminders of her "little cricket" everywhere: her tiny spear propped against the wall of the hut, her horse as it grazed in the pasture, and her small flute that lay on the mantel.

While they sat around their hearth one night, Sede spoke with words that trembled with emotion. "I need to go to the forest and find my heart once more."

Sadly, Shem searched her face. It grieved him to see her hurt so deeply. "I wish I could be your comfort, Sede." He began to softly cry.

She leaned into him, touching her forehead to his. "Oh, my husband. You are such a wonderful man. You are strength to me always. But in this thing, I must find my comfort from Yahweh himself. Please don't misunderstand this. I know that my heart needs the words of Yahweh."

Shem closed his eyes. He knew she was right for he had found the words of Yahweh for his own heart the day they buried Ne-el. Yahweh came to him on the breeze and said, "Fear not, Shem, your daughter is in the safest place in the universe. She is in the arms of love…my arms." All of Shem's grief was broken when he heard those words. He had heard them once before. It was when he had to trust Yahweh to keep Sede safe when she had been taken from Sidon. Now, instead of piercing loss, all that now remained in his heart was peace. His precious daughter *was* in the arms of love. His Sede must find this peace too.

She left in the morning, climbing the plateau that led to the forest. She had her bow, cloak, and leather bags for food and water. Just as she had found a place of rest for Playtheus and her father, she would search for a place of peace for her daughter. Two weeks she stayed in the forest. The gentle breeze blew through the tall pines, and the nearby brook sent forth the soothing sound of peaceful, flowing water. Every day she walked alone on the deer trails that led through the woods, and at night she slept by her fire. The forest had a way of speaking to her that no human ever could. She knew her soul was receiving the language of solace and rest.

One night as she lay by her fire, she felt a presence. Materializing before her, she saw him—the same Watcher who had appeared to her before. Startled by his appearing, but then relieved, she waited for him to speak. "Hail, Sede, mother of her people." Sede felt the sweet comfort of the Lord streaming from this beautiful angel. She began to weep, not holding back her sorrow and pain of loss. "Yes…let your sorrow flow from you, Sede. A mother's grieving heart is dear to the heart of Yahweh."

The Watcher waited for Sede to look up. "Your heart has been broken, Sede, but Yahweh has sent his comfort for you. Receive from the very heart of God." He stepped forward and embraced her. Light shot from his being, lighting up the dark forest all around them. She felt the penetrating shafts of love that were intermingled with the light. All her sorrow melted away, and she felt peace flood her soul. With this wonderful peace came a beautiful vision within her spirit and a gentle, quiet knowing. No longer did she see within herself the image of Ne-el's limp little body in Shem's arms but rather she saw her playing with other children. They were skipping and running over rolling hills of soft meadow grass. She saw her dear father and mother standing in the distance beneath a beautiful tree, holding hands and watching their granddaughter play. As more understanding came to her, she knew that when her days were fulfilled on this earth, she would be greeted by them and hold her daughter once more. They were there, waiting for her. The peace she sought had come.

As the Watcher released her, he motioned for her to sit by the fire. He seated himself next to her in silence, giving her time to absorb what Yahweh had given her. When he knew the time was right, he continued. "I have words from Yahweh to give you, Sede. You are the mother of your people, and Yahweh knows he can trust you. This is only for you to know. You are not to share this even with your husband. It was Yahweh's intention to begin anew with mankind, a fresh world, washed clean from the corruption that had infested it. But as you know, sin will always try to rule the hearts of mankind. It is only through intentional faith in Yahweh that any person can be free from sin's destructive snare. Your new village is like 'heaven on earth,' but this will change."

Sede began to cry. It was as if she knew what he was going to say and didn't want to hear it.

"Yes, Sede, a division is coming among the sons of Noah. Each son will part their ways. An even greater division will come in the far future when only one family from Shem and your descendants will hold true to Yahweh. Japheth and Shoda will not see this in their generation, but after their death, their children too will abandon Yahweh and seek their own gods, desiring pleasure instead of faith. Ham's descendants will be the most corrupt. They will actually persecute yours and Japheth's families. Ham and his son Canaan will learn the dark knowledge of the fallen ones. Through this knowledge, they will cause a division in the families of Noah, lusting for pleasure, power, and glory. This will be the desire of their heart: to be exalted king over the people of the earth."

She began to weep, holding her hands to her face. With trembling words, she asked, "Why can't Yahweh stop this before it goes this far? He is all powerful and could prevent this!"

"Yes, Sede, He is all powerful, but He has given people the sacred right to choose, and Yahweh will not violate the power to choose. It is an everlasting dictate He has declared. When He created man, this was the one thing he gave them: the power to obey or rebel. From the very beginning with Adam and Eve, it has been so. They chose to rebel against his commandment concerning the tree of knowledge of good and evil. The generations that will come from Noah's descendants still have that same choice: to obey or rebel. Yahweh knows the end from the beginning. He knows that Ham will choose to exalt himself."

"From the very beginning, it has been Yahweh's plan to fulfill the promise he made Eve…that the 'Promised One' would come and destroy the 'wicked one.' His heart of love did not leave mankind without the hope of redemption. Your seed, Sede, throughout each generation, will continue until that 'One' is born. Each generation after you will continue this lineage. They will have the witness of the Lord in their lives. Yahweh will raise up, in the far future, a people that will someday call him 'Abba Father.' He will have the family He has always wanted, and they will be mighty in the earth:

in righteous, peace, and joy." He paused, allowing her to absorb the words he had spoken. He then continued, "You have been told all of this so you will remain strong in the face of these coming changes, helping your husband as he establishes the 'way of the Lord' for your posterity. Yahweh sends you back to your family now, knowing what is to come. Enjoy what remains of the peace among your kin, but do not fear the future. Yahweh goes before you to prepare the way. All you have to do, Sede, is walk in the way He shows you." As he finished speaking, he tenderly smiled and disappeared.

She sat for a long time, rehearsing in her mind what had just happened. No longer was her heart filled with sorrow for her precious daughter. She knew her "little cricket" was happy and carefree, playing in the meadows of heaven while her father and mother watched nearby. She now had the comfort and peace she had been searching for. She would return to the village, watching and praying. For as she had come to know, Yahweh's word would surely come to pass. What a wonder. He had taken the burden of loss from her, giving her a loving vision to remember. He had shown her what was to come and trusted her with this knowledge. Even though it was sorrowful to consider, there was still this shining hope: The "Promised One" would come.

Chapter 18

Ham's Rebellion

When Sede arrived at the village, everyone left their huts to embrace her. Shem and their children were overjoyed to have her home. They were together again. She soon joined the hunt with Shem, along with their young hunters, and life settled down once more to peace and small village life. She let each day with her people fill her heart with love and joy. As the months turned into years, Sede thought that perhaps they would live centuries before the division of their people would come to pass for even after the flood, they continued to have extended longevity of life.

But one day she began to see a change in Canaan, Ham's son. His countenance seemed to carry a "brooding way" about him. She remembered what the Watcher had said about Canaan in particular. Could sin be crouching at the door of his heart, as it had with Cain when he hated his brother Abel and killed him? Sede remembered the teaching Noah had shared with them while they were on the ark. He had said they were royalty, priest, and prophet. As prophet, they were to keep a watchful eye on their people and deliver the word of the Lord. She waited to approach Canaan, wanting to be in Yahweh's perfect timing. The time came one night as the families were leaving the council fire to return to their huts.

Sensing the moment had come, she approached Caanan. "May I speak with you, Nephew?"

"Yes, Aunt Sede. We can sit here." He motioned to a large log near the fire.

She sat and intently looked at him. "I have noticed a change in you, Canaan. You seem downcast. What is troubling your heart?"

He looked surprised that someone could see deeper than the outward appearance. He fumbled for words and finally confessed, "I'm angry about the honor I'm denied among my brothers. Because I'm the youngest, I'm treated as though I know nothing and that I have no value."

Sede was troubled by what he said. The words and actions of his brothers were as weapons afflicting his soul. This young man was being attacked spiritually and had no defenses. "Oh, Canaan, the words and actions of others can be as spears and arrows that wound the heart, but it's within your power to quench them. If you know the truth about yourself, nothing can wound or harm you. You need to shift your focus from what others are saying about you and know what Yahweh has said about you. Because you are a Sethite, you are royalty—a child of the "Most High" God. You are now a grown man of God and coming to the age of choosing a wife. Soon you will begin a family of your own. Your brothers' words and actions will mean nothing then. You will be the elder of your own family, with a wonderful wife and children to nurture and inspire."

The revelation of her words broke through, and Canaan's face shown with light. He knew what she said was truth and the counsel of the Lord. He threw his arms around her neck and hugged her thankfully. "Oh thank you, Aunt Sede. I see the truth in the words you have spoken."

Sede held his hand and patted it. "The next time you're tempted to believe what other people say about you, always remember to look to Yahweh and remember what He has said about you, okay? You are royalty, Canaan."

"Thank you, Aunt Sede."

She smiled and bid him goodnight. While she lingered by the fire, a profound pleasure settled within her heart. Yahweh had given her opportunity to counsel him, and he had received her words. It occurred to her that this was the first time she had been a "mother to her people." It felt good to help her kin.

Ham's Rebellion

Canaan was his father's favorite, although Ham had other sons: Cush, Mizraim, and Phut. He showed Canaan the favor of firstborn though he was the youngest. This favoritism created an undertow of competition and contention among Ham's now grown sons. It was no wonder the older sons were jealous and tormented Canaan. Ham praised him openly before them, knowing that it made them jealous. It was Ham's desire to only spend time with Canaan. They journeyed often to the wilderness, hunting and exploring together, and even now they left the village in discovery of a new adventure.

It was on this trip, as Ham reclined by their campfire, that Canaan came running and dropped at his feet, breathless. "I came as soon as I could! It's amazing, Father!" He could hardly catch his breath for the excitement he felt.

Ham could see his son had seen something that truly excited him. "Take your time and calm yourself, Son. Tell me what you've seen."

"I've seen a cave. Come with me, and I'll show you." Canaan pulled at his father's arm to help him rise.

"Son, you're always finding things that amaze you. What is it this time?"

"Nothing like we've ever seen before. Truly, this is a wonder!" Canaan had Ham's attention now.

He followed his son, led by the light of his torch.

"We have to climb from here. Follow me." He tossed his torch upward, and it landed in the mouth of the cave. Canaan started climbing, leaving his father far below.

"Wait up. Remember that I'm not as young as you!" Ham softly laughed. As they stood at the entrance, Ham gasped.

The cave was filled with crystals that glowed from the inside. The torch light wasn't needed. Ham suddenly remembered he'd seen this before, many, many years ago when he and Dollo were in the great City of Lights. "Oh, my son, I've seen this wonder before—long ago!"

"It's truly a wonder, is it not, Father?"

"Yes, Son, a wonder…." His voice trailed off hesitantly.

They began walking in the chamber, past scrolls of parchments, works of art, strange objects, and statues of the Renown that Ham still recognized. The atmosphere in the air was charged with a strange and compelling energy. There, at the far end of the chamber, was a golden pedestal. A large, leather-bound parchment rested on top, having golden symbols embedded into the covering. Light streamed from it in all directions.

Behind the pedestal stood the marble statue of Castius. Ham gasped when he saw him. The statue glowed within its chest with swirling amber, red, and yellow light.

"What is all this about, Father?"

"I know what this is, Son. It's the dark knowledge of the world Yahweh destroyed with the flood. The fallen angels saved all this, knowing their world was about to end. The earthquake we felt a few days ago must have opened the entrance." He couldn't believe what surrounded him. It was the accumulated knowledge of the fallen ones.

"We must leave this place, Canaan, before some evil overtakes us!" Ham pulled at his arm, stepping toward the entrance.

"No, Father," he defiantly protested, jerking his arm loose from his father's grip. "I want to discover the meaning of all of this. You'll not deny me this discovery. I feel strangely drawn to know what's written in these scrolls. Don't you feel the power that surrounds us?"

"Yes, Son. That's why we must go!"

Suddenly, from Castius' statue, came his misty spirit and stood before them, hovering just above the ground. Ham trembled at the sight of him, but Canaan was in awe of his beauty and majesty.

"Who are you?" Canaan spoke as if mesmerized.

"I am a Great One from the "old world." You can know the hidden secrets of the universe hidden within these scrolls. And if you choose, I will usher you into greatness, fulfilling your heart's desire."

Ham trembled, knowing he and his son were in great peril. He felt frozen and couldn't move.

Castius waved his misty hand, and a vision appeared. Both Ham and Canaan saw themselves being paraded down a street with thronging crowds shouting their praises: "Great are our kings. Glory be to their names. We exalt you!" They were seated in golden sedans, carried on poles over the shoulders of men. Flowers and petals were lavishly strewn before them, and those who stood near strained to touch the tassels that hung from their chairs. They wore exquisite kingly robes made of fur and jewels. Upon their heads were crowns of gold that streamed with light. Each held a jeweled scepter in his hand that was pressed to their chest. They exuded beauty, masculinity, and power. As they approached an elevated platform, exquisite thrones awaited them. Graciously they stepped forward and seated themselves side by side. Below their feet bowed Noah, Shem, Japheth, and Canaan's brothers as they gave homage. They extended their scepters toward them, and their family broke out in worship, hailing their greatness with unfailing love. As both Ham and Canaan watched this vision, they felt the power of the worship being given to them. It satisfied the deepest longing in their hearts.

They trembled with pleasure, knowing their family finally acknowledged their importance and majesty. This was the secret desire they shared: Canaan to be exalted above his brothers and Ham recognized as king over all. Within themselves they knew…they *were* worthy to be these royal kings. All the counsel Sede had given Canaan evaporated. This is what he truly wanted. He cared little that his identity was in what Yahweh said about him. He wanted the acclaim of others.

But Ham knew there would be a price to pay for all this glory. He knew he would have to forsake Yahweh and the way of the Sethites in order to have what he desired. He felt his will beginning to surrender to temptation. And as the moment lingered, he chose. He knew, in his heart, that any price he would have to pay would be worth having this kind of acclaim, praise, and glory. (Dark Deception had done its deed. They were deceived, and darkness had found its entrance into the hearts of men.)

"Oh, this is wonderful, Father. You and I are royal kings over all. They see our greatness and worship us!"

Castius knowingly smiled. "You will be given the knowledge to be such kings. Here in this cave are the secrets to power and glory. None can stand before you, for you alone will rule the earth." His words were smooth and hypnotic, pleasing in every way.

Ham and Canaan looked at each other, knowing in their hearts they wished to have what they had seen. Ham knew that Shem would to be the leader of all the peoples of the earth when Noah died. He had envied the honor his father and their kin showed him. If only he had been the firstborn, he would have received the position of leadership, ruling their people as supreme. This was the one reason he showed such favor to Canaan; he knew what it was like to be overlooked because of birth order. But now, in this image before him, *he* was the ruler, and his son was at his side. With all his heart he wanted this vision to come to pass. *This* was his future!

Castius looked intently at Ham. "This is the wish of your heart, is it not, Bromos?"

Surprised that he had called him by his Atlantis name, but still dreamingly transfixed, he yielded. "Yes… I do. I, Bromos, wish with all my heart to rule the earth!"

"Well then, it is as you have said. By your own words it will done!"

Instantly they felt a change within themselves. Something left them, and something else entered. An exchange happened. Icy cold darkness flowed from the top of their heads, down through their chest, and into their arms and legs. No longer were they the innocent of Yahweh. They had purposely surrendered their wills in exchange for power and glory, yielding to temptation. They were now subject to the lord of darkness. He had found his entrance into Yahweh's world once more. The first time was through Adam and Eve. This time it would be through Ham and his seed.

Castius, with his angelic knowledge, knew that only through the words of a human could a link between the unseen world and the natural world take place.

Ham's Rebellion

Ham should have remembered Enoch's teachings. Yahweh had created the natural realm with his spoken words; these words, though unseen and invisible, were spirit and life. All creation was manifested from an unseen reality into a natural reality through the words Yahweh had spoken. The angels of darkness knew this spiritual principle, and it had been taught to the Sethite people. But Ham made a conscious decision to choose what he *wanted* rather than what he knew was *right*. He was fully aware that he was choosing a different destiny for himself and his descendants. This dark knowledge would lead them in a different direction from the Sethite way he had been taught. A true leader would have considered his people, but Ham chose to consider what he wanted.

Castius' misty body began to solidify into the Nephilim that now stood before them. With his fingertips, he touched Ham and Canaan's foreheads, sending another wave of cold, icy evil through them. "I give you power to learn the knowledge that will make you great. This chamber I give to you. Share it with no one. Stay here and learn the knowledge of greatness. In time, you will become established as kings and rulers over all the earth!"

The soft whispers from within the scrolls could be heard as Ham and Canaan staggered on their feet from the waves of power pulsating from them.

Castius spoke once more, asking them, "Are you willing to release the three 'Mighty Ones' to be among you?"

Ham and Canaan looked at each other dumbfounded. Were they this important that this mighty being needed their permission? With willing eagerness, they said in unison, "Yes, we are willing to release the 'Mighty Ones'!"

From the great parchment on the pedestal, three misty images began to materialize. They were Talimus-qua-tam, Masta-lovid, and Satsum-kedesh. Brilliant blue light radiated from their bodies. Their tattoos sparkled with flecks of red light pulsating from their foreheads. They exuded beauty, masculinity, majesty, and power. Ham recognized Talimus-qua-tam. This was the same mighty angel he had seen in the City of Lights. It was he who had stood at the gazebo at the marketplace and disappeared with his newly bought Sethite maiden.

Ham and Canaan bowed in awe before them, compelled to worship them. They felt the adoration from their hearts leave them and flow to the angels, who willingly absorbed the invisible, yet powerful, love and worship they gave them. The angels, in return, glowed brighter, and the chamber filled with music coming from one of the parchments. Ham slowly stretched out his hand to touch the feet of Talimus-qua-tam. A surge of power shot through him, and he gasped from the ecstasy he felt! For even though they were fallen angels, they were powerful and possessed dark glory.

Great envy stirred within Ham's heart. Outwardly, he was giving these angels his worship, but secretly, he desired to *be* as the angels: beautiful, strong, and mighty. (The "lord of darkness" had found a heart to be at home in. Just as with Adam and Eve, he tempted Ham to be something more than what he was created to be. Adam and Eve were told they would be *like* the "Most High." Ham's temptation was the same: to be something he was not created to be—a *king* to rule over mankind.)

The three angels were finally free from their confinement. They would begin their work in this "new world" as they had in the old one. There were fewer of them this time, but their arrogance and pride would not stop them from having their hearts' desire. There was a knowing within them that "the day of days" was yet to come for them. But defying the inevitable, they would strategize and make new plans. They would go about establishing families of their own and see generations born to them as they had before. They would take for themselves new human wives: wives that would give them Regal sons.

Castius and the three fallen angels disappeared while Ham and Canaan remained alone, kneeling in the cave. "We are changed, my son. Changed into men of greatness!" Ham still felt the power he had experienced when he had touched Talimus-qua-tam. As they stood, his emotions exploded. Raising his voice with a shout of triumph and shaking his fist in the air, he declared, "We are men of greatness! We *are* mighty in the earth!" Canaan blinked in wonder at the strength and power radiating from his father. "Come, Canaan, we have much to discuss."

They returned to their campfire below, adrenaline pumping through their veins. Never had Ham felt such power. He knew within himself that he *was* a royal king, even before he would see it come to pass. He and his son would rule the whole earth. They talked late into the night of their greatness and how they would finally be recognized and worshiped for the truly great kings they were.

During the days and weeks that followed, they stayed within the cave's chamber and began to read each scroll, discovering knowledge that had been hidden from mankind. They practiced incantations and learned the art of divination. They saw power manifested from merely speaking certain words. They experimented with the fetishes left behind, learning the secrets of each one. But it was the drums that gave them access to unspeakable pleasure. This knowledge became like a drug, causing them to want more and more.

It was from the scroll written by Satsum-kedesh that Ham and Canaan learned of blood-letting and the power it possessed to summon demons. They drew their knives and cut their forearms. Catching the blood in a bowl they drank each other's blood. This was in direct rebellion to Yahweh's command concerning His covenant. Yahweh had given them the express commandment *not* to drink the blood of the flesh. The very moment the blood was swallowed, a great rumbling resounded within the chamber. Wide eyed, they looked at each other. Ham knew they had now passed into a realm of power that only the elite Regals of Atlantis had possessed. He smiled wickedly at his son, who returned the same devious smile. They felt a strange but alluring transformation within themselves. Something within them had been awakened and released.

What little light and sound reason that was in them left, and was now quenched by the darkest evil. No longer were they the men they had once been. They had become someone else. It was as it had been with Ka-sta; they were transformed in every way.

Stunned, but lustfully eager, Ham whispered to Canaan, "With this knowledge, Son, we will have whatever our heart's desire, not only power but pleasure as well!"

Using the drums, they began to beat a mystic rhythm they had learned from the scroll of Diatus. Demons began to rise from the ground and surround them, circling them, dancing to the hypnotic sound. They sensed these two humans were eager to embrace the evil they possessed. Ham and Canaan began to wildly dance and drew their knives. Cutting their forearm, the blood flowed. As it had been in Taasa-toka among the defiled Sethites, so it became with them. Ham surrendered to the evil surrounding him, and laughed, remembering how foolish he thought the elders of Taasa-toka had been, but now, his only desire was to know what they meant when they said, "They give us both pleasure and pain!"

Castius materialized. Smirking, he watched sin manifest before his eyes. He despised human men. To him they were inferior to Regals and their supernatural fathers. The only value he held for humans were for their women. They served a purpose for breeding with animals and hosting a body to bear children for their angelic fathers. It brought him twisted pleasure to see the crowning jewel of Yahweh's creation loose the innocence they had possessed and take on the dark nature of demons. It had come to pass as the Watcher had told Sede: Ham and his descendants would lust for pleasure and power. But this was only the beginning for Ham and Canaan's descendants. What they would learn from the scrolls and the evil of demons, would personify what the world would come to know about the Canaanites as a nation of people, and their future cities of Nineveh and Sodom and Gomorrah.

Ham and Canaan soon forgot about their village and, like addicts, were compelled to crave more and more knowledge from the scrolls. Their craving was like a sickness that they didn't know they had. The only time they ventured from the cave was to find food and water. Their hair began to grow long, with beards that hung over their chests. No longer were their faces smooth and fair but wrinkled and aged, looking older than their years. They hardly resembled human beings. They tattooed their bodies with strange symbols that gave them access to hidden powers and wore only a small loin cloth. Both were deceived, believing themselves to be beautiful in power, masculinity, and appeal. They began to live for their next sensual high, and then the next, and the next, longing to experience more intense pleasure and pain.

It had been six months since they had gone missing, and Noah felt he must do something. He called a council meeting.

"We must look for Ham and Canaan. I fear they have perished."

It was decided that Shem and Japheth would search for them, and left in the morning, bidding their families farewell. They searched for over a week when they caught sight of two strange creatures huddled together over a carcass, devouring its raw flesh. As they drew near, they felt sickened when they realized who they were. Shem felt as though he was going to throw up. It was his brother and nephew!

"Japheth, our brother and his son have left all reason and have become as wild beasts. It is as Father suspected; they have succumbed to foul play. We'll have to hunt them like prey in order to capture them."

They hid in the cover of trees until late that night. Creeping to the mouth of the cave, they peered inside. There, Ham and Canaan slept on strange beds made of hot coals of fire. As Shem looked upon them he felt sickened by the evil that radiated from their bodies. Nodding to Japheth, they grabbed their leather ropes and quickly bound their wrists and tethered their feet. They were amazed that neither of them moved or roused from their sleep. They rolled them from the hot bed of coals when suddenly both of their bodies jerked and were awakened. It seemed one moment they were not in their bodies, and the next they were. And indeed they were not in their bodies, but their spirits had left with the demons to unknown places of darkness. When they realized they had been bound and that Shem and Japheth were holding them captive, they began to curse in a strange language and struggled against the ropes. Even though Shem and Japheth didn't understand their words, the fierceness in their tone communicated anger and hate.

They drug them from the cave and tied them to a tree in the open air, waiting for dawn. In the light of the campfire they tried to calm them, only to be kicked and spat upon. Feverously they pulled against their ropes, making their wrists and feet bleed. Every attempt to sooth them was met with contempt and hate. During the long night they took turns standing watch, praying as tears filled their eyes. It was devastating to see their brother and nephew so changed and degraded.

When the sun rose, the full impact of what had happened to Ham and Canaan was evident. They didn't resemble the same people they knew. They were aged beyond years; scars marred their bodies, and they could feel the evil energy that exuded from their tattoos. Ham hissed at them and spoke in a strange language. Canaan spat at them and thrust his body at them in blatant gesture. Shem and Japheth began to cry and wail. They fell to their knees, weeping, their heads bowed to the ground. Oh, the travesty, the unbelievable horror of what had happened to their kin! What had overcome them in this wilderness place to transform them into the evil creatures they saw?

They cried as they worked. Shem held them while Japheth cut their hair and shaved their beards with his knife. They brought water from the stream and tried to wash them only to have Ham and Canaan kick at them and spit in their faces. They finally pulled them by a rope, dragging them through the stream; washing the dry blood and filth that covered them. They were emaciated and looked to be starving. It was a most pitiful sight.

Shem and Japheth knew they couldn't take them back to the village like this and decided to take them to the ark. Somehow they knew they would find some kind of answer there. By ropes, they pulled them behind their horses, making their way through the mountains to the ark. They could hear Ham and Canaan chanting strange words and singing dark songs; it made their skin crawl. With tears in their eyes, they, too, spoke their own words—words of love. They both prayed as they rode, pouring their souls out to Yahweh for the devastated ones they led at the end of their rope.

After a week of traveling, they reached the empty ark; the sun was going down as they entered the great door. Japheth started a fire at their old gathering place, and Shem tied Ham and Canaan inside separate stalls. The brothers would finally get some rest; they were weary from a week of emotional turmoil with family they no longer recognized.

During the night, Ham began to cry. Memories aboard the ark came flooding back to him. It was though his mind was clearing and he could think for himself. Shame filled his heart as he reviewed his degrading behavior with demons and his own son. He had drank his son's blood and joined himself with the dark knowledge. He had become a part of all he had loathed when he was in Atlantis. He was as horrible as Castius and the devious breeding he had despised. How could he ever be with his sweet wife, Ne-el, again? He was feeling the wages of sin, and it was bringing death to his soul. The burden of shame and regret weighed heavy upon him.

That night a great war raged within him, and he saw two paths set before him: repentance and returning to Sethite life or the dark pleasure he had so eagerly embraced. He knew within himself that Yahweh, in His mercy, was giving him this opportunity to turn from evil. Would he take it?

But as the night wore on, he made his choice. For though he saw the evil he had done and had regrets, he wanted no part in repenting from his deeds. The memory of his pleasure and pain burned hot within him, stirring him and compelling him. He longed to again experience the pain that was so dear to him. He loathed the idea of returning to the village and being a part of Sethite life again. He wanted no part of Yahweh's will, for he had his own will to pursue—that of a king. This is what he would do: take his sons and daughters and leave the others. They would build their own village and live apart from his father and brothers. There he would see his dream fulfilled: king of the earth. No reminders would surround him of conscience or restraint, like this ark. He would be able to pursue "every imagination of his heart."

When the first light of the morning filtered into the gathering place, Shem and Japheth stood over Ham, watching him as he slept in the stall.

When he woke and looked up, he confessed, "My mind has returned to me, brothers, and I know what I must do. I and my family will separate from the rest of you and build our own village in a far off land."

Shem and Japheth were relieved that Ham's sanity had returned and that he was at least speaking in a language they could understand. Canaan, too, began to think more clearly, accepting food and water without strange and bazaar gestures.

"The village is not going to understand what has happened to you in the wilderness. *We* don't even know what happened to you," Shem said as he tried to control his emotions. "This will break Father and Mother's hearts, as well as the rest of our kin. How could you have yielded to sin, Ham? Your responsibility was to protect Canaan's innocence. I sense you stole it by some vile act. You have become a Cainite. How can you rectify what you've done? I worry for you, my brother. How will you find a place of peace again?"

Shem began to weep, burying his face in Japheth's chest. Ham could see how much his brother really did love him and saw his broken heart, but he set his jaw and hardened his heart.

When he had composed himself, he continued, "I must bring Father to the ark. We'll decide together what must be done."

Japheth stayed with Ham and Canaan, bringing them food and water but keeping them bound. When Shem returned with Noah, he wept when he saw how corrupted his son and grandson had become. The tattoos on their bodies he recognized from the day they stood before the defiled Sethites in Taasa-toka. He knew within his heart what Ham had done to his own son. His beautiful son, whom he loved, had abandoned Yahweh and corrupted his own son. They had become Cainites. At that moment he knew how Adam must have felt when his own beloved son Cain, killed Abel. Cain was lost to Adam, just as Ham was now lost to him.

Noah discerned the time had come when his three sons would part their ways and be dispersed on the earth; he knew what he must do. Releasing Ham, but keeping Canaan bound, he wrapped his own robe around his son and called them to council. They sat at the gathering place where they had gathered so many times before.

"It is time to appoint your inheritance, seeing this division has come." Drawing stones from a small bag, he said, "You will choose lots for the earth; 'For the heavens belong to the Lord, but the earth he has given to man.' This earth is our inheritance, my sons. The whole earth will be divided three ways." Each stone had one of the Sethite symbols for northern land, middle land, or southern land.

Each son withdrew a stone from the bag, starting by birth order. Ham inwardly seethed with anger, knowing Shem would have first choice, as he always had. Shem drew the middle land, Ham the southern land, and Japheth the last stone—the northern land. "You will now pledge with an everlasting oath that cannot be broken by you or your generations after you. You will honor each other's inheritance and not covet them for yourselves." With power in his voice, he continued, "I will pronounce a curse upon you if you break your oath!"

His sons looked wide eyed, for never had he spoken to them with such authority and power. They sensed the severity of the oath they were about to take. One by one, each son made their everlasting oath to honor each brother's right to their inheritance, swearing not to covet or take it by force.

"Ham, I cannot allow you or Canaan to return to your kin right now. Your behavior is still strange. You will stay with me until arrangements are made to gather your family and leave for your inheritance. We'll prepare a feast to send you on your way."

They stood to leave. Noah loosened Canaan's bonds and wrapped a cloak around his shoulders. The look of mistrust was obvious in Canaan's eyes. He still held to the dark knowledge that resided deep within him. By his grandfather's gaze, his corrupted soul was pierced, and the light of righteousness reflected his corrupted heart. Canaan could only look away.

The village wailed when they heard the word that they were to be parted by families. It was unthinkable! The thought that they would no longer "go out and come in" together was heartbreaking. They prepared for the feast and tried to settle their hearts on this tremendous change that was about to take place. The food was brought to the council fire, and they feasted. As a gesture of love, Noah wished to bless them with the fruit of the vine, and Ezmere lovingly served them. They toasted to each other and made their way to their huts.

As Noah returned to his hut, he was sad of heart. His family would no longer be together. One man's sin had affected them all. Ezmere was so distraught at her son and grandson's evil transformation that she couldn't bear to sleep in the same hut. She stayed with Shem and Sede that night. As the night drew long, Noah drank more and more wine to sooth his sorrowful heart and then finally fell into a deep sleep on his furs.

In the morning, as Shem and Japheth were passing his hut, Ham stood outside with a smirk on his face. "What is happening, Ham? What is this I see in your face?" Shem asked with suspicion.

"Father is uncovered in his tent. I've seen his nakedness that Canaan was delighted to show me." A depraved gleam was evident in his eyes.

Shem and Japheth's faces blanched white with horror! How could Ham have looked upon his own father's innocence and allowed Canaan to uncover him? *And* to so lightly speak of it?! In great wrath, Shem lunged toward him, only to be held back by Japheth's restraint. Ham slinked away, laughing at Shem's anger. Shem and Japheth wept as they took a fur robe and walked backwards, covering their father's body.

When Noah woke, he knew Ham had mocked him and what his younger son had done to him: revealing his innocence. To a Sethite, this was beyond vile. To have their innocence looked upon and mocked was more profane than any other act that could be committed. Everything about the Sethite way of life was based on innocence and protecting it. By committing this act, Ham knew its symbolism. He and his son were openly defying the Sethite way of life and its leadership. They were establishing their supremacy by humbling the leader in the eyes of the people. Ham knew the subtle manipulation of his act.

With fire in his eyes, Noah called his sons and Canaan to the council fire. The rest of the village heard the commotion and gathered around. It was Noah's intent to dispel the darkness with light. With a loud voice for all to hear, Noah shouted with great authority, "**Cursed** be Canaan, a servant of servants shall he be unto his brethren! **Blessed** be the Lord God of Shem; and Canaan shall be his servant. God shall enlarge Japheth, and he shall dwell in the tents of Shem; and Canaan shall be his servant!"

Canaan laughed and huffed off, speaking in the dark language he had learned. What did his grandfather know about curses? He knew a thing or two about curses from the dark knowledge of the scrolls. He no longer held Noah with any regard. His only regard was for more knowledge and his future greatness as a royal king. Ham smirked for he knew the damage had been done. He had humbled Noah. He cared little that his father had cursed him.

Ne-el was in tears, confused with what was happening. Her life was being ripped apart by a husband who was estranged from her and a son she didn't know anymore. What was she going to do?

Sede and Shoda saw her distress and came to her side. With yearning in her voice, Sede spoke, "You don't have to leave with them. You can stay here with us. You can become part of our family." She held Ne-el's hand to her cheek. "I love you so much and don't want to see you live your life under the shadow of the foolish and evil choices your husband and son have made."

"That's right, Ne-el, you don't have to leave with them," sobbed Shoda. "We are, and will always be, your family."

Ne-el burst into tears. "How can I leave my grandchildren to the leadership of such corrupt men? My little ones will be truly lost if there is no 'light' in their lives. I will be the only light they have."

Sede and Shoda wept for they knew it was true and would say the same thing if they were in Ne-el's place. "We can't let you go, Ne-el, we can't," Sede and Shoda sobbed at the same time.

Then Sede remembered the words her Aunt Marah spoke to her the day she whispered in her ear at Playtheus' funeral ceremony. Sede touched Ne-el's forehead with hers and whispered through her tears, "Ne-el, may Yahweh richly bless you all the days of your life and hold you in the palm of His hand. I will never forget to pray for you and send you my love in the spirit."

Shoda wept bitterly for she knew their lives would never be the same. She held her sister, weeping on her shoulder. Would she ever see her again? Embracing one last time, they said goodbye.

Sede entered her hut, hardly believing what had happened. It was though a whirlwind had blown through their lives and scattered her emotions everywhere. The Watcher had told her this change was coming, but she was so unprepared for its full impact. As Shem held her that night on their furs, hot tears filled her eyes. Would life always be this hard? She had lost Playtheus, her father, Dosta, and her sweet little girl, and now she was losing her sister along with all her children. "Oh Shem, the loss of our loved ones is so great. How will we recover from this? I found sweet comfort from Yahweh for our 'little cricket,' but we are losing our kin!" Shem kissed her sweetly on the forehead as he held her close to his heart. Softly, he spoke...

"To everything there is a season; and a time to every purpose under heaven:

> *a time to be born, and a time to die;*
> *a time to plant, and a time to pluck up what has been planted;*
> *a time to kill, and a time to heal;*
> *a time to break down, and a time to build up;*
> *a time to weep, and a time to laugh;*
> *a time to mourn, and a time to dance;*
> *a time to cast away stones, and a time to gather stones together;*
> *a time to embrace, and a time to refrain from embracing;*
> *a time to get, and a time to lose;*
> *a time to keep, and a time to cast away;*
> *a time to rend, and a time to sew;*
> *a time to keep silence, and a time to speak;*

a time to love, and time to hate;
a time of war, and a time of peace."

"In the same way we survived the hardships of being separated when you were captured, we will somehow survive this, Sede. We don't have to do this alone. This time we have each other."

As she listened to his words, she felt them penetrate her heart. She would not be alone to experience this. She would have him. The remembrance of a prayer he prayed so very long ago came back to her. It was when they had said goodbye within their hut, before they entered the ark. She let the memory of his prayer wash over her like warm, soothing oil: 'Help us bend like a reed in the wind to the changes that lie ahead of us. Give us the courage, strength, and love to see the end of our days.' As she pondered his prayer, she knew they would somehow live through this, bending like a reed in the wind of loss and change.

Chapter 19

Evil Revealed

That night Sede couldn't sleep. Ne-el would be leaving in the morning. What kind of life lay before her with no mother, sisters, or fellowship of kin to comfort her? She rose from bed and grabbed her cloak. She needed to think. In the quiet of night, she walked the familiar streets. The moon was full, casting a warm glow on the peaceful huts. She pondered how that peace would change when Ham's families left in the morning.

As she passed Noah's hut, she saw a low fire burning near his entrance. Ham and Canaan were huddled near, whispering. The light from the fire sent strange and eerie shadows over their faces.

They abruptly stopped and acknowledged her. "Come, sit. Warm yourself, Sede." Ham motioned to a place next to him. It was hard for her to accept how they looked. They were visibly different—older and hardened. Although they wore robes, she could see the tattoos on the top of their hands and around their necks. There was no covering the tattoo on their forehead. It was all too familiar. They were, as it had been with Ka-sta, "changed in every way."

She sat on the log and felt the warmth of the fire. As Ham poked the fire, stirring the embers, she felt her own emotions stir within. After a few moments, as if her emotions forced themselves into words, she blurted, "I'd like to know something, Ham."

"What would that be, Sede?" he responded in a mocking tone, knowing she was troubled by their appearance.

With sadness and compassion in her voice, she nearly cried, "How could you fall so far into sin, knowing what you knew about Atlantis' great evil and having been delivered from it? You were so happy to be restored to your father and mother and the rest of our kin. You even thanked me for finding a way for us to return to our village. What has happened to you?" She could hardly hold back the tears.

Slowly poking the fire, he thoughtfully considered her questions. He then answered. "Sede, I saw the future glory that would be Shem's. He will be ruler over our people, and I will be but an elder. I have felt deep jealously over the honor given him and denied me. He has been first at everything that matters: firstborn son, first to have a child, and first to choose our inheritance. Always he was honored at Taasa-toka's council meetings, while I was overlooked. They considered his counsel, and mine wasn't even requested. Even now, in our festivals, he is mentored by Father to officiate and tell our ancestral stories. I hate him, and Father, for what they've done to me. All that has happened to me and my son is *their* fault. Castius offered me power and glory, and I took it!"

She looked at him in horror, her face paling with the thought. She felt frozen with fear. "What? You've seen Castius? How could he have survived the flood? All that drew breath were destroyed!"

"True enough, Sede. All who drew breath *were* destroyed. But Castius' spirit was hidden within his statue—the same statue that once stood on the steps of the Pavilion, remember? This statue was hidden in a cave along with the treasures from the world of Atlantis. The angels sealed it, preserving it from the flood. We found the chamber within the cave and read the parchments containing dark knowledge. Canaan and I know their secrets. By our spoken words, we released Castius and three "Glorious Ones." They, too, had hidden themselves. They were not judged with the rest of the 200. In exchange for releasing them, we were promised to be kings and rulers over the earth."

Sede looked down at her trembling hands and clenched her fists to keep them from shaking. What would this mean to the world? She knew the power these angels were capable of and what they would probably do. Playtheus had told her their greatest desire was to have families of their own. She could hardly believe what he was saying.

"Ham, how could anyone in their right mind release such evil knowing the corruption it caused in the old world? How could you have been so deceived? You were already going to be a king and ruler over your own tribe of Sethites when our families divided the earth and each brother began their generations. What have you really gained? I see only broken relationships you will be leaving behind in the morning."

He looked at her coldly and replied, "Sede, you know nothing of the glory, honor, and majesty that I will possess. Castius showed us what we will become. I no longer wish to follow Yahweh. I now possess the knowledge for my own destiny. I am relieved to be leaving in the morning so that Canaan and I can return to the pleasure and pain that satisfies our souls." He rubbed his son's knee and smirked when he saw Sede's horrified reaction. He knew her innocence was being assaulted, and it brought him twisted pleasure. Sede felt sickened seeing him touch his son in such a way. It was the same feeling she felt the day they stood on the platform in Taasa-toka years ago, seeing Ma-la, Te-mar, and Ro-nad openly display their debauchery and intentionally taunt her innocence.

With her voice cracking from emotion, she pleaded, "Ham, I knew you when you were just a boy. We grew up together; we hunted as a pack. We worshiped together at festivals and competed in games. Side by side, we worked together on the ark and traveled to fill it. It was your help that made that possible. Yahweh spared your life over humans that acted as you do now. Are you that willing to throw away your loving past for some promised future by a Regal who probably secretly hates you? Surely there's some of Yahweh still in you."

He looked at her coldly, refusing to respond.

Distraught, she stood to leave, visibly shaken by the hardness of his heart. Ham and Canaan stood as well, smiling that his subtle power to manipulate her emotions had caused her pain.

Looking at Ham, she said with great sorrow, "I will pray for the brother I once knew. I bid you farewell."

"I don't want your prayers, Sede. I would much rather know you as my brother has—intimately." He grabbed her by her wrist and pulled her to his chest. She could feel his heavy breathing and pounding heart. She couldn't believe her ears. Panic gripped her while the crazed look in his eyes filled her with terror!

He continued in fevered excitement, "Our old village recognized you as the finest Sethite maiden, and you were given to Shem through father's arrangement, where I had to settle for a patched up union with Ne-el after Japheth took my rightful bride. I have lived long enough in the shadow of a man who I was meant to be. By taking you, I'll have some measure of revenge, and wound him as well. He will carry my act of defiling you for the rest of his life. I will get even where it really counts—in his heart!"

Then Canaan moved in close to her ear, whispering with his own fevered words. His breath smelled of blood he drank before she arrived. "Yes, Aunt, Father has introduced me to the dark pleasure of defiling innocence. I will savor seeing you lose yours, and know that Shem was wounded too. I delight to feel the dark and searing pleasure when violence invades a helpless soul and the light of their innocence is possessed.

But in the split second that followed, something shifted within her. A strange strength rose up. She felt panic flee, and in its place: the fire of Yahweh! The heat of rebuke was in her mouth. She twisted her wrist free from Ham's grip and stepped back. Raising her palm in front of her, she commanded with great authority, **"Yahweh rebuke you both, you Cainite sons of corruption!"**

Her words blasted their bodies, and they flew back, landing on the ground! After the last word left her mouth, the Watcher suddenly appeared and stood between them. In the blinding light of his countenance, they scrambled and fled inside the dark, empty hut, cowering in fear. Sede began to tremble, realizing how close she had come to being ravished by her brother and nephew.

Evil Revealed

The Watcher spoke calmly and with reassurance. "Sede, it is as I told you in the wilderness; Ham and Canaan have forsaken Yahweh and desire only pleasure and power. Return to Shem, and may Yahweh's peace bring rest to your troubled heart."

He softly blew upon her. As his heavenly breath touched her face, she felt peace settle and calm the terror she had felt. The Watcher then said, "I will stand vigil so they harm no one. Noah and Ezmere are with Japheth and Shoda. These two are going nowhere. Be at peace, Sede. They will leave at dawn."

He stood by the fire with his legs planted apart and his arms folded at his chest. Power and glory radiated from his body. As she looked at the hut, she saw them fearfully peering through the cracked door. As was the Sethite custom to show rebuke and shunning, she removed one of her sandals and shook the dust from it. Ham and Canaan knew what it meant.

Peace calmed her as she walked back to her quiet hut. She could feel the terrifying experience she had just had becoming a blur in her mind. This was more than likely from the heavenly peace the Watcher had breathed upon her.

As she lay next to Shem, she listened to his slow and steady breathing, watching the rise and fall of his chest. Somehow just the calm and constant rhythm brought comfort to her soul. It reminded her of his steadfast faith and strength—so constant, so sure. Her mind drifted back to when they were in the Cave of Treasures before the flood. His words echoed in her memory: 'I wish with all my heart to be a man of God. I make this covenant with you, Sede...I will lead our family in righteousness and truth.'

As she lay there beside him, she felt so very safe. He had said in the cave that day, 'I am your covering, as Adam was to Eve.' As she fell asleep, she knew there was safety in the promises he had made her. She didn't have to fear he would fall into sin as his brother had. And concerning Ne-el, she knew that just as Yahweh had helped her in her most desperate hour, He would be there to help Ne-el as well. (For Yahweh's eye is upon the righteous, and His ear is open to their prayer.)

As dawn broke, Ham and his sons, along with their children and belongings, loaded their camels to leave. He separated the herds he had bred, dividing them equally between Noah, Shem, Japheth, and himself. Litters trailed behind horses, camels, and oxen as the caravan of "Canaanites" departed. Ham had declared that he would give this honor to his son: to name all of his own descendants after the name of his favored son, Canaan. As could be expected, his other sons despised him for the dishonor it reflected upon them.

Sede told Shem what had happened the night before. A bruised wrist was all that remained of the evil encounter. He was livid with anger. He felt the same rage he had when Ham had shamed their father. Any compassion he still had for his brother and nephew was gone. They had become contemptible Cainites. His beloved brother was dead to him. He knew the choices Ham had made would only lead to his own destruction. Through the wisdom he had gleaned from Enoch's writings, he knew that the wages of sin brought death and that what is sown in the life of a person is what they will ultimately reap. The only hope of reversing this inevitable principle is true repentance. He knew his brother would never humble himself and repent. He was deeply troubled when he heard that Ham and Canaan had knowingly released fallen angels and a Nephilim into the world. What would this mean to their future generations?

They stood in the doorway of their hut and watched the long line of people and animals disappear over the hills. Who their kin had been to them was now lost. Shem put his arm around Sede's shoulder and whispered as if talking to himself, "It's a fearful thing that one man's sin can affect a whole nation. The burden of judgment on his descendants rests on him alone. He is responsible for what they will know and believe. Whatever they become as a people is a direct result of what he surrendered that day in the cave. He had a choice. He chose himself instead of them!"

Tears ran down their cheeks as they held each other. Their hearts were broken for the people they once called kin, and the Sethite innocence that would surely be lost in their descendants. They both perceived the unsavory future that would become theirs.

Evil Revealed

Village life continued as Shem and Japheth's families remained with Noah. They knew they would eventually part. But for now, they would continue to live together until the right time came to separate. Both Shem's and Japheth's sons had grown into fine men with families of their own. When Shoda had come of age and married, it was Shem's delight to prepare the wedding tent and sing the "Father's Love Song" as Tolmaka had done for Sede. And it was Sede's delight, as one of the elder women, to instruct her daughter in the ways of married life.

Both Shem and Sede had stepped into leadership among their own children. They no longer hunted. They had turned "the hunt" over to the next generation. They were now the elders of their people and focused on mentoring their children, who had become elders and leaders of their "**Shem**ite" kin.

Hundreds of people now lived in Tolma-toka, as they called their village. Noah had chosen the name to honor his dearest friend, Tolmaka. It had been over a hundred years since the flood, and they had truly been blessed and multiplied upon the earth. Yahweh's blessing of "being fruitful and multiplying" had been upon the four women. Ezmere herself continued to have more children, to the delight of Noah. There was a unique blessing that rested on the original "eight." They didn't seem to age as their children were. Their appearance was one of middle age—vibrant and strong.

Chapter 20

The Center of the Earth

One night Noah called Shem and Japheth to the council fire. They were to bring their eldest sons. As the men sat cross legged by the fire, Noah began: "I have called this council to discuss your futures. Ham has long departed from our midst, and our lives have returned to the peace we once knew. I wish for each of you, Shem and Japheth, to take your wives and travel to the land of your inheritance. Seek out a place that you will call your "beginning"—a starting place for your people that will become your generations. You, my grandsons, will remain behind and care for our people here. Shem and Japheth will probably be gone for months, so prepare yourself and your own families that you will lead them now. This will also give you experience as elders among your kin.

That night after Noah had dismissed the council, he asked Shem to call Sede and join him in his hut. As they sat, Noah was silent for a long time. Then, as if he'd made a decision within himself, he said, "Shem, it is time to find a final resting place for Adam and his treasures. It has been on my heart for some time now to do this. You and Sede will secretly take Adam with you when you leave. I want no one else to know but you and Melchisedec, who has agreed to go with you. Yahweh has shown me that he has been chosen to know this secret concerning Adam and be his guardian. He will remain at this special place, and you will return to us.

Sede and Shem clasped hands and, with knowing eyes, smiled at each other. The day had come for them to take Adam to his final place of rest, just as the Watcher had told them so long ago. Noah continued, "We will go in the cover of night and gather Adam and Eve and conceal them with the cargo for your journey. Yahweh will send a Watcher before you and show you the place He has chosen."

In the dark of night, Noah led Shem, Sede, and Melchisedec to the ark. There it lay, silent in the night, like a sleeping giant. The shadow from the moonlight silhouetted the outline of the great structure, making it look even bigger. As they walked the corridors, their footsteps echoed in the darkness. It gave Sede a cold and sad feeling. This ark had once been so full of life, with people and wondrous animals.

When they arrived at Noah and Ezmere's nook, they started to remove the flooring. It was surprising how easily the boards were removed. When they lifted the last one, they saw why it was easy to remove them. Someone had discovered this secret place. Adam and Eve were still there, but the gold, frankincense, and myrrh, along with the lambskin aprons and emerald rod, were missing. Enoch's leather parchment scroll had been tossed carelessly to the side, and the jeweled box had been turned upside down, the spices and leaves left in a pile on the floor.

Sede began to weep. "Who could have done this? Why would anyone steal from father Adam?"

Noah and Shem looked at each other. They knew it was Ham, and probably Canaan, who had plundered Adam's treasures. "They took what they considered most important, but what they left is the real treasure," Shem tearfully mumbled.

Tenderly, he grasped Enoch's scroll, bringing it to his lips and kissing the cover. Tears came to Noah's eyes as he saw the reverence his son was giving to what the Sethite people held dear. "Yes, the true treasures still remain," Noah whispered to himself. He not only meant Enoch's priceless scroll but Shem's pure and innocent faith.

Sede carefully scooped up the spices and leaves, gently returning them to the jeweled box. Closing the lid, she stroked it with her fingertips, remembering how she had felt the first time she'd seen it. She had felt such wonder considering why Adam would save such a thing. Carefully, they removed Adam and Eve, and made their way back to the village. There, they concealed them among their belongings and prepared for the long journey.

At dawn Sede walked across the village to Shoda and Japheth's hut. It was in her heart to say goodbye to her dear friend and sister.

When she arrived, Shoda was helping Japheth load their camels. She smiled when she spotted Sede. "Sede, I'm so pleased you came to see me. I hoped to see you before we left on our journeys." They hugged each other and began to walk arm and arm.

"I will miss you as we part," Sede said, her voice cracking with emotion.

Shoda gave her a gentle squeeze. "And I will be missing you, my sister. This journey will begin a new chapter in our lives. It is always hard to let go of what is comfortable and embrace a new beginning. My only consolation is that Yahweh is with us. I have watched your life, Sede, these past years, and I've seen you mature into such a wonderful mother of your people. When we begin our separate tribes, I know your generations will continue in the ways of the Lord. This gives me peace for I don't have that assurance for Ne-el's generations. She is always on my heart."

"Mine too, Shoda. It does bring me some measure of comfort that not all of Ham's sons were cursed. Perhaps Cush, Mizraim, and Phut will hold to the ways of the Lord and be a blessing to the mother of their people."

They continued to walk along the street as they shared their hearts with one another. "Oh, we're back!" Sede said, surprised she was now at her hut. She had been so caught up in their conversation that she hadn't noticed where they were walking. "Be blessed, my friend and sister, as you journey into your future."

"And you as well, dear Sede." Facing each other, they spontaneously clasped each other's forearms and said as they touched foreheads, "Took-la-say-a-la-nay." Both paused and smiled with a twinkle in their eyes. Touching foreheads once more, they whispered the call to adventure— "Ha-la-lah!"— for their future would be as their hunts had always been—an adventure!

By mid-morning each brother was on their way to discover their inheritance. Japheth turned north, while Shem turned south. Neither of the brothers knew how far to travel in discovering their lands. It would be Yahweh's Watchers who would tell them when they arrived at their place of "beginnings."

Shem, Sede, and Melchisedec traveled every day from early morning till dusk. This remarkable young man was Shem's younger brother Uzza's son. Noah and Ezmere had Uzza twenty years after the flood. His son Melchisedec had never married but spent his time in the high forest, seeking Yahweh in prayer and studying Enoch's writings. He had copied passages from Shem's parchments so he could meditate and study the principles of Enoch's instructions. Shem had perceived that his nephew was marked by Yahweh for a special destiny, and now he knew what it was.

Each night as they built their fire, their conversation was rich in fellowship. They joyfully exchanged stories about Yahweh, and Melchisedec listened as Sede told about the first time she heard Yahweh on the warm breeze from her window. It was a starry night after a festival, and her heart welcomed His loving words. From then on, she came to rely on hearing Him to help her through great peril. He had watched over her and cared for her. While she had been captured, He had sent his Watcher to make a way for her when there seemed to be no way. It was with loving memory that she told of seeing Adam and Eve within the Cave of Treasures and what it was like to hear Yahweh sing his love song to Eve. Tears misted in her eyes as she visited those memories once more.

As Shem shared his understanding of Enoch's writings, Melchisedec paid close attention. He felt faith stir within him, and he longed for the same deep understanding of Yahweh and His people. Shem retold how they labored building the ark and traveled to a distant land to fill it with grain and supplies, preparing for the flood to come, and how Yahweh cloaked their returning caravan, Nephilim coming but feet from where they stood. Yahweh had saved them within the ark, and then gave them His everlasting covenant with the great rainbow as a sign and memorial. As though he were a sponge,

Melchisedec absorbed every word that fell from Shem's lips. He listened in wonder and could only image what kind of faith it took to believe all that Yahweh had promised them.

And when it was Melchisedec's turn, Sede and Shem listened to his stories of discovering Yahweh in the lonely places of the high forest. Although he had been alone there, he was never really lonely. Always he felt His presence with him. He saw Yahweh reflected in the living things around him. The breeze that moved through the tall pines and the laughing water that swirled around smooth stones in the streams, all gave testimony to him. He saw Him when a mother deer nuzzled her newborn to stand for the first time and in the power of a thousand hooves thundering over rolling hills. But he especially saw Yahweh after a rain, when a magnificent rainbow stretched across the sky. His times in the forest had shown him a part of Yahweh's heart he could have never seen in the village. He loved his kin, but always he heard Yahweh woo him to the still places, desiring communion with him. His words were pleasing to Sede and Shem. They were so very thankful that such a one as Melchisedec would be trusted to care for Adam's final resting place.

They had journeyed for over a month when they reached a high ridge. It overlooked a great and glorious land that stretched as far as the eye could see. It was lush with rolling grassland, trees, and streams. Great herds could be seen in the distance, looking like small speaks roaming on the great sea of grass. Shem felt his spirit leap and instinctively looked at Sede, who knew as he did. It was at that moment the Watcher who had appeared to Sede, so many times, stood before them.

Surprised, Melchisedec gasped.

"Hail, Shem, 'father of his people'!"

Not since the time they were in the forest, after their wedding, had Shem seen him. He could feel his mighty presence and the great peace that exuded from his being.

"I have appeared, just as your father said, to reveal your inheritance to you. The land before you has fallen in your lot to inherit, Shem. I will lead you south from here for Ham has encroached upon your land. A Watcher appeared to him and revealed his inherited land, but only his sons Phut and Mizraim have settled there. Ham knows this land is not his but cares little for the oath he pledged. The curse of your father will rest upon him and his descendants for he has broken his word."

Sede began to cry, for she knew Ne-el would be directly affected by such a curse. "Weep not, Sede, for the sister you once knew. She has passed from this life and is now with Yahweh. She has joined Gruetat, Mersta, and Adat. Grieve not for her, for she has been spared the corruption that follows the choices of her husband and son. Yahweh did not allow her body to know their newfound ceremonial practices for the dead but sent a Watcher who buried her in secret. Precious in the sight of the Lord was the death of his favored one. Just as you said when you prayed for her, 'May Yahweh keep you in the palm of his hand,' she is now there. When you return, comfort Shoda with these words."

"Yahweh will judge the descendants of Ham in a future generation. Your descendants will reclaim this land that was rightfully promised to you and your offspring. When you separate from your father, Noah, I will lead you to where you and Sede will live to the end your days, living to a good old age, full of years. You will be instrumental in helping the 'seed of promise' in the next generation. Your great grandson Eber, who will be born to your grandson Salah, will live with you and be the one from your great lineage to pass on the 'ways of the Lord' among your people."

"You, Melchisedec, will be priest of the 'Most High.' When Adam is laid to rest in the center of the earth, you will remain there, offering prayers and supplication for mankind. You will find great blessings in being separated unto the Lord. There will be no lineage from you, and you will be remembered no more for having father or mother, and will not be counted among your people for an inheritance in the land. The 'Most High' will be your inheritance. This will satisfy your soul in a way no earthly inheritance ever could. You will walk in the presence of the Lord every day of your life. You, like Enoch, will know no end of days."

The Center of the Earth

Sede and Shem looked at each other, hardly believing what they were hearing. They were hearing the prophetic future.

The Watcher remained visible to them. As they rode their camels, he walked beside them. Just being in his presence every day brought heightened awareness. Everything seemed more alive; the sky seemed bluer and clearer, the grass greener and more vivid. Even the water tasted more refreshing. Every night he sat with them and talked of the glories of heaven and the great Yahweh he worshipped and served. His passion, love, and great devotion to Yahweh was beyond words to describe.

One night as they were resting before the fire, Sede desired to ask the Watcher a question. She hesitated. She had desired to know this answer for a long time, ever since he had appeared at Eden's wall. Stirring up the courage to ask, she finally forced the words from her mouth. "What is your name, Watcher of the Lord? I know that Yahweh has named the angels for father Enoch recorded some of them in his parchment that has been passed down to us. Instead of calling you Watcher, I wish to call you by the name Yahweh has given you."

The Watcher's eyes fell graciously on her. "Sede, 'mother of her people,' I don't think you could pronounce it. I will ask the One whom I serve if I am allowed to tell you my name." He disappeared and then reappeared within minutes. When he materialized, he glowed with an intense and brilliant light for he had come from the very throne of God. "Yahweh has given me permission to tell you my name."

The three eager humans inhaled in anticipation. "As your formal name is Sede-quete but Sede among those within your inner circle of friends, my name is the same. My formal name is Plaqualah-lanay, but you and your husband, as well as the servant of the 'Most High, are allowed to call me Plaquanay." The air vibrated with power as the words left his mouth. Even the ground beneath them rumbled. They trembled at the power of hearing his name spoken. Oh, what a wonderful privilege... They had just been told a secret that Yahweh himself had approved for them to know.

"You won't be allowed to share my name with others, for there is temptation with mankind to worship the angels. You saw this in the old world, Sede, among the fallen ones. Humans eagerly worshipped them. We angels were not created to be worshipped but rather to be 'ministering spirits' sent to minister for them who will be heirs of salvation.'" Again the ground rumbled as he spoke. "He sends us on assignments, helping His sons and daughters. It is my great joy to obey Yahweh's every word. I am fulfilled when I obey.

The night drew long and they fell asleep, pondering the things he had spoken. They were beginning to realize this journey was becoming more than just discovering their inheritance.

They traveled south for several more weeks, and slowly the terrain began to change. The trees were more abundant and gradually turned into a great forest. The great cedars whispered in the wind, high in the lofty branches. The forest sounds below were hushed while they followed the winding trail. Occasionally they heard the snap of a twig or rustle of leaves. This forest held a mystery. All of them felt it. At any moment they wondered if they were about to meet or see something out of the ordinary. For seven days they traveled through the whispering trees, and then they saw it! In the clearing ahead, a mountain rose high above the forest floor. They knew *this* mountain was the unexpected thing they were sensing.

Plaquanay led them forward as they began their ascent. When they reached the summit, the Watcher announced, "We have arrived. This is Mt. Moriah, the center of the earth!" As the last word left his mouth, heavenly music burst forth.

All three immediately fell on their knees and began to worship the Lord. The power of Yahweh's presence fell upon them, and they could no longer stand. Unbelievable love and worship filled their hearts and flowed like a song from their lips, adding to the heavenly music that permeated the air. They sensed that something wondrous was about to happen.

It was then the heavens opened! Above them the clouds parted, and a misty staircase led upward as far as the eye could see. They felt a tingling sensation, and supernaturally they felt their spirits lift from their bodies. Hand in hand, they followed Plaquanay and began to climb the staircase. Could this really be happening? Awe filled them, realizing they would see heaven... just as their forefather Enoch had.

When they reached the top stair, glory filled them, and they fell prostrate. Before them was the throne room of God. A great sea of crystal glass spread into the distance, encircling the great Throne. The sea of glass was alive with fire and moving color, shining and reflecting the glory of the throne. Spread over this sea were worshipers prostrate before the God of their love. There, in the middle of this glassy sea, sat the "Most High" upon His throne. The glory cloud surrounded Him, shrouding His image. Above Him was a rainbow of emerald arching over his magnificent throne. It was though it had its own glory for it vibrated and sent out wave after wave of sparkling light. Glorious beasts, filled with eyes, were at his right and left, and 24 elders lay prostrate before his feet. Seven lamps burned around the base of the throne, and, above, angels hovered in the air, their wings gracefully swaying back and forth to keep their position. The same heavenly song Sede and Shem had heard from Eden's seed filled the air, and the identical fragrance they had experienced in the Cave of Treasures now filled her lungs.

Plaquanay touched their shoulders, and they received power to stand. He ushered them forward, past worshipers prostrate on the living glass. Their bodies glowed with pulsating light, and Sede knew they were experiencing the exchange of love with Yahweh. He was loving them; they were loving Him. The closer they came to the throne, the greater they felt His glory. Their spirits absorbed His warm, pulsating love, and they began to weep. They fell once more on their faces, basking in His glory. Plaquanay, too, fell prostrate, breathing his praises in his own angelic language.

It was then they heard the voice of the One they knew so well; it was the same gentle voice that had come to them on the breeze so many times before. When He began to speak, they felt whole and complete, filling something that had been missing all their lives. "My precious children, long have I waited for this moment in time for you to come before Me. As you now feel fulfilled receiving my love, I feel fulfilled giving it."

Wave after wave of love moved through them as He spoke. They felt soothed and comforted, as a child that is held next to its mother's breast, listening to her heartbeat of love and lovingly cradled in her arms.

"This is your true home, children. Here with me. When your days are fulfilled, here is where you will come and be with me forever. Your life on earth is a witness for all to behold. Every choice you make—when you choose love over hate and light over darkness—you witness of me your Creator. The impact of your lives has only just begun. Before you, in your future, lies a multitude, to love and influence. Through your witness, many will see me for who I am: a God of love and great compassion. I am that I am. I am Love. Shine as lights in a dark world, children, for I have no other witness but the ones who love me. When your days are fulfilled, I will hold you in the arms of love. Be refreshed now in my presence for I delight to see you fulfilled."

For what seemed a long time, they lay there while wave after wave of love continued to minister to them. Plaquanay gently touched their shoulders. "There is one last place Yahweh wishes you to see."

Immediately they were transported, and now they stood on a grassy slope overlooking a familiar place. Sede and Shem both looked at each other with unbelievable joy. It was their old village of Taasa-toka before it knew ruin! They recognized the familiar places: Seth's altar, the council fire and platform, and Noah's hut high on a hill. Sede saw her own hut where she grew up, the walls, and great watchtower. The streets were filled with people they recognized, those who had died long ago. From even this far away, she knew she saw Dosta carrying a water skin and Ne-el walking hand in hand with Adat. Tears fell from her eyes to know such a place existed. She looked at Plaquanay, who was waiting for her questions. He smiled, knowing she was now ready to hear his answers.

"Yes, Sede. This awaits you and Shem. You will be reunited with your kin once more when your days are fulfilled."

She turned to Shem, and they embraced in joy. To think that their hearts' desire would be fulfilled. For neither of them had shared with the other that this was their deepest desire: to live as Sethites once more in the love and peace of their old village. And then she heard it. It was the call of the hunt. She knew it was her father's horn. Every cell in her body ignited with a thrill. "Oh Shem, I long to respond to that call. I want to join them and hunt with my father once more!"

Plaquanay smiled and said, "Yes, Sede, all that your heart desires will be fulfilled here in your home in heaven. But you and Shem have you days to fulfill, and like Yahweh has said, 'many to influence with His love and compassion. You are the only "light" they will know.'" With knowing acceptance, she nodded. She knew within herself that she and Shem had more of life to live before they could return.

Both of them knelt. There, overlooking the heavenly village, they gave thanks for what Yahweh had shown them and what was waiting for them. Plaquanay touched their shoulders once more, and they were now back in their bodies, kneeling on the top of Mr. Moriah. It was hard for Sede to know how long they had been caught up in the heavenly visitation, but the sun was now setting over the tops of the trees.

The Watcher gathered wood for their fire, and taking his staff, touched the wood and a fire began. Sede, Shem, and Melchisedec reverently gathered around the fire. As they waited for the Watcher to speak, the glow of what was still in their hearts satisfied their soul in an indescribable way. Yahweh's presence had lifted them to a glory none of them had ever experienced before, and they saw their future home. This was what father Enoch had experienced when he had been in the company of angels and visited heaven, seeing the very throne of God and the mysteries of heaven.

Plaquanay began to speak. "We have arrived at the center of the earth. It is here that Adam will rest, along with his beloved. The only treasure Adam will be buried with will be Eve. Yahweh wishes for Melchisedec to have Enoch's parchment scroll. This scroll will become your treasure, Melchisedec, as you search and study all that your forefather wrote. Yahweh will give you wisdom and understanding, and you will grow in grace and knowledge. Sede, you are to have the jeweled box. With the precious spices and leaves, you will anoint the body of Noah when he passes from this life. You will also use them for Shem, when he, too, has fulfilled his days. You had desired to know why Adam had saved them. You will now know…he saved them for the fathers of his people. He saw into the future and saw the faithfulness of Noah and his son, Shem."

Shem began to weep. He felt so very humbled. To have such an honor bestowed upon him and to be counted worthy of such a gesture of love, was beyond belief. Sede, too, wept for she realized that Shem would pass from this life before she would. The thought of being separated from him was almost unbearable.

"Weep not, Sede, for the loss you are considering. 'Yahweh makes all things new.' You will have the grace to endure Shem's death when it comes. You and Shem will have many wonderful years together, and that will be your comfort when his time comes."

Shem clasped her hand tenderly. He could feel her trembling as he brought her hand to his lips. Kissing it sweetly, he gently spoke. "We won't be parted for long; I know this within my heart."

"You are right in saying this, Shem, for the time will be short until you hold each other once more. Yahweh has numbered each of your days, and they must be fulfilled."

"Tomorrow we bury Adam and Eve, and you, Shem and Sede, will return to Noah and the others. Now sleep, children, for you have been given much to ponder. Tomorrow will dawn a new day."

They settled upon their furs and soon fell into peaceful sleep. Plaquanay took his stance of sentry, with arms folded across his chest and legs planted firmly on the ground. He radiated strength and glory.

With the first light in the east, they woke with great anticipation. What would this day hold? After they had eaten their morning meal, Plaquanay said, "It is time. Bring forth the 'First of Creation'!"

The Center of the Earth

Shem and Melchisedec carefully carried the bodies of Adam and Eve and laid them at the Watcher's feet. With his staff, the Watcher touched the stony ground before him, and the earth opened, forming a giant cross. As his hands rose slowly in the air, the body of Eve rose and then descended in the very center of the cross. He then repeated the same with Adam.

Shem whispered in awe to Sede, "Adam remains her covering still, even in their final resting place."

A tear rolled down her cheek as she remembered that he had said this before when they had seen their bodies in the Cave of Treasures.

With the bodies laid gently in place, Plaquanay touched his staff on the ground. The stone closed, sealing any trace of what lie beneath. "This is a holy place," Plaquanay said in a whisper. "The 'first Adam' is now buried here. In the far future, the 'second Adam,' the 'Promised One' to come, will also know this place. On this mountain, he will offer himself as the ultimate sacrifice: the perfect, spotless Lamb of God. This holy mountain, and the surrounding area, will have known his footsteps. It will be called Jerusalem, the 'City of Peace'."

Turning to Melchisedec, he instructed, "You will remain here. Yahweh has prepared a cave for your dwelling place. In the future, when these lands become populated, the people will recognize you as the 'priest of the Most High.' They will name your dwelling place Jerusalem for it will be a city of peace."

Melchisedec knelt and raised his hands to heaven. "I am your servant, Yahweh. As you have spoken through your messenger Plaquanay, may it be so!" He then rose and embraced his aunt and uncle, kissing them on each cheek. "Farewell, mother and father of our people. I know we will see each other again."

Shem and Sede saw a cloud of glory descend. It was the same glory cloud they had seen at their sacrifices, and had shrouded the "Most High" as he sat upon His throne. They felt its pulsating divine love and power. It surrounded Melchisedec, who now glowed with a countenance that made Sede and Shem gasp.

They heard the words of Yahweh: "This day, Melchisedec, you have been ordained a 'priest of the Most High.' You will walk in my presence from this day on, offering prayer and supplication for my creation…the sons and daughters of Adam and Eve."

The Watcher touched his shoulder with his staff, and Melchisedec disappeared before their eyes. He turned to Shem and Sede. "The priest of the 'Most High' has now entered his ministry. He now abides in the place Yahweh has prepared for him and will know great comfort and peace. It is now time for you to return to your people."

With reverence, Shem and Sede prepared to leave. No longer would they think of their nephew as Uzza's son but as Melchisedec, the great "priest of the Most High."

Chapter 21

Inheritance Claimed

When Sede and Shem drew near their village, they heard the horn blow from the sentry tower. The welcoming sound echoed through the valley and brought a thrill to their hearts. They were back. Their months of traveling from Mt. Moriah had gone smoothly and with great ease. Plaquanay had accompanied them to the hill that overlooked Tolma-toka and then disappeared. They looked forward to the embrace of their kin once more. Japheth and Shoda had arrived a few weeks before having found their place of "new beginnings." They had been eagerly anticipating Shem and Sede's return.

That night a great feast was given for the families were together again. Both Shem and Japheth described their wonderful inheritance, sharing about the sights they had seen. Japheth's land, like Shem's, included great pasture lands, forests, mountains, and mighty rivers. Noah and Ezmere eagerly listened, rejoicing in what they had received—all because Yahweh intended them to have it.

Shem told of Ham trespassing on his lands. The Watcher who had guided them had told them a time would come when their descendants would drive them out. Shem held Sede's hand throughout his speaking and squeezed it gently when he spoke of the Watcher. He purposely withheld his name as they had been instructed.

They wept when Sede told them about the death of Ne-el. Their hearts were broken that she had died alone, without her loving sisters and mother at her side. But Yahweh had sent a Watcher to bury her in secret; Ne-el had remained a true Sethite to the end and would not be dishonored by Ham's newfound religious practice for the dead.

Shoda struggled the most with the news. Japheth, as if covering her with an invisible blanket of love, held her in his arms while she wept. Sede heard his whispered words, "When the time comes, most precious wife, you'll see your dear sister again, along with your father and mother and sweet Adat. Her days of pain and grief have known their end. She now rests in the arms of love."

The tears fell from Sede's eyes for Plaquanay had spoken those very words. The next day the great host of Noah's family honored Ne-el with the custom of the dead. They mourned for three days and hung the black banners outside their huts—the very ones she had made. Then the three days of celebration began as they remembered the beautiful life she had lived among them.

That night Sede couldn't sleep and decided to walk the path to the altar. She loved the sight of their village from this high vantage point, especially at night. A sadness still hung in the air for it was no small thing that the mother of the people they once knew, had passed from this life. As she walked, the warm evening breeze blew softly and she heard the voice she had come to know so well. It was Yahweh.

"Yes, go to the altar, child. There you will find Shoda weeping. Tell her the glories you witnessed in heaven. Your words will bring her comfort, and she, too, will find peace for her loss, just as you did when your precious daughter came to my embrace.

She climbed the hill in the glow of the moonlight. The night was so clear and calm. As she looked up, she saw the altar silhouetted in the moonlight. Shoda was at the very top, kneeling with her hands lifted to heaven and singing. Her voice was so pure and holy. Sede sensed the unseen glory flowing from her friend. She was hearing Shoda's secret place of worship. She sat on the first step of the altar and listened as her friend poured out her vulnerable and broken heart:

Yahweh, hear my song as I weep in the night
My sister is gone and has died alone in the dark
My heart grieves because I was not there
To hear her last breath and send her to you with a prayer

What was it like for her so far from her kin
Alone, afraid, and no hope of return
Oh, the sins of her husband, who caused such pain
His thought was not of her but what he could gain

How will I ever find peace in my heart
For I am broken, distraught, and cast down
I need sweet rest for my soul
Only Your touch can make me whole

As Sede listened, tears rolled down her cheeks. It was all too familiar. It was the same pain she had felt at little Ne-el's death. Oh, it broke her heart. She brought her hands to her face and began to openly weep.

Shoda heard her from above. Tearfully, she called out, "Come to me, Sede. Help me in my sorrow."

She slowly climbed the winding steps, and at the top, she held her friend. In great grief and pain, Shoda wept. Her sister had died alone…she wasn't there to love her in her last hour…she would never see her again….

When she could cry no more, they sat in silence, looking over the quiet village below. Lamps from the dark huts cast a soft glow, and the moon reflected the great valley that stretched beyond. It was though they could see the whole world from where they were.

Taking Shoda's hand, Sede realized she and her sisters had been through so very much. Her memory drifted back to that day they sang over the grave of Shoda's mother and father as little Adat rested in their arms. Shoda, like Sede, had known great loss in her life.

Knowing she could now speak without crying, Sede began, "Shoda, there is something Yahweh wishes for you to know." She could feel Shoda relax in her arms and knew she was prepared to hear what He would say. Shoda, in her rich relationship with Yahweh, knew how to receive from Him.

"When Shem and I journeyed to our inheritance, our Watcher led us to a mountain. There we worshipped. While the presence of Yahweh was resting upon us, the heavens opened, and a staircase rose from the earth to the clouds above. Our spirits left our bodies, and climbed the stairs to heaven, where we stepped upon a sea of glass filled with fire and glory. Before us was Yahweh upon His throne. Angels hovered above Him, and the glory cloud covered his form. The music of heaven filled the air, and we inhaled an aroma like no other. But more than what we saw and felt was what we heard: the very words of God. He spoke to us with gentleness and love. His words could be felt and were full of warm, soothing love that gave us encouragement and courage. We were to establish our people for generations to come, teaching them what we, ourselves, knew. Because we know who He really is, we are the only testimony the world has. He declared himself to be: 'I am that I am. I am the God of Mercy and Love and have not left the world without hope of redemption. The "Promised One" will be born!' With all my heart, Shoda, I wanted to stay in that place of glory, love, and wonder. It felt like home. And it will be someday."

She paused, allowing Shoda to absorb her words. She then continued, "This is the part of heaven I believe Yahweh wants you to know so that comfort might sooth your sorrowful heart. The Watcher showed us something that thrilled our hearts. It was our village of Taasa-toka before it knew ruin. It was the same in every way. It had the altar of Seth, Noah's hut on the high hill, the council fire and platform, the walls, and the watchtower. I saw my father's old hut. There were people from our past walking the streets. And two of the people I recognized were Ne-el and Adat. They were walking hand in hand and were so very happy. And then I heard it. It was the call to the hunt. I heard my father's horn. Everything in me wanted to join him and hunt once more. The Watcher said my time was not yet fulfilled and that Shem and I had much to fulfill before we joined our kin. It is my hope and prayer, Shoda that you will be comforted to know that Ne-el is blessed. She is in the arms of love. She is in the arms of God!"

Shoda burst into tears, her words flowing like praise. "Oh, the glory of God, to send me such comfort. My sorrow is released, and peace now floods my soul!" She continued to cry, feeling more release as her tears flowed.

Sede lovingly sighed, knowing what she was experiencing for she, too, knew comfort's release and the peace that followed. 'Oh the glory of the ways of Yahweh!' she thought. He had allowed her to be a prophet once more, just as Noah had said they would be, keeping a watchful eye over their kin. And oh, how blessed she felt knowing He had allowed her to be a part of her dearest friend's comfort.

"My heart is settled," Shoda sighed in relief. "I will forever have that vision within me of my sisters walking hand in hand through our heavenly village. Thank you, dearest of friends, for the love you have shown me this night. Truly, I will never forget it!"

Slowly, they descended the altar and returned to their sleeping husbands. Shoda, like Sede, had reached out to Yahweh in her darkest hour, and He, in faithfulness and love, had comforted her.

* * *

Village life soon returned to the peace they had once known. Many years passed, bringing more grandchildren and great-grandchildren born to "the house of Shem." They rejoiced to welcome their grandson born to their daughter Shoda and Magog, Japheth and Shoda's son. Joyfully, they named him Noah after their beloved patriarch. Elem, Assur, Arphaxad, Lud, and Aram were also blessed as they continued to have more children. And Arphaxad's son, Salah, and his wife, Maheda, had their firstborn son, Eber. Arphaxad was now a proud grandparent. This was the very child the Watcher had prophesied to Sede who would one day lead their people in the "ways of the Lord." It had been 200 years since the flood, and the village had grown and became a bustling place with family huts and commerce. Shem and Sede's twin sons, Elem and Assur, had moved their wives and children to distant pastures, living in tents. Japheth's eldest son Gog and his family also followed their herds to green pasturelands. The village herds had become too great to feed in the surrounding hills. Both Sede and Shem knew the time was near when they would be saying farewell and moving to their inheritance.

And that time came. One night Noah, Shem, and Japheth all had the same dream. In the dream, a Watcher stood before them reading a scroll. They knew he was about to read the word of the Lord: "Do not sorrow to separate from your beloved family. You will gather again at a new feast that I, Yahweh, will decree among you. It will be called the 'Feast of Jubilee.' Every 50 years you will return to Tolma-toka. You will feast together and offer a sacrifice that commemorates the 'Rest of the Lord.' When you gather for your Jubilee celebration, you will find renewed strength and joy in your faith as Sethites, 'the righteous people of my joy.' When you come back to the village, you will stay for a full year. Your lands will rest while you are away, and this will remind you that I rested on the seventh day after creating the world and all that is within it. You will celebrate with seven trumpet blasts on the seventh day of each month throughout the year you are gathered. After the last trumpet blast, you will offer your sacrifice upon the altar. I will give Shoda a song for all Sethites to sing when the trumpets will sound. Now comfort your hearts and the hearts of your wives for Noah and Ezmere will send you into your inheritances with joy and gladness, and I, too, will rejoice over you with singing. My blessing will rest upon you, my sons!" When the Watchers had finished, he rolled up the scroll, and the dream ended.

In the morning, Noah called for a council meeting. Shem and Japheth, along with their sons, who were now established elders, assembled together. Noah explained to a now great host of elders what Yahweh had revealed to him and his sons. He would bid them farewell in seven days. By his word, great anticipation filled the hearts of all the men as they rose. Soon the news spread throughout the village, and word was sent to Elem, Assur, and Gog, who were migrating with their herds. Joy filled their hearts too, as they knew the time had come to enter the land of their father's inheritance.

The day had come, and they were on their way. They had said their goodbye to mother and father, brother and sister, and family that Noah and Ezmere had after the flood. With tears, but also with joy, they parted. Japheth turned north and Shem south. A long string of camels, horses, and herds trailed behind them as they led the way. All their sons and their wives, their children, grandchildren, great-grandchildren, and swaddled great-great-grandchildren followed. Shoda had left with her husband Magog in Japheth and Shoda's caravan. Her parting had been bittersweet for they knew it would be many years before they would see each other again.

As they left, Noah and Ezmere climbed the sacrifice altar. They watched as their two sons parted, moving their great caravans in opposite directions on the plain far below. Holding hands, they pondered how royal their sons and their wives looked riding atop their graceful camels. Their robes were richly embroidered, and their feet were covered with the finest skins and fur.

Noah brought Ezmere's hand to his lips, kissing it sweetly. His words were soft and held more meaning than he knew. "As they are in the spirit, they have become in the flesh. They *are* Royalty, Priests, and Prophets."

With loving tears, Ezmere rested her head on his shoulder, considering his words. Her own words fell from her lips as prophecy. "Our children have seen a new day. Their seed will fill the earth, just as Yahweh declared when we stood at the door of the ark. This world will know the birth of the 'Promised One' through them. And through Him, the knowledge of the glory of the Lord will fill the earth!"

As they lost sight of the last of their caravans, Noah and Ezmere heard a sound. It was Shem, blowing the horn Noah had given him when they had entered the ark before the flood. As the beautiful sound echoed through the valley below, they heard its reply. It was Japheth answering his call. They held each other, overwhelmed by what they felt; that crystal clear sound called from their past. It was the sound that would forever connect their family's hearts. Their children would always remember where they had come from and how deeply they were loved.

Noah and Ezmere remained in Tolma-toka with their other sons and daughters and their children, grandchildren, and great-grandchildren. The huts that were now empty and still would someday know the sound of fellowship and love once again, when Jubilee would be celebrated. Through the years it would be their joy to keep them clean and repaired in anticipation of their children's return.

Shem led his family for nearly a week before Plaquanay appeared. Their children, along with the rest of his family, were overjoyed to finally see a Watcher. They had heard so many stories about these mysterious angels. Because he carried heaven's presence, the little ones ran to hold his hand and hug his leg, drawn to the reflected love of Yahweh. They never tired of looking into the shining face of an angel.

Every day he walked beside Shem and Sede's lead camels, and at night around the campfire, he told the young children stories about their ancestors. They were tales of the children of Adam and Eve and how he and other angels watched over and protected them when they were young. The children hung on his every word as he retold the adventures of saving them from many dangers.

There was one particular story they wanted him to tell over and over. It was the story of saving the young boy Seth when he tried to cross a dangerous river. A waterfall fell from high above the river, filling the air with a misty cloud, and trees crowded the river's edge. The only way to the other side was by fallen trees caught between boulders that bridged the distance from bank to bank. As the young boy started to cross, he weaved and wobbled to balance on the wet bark. Through the thundering noise of the waterfall, an eagle called, soaring high above the mist. Looking up, Seth slipped and fell into the raging white waters. Hidden whirlpools pulled him under as he struggled to grab at slippery boulders only to be swept away by the powerful current. With his angelic assignment to watch over and protect, Plaquanay transformed from the invisible to the visible and walked on the water to save him.

Pausing from his story, he reached down and raised one of the listening children to sit on his shoulders. With a broad smile, he took exaggerated steps, showing the children how he walked on the water, saving the drowning boy who rode safely on his shoulders. The child raised both hands in triumph while Plaquanay continued his long strides, pretending to walk across the river. The other children, as well as the parents, joined in the fun with cheers and clapping, their hearts being knit together by the wonder of a past they were connected to.

As Shem and Sede happily watched, he leaned and whispered in her ear, "These stories will be added to the ancestral stories told during festivals. These new stories will become the ancient stories told to our future generations."

With tears in her eyes, she squeezed his hand. They were living in the "now" but making history for their people at the same time. Seth's life had known his stories; this was theirs!

They journeyed for a month and camped for several days on a high ridge overlooking their inheritance. This was the same place the Watcher had shown them when they had been with Melchisedec. It was where their inheritance began. They could see on the horizon the evidence of man. Small threads of smoke rose in the far distance, evidence of Ham's presence.

The Watcher told them that Ham's descendants had greatly multiplied. Cush, Ham's eldest, had a son named Nimrod, who had become a mighty hunter/warrior among them. With the stolen treasures of Adam and Eve, he had used the anointing that still remained on them to gain favor and position among his elders. He used the emerald rod as a scepter, and from his belt, he carried the lamb skin coverings. He told them there would be a day when these two treasures would be repossessed by the righteous just as his inherited land would be.

Shem's caravan moved south, following the lead of Plaquanay. They had traveled for several more months when they saw a peaceful open land. The soil was rich and fertile, and the grassland went on as far as the eye could see. A great river passed through the valley, and a forest lay to the south. Rising above the beautiful land was one lone mountain positioned like a sentry over the surrounding area.

As Shem brought his camel to a stop, Plaquanay said, "We have arrived. You and Sede will find your dwelling place on the mountain. In time, your people will stretch out over these lands." He slowly moved his hand in an outward motion across the expanse before them. "Your dwelling place on the mountain will be as a beacon for your descendants, who will rejoice to know that 'the father and mother of their people' watch over them."

A thrill surged through both of them, and they looked at each other, feeling an instant connection with this place. The mountain seemed to call to them. This was their inheritance: the place of "new beginnings" for them and their generations. It was as though they knew they were home.

It took nearly another week of traveling to finally reach the mountain for the distance was great across the open land. As each day passed, Shem and Sede grew in anticipation of what they were going to experience when they finally got there. When they approached the base of the mountain, Plaquanay led the slow ascent. There was a natural trail, most likely the path of deer. They followed as it meandered and turned, leading higher and higher. He stopped at the entrance of a cave, and with a loving smile, announced, "This is your new dwelling place. You and Sede will live within this cave, but your children and their descendants will live on the plain below. There, they will build huts, while others use tents, roaming with their herds."

When they stepped forward to enter, they felt the presence of the Lord. It was as though Yahweh was welcoming them. What they saw was breathtaking. The walls were polished vertical stone; the light from above seemed to dance off the marble surface. Around the circular perimeter were small alcoves lit with streaming light from above. Looking up, they saw a natural cathedral ceiling with openings to allow light to enter. There were slits in the stone forming a beautiful wagon wheel pattern. The sunlight streamed down, creating a pattern on the marble floor. They were standing in the very center of the wheel's light. They both sensed this cave had been created just for them. And in a way, it had been.

Overwhelmed by the joy he felt, Shem scooped Sede up in his arms and whirled her in a circle. Throwing his head back, he laughed with great joy. She burst into tears, laughing too, with a happiness beyond description. They were home! Plaquanay stepped back, silently watching as they shared their joy. He glowed with a warm, soft light; Yahweh was blessing His own!

Returning to the entrance, they looked below. There, the whole plain stretched before them. They both sensed that from this day on, all that happened within their families would be overseen and protected from this lofty place: the camp of Shem, who was the son of Noah, the son of Lamech, the son of Methuselah, the son of Enoch, the son of Jarad, the son of Mahalaleel, the son of Cainan, the son of Enos, the son of Seth, the son of Adam...the created son of God.

The first thing Shem did was build an altar at the highest pinnacle of the mountain. His sons helped him gather the stones, arranging them to resemble the altar in Taasa-toka and Tolma-toka. Around the altar was a natural plateau of open space. This would be as the knoll around their old altar at Taasa-toka. When the altar was built, Shem chose a perfect, spotless white lamb, and they sang the song they had been taught from their youth: the "Song of the Chosen and the Blessed." Lifting their hands and voices to heaven they sang...

From the altar of our hearts,
The fire of love ascends   the **women** sang the heart of the Sethites
Flames of the called, the chosen,
The welcomed, the friend

Sede, Seed of Eden

From the altar of my heart
The fire of love descends   the **men** sang the heart of God
Flames consuming Eve's promised one
For sins choice, amends

Our burning altars now are one
The fires of love unite   men and women sang in **unison**
Flames of yours, mine and ours
Restoring Eden's light

Plaquanay stood at a distance and watched as Yahweh's children gave honor to the God that he himself loved and served. As he watched them, he saw Yahweh's glory reflected. There they were, His glorious children, loving Him. With holy tears, he wept for joy, knowing Yahweh's heart was fulfilled. He felt deep satisfaction knowing he was fulfilling his own created purpose. He had delivered the word of the Lord and was watching over those who would become heirs of salvation.

From where he stood, he watched as a lightning bolt of fire flashed from heaven and knew in his spirit the thrill of Yahweh's approval. Their sacrifice had been accepted. He heard their shouts as the fire consumed the sacrifice and saw them raise their hands and faces as the glory cloud descended upon them. Oh, he saw their happiness! He knew this was the closest thing to heaven they knew: to experience Yahweh's presence through the glory cloud. He watched as Shem pronounced his blessing over his children, grandchildren and great-grandchildren, and their children. Plaquanay had watched over Sede all her life. And now her husband would lead the people of God. Holy satisfaction filled him, and he bowed his head in worship.

Shem and Sede held hands, remembering the glory cloud they had seen in heaven. Oh, that Yahweh would share His glory with them. After Shem spoke his blessing over his great family, they formed a line to receive the mark of ash on their forehead and heart. As Sede stood before him, he leaned forward and said, "You, Sede, are the blessed seed of the Lord!" He had no way of knowing that Noah had once told her the same thing so very long ago. Thanksgiving welled up within her as she pondered how Yahweh could weave the memories of her past into the present. It made her love Him even more.

When he finished ministering, he felt Sede at his side. Slipping his hand into hers, they began walking among their people; their loved ones touched them as they passed, smiling with a sense of wellbeing and peace. With tears in his eyes, he whispered to her, "I am so very happy, Sede. This is how I dreamed it would be, and to see it now before me...my heart is overwhelmed with thanksgiving!"

As they continued through the glory-filled people, he was filled with reverent awe. He whispered to her once more, "All of these precious people, Sede, have come as a result of the love between you and me. Who are we to know such glory?"

Squeezing his hand gently, she was reminded of a time long ago when he had taken her hand and they had walked together through the crowd at the competition games; it was at the last feast celebrated at Taasa-toka. The elders had stopped that day to honor and encourage him for they knew he would one day be the leader of the people of God. Sede remembered how gracious he had been, showing them great respect. Now he was the leader, and all their people would look to him to guide them. Tears filled her eyes. How thankful she felt at that moment to be his wife and to know his heart. He truly was a man of God and had led them in righteousness and truth.

She happened to look up and saw Plaquanay standing in the distance, watching over them. He looked so mighty and majestic. The joy and activity around her seemed to disappear as she slowly raised her hand in recognition. With a knowing and loving smile, he raised his in return.

Chapter 22

Progeny

As time went by, Shem and Sede's family grew and became a great people. When Eber had twin sons, Peleg and Joktan, Shem divided his portion of the earth to form nations among his sons. They drew lots as Noah had done with his sons according to birth order. Elem drew first and then Assur, Arphaxad, Lud, and Aram. Each son was now a great nation. As their own sons became elders and leaders of their families, they became nations within these nations. Their dwellings were from Mesha to Sephar, a great mountain in the east. Only Eber's family remained near Shem and Sede, at the bottom of their mountain. This fulfilled what the Watcher had prophesied to Sede those many years ago. Japheth, too, divided his inheritance for his sons, who had also become great in number. Ham's sons, Mizraim and Phut, divided their lands among their sons. This land was the part of the earth that Yahweh had originally intended for Ham to possess. And as for Ham and Canaan and Cush, they continued to be squatters on Shem's inheritance, calling it their own and filling it with their descendants.

Shem and Sede were able to see their sons and their sons' extended families at the great Jubilee celebration held in Tolma-toka every 50 years. But for them, this was too long to wait to see their families. They wanted to welcome the beautiful new faces born within each family and get to know them by name. They left their peaceful cave and visited them for five months out of the year, staying a month with each son's family. While they visited, Shem encouraged his sons to hold the feasts and sacrifices that united their people in faith to Yahweh.

He passed on to them the "ways of the elders" that he had learned on the ark; what Noah had taught him and his brothers. He began to see each son mentor their own grown sons, becoming elders in their families. And last of all, he found the deepest satisfaction in instructing those who desired to study Enoch's parchment. He willingly shared the revelation he received during his many years of studying and saw the light of understanding come to his progeny.

While Shem gave counsel to the men of their family, Sede oversaw the women. It was her joy to help with the birthing of another generation coming to life among them. And as one of the elder women, she mentored the young maidens going through their "preparation for marriage." These innocent women delighted to hear her stories of how she and Shem's love had grown through their many joys and sorrows.

But her greatest joy came from mentoring the hunting packs within their sons' families. The fire of hunter/warrior was still alive in her as she shared her knowledge of the "old ways," instructing them not only in hunting but warfare as well. Because of Yahweh's great blessing commanded on the original "eight," she was still strong, powerful, and quick even after all these many years. She demonstrated her skill with different weapons and the art of attacking and defending in close combat. She passed on the stories that her father had told; of the Nephilim attack on the ancient village of Taasa-toka; and of the attack her village endured before the great flood. The hunter/warriors had fought against a female Nephilim and her host of Hagonoths. Although they were overcome, they fought valiantly, protecting the people, their village, and their way of life.

Every year she came, those who desired to be trained in warrior skills lined up to greet her. She soon realized these young men and women preferred this training over hunting. Each time she came, they were ready for her. They stood in precision rows at attention with tall bows and spears at their sides. When she came to review their troops, they would pound the ground with their bow or spear and chant the warrior's song they had created just for her.

Progeny

Our mother has come to teach her young
The willing, brave, and strong. (thump, thump went their spears and bows)
We'll fight to defend our homeland and kin
Her warrior cry is our song. (thump, thump went their spears and bows)

The enemy may come from near or far
With rage and war in hand (thump, thump went their spears and bows)
But we will rise to the battle's cry
And by her banner stand. (thump, thump went their spears and bows)

Over and over they sang and thumped the ground with their weapons, and when finished, a mighty cheer rose in honor of her as they waved banners with the Sethite symbol. She felt such a warm and wonderful pride seeing such willing, strong warriors—just as she and her pack had been so very long ago. It made her long to talk with each one for she knew that they, too, had their own stories of adventure, danger, and victory. She recognized the leaders among them and appointed them as captains. They became much like an elder, overseeing their troops.

Every year she would leave them with the exhortation: "Always be alert to fight for the sake of our people and the Sethite way of life." Everything that Shem and Sede had lived within their own lives was now being duplicated in their descendants. They found a deep and profound satisfaction during this time of overseeing their families.

As more years passed, Sede and Shem desired to visit Japheth and Shoda. They wished to see their home and the inheritance Yahweh had given them. They also yearned to see their beloved daughter, Shoda, and her growing family. With this desire, they prepared to leave for the north lands. Shem supervised the preparations of camels and supplies, knowing they would be gone for months and perhaps not returning for a year.

The night before they were to leave, Shem and Sede stood at the entrance of their beautiful cave. As they had so many times before, they watched the twinkling lights of the huts far below in the valley. They loved this vantage point, looking down on Eber's family, who had become a great people. "I will miss this place while we are gone," she whispered, laying her head on his shoulder.

The last of the light from the sun had faded, and stars were beginning to appear in the eastern sky. As the great expanse of land met the horizon, it brought wonder and awe to their hearts. It was though they could see the whole world from where they stood. "I love this place we call home," she softly sighed.

Shem wrapped his arm around her waist and drew her close. The warmth of her body felt so good. He marveled at the beauty of her face and smiled. "You're so lovely tonight, my wife. Your eyes tell me the story of what is in your heart. This is a soft and tender moment for you. I wish to greet your tenderness with my own heart."

She loved the way he spoke to her when they shared such intimacy. Searching his face, she saw in his eyes the softness of love. As she absorbed the love he was expressing, she tenderly said, "I love you, husband."

Smiling, but still with the most tender of words, he answered, "I love you back, wife."

They kissed, and both touched the great depth of love that had grown between them over the years. A sweet smile rose on his face, and he whispered, "Tonight as I hold you, I'm reminded of our first night together, long ago, in the wedding tent your father prepared for us. Your innocence rose to embrace me and was ecstasy for me. As I look back, I see that we were both so very dear in our innocence toward each other. Our love through the years, Sede, has become like that seed Father spoke of: a seed that would become a mighty tree bearing much fruit. From our roots, came the tree. You have brought me so much fulfillment. What would I have ever done without your love for me?"

He saw the slight reflection of light glistening from a tear in her eye and drew her to his chest. She could feel the beating of his heart, and it made her feel so safe—so loved. "You are wonderful beyond words, Sede. I love you so much."

Progeny

Emotions rose within her, and she felt as though she would cry. His words were her own heart reflected. She loved him so very much. She held him tight, wanting to capture this moment and hold it forever. He led her to their furs, and as he held her in his arms, they lay in silence, taking in the panoramic view of the heavens—a multitude of stars in the night sky. Yahweh *had* given them a wonderful life!

As the sun rose to greet them, they felt a sense of excitement and anticipation. Saying their goodbyes, they mounted their camels and began to travel the caravan route to the crossroads of Tolma-toka. From there, they turned north. Passing through Japheth's inherited land, they were in awe of what he had been given. They crossed great mountain ranges and forests as they followed the North Star. Noah and the elders of old had known about the movement of the stars and constellations; given them from Enoch's writings.

There were nights they traveled by starlight. The earth was so quiet, and the expanse of the night sky gave them a sense of Yahweh's greatness. On one of these nights, Sede felt a song of praise rise within her. As the camel gently rocked with smooth and steady strides, she clasped her seed necklace that rested on her chest. Lifting her gaze to the starry sky, she softly hummed her sweet melody. Then it was though words filled her mouth, and she began to softly sing, lifting her love and praise to the very stars above her...

> As I travel under this canopy of night,
> I ponder your glory, your hand of might
> You not only made the earth but this sky
> You, who lives in your dwelling on high
>
> I see your greatness in this vast array
> A multitude of stars in twilight display
> Who am to be remembered by You
> And be counted with the "eight"—so few

Sede, Seed of Eden

The seed you gave me at Eden's wall
Still holds a promise; I hear its call
As these brilliant stars witness above
Your seed still speaks of your love

I feel so small beneath this wondrous sky
But my love is great; I lift it high
The heavens declare your glory
And with my last breath, I'll tell your story

As Shem listened, he hummed the melody she sang. His own heart reflected the praise she was offering. In some special way, their hearts united in wonder and praise; on this quiet night, as they journeyed north.

On the nights they camped, Sede enjoyed the connection she felt to the land and the sounds of the wild. She was still a hunter at heart. She and Shem had brought their old hunting weapons and enjoyed fresh game along the way. It brought sweet memories back hunting once more. As they watched the herds thunder over the hills, they marveled that these were the offspring of the animals they had once cared for on the ark.

While they waited in the cover of tall grass, Sede thought of her father. She had loved their talks while they waited for the herds to move. There was a place in her heart that ached to see him. She now understood what he meant when he once told her he longed to see his kin of old. There were times too that her heart ached for little Ne-el. Although she had peace about her death, something pulled at her heart. She wanted to hold her "little cricket" once more and to feel her small arms around her neck. Perhaps it was because they were away from their busy lives that her heart longed for those she dearly missed.

They traveled for a month and began to see the signs of Ham's descendants. The land looked ruined and ravished. The pastures had been eaten too low, and the grass had died, leaving barren and windblown lands. The shepherds who had grazed their flocks had not been good stewards of the land. Shem wondered why Ham would neglect such things knowing what he knew about the ways of animals. Ham knew very well, that animals could not be left to graze too long in one area but should be rotated to different pastures. They saw abandoned villages left in ruin. It was the result of staying in the area until it was depleted and then moving on to new lands. It made Sede sick of heart to see such neglect and disrespect for the earth. Perhaps Ham didn't care. It really wasn't his land anyway.

They camped one night on a rock escarpment that overlooked a great valley. Below was a city that sprawled over the land. As they built their fire and settled on their furs, the sounds of the city rose in the night. It was not the sounds of melodic music but rather drums that beat in strange rhythm. They both looked at each other with a sinking feeling. It was the same sounds of Zadanim and ruined Taasa-toka before the flood. They packed their camels and led them farther into the wilderness, making their camp in peace.

When they left the region, they saw no evidence of man for the next week. It was an amazing feeling Sede experienced, and it continued for a whole day. It seemed to her she and Shem were the only two people on the face of the earth. She had a sense of what Adam and Eve must have felt knowing they were the only two people on earth. The whole world was a vast and open place, and it belonged to them. She shared her thoughts with Shem, bringing a smile to his face.

"Isn't it amazing to think the whole earth belonged to just one man? And now one third of the earth belongs to us, Sede, and to our descendants!"

Early one morning as they crested a high plateau, they saw a great city below. Shem smiled and with joy nearly shouted, "This is it! I know in my heart this is my brother's city!" With a broad smile, she knew too.

They made their way down the winding trail that lead into the city. The sentry's horn blew as they approached the gate and guards ran to meet them. When Shem told them who they were, one ran ahead to tell their patriarch who had come.

Sede, Seed of Eden

Japheth and Shoda stood in front of their palace steps to greet them, joy filling their hearts. Shem and Sede looked radiant as they approached on their camels. They had worn their finest to greet their brother and sister. As their camels lowered to their knees, Shem and Sede stepped to the ground. Japheth and Shoda ran to greet them, tears filling their eyes. Their happiness seemed to ignite the air around them. Instinctively, each greeted the other with their familiar pack greeting: arms to forearm, touching foreheads, and a "Ha-la-lah." Oh, how wonderful to be together once again!

As they reclined together at their meal, Japheth and Shoda shared how their lives had progressed from when they first settled in their inheritance. Like Shem and Sede, they had known great blessings, seeing their family become many nations. They had built their village that gradually became the great city they saw from the high plateau. They had a culture as of Taasa-toka: with elders, hunting packs, and the ceremonies of the ancients.

As the days went by, they gave Shem and Sede a tour of their city. Everywhere they went their posterity gave Japheth and Shoda great honor. It pleased Sede to see such honor for they were the loving father and mother of their people and worthy of respect. They saw the altar that Japheth and his sons had built when they first arrived to offer the sacrifice that Seth had instituted. Japheth was proud to show them the vast fields that he and his sons had developed over the years. It was still his delight, as it had been in the early years at Tolma-toka, to grow grain and see the seasons change with seedtime and harvest. They had great storehouses for their surplus and much commerce within the city market. Japheth's sons also bred great herds of horses and built beautiful stables to house them. It brought back sweet memories to Sede. The magnificent horses she was seeing were from the great Fallon and Mora.

Sede was able to spend time with her daughter Shoda, now a great-grand-mother herself. She had seen three generations come from her love with Magog. Sede took long walks with her in the beautiful gardens at their estate outside the city. Magog was the only son that remained close in location to his parents. The other sons had parted and claimed their divided inheritance. Wonderful days melted into one another as fellowship was enjoyed between them.

It was at one particular evening meal that a messenger came to the great palace with urgent news. As Japheth read the parchment, his face blanched white. His sons Gomer, Madai, Javan, Tubal, Meshech, and Tirus had all been invaded and carried away captive by Nimrod's army. He stood to his feet and sent word to blow the horn of assembly. Shem joined him as they hurriedly walked the crowded streets to the altar platform.

When the men had gathered, Japheth made a loud proclamation, "We will mount up on wings of eagles. We will ride our swiftest stallions and come to the aid of our families!"

Shem stepped forward and, clasping his brother by the forearm, said, "I and my house are with you, my brother!"

As Japheth's men prepared to leave the city, Shem told Sede what had transpired. They would leave at once on Japheth's fastest horses, returning to their own lands to rally help for their brother's family. They would meet in Tolma-toka. During this time, Japheth would send messengers to gather more information, and Shem would gather his men. Noah's other sons would surely help. Embracing her beloved friend and her daughter, Sede left with Shem.

Their journey home was swift. The horses were strong and fast, unlike the slow-plodding camels. When they arrived in their village, they learned their sons, too, had been invaded and taken captive. Sede felt great panic. She feared not only for their sons but also for their wives, children, and grandchildren. Had they all been taken or just the men?

It was but a few days after their return that they discovered the extent of the raids. Nimrod had invaded their lands and captured all the people. Their villages were deserted, and the only thing that remained were the dead warriors. They had died defending their people and villages. The scouts had buried the brave young men and women. This especially broke Sede's heart. She remembered their great zeal and love for her when she came every year to train and encourage them.

Now the only free people remaining in their families were the descendants of Eber living at the foot of the mountain. Nimrod had not ventured this far south. Eber would stay and stand guard over their remnant family. As he prepared to leave, Shem wished to bless Sede before he left. But through her insistence, she would not be left behind.

"I was trained as a warrior as well as a hunter. If our great-grandchildren were brave enough to fight for our families, how can I do less? It is my place to be at your side. I *must* be at your side!"

Shem could see there was no convincing her otherwise. They would be leaving together.

When they arrived at Tolma-toka, Japheth and his men were waiting. Noah's other sons, Uzza, Adall, Omarh, and Dedal, were also prepared to leave with their sons. Before they left, Noah laid hands on all his sons and prayed, "Oh great and mighty Yahweh, be with my sons. Be their shield and exceeding great reward. Keep all who go with them safe to return to their promised land you gave them. Deliver their families out of the hand of the enemy, and exact your judgment. It is as I proclaimed: 'Canaan is **cursed** with a curse and <u>all</u> who stand with him.'"

"Now be blessed, my sons, for Yahweh goes with you!" In their gentle frailty, Noah and Ezmere embraced them, tears running down their cheeks.

Chapter 23

Tower of Babel

It wasn't hard to follow the trail of the captured. They left signs along the way: broken litters and discarded clothes, dead animals from being driven too hard, and, saddest of all, grave mounds of the dead. They wept as she realized their beloved families had been ravished. She saw the graves of her brave warriors, their weapon belts laid upon their burial mounds. They had fought their captors and tried to free their people.

They followed the trail that led them to the great plain of Shinar in the southeastern region of Paddan Aram. It was there they saw an unbelievable sight. Even though they were miles away, a mountainous tower rose out of the ground and ascended into the clouds. Its base was immeasurably huge and gradually narrowed by spiraling rings forming a point at the top. Sede overheard Shem tell his brothers, "This is why our people have been stolen. They needed laborers to build this great tower. What has Ham been up to? I know he's behind all this."

They kept hidden in the forest, knowing they could easily be spotted from a high vantage point as the tower. Under the cover of trees, they concealed themselves while they made their plans. That night Shem and Japheth, along with their brothers Uzza, Adall, Omarh, and Dedal, met for counsel. Their combined families were too few to attack such a great fortress and Nimrod's hordes. They decided to send in spies to gather information, and then make a plan. Shem and Sede would go disguised as a traveling couple. In preparation, they changed into traveling garments and packed their horses as though they had journeyed for a long time. Sede wore the cloak she had kept all these many years, and Shem donned desert garb worn by their family that possessed the Eastlands.

When they arrived at the tower gate, sentries lowered their spears, not allowing them to pass. "State your business," demanded the gruff guard.

Shem bowed and graciously answered, "We've journeyed to see the 'Majestic Tower,' famed in our far Eastern lands. It is this wonder we wish to behold." Shem passed them a pouch of gold, and the guards lifted their spears and waved them through the gate. For more gold, they received a token to spend the night in an inn farther up the road, past the marketplace. He also told them that if they wanted to see the tower in its entirety, it would take three days to walk the circumference. It was unbelievably great in size at a distance but even more unfathomable up close.

The great spiraling road made a gradual ascent that followed the outer wall of the tower. The marketplace the sentry had told them about went on and on. Every imaginable thing was sold—food, of course, but other things that spoke of the strange religion of this place. There were booths after booths selling small idols and what looked like objects of divination. Small shrines were set back behind the booths, where people bowed and worshiped idol statues. Sede recognized the image on the idols. They were the likeness of the fallen angels that Ham had released into the world.

The higher they walked, the more they saw. Strange weapons and armory: curved swords, crossbows, and habergeons were displayed for sale. She recognized the flaming swords from Atlantis of old. The merchant wheeled one through the air while flames flared from the blade. More booths displayed clothing and fabric she knew came from dark knowledge. It shown with light that was supernatural and made a sound when touched. Large cages held strange animals that only Castius could have created. They were a blend of one species to another and animal to human. There were winged lions, dragons, and horses. Some of the animals were fierce. Half human bulls snorted and lunged against their chains, shouting profanities. The centaurs looked so very sad. They knew they were not what they could have been had they been wholly human.

After they passed the market place, they found the inn; the symbol on their token matched the symbol on the door. They stabled their horses and waited for the quiet of night. This great tower was like a city that never slept. Even in the wee hours of night there were constant sounds of construction. Laborers moved their great pallets of brick past their door, and the sounds of saws and hammers, along with foremen shouting orders, caused such a noise it made it impossible to sleep.

They decided to search for their kin and left the inn. They crept through the streets, hiding from laborers and those who socialized outside their homes. The spiraling road led them higher and higher. For three hours they snuck and hid to avoid detection, all the while looking for signs of their families. They passed palaces and great works of architecture. How could there be open and vast gardens with great trees and waterfalls so high from ground level? It was a wonder to behold. There were trees that had crystal leaves that created tinkling melodies when the breeze blew through their bows. Sede could only imagine it was again dark knowledge that made this possible. They continued until they felt moisture in the air and then realized they had arrived at the cloud level of the tower. Looking behind them, they no longer saw the road but only mist from clouds.

It was here, at the very top of the tower, that they saw a temple. It was magnificent in architecture and wonder. Made of white marble, it rose 400 cubits in the air. It was so tall they strained to see its pinnacle. The breadth spread as far as they could see in opposite directions, with columns following the exterior wall. Pagan symbols were embedded in gold over the entrance— the same symbols they recognized from Zadanim. The steps that led to the entrance were solid gold, with flowing water cascading down each side of the steps, creating a soothing water sound. Three giant statues were enshrined within alcoves built into the temple's exterior. A muted light swirled within each chest of the statues—in glowing yellow, red, and blue—like burning flames.

But even amidst all the beauty they saw, they felt evil pressing upon them. It was a feeling of dread and woe, as if something bad was about to happen. Hearing the sudden pounding of drums, they hid behind a great stack of bricks. Nearby, a large pot of slimy tar mortar hung over a small fire. This is what they had used to seal the bricks, making it waterproof and impregnable.

Shem whispered to Sede, "Why would anyone build such a structure and seal its stones in such a manner? What would be the purpose of such a feat?"

She considered his words and then remembered what the Watcher had told her about Ham's descendants: They would worship other gods. Perhaps this was built for their worship. Perhaps they feared another flood by water-proofing the stones, attempting to secure for themselves a place of refuge. In her heart she sensed that what she was seeing, was in defiance and rebellion to Yahweh.

As the noise grew louder, several people stepped from the entrance. The illuminated temple was so brilliant with light that it silhouetted their form. A bright cloud followed them, rolling and billowing as it moved. The heavy scent of incense filled the air. It reminded her of the oil that was poured on her hair when she was prepared for the market in Atlantis. She felt sickened in the pit of her stomach. With the light behind them, it was hard to see who they were until they drew close. When their faces became visible, terror struck her. To her utter horror she saw him…Talimus-qua-tam! He was glowing with radiant blue light, and the tattoo on his forehead burst with red flecks.

Pressing herself against the bricks, she held her breath, holding her hand to her mouth to keep herself from screaming. She instinctively gripped Shem's arm. When she could finally breathe again, she whispered in fear, "It is one of the fallen angels from the old world!" Her voice was trembling when she spoke, and her grip was frozen to Shem's arm. "It's Talimus-qua-tam, Playtheus' father. This is the same angel who kidnapped our Aunt Marah."

Shem froze. The reality of her words hit him with full impact, and he now understood why she was so terrified. This fallen angel exuded evil. He felt it from where they were hiding. Evil flowed from him, rolling in waves. He, too, pressed himself against the bricks in terror.

At Talimus-qua-tam's left walked Ham and Canaan. To Sede's utter amazement, they looked completely different from the last time she had seen them, the night they accosted her in front of Noah's hut. They had looked so aged and hardened. But now she saw men who had been transformed. They were young, strong, and virile, with a seductive aura about them. It had to be sorcery to have brought about this kind of transformation. She didn't recognize the man at his right. He was as tall as Talimus-qua-tam and wore a golden crown. He carried Adam's emerald rod, and their lamb skins hung from his belt. He was strikingly handsome—the perfection of masculinity. He reminded her of the Renown from Champion Hall. Could he somehow be a Nephilim?!

"That must be Nimrod," Shem whispered under his breath. "The one Plaquanay told us about."

They held their breath in fear of discovery. As Talimus-qua-tam passed the stack of bricks, he paused. He was sensing something he hadn't felt in a long time. It was the presence of innocence. He saw nothing and was reluctantly drawn away by his companions as they continued down the road.

When they were out of sight, Shem exhaled, "What a relief they're gone. The evil from that angel rolled over me in waves. I felt frozen inside!" In amazement, he uttered, "Oh, how did you survive being in his presence?" When he knew they were safe he whispered again, "We need to leave this place and go back to the inn. In the morning we'll question the sentry guards. I'll trade gold for information about the captives and why this tower was built."

They made their way down the road, keeping out of sight. When they had gotten below the clouds, they heard a crashing noise behind a garden wall. Cries could be heard that sounded like children. Looking around the corner, they saw a small group of children huddled together. They were going through garbage left outside a back door. A stack of barrels lay about, and a small child held his ankle, obviously from falling from the barrels. Another knelt before him trying to offer comfort. Sede and Shem looked at each other, hardly believing children would be awake at such an hour and alone. Why would they be going through garage?

They left their hiding place and approached the children. When the children saw them approach, they became frightened and huddled in a tight circle. The older ones instinctively took a protective stance in front of the younger.

Sede called to them in a soft and caring voice. "Hello, children. What is happening here? Can we help you?"

Shem knelt on one knee to help the young boy who held his ankle. "I'm going to feel your ankle to see if it's broken." He gently felt the small ankle, moving it slowly back and forth. "I don't think it's broken. Can you stand?" he asked as he helped the boy to his feet. A smile broke out on the boy's dirty face.

"What is your name, young man?" Shem asked.

"My name is Uzziel."

"Well, Uzziel, why are you here so late at night, and where are your parents?" The children looked at each other, puzzled. One of the older children stepped forward.

"My name is Mahlel. We have no parents." Sede and Shem looked at each other in horror and realized these children were orphans, and homeless.

"Of what Sethite tribe are you?" asked Shem.

The oldest boy, Shanini, spoke up. "We are descendants of the tribe of Cush, son of Ham. We don't remember our parents. They abandoned us when we were very young. They left us to seek their 'pleasure and pain.' They now live in the temple and serve the gods. It has been the older among us who guard the younger. We lose our guardians when they, too, become old enough to seek their own 'pleasure and pain.' Together, we search the streets for food and a safe place to hide and sleep. We fear being captured by the fierce dark angel who preys upon abandoned children. He and the elders of the temple use them for sacrifices and hurt their bodies.

Tears rolled down Sede's face. She felt as though her heart was breaking. In this young child's innocence, he described the unthinkable. Who would keep them from a fate of sacrifice and abuse? Who would protect their innocence? How could this be? She looked at Shem. The pain of what she felt was evident in her eyes.

Shem gathered young Uzziel in his arms. "You don't have to be alone anymore. There is someone who loves you and will take care of you." The children could hardly believe his words. They looked at him intently, wanting to know who this was.

Finally, Shanini asked innocently, "Who loves us and wants to take care of us?"

Sede spoke softly, looking into their eyes and stroking their dirty cheeks. "Yahweh loves you and will take care of you, dear, dear children. You no longer need to scavenge for food and hide in the dark."

The children looked at each other, bewildered. They didn't understand what she meant.

"Who is Yahweh?" asked little Uzziel.

Sede began to softly weep. She couldn't believe her ears: Sethites who hadn't heard the name of their God.

Shem stood to his feet and met Sede's eyes. "They'll stay with us tonight, and tomorrow we'll find a home for them among our kin. These Sethites will enter into the knowledge of who they are and the One who loves them with an everlasting love. They will learn they have a higher purpose than mere survival."

Cautiously, the little band of orphans was led down the great road to the inn. Sede brought water in a large bowl and washed their face and hands. From her saddle bag she found her comb and groomed the girls. Shem used his knife to trim the young boys' hair and made small sandals for their blistered feet. He used the leather from their bags and strips of jute from their rope. The children could hardly believe that strangers would show them such kindness. The children wept as Sede and Shem hugged each one saying,

"You are no longer alone but have a family among our kin. You will be shown the honor due to the sons of Adam and the daughters of Eve."

Shem started a small fire in the hearth, and Sede prepared food. Tears filled her eyes as she watched them hungrily grab at the food and swallow it, hardly chewing. When they had finished eating, she laid their bedding furs on the floor for the children. She and Shem would sleep in each other's arms, leaning against the wall and watching over "the innocent" of Yahweh. One by one the children fell asleep, and their rhythmic breathing brought a calm to the lonely room. What a strange place this tower was. Nothing in the room or on the road they passed reflected anything about Yahweh. This was not a Sethite culture but a Cainite one.

Tears rolled down her face as she whispered her heart. "Oh, Shem, these are probably but a few of a multitude of children roaming this great tower. How could Ham neglect the greatest responsibility of what an elder should do: protect the innocent? This was taught to him from his youth. What kind of man and leader has he become? I sensed his evil when he tried to attack me in front of Noah's hut, but this is even worse than what he tried to do to me. This is a sin against a helpless generation that doesn't even know the name of Yahweh!" She leaned her head against his shoulder and sobbed.

Taking her hand and tenderly kissing her folded fingers, he whispered his comfort, "Yes, Sede, it is a grave sin we see lying on the floor before us. I'm thinking it's even worse than we suspect. If Ham had no regard for his own son's innocence, why would he care about children he doesn't even know exist? Remember what Yahweh told us in the throne room, when we were before Him in worship? He said there were many who needed his love and compassion. I'm thinking these innocent ones are some of the needy He meant. After we learn more in the morning, we'll find the answers to these haunting questions. Yahweh will show us what to do."

She felt the counsel of his words, and it brought her comfort. This was the same kind of comfort she had felt with her father's counsel. How relieved she was that he was so capable and willing to lead. He had become her elder even though he was her husband. Whatever they discovered tomorrow, Shem would know what to do.

They had gotten but a few hours of sleep when they woke to the sound of pounding drums and the noise of a crowd. Stepping to the door, they saw a parade. It was spectacular in pomp and extravagance. Shem instructed Shanini to keep watch over the others until they returned, even if it took all day. They slipped into the crowd and followed the parade. Somehow they knew that at the beginning of this procession, they would find the answers about their missing kinsmen.

As the parade slowed, they saw them. There, on the shoulders of very muscular men, were golden sedans carrying Ham, Canaan, and Nimrod. They wore golden crowns and carried scepters. Their garments were exquisite: embroidered robes with jewels and the rare fur of the glendak—pale blue and velvety soft. It was Nimrod who carried the priceless emerald rod. They were being paraded through the streets as the crowds thronged them, praising their greatness. People pressed through, struggling to lightly touch a tassel that hung from their elaborate sedans. Others threw beautiful flowers before them on the street. They were lavishing their worship upon them, openly hailing Ham and his heirs with their praise and loving them with all their hearts. As she watched, Sede knew this was the fulfillment of what Ham meant when they talked in front of Noah's hut. He was a king. This is what Castius had promised him and what he had sold his soul to get.

As she watched the eager people falling over each other for just a touch of a tassel and crying with tears of love in their eyes, it sickened her. People worshipping other people and not giving their worship to the rightful One—Yahweh; she was not only appalled but disgusted! She sensed the blasphemy in it all. People were worshiping the creature rather than the Creator. She turned to Shem and vented her hot anger. "People are to worship the Lord God with all their heart, mind, and soul, not their kin!"

He saw her great defiance in what she saw and admired her righteous indignation. He, too, was appalled by his brother's arrogance. To think he would allow, let alone welcome, his descendants to worship him. He knew then, in that moment, that his brother had fallen from the grace of Yahweh, and there would be no going back for him. A great horror filled him knowing there would come a time when Ham would reap judgment for what he had sown.

The great host of worshippers now stood well above the clouds. It was though what was about to happen was taking place in the heavens. The road below them seemed to have disappeared in the clouds. When the procession stopped, the strong bearers lowered the sedans to the ground. With great pomp and pounding of drums, they gloriously ascended the platform and seated themselves upon three magnificent thrones. Ham's throne was positioned highest, and the other two were on each side. The drums slowed their beat and stopped, as great blasts sounded from silver trumpets. All the people—old, young, and infant—fell prostrate to the ground in silent adoration.

As Shem and Sede looked around, they were the only ones standing. Whispers from the crowd turned into rumbled mumbling as all eyes fastened on them. Ham saw two people standing at a distance and stood to his feet, extending his scepter toward them. With authority, he boomed, "Bring them before me!"

The royal guards ran to bring them. As the guards stepped from before them, Ham now saw who stood before him. With a sinister laugh that echoed over the backs of the prone worshipers, he mocked, "So…it is *you*, Brother, and your simple wife." In full confidence and authority, he extended his scepter and proclaimed, "You may kneel now."

Shem and Sede stood tall and still. Neither moved. The silence was profound. Never had Ham's word been challenged since declared king. He felt humbled by their defiance and it reflected in his countenance. "This will not be tolerated!" he thundered, trying to regain composure. "You *will* bow, or you will *die!*"

Shem spoke loud and clear. His voice carried an authority that even caused Ham to tremble. "I will have you tell me first, Brother, why you have trespassed on lands that were given to another, and ravished your Sethite brethren, taking them captive. It is not befitting the sons of God to act in such a way upon the earth!"

Silence gripped the air, waiting Ham's response. Then, a laugh bellowed from Ham as he turned to look over his shoulder at Canaan and Nimrod. They smirked, knowing that as king, he would exercise authority over such impudent behavior. "You know nothing of the earth, older brother. **I am** now king of the earth, along with my son and grandson. The 'Mighty Three' have made their decree. I care little for the rights of the sons of God. Your people, along with Japheth's and our feeble father's other sons, will serve me and finish this tower. This is my dictate, and this is my decree! It is the desire of the great Satsum-kedesh that we build a gateway to heaven and make war on the 'Most High.' He, Talimus-qua-tam, and Masta-lovid will establish their thrones on high. They will rule the heavens, and I and my heirs will rule the earth. On a clear day, from this throne, I see the whole world and it has become mine. **I am** king over all!"

Sede was aghast at his words—the blasphemy in what he was saying; and that he and the angels would dare wage war on the "Most High"! It made sense that Satsum-kedesh would try to rule from the heavens. He had the knowledge of the stars and knew the power of heaven's lights. This tower was evidence that he and the other two angels had manipulated mankind to build this gateway to heaven—this tower of abomination. The blind arrogance of these angels was unbelievable. Ham should have remembered that Yahweh was greater in power than these angels and destroyed what they had made upon the earth: their cities, their culture, and their sons. (But, evil has a way of blinding the eyes from seeing the truth. Ham could only see his lust for power and glory.)

Just then Talimus-qua-tam materialized before the thrones! Ham, along with Caanan and Nimrod, stumbled and fell before him and began to worship, reaching out to but touch his feet. They visibly trembled in ecstasy and groaned with pleasure. Just being in his presence triggered a physical response in them. They obviously were used to worshipping him with all that was within them. The only ones, again, who still stood were Shem and Sede. Sede's forehead began to glow with a brilliant white light, and the symbol of "Tella-la-no-ah" could be seen on her forehead. Her body radiated a soft, sparkling light that pulsated. Shem was amazed and captivated by what he saw. He felt his spirit respond to hers in warmth and love.

Ham and his son, along with Nimrod, stood to their feet. What they saw had a hypnotic effect on them. They were visibly drawn to the manifestation of her innocence. No longer did Ham's derogatory remark about Sede being Shem's simple wife hold credence. Desire for her innocence burned within his heart, making his palms sweat and breathing deepen. Canaan and Nimrod both felt the same burning desire. In all the corruption they knew and practiced, it was still innocence that captivated them.

Talimus-qua-tam drew near with his intimidating presence. His evil pressed upon them, suffocating them. They trembled with each step he took toward them as wave after wave of evil swept over them. "Ah, it is you, Sede-quete. I remember seeing within your soul the day you were declared high companion. What desirable innocence and exquisite essence you possess!" He slowly circled her and leaned in, inhaling next to her neck. Both Sede and Shem were frozen in fear. With a lustful groan, he uttered, "Umm…it was *you* my son had set his love upon. Perhaps I will grace you with *my* special attention. It has been a long time since I've inhaled the essence of one as priceless as you. The last time was Ba-nea. You do look queenly in her robe!"

He brushed his forefinger slowly over her breast, where the symbol for "Angelic Queen" was embroidered. Although Sede had appeal for her priceless innocence, she was still breathtakingly beautiful. Though middle aged according to the longevity of the ancient Sethites, the great blessing of Yahweh given them the day of the covenant still remained on her, giving her vitality and youth beyond her years. Her physical beauty was made even more magnificent by the beautiful innocence rising from within her spirit, making her truly "Tella-la-no-ah"—unlike any other women in the crowd.

Little did he know when he brushed the symbol over her breast, he moved her seed necklace that lay beneath her robe. As she felt the seed move, it was as though time stood still, and everyone and everything around her froze. Simultaneously, everything unfolded. She immediately felt a great composure settle over her. Her breathing calmed, and no longer did she feel frozen with fear. Then the sweet remembrance of Yahweh's promise came to her. *She* was the chosen seed in this generation. Her destiny was secured by Yahweh himself. Who could dare attempt to change what Yahweh had declared? She then sensed the heat of Shem's anger from the lustful advances of Talimus-qua-tam and could almost hear his thoughts...'How dare he touch my wife!' She instantly knew he was willing to risk his life to protect her. But before Shem could react, from somewhere deep within her, a strength of power and fire rose. Clasping her robe around Eden's seed, she held it tight against her chest. She knew *who* she was. And she also knew *who* this fallen angel was.

As this frozen moment in time was released, she planted her feet. Holding her ground, and no longer intimidated by his presence, she faced him with no fear. This sudden change perplexed him. He had the power to instill fear, but somehow she had broken it. Then, with the strength that had risen within her and still clutching her seed, she spoke with authority and power: "**I** am the chosen seed in my generation. **I**, a child of the 'Most High,' am not afraid of a disobedient angel, who was created not to be a ruler but to be a servant, and messenger to those who would be the heirs of salvation!"

She could hardly believe what her own mouth was saying. Shem stood in awe of her boldness. Her words of prophecy continued, "This day you will be chained, as were the 200 when Yahweh pronounced judgment on them. You will not escape this day. For '**The Day of Days**' has come for *you*, Talimus-qua-tam. **I** will worship the 'Most High' upon the sea of glass with those who fly above his throne, but as for you, **you** will be brought down to the lowest hell!"

The air reverberated with the rumbling power of her words. The spoken energy rippled waves of power over those who were standing next to them, staggering on their feet to regain their balance. Talimus-qua-tam's mouth dropped open in astonishment. How could a mere human know the ways of angels, and their judgments, as well as the knowledge of the sacred throne room of God? Eons ago, he had been one of the angels that had gracefully hovered over the throne of the "Most High." The reality of the loss he had incurred through his rebellion was before his spiritual eyes. Never again would he worship in that secret place. He trembled and was visibly shaken by the reality of the moment and the boldness and veracity of her presence. Instead of intimidating her, she was intimidating him! There was *fear* in his eyes. The brilliant blue light that emitted from him faded, and his face slowly became dark and cold, as he was in truth—no longer shrouded and disguised by his deceptive light.

It was then, after she had finished speaking, that a flash of light ignited before them. Plaquanay appeared at her side! Smiling, he commended her: "You have well spoken, chosen daughter of the 'Most High.' Today this disobedient one will know the judgment of Yahweh!" With authority and power, Plaquanay pulled a chain from his belt. Just like the chains that were used in the cavern of Arnon, this chain glowed with the light of fire within it. He bound the weakened and fear-filled angel around his shoulders, over his body, to his feet. He stood mute in the captivity of judgment.

Shem drew near Sede, who was still clasping her seed. She slid her hand in his, feeling the strength of his grip. It sent a thrill through her! They had stood in the face of evil and prevailed. It was then that a great quiet fell upon the crowd. It could almost be felt. Their kings stood mute, sensing something was about to happen. Everyone was held in the moment. There was no sound: not a whisper of a breeze, not a flutter of bird, or a muffled word. It was as though the whole earth held its breath, waiting for what was about to happen.

It was then the voice of God fell upon them! Some thought they heard but a whisper; others heard a great booming voice; and still others heard what sounded like lightning crashing through the sky. **"Let us go down** and see what the children of man have built. The people are one, and have one language, and this they begin to do. Now nothing will restrain them which they have imagined to do. Let us go down and confound their language so they will not be able to understand each other's language."

The heavens that were clear now became dark with ominous rolling and billowing clouds. Great lightning flashed, sizzling and crackling in every direction. Suddenly, a great tremor shook the base of the mammoth tower, sending violent vibrations beneath their feet. Plaquanay and Talimus-qua-tam disappeared!

In terror, Ham, Canaan, and Nimrod looked at each other, and without a word exchanged between them, bolted for nearby chariots. Cracking the whip over the horses, they sped down the great road. Frightened people flew backward to escape the pounding hooves. The screaming crowd began running in fear as the tower beneath them continued to shake. It was mass chaos. People grabbed each other, screaming in words that were foreign and strange! No one understood each other! A flood of terrified people descended the great wall road. Multitude upon multitudes of people flowed through the gate, like water released from a dam, spreading over the flat plain before them. The terrified people began to find others who understood the words they were speaking—those who spoke the same language. Soon groups began to huddle and cling together, separating themselves because of the fear they felt, while the lightning continued to flash and the earth rumbled and shook.

Shem and Sede were swept along with the terrified masses, racing down the tower road. When they saw the inn, Shem held her hand and pushed through the hysterical crowd. They found the trembling children huddled in a corner. They, too, had heard the "great voice." Reassuring them, they led them from the gate to their kin. When the last of the people had passed through the tower gate, a mighty earthquake cracked the tower's foundation. The ground opened, and a third of the tower sunk below the surface. Then fireballs fell from heaven, setting what remained of the tower on fire.

The flames rose toward heaven as the bricks melted like lava, leaving only a rubble of melted bricks. The tower of defiance had been turned into a ruined monument of disobedience.

Ham escaped the city with his deposed kings. His great angel, Talimus-qua-tam, had been captured before his very eyes. He felt within his heart a yearning to be in his presence and to but touch his feet once more. He had lost his god! Even though he didn't want to retain the knowledge of Yahweh, he couldn't deny that Yahweh had shown Himself to be the "Most High" over all. In that moment, Ham knew that Yahweh had given him up to his own vain imagination. By his own choosing, he had exchanged the truth of Yahweh for a lie: worshipping and serving the creature rather than the Creator. He knew, deep within himself, from the teachings of Enoch and the elders: that those that refused to retain God in their knowledge would be given over to a reprobate mind to do what was unclean through the lusts of their own hearts. And he knew it had become so with him. This was the full weight of the curse Noah had pronounced on him. It came according to Yahweh's timing. What Ham had sown, he now reaped.

Shem and Japheth soon found their sons, along with their families, huddled in the valley of Shinar. It was to their great astonishment that their sons spoke different languages. They no longer spoke the ancient tongue of the Sethites. It was only Shem and Sede, Japheth, Noah's other sons, and the rescued children that retained the language of the Sethites. As best they could, they communicated with their sons and helped them back to the land of their nations. It took nearly two months to see them settled in their homes once more.

During this time, Shem and Sede nurtured the rescued children. They responded to the love they received much like a starving animal would respond to a feast set before them. When they returned to their mountain, Eber embraced the children, declaring them his own. Shem and Sede spent many nights around Eber's council fire while he learned about the great wonder Yahweh had done at the tower that everyone was calling "Babel."

Tower of Babel

Although the people of the earth no longer spoke one language, Yahweh had chosen to keep the ancient tongue of mankind within a small group of people. The holy language of the Sethites would not be lost.

Chapter 24

Jubilee

Years blended into years and more years until it was time for the families to gather at Tolma-toka. It was the fiftieth year and time to celebrate Jubilee once more. Shem wasn't sure how they would communicate between the families, but they would still gather and honor Yahweh with celebration. This would be the third Jubilee that they had observed.

Sede had an "inner knowing" she was to bring the jeweled box the Watcher had given her. She somehow knew this would be the last time they would see their father and mother. Spring came early that year, and it was with great excitement that Shem and Sede helped Eber prepare his family for the journey to Tolma-toka. As they traveled the caravan route, they joined other families journeying to celebrate Jubilee.

Tolma-toka was again filled with people. Multitudes of tents pitched on the surrounding hills to accommodate Noah's great and expanding family. They would be together for a year, enjoying each other and learning how to communicate. There *is* a language that is universal, and that language is "love." Shem and Sede would show love to their children as they always had, even if they weren't able to understand their words.

On the day of the sacrifice, Shem and Japheth helped their elderly father with the lamb. It was a beautiful sunset as they placed the sacrifice upon the altar. Before they began, the trumpeters surrounded the altar and faced outward toward the people. Lifting the long silver horns to their mouths, the chosen elders blew the horns of Jubilee. The crystal clear sound rang out over the valley and through the hills. It brought a hush as every ear heard the seven blasts. Noah then motioned for Shoda to come forward. As she stood high on the platform, she led the people with her beautiful clear voice. Each nation, in their own language, sang together. Musical instruments played by her children, grandchildren, and great grandchildren created awe-inspiring music that accompanied the "Song of Jubilee":

> *With silver trumpets, great blasts of glory sound*
> *In loving fellowship, we worship on holy ground*
> *The year of Jubilee has begun*
> *Remembering Yahweh's rest has come*
>
> *Six days you labored, and then were blest*
> *On that seventh you reclined to rest*
> *It was not only good…but very good*
> *The joy within your heart, you understood*
>
> *Now we your people rejoice and sing*
> *And honor you, the Creator of all things*
> *We enter our rest, as you did yours*
> *Our labors cease; your peace is ours*

Tears filled Sede's eyes as she looked out over the surrounding hills filled with a multitude of tents. They were all her family and kin. As she pondered the vast number of them, it occurred to her they were all the result of the love between Noah and Ezmere. Their love had created the people of the earth.

Through the crowd, she saw Ezmere carried on a fur-padded cot to watch the sacrifice. Sede drew near to hold her hand and kneeled at her side. As they softly sang together, Sede's heart rejoiced for this sacred moment between them. She felt her heart bond to Ezmere's in way she couldn't describe. Looking into her ancient face, she saw the beauty of her spirit. The peace and love that surrounded Ezmere drew at something deep within Sede's heart, making her weep.

As Ezmere finished singing, Sede watched as she peacefully closed her eyes. It happened so naturally and with such ease. At that moment she knew her mother had passed from this life. 'What a glorious way to die', she thought, 'Offering praise to Yahweh.' With tears in her eyes, she drew her mother's wrinkled hand to her lips and kissed it tenderly.

Shem stood nearby and noticed her act of love and instantly knew. His mother was now in the arms of God. Tears rolled down his cheeks as his eyes met Sede's. As the "Song of Jubilee" continued to be sung, he drew near and knelt at his mother's side.

"She is now with her kin of old," Sede softly whispered. "How beautiful that she gave praise in song before she left. Truly it is what Enoch said, 'Precious in the sight of the Lord is the death of his favored one'."

Shem lay his head on his mother's chest and whispered as if it were a prayer, "Goodbye, Mother. You gave me life, and you gave me love. I love and cherish this moment of your passing. We will be together again in our heavenly village of Taasa-toka."

Sede felt as though her heart would break. She kissed the top of his head and rested her cheek against his hair. "Dear husband, how wonderful is it to die in the arms of God. We Sethites have the greatest of hope. We will live again!"

As she began to weep, fire flashed from heaven and a great roar echoed throughout the valley into the hills. Yahweh had received their sacrifice. And then the glory cloud descended. Its sparkling mist rested on the people, filling hearts with great peace, comfort, and love. Shoda and Japheth saw Shem embracing their mother and knew....

They took Noah's hand and drew him near. Shem and Japheth raised her cot so Noah could draw close. He bent and kissed the cheek of the one he had loved all his life. Ezmere was his beloved, as he had been hers. He whispered softly, "How fitting you would depart in the glory cloud, my love!" He slowly touched his forehead to hers in a loving Sethite gesture.

That night as Sede and Shoda prepared her body for burial, Noah called Shem and Japheth to his hut. He wished to bless them. When they entered, they saw their father lying on his furs near the hearth. The fire cast a warm glow, and they felt the love that abided within the hut. This had been their parent's home since the flood, nearly 350 years ago. As they knelt at his side, they could hear the gentle melody of the musicians playing in the distance. It was the "Love Song of the Dead." Somehow it comforted their hearts to hear the familiar song and know it was being played for their dear mother.

Noah feebly grabbed their hands and gently squeezed them. "My sons, my time is near, as was your mother's. Soon I will join her and know the happiness waiting for me. It will be a life where she and I will be forever young. I will be with all those I love—my God, Yahweh, and my kin of old." Clearing his throat from the emotion he felt, he tried to speak. "And now for you, my sons… It was Yahweh's intention to save you from the flood and bring you to this 'new world.' And he has blessed you both, making you the great people you are today. It has been my joy to watch your lives and see you honor Yahweh with all you have set your hands to. You have loved your wives and your children, leaving them a legacy of faith. A father could wish for no more. I am proud of you, my sons, and love you with all my heart. 'May the Lord bless you and keep you. May the Lord make his face to shine upon you, and be gracious unto you. May he lift up his countenance upon you both, and give you peace.' Amen and amen, my sons."

He drew them close to touch their foreheads to his. Bowing their heads, they both began to weep. They knew he was dying and that he had given to them the best of what he had: a father's blessing. As he closed his eyes, he breathed his last breath. Their father, and the father of all the people of the earth, was gone.

Sede and Shoda stood outside the hut and heard his last words. Soft weeping drifted from within the hut, and they knew their father was now with Ezmere. They had lost their mother and father in the same day. They joined their husbands and solemnly held them, weeping in their arms.

The two couples slept in their parents' hut that night, near the beautiful body of their father. In the morning they would send the word out to their families and begin the ceremony for the dead. But for now, this night was for them alone. They had shared something with Noah no other person could really understand. Not only was he their father, but they had survived the flood with him. They had started humanity over with just the eight of them. Their father had been the strength and foundation of what they now walked in. It was hard to pinpoint, but deep inside, a piece of who they were seemed to have died with him. They saw their own end in his.

The next day as they prepared Noah for burial, Sede took the jeweled box and placed some of the spices and leaves on his peaceful face and in each of his palms. Then gently Shoda laid a veil over his face, holding Adam's gift for him in place. It had been his face that had shined upon them throughout their lives, and with the touch of his hands, he had blessed them. How fitting that the beautiful spices and leaves should rest there. To honor their mother, Sede and Shoda took two small leaves and placed them on each eye lid, and then veiled her face. Their mother had watched over them all their lives and had seen them through the eyes of love. It seemed so right that they were together, lying side by side in the small cave where their bodies would rest.

And with the days that followed, during the days of mourning, a continual line of relatives passed by the cave offering their prayers of love and thanksgiving for the great patriarch and matriarch of their families. Some of their grandchildren, great-grandchildren, great-great-grandchildren, and many more greats brought tokens of their memories to leave in their place of rest. These were things that Noah and Ezmere had made them, or special treasures they had kept from a walk they had taken, or a skill they had learned from their mentoring long ago in their childhood. There were small knives and horns, tiny woven scarves and scrolls, whittled animal figures, and even small arks that floated down a stream on a special day the child had heard Noah's stories. Soon their cave floor was covered with these many gifts of love. And when the large stone sealed the cave, a heavy peace and calm hung in the air that blessed those who passed.

The Jubilee continued that year, and the great host of Sethites settled into life without their ancient father and mother. Every month the seven trumpets blew the seven blasts on the seventh day, and the sacrifice was offered. Shem officiated as Noah had mentored. Throughout the year, Shem and Japheth's hearts were comforted from the death of their parents, and they saw many of their great-great-great-grandchildren marry between their families, bringing them happiness to see their seed continue in yet another generation. They were seeing Yahweh's commandment come to pass: 'Be fruitful and multiply, and replenish the earth'.

* * *

Ham and his descendants continued to migrate to the Mesopotamian basin of Shem's middle lands after recovering from the upheaval at the Tower of Babel. He again established himself as king, along with Canaan and Nimrod. Through great wealth and demonstration of power, they reigned from their tri-city domains of Erech, Achad, and Calneh. As exalted king, Ham developed Baal worship among his descendants; this worship was central to their culture. It included the worship of the two remaining fallen angels and their leader: the "lord of darkness." Ham's descendants saw this "lord" as supreme—ruling from heaven. They believed that the Tower of Babel had been the gateway he used to usher his rule to earth. Ham led them to believe that this "lord" made war on Yahweh and deposed Him, ruling now in His stead. After he won this battle in heaven, *he* then destroyed the tower. It was *his* power that opened the earth and swallowed the foundation. And it had been *his* power that called down fire from heaven, burning the tower into melted bricks. Through his magnificence, he granted new and diverse tongues for the people to speak. (He was, as he had been from the very beginning with Adam and Eve, a liar and the father of lies!)

Baal worship was based on fertility, blood-letting, and human sacrifices. All the firstborn of any family was offered to their gods: the "lord of darkness" and the two fallen angels. The people eagerly gave them their wealth, hoping to gain their favor. With this accumulated wealth, they built their temples of gold and lived in ivory palaces. In one particular temple, the treasured scrolls from the secret chamber of the 200 were kept. Ham and his heirs continued to practice the dark arts that gave them favor with their people and satisfied every imagination of the heart. They sought both "pleasure and pain." Their blood-letting brought them their hearts' desire.

But word came through a trading caravan one day that Ham and Canaan were dead having died in a shroud of mystery. It was rumored Nimrod was responsible. And in truth, he was. Through patience and manipulation, he had planted a seed of suspicion between Ham and Canaan. With secret knowledge he discovered within the angelic strolls, Nimrod set up a series of events that led both of them to believe the other desired to kill them in order to rule supreme. It was easy really. He conspired with them both to depose the other. He provided the poison they used. Nimrod didn't have to kill them; they killed each other.

During Nimrod's new reign, more evidence of the two remaining angels was revealed. He was in league with them, propagating their desire to fill the earth with their *own* children. In exchange, they granted him more power and manifested majesty. And truly, there was none like him in all the earth. He was a mighty hunter before the Lord, but not in a righteous sense. What he hunted was His people's innocence. He had learned from Talimus-qua-tam's scroll how to withdraw the innocence of man as well as their essence. He had become a "Mighty One" in the earth. He captured and ensnared the righteous, turning them to serve him and the angels. His greatest delight was to bring them before the "dark lord" and hear them renounce Yahweh and confess *him* as lord.

He had made a law and dictate that every young virgin who wished to marry must first lie with him or the angels. The maidens were eager to please their king and honor their gods in such a way, believing they would receive their blessing for many other children and long life. From offspring born to Nimrod, the maidens sacrificed their firstborn to Satsum-kedish or Masta-lovid. If the maidens bore offspring from the angels, they became the majestic Renown or the undesirable Hagonoths.

These brutish giants paid Castius wealth untold, to find the link for them to propagate. In doing so, they intermingled their seed with more of Ham's seed to the point where there were few that remained of Ham's pure seed. Their lands became filled with this mingled seed. Unlike the age of Atlantis, where the giants roamed and raided, these giants formed clans and settled in regions. They were known as the Rephaims, and the Zuzims, the Emins, Avims, Horims, Caphtorims, and by many other "ims." History had repeated itself, all but for one thing. Yahweh had given Shem a promise: In the far future, his people would regain these lands and drive out the inhabitants from his rightful inheritance. The mingled seed of the Canaanites, along with the giants, would be destroyed, and Shem's seed would produce the 'Promised One'.

Even Mizraim and Phut's seed became polluted. Only three generations had prevailed to keep the ancient ways of Seth, and after that, they were seduced to worship the dark angel, Satsum-kedesh. It was only in the desolate and wilderness places that a few faithful tribes still worshipped Yahweh. The kings and Pharaohs that rose to rule Mizraim's and Phut's descendants began to reflect the inbreeding with Satsum-kedesh and were in actuality Regals that had been appointed by their father. They were beautiful, strong, and magnificent. There characteristics were common to the Nephilim: elongated head and additional digits on the hand and foot along with great stature. It was in Egypt that Satsum-kedish established his favored place upon the earth. In their temples of worship, they planned and charted their days according to the movement of the heavenly bodies. He instituted the worship of the sun, moon, and stars and the journey of the afterlife for the chosen ones among them: his Regal sons and daughters who were their kings and Pharaohs. These Regals, too, used the dark knowledge from the ancient scrolls to build great monuments and architectural wonders.

Masta-lovid chose to establish his kingdom from a mount in the fertile lands of the Canaanites. Mt. Hermon it was called, and it had been sacred to the 200. It was the first place on earth their foot had touched when they descended from heaven. Although the flood had covered the land, the mount still remained. His elaborate temple, built on the summit, faced north toward the Great Sea. The Canaanites saw him as god of the seas and rain. By his dark knowledge, he controlled the wind that swept the rains inland from the coasts. He instituted the worship of the seas and the mighty creatures within it. His Renown children were mighty navigators, as Shoal and Fathom had been. He, too, accepted human sacrifices and traded his dark knowledge for a night with the fairest of women. These women, in turn, became witches and practiced their sorcery, controlling regions to please their master.

It was through the process of time that the aggressive Canaanites desired more of Shem and Japheth's lands and took it by force, although this was in direct violation to what Ham had pledged when the earth was divided among the three brothers. The **"Shemite's"** would have to become warriors in order to keep what Yahweh had given them. All of Sede's mentoring would now be used to fight for their rightful inheritance. And Shem's spiritual mentoring would help them to fight the "good fight of faith." For as Shem's descendants migrated into more of his inheritance, they bordered the tres-passing Canaanites. Their dark religious practices were a stark contrast to the pure and simple faith in Yahweh.

* * *

As the years passed, Shem assumed the position of patriarch according to the Sethite custom of firstborn. The great families of Shem and Japheth celebrated two more Jubilees, but each Jubilee saw fewer family nations attend. Their far-reaching descendants had dispersed to uncharted parts of the earth, discovering new lands and great islands of the seas. Each Jubilee was celebrated by learning about new family members and the blessings that Yahweh had given them.

When the second Jubilee under Shem's leadership drew to an end, the brothers desired to see each other before they departed. Shem and Sede made their way down the busy street to Japheth and Shoda's hut, built like theirs, long ago, after the flood. It held mementos of when their children were young. Tears filled Sede's eyes as she saw the small musical instruments that hung on the wall and carved pictures of animals that Riphath and Togarmah had made when they hunted with her and Shem. As the four of them embraced, none of them could speak out what they were all sensing and knew…this was the last time they would see each other. The next Jubilee would be celebrated by their sons but not them.

As Sede and Shoda faced each other, Sede struggled to hold back her emotions. She wanted to leave her friend with words from her heart. "Dearest Shoda, it has been my joy to call you friend and sister all my life. If I could leave you with anything, I would leave you with this…I love you!" Looking into her eyes, she lovingly stroked Shoda's beautiful, wrinkled cheek. "It has been my joy since I was a young child, to know that through our fathers' arrangement, our lives would always intertwine and be connected by marrying brothers. You have become such a gracious mother to your people and have passed on to them your love of worship through song. You leave them such a wonderful legacy. I honor you, my sister; my friend." Sede knelt to one knee and clasped Shoda's frail hand and kissed it sweetly.

Shoda burst into tears. "Who am I to have the mother of our people kneel before me? It is you who should be honored, Sede. Please stand and receive the embrace of one who loves you dearly!"

As Sede stood, Shoda threw her small, frail arms around her neck and held her as she wept. Through her tears of love, Shoda whispered, "Farewell, my sister, my friend. We will meet again, when we pass from this life. It will be my joy to see you in our heavenly village as the young hunter you once were. I have never forgotten that day we met in the forest after you and Shem had married. That was our last time in the wilderness before our village was raided. I told you that day, 'I will always remember you as you are today, in your skins, young and strong, a mighty hunter among our kin.' I still remember you that way." Sede could hold her tears back no longer. They fell hot upon her friend's neck as she softly sobbed.

The brothers held each other in strong embrace, their manly sobs echoing from the walls. As Shem looked into the aged face of his brother, he lovingly said, "We have journeyed long together, my brother. Our days come to a close as they did for our father. It has been my honor to not only have known you as brother, but friend." He gently pulled Japheth close and touched his forehead to his. Softly, they whispered to each other, "Took-la-say-a-la-nay."

"I love you, my brother," Japheth whispered, his voice breaking with emotion.

They left the hut that day, leaving a piece of themselves with the family they loved so much. As they began their long journey home, Japheth turned north and Shem south. Through the distant valley rang the sound of Japheth's horn, clear and true. He would sound the last farewell, and Shem would echo its call. Noah's sons had known the bond of love and family.

As they journeyed home, the comfort of Yahweh rested upon them, and sweet memories reviewed before them of the lives they had lived together. They had begun as sheltered children in the lovely village of Taasa-toka. Loving parents had nurtured them, and they grew up guided by godly elders and customs of their people, the Sethites. They had their stories of the ancestors, the sacrifices, the festivals, and their courageous hunts. They had survived the flood and begun anew in that first place they knew as "heaven on earth." A great many years had passed as they saw their families grow and become a great people who would cover the earth. These were the memories they held close as they journeyed home.

Chapter 25

The Seed Revealed

As time passed, Sede and Shem spent more and more days in their beautiful cave, resting comfortably and entertaining those who journeyed to visit them. One day as Sede was caring for Shem, she saw a caravan approach. Something within her spirit leapt. She knew it was good news. As the travelers ascended the winding trail, she recognized her. It was Shoda, her daughter! In laughter and joy, they embraced. Oh, to see each other face to face. After their hugs and tears were soothed, Shoda introduced the young maidens she had brought with her. She had mentored maidens in the ways of the Lord for many years and had thought to bring this new group of maidens to hear the stories of the ancients from the father and mother of their people. She also came to care for her parents for she desired to minister to their needs.

After she settled her maidens in the many alcove chambers within the cave, she shared with her parents about her husband Magog's passing, and how her life had changed after his death. She had cared for Japheth and Shoda in their old age until they too, were laid to rest. She spoke of the beauty of their deaths. They died in each other's arms and had simply fallen asleep. Sede's eyes filled with misty tears. So…her friend had left this life. A gentle and peaceful calm held her heart as she pondered. It seemed right that Yahweh would give her and Japheth a glorious end… in the arms of the one they loved. Shoda and Japheth had known a love as great as she and Shem.

Her daughter's words became muffled and distant as her memory took her back to the last time she saw her friend. It was when they parted at the last Jubilee. She remembered the great love they exchanged in their farewell and the sadness she had felt knowing she would never see her again. But now, Shoda was in paradise, waiting to embrace her when her own days had known their end. The thought filled her with loving comfort... As her daughter's words became audible once more, she heard Shoda say it had been after Magog's death that she began to mentor maidens in the wisdom of the ancients, the knowledge she had learned from her. She realized that Sede and Shem were aging and knew their stories and knowledge would be lost unless it was passed on to those who would value and treasure it. But, even more than this, she desired to care for her beloved mother and father. With tears in her eyes, Sede welcomed her daughter's gift of care. She had often felt weak as she cared for Shem. It would be a blessing to have their daughter minister to them.

Sede and Shem's days continued in peaceful comfort. Shoda attended to their every need, and they enjoyed the young maidens who gathered around the hearth in the evening. As Shem held Sede in his arms, they eagerly listened as the maidens told stories of their lives in faraway lands. They told of great cities filled with people and others who lived with their kin in tents, following their herds. Some had come from remote villages hidden in the wilderness.

Two of the maidens had come from remote villages of the tribes of Mizraim and Phut. They told stories of the great mother of their people, Ne-el. She had guarded Mizraim and Put's children when Ham threatened their innocence. Her sons would not accept his perverted ways and held true to Yahweh and the Sethite way. When she died, refusing to surrender the young ones to Ham, an angel appeared, filling the whole sky with glory. He carried her away in his arms to bury her in secret. Ham fled in fear, and their families were saved from his corruption. Sede's eyes filled with tears. Now she knew the story of how her sister had died.

She remembered Ne-el's last conversation when they said their farewells. "My little ones will be truly lost if there is no light in their lives. I will be the only light they have." Ne-el was truly a Sethite, brave and willing to stand alone, and her legacy was evident in these maidens.

Others told of the influx of caravans bringing goods and news into their villages and cities. By these caravans, their parents learned of the growing Canaanite influence and how more and more Sethites were abandoning Yahweh for a new god named Baal. Their families had felt the threat upon their children's beliefs and wanted them to learn the ancient Sethite ways and customs. They heard of Shoda's gift of mentoring, and sent them to learn from the daughter of the great patriarch and matriarch of their people. They had come from the far north, the east, and the hidden wilderness places of the south. It warmed Shem's and Sede's hearts to know, though Ham's influence was present, their descendants were still encouraging their young and watching over their innocence, seeing that they learn the ways of their people.

There were many nights around their hearth that the young maidens desired to hear the stories of the world of long ago; of an ancient village called Taasa-toka and a young maiden that hunted with her father; of a corrupt world Yahweh had to destroy and the ark that saved them all. How did they make a new world of fresh beginnings with only eight people? What was it like to hear Yahweh's voice from heaven, from on top the tower of Babel? Did everyone really speak the same language at one time?

It was during these times that Sede read from her ark diary. The maidens were held captive as she read of their months within the ark, waiting for the new world Yahweh had promised. Tears filled Shem's eyes as she read of the love and trust she had in him, and how he always made her feel safe. Through her words of long ago, he saw her precious innocence once more, bringing sweet remembrance of the tender love they shared.

Sede especially enjoyed a sweet young maiden named Sarai. She came from the family lineage of Eber's son, Peleg, from the far away land of Ur. She had a tender heart and showed great interest in how to hear Yahweh's voice and believe His promises. Sede perceived that there was something special about this young maiden for her questions where not like the other maidens who only wanted to know about their adventures, but rather, Sarai wanted to know how she came to trust Yahweh in all things.

Sede began to make the connection who this maiden was. Her father had sent his son, Abram, when he was young, to learn from Shem and Eber. Through the course of time, Shem discerned that Yahweh's hand was upon this young boy. Shem had discerned this with Abram, and now Sede was seeing the hand of Yahweh upon Sarai; both from the same family. She sensed that some special destiny would tie them together.

As Sede pondered their connection, she remembered what Shem had told her that took place when he mentored Abram. He had encouraged him to learn the language and traditions of the ancient Sethites, and in time, after showing great interest in Enoch's parchments and several years of instruction, Shem felt he should take him to counsel with Melchisedec.

They journeyed to that far off place, "The Center of the Earth," where destiny was to meet this young man. Shem remembered the landmarks that brought them to the mysterious forest of whispering pines. When they stepped from the trees, there it stood—the mountain! The only thing that had changed was that now a small village nestled against a ridge halfway to the summit. It had been built for Melchisedec, just as the Watcher had foreseen. By all appearances, it seemed an ordinary village, but there was something special about it. The very air seemed charged with life, and a sense of peace permeated everything within its whitewashed walls.

While they stayed with Melchisedec, Abram began to grow in the grace and knowledge of Yahweh. He leaned about offering a sacrifice and the meaning of the lamb. It was only the spotless and best that could be offered. In the distant future, the perfect, spotless lamb would come—the "Promised One." He would be the ultimate sacrifice.

Melchisedec instructed him about hearing the voice of Yahweh—a still, small voice that always testifies with the heart: "Something within you will just know it is Yahweh." And last of all, the wisdom of the elders, of being Royalty, Priest, and Prophet. The greatest glory in life is to guide your family and watch over your children's innocence until it has grown full bloom, becoming strong, beautiful, and mature.

There were many holy Sethites who lived in the village with Melchisedec, whom he called "prophets of the Lord." Shem was fascinated by their pure and devoted faith. They possessed great peace, and their sense of reverence seemed to still the atmosphere around them. It was among the prophets that he saw Shanini. His heart filled with great joy to see the man he had become. He had grown up in the house of Eber, and when he came of age, desired to separate himself unto the Lord. He heard of Melchisedec and longed to be mentored by him. He left his father, Eber, and journeyed through the wilderness in search of Jerusalem, the City of Peace. A Watcher appeared to him and showed him the way. With great respect and reverence, Shanini embraced Shem, thanking him for rescuing him from the tower of Babel and showing him what real love was. It was his and Sede's act of love that turned his heart to know the one true God.

Before Shem and Abram prepared to leave, Melchisedec desired to lay hands on young Abram and bless him. As he spoke his words of prophecy, Shem wept. He was beholding the next link to the "Promised One" to come through his and Sede's seed. Abram knelt as Melchisedec rested his hands on his head. Looking to the heavens, he prayed: "Yahweh, Great and Mighty God, this day you declare Abram blessed. I discern you will trust him to lead your people in righteousness and faith. In generations to come, they will call him 'Father of the faith' for great kings and nations will come of him that will believe in you as he does. All that You promised Shem concerning his inheritance, Abram's seed will possess. They will rise to live in this land and fill it with *their* seed. Bless now this chosen one, who will be 'father' to a people who are yet to come!"

When Abram opened his eyes, he saw Shem prostrate and weeping on the ground beside him. A holy awe filled him as he suddenly understood what had just taken place; his future had just been declared by Yahweh, the "Most High." He knew that what had rested on Shem, for their people, had now been laid upon him. He now wore the mantel of "father" for their people. As this revelation settled in his soul, the presence of the Lord filled him, and he fell prostrate next to Shem. There he lay, lost in the glory of God.

It wasn't long after that that Abram returned to his father in Ur. But for Shem, the memory of what took place that day was ever present with him. He saw his own future in Abram.

* * *

Weeks turned into months as Shoda's maidens were embraced as part of Sede and Shem's family; for in every sense they were. Their presence within the cave, and Eber's village below, was one of love and joy; giving Sede and Shem renewed hope for the future generations to come.

It was on a beautiful starry night as Shem held Sede in his arms, laying on their soft furs and facing the eastern sky, that she sighed, "The stars are so beautiful tonight, just as they were that night long ago when we traveled to see Japheth and Shoda. Somehow, looking at the night sky, I feel so cared for, so loved."

Shem smiled as he listened. He had just thought of that same night when they had traveled in the light of the stars.

"Little cricket once asked me, 'Who made the stars, Mommy'? When I told her Yahweh had, she then said in childlike wonder, 'The stars are like candles in the sky.' I think of her words often when I see the lights of heaven."

He hugged her gently and thoughtfully said, "I look forward to holding her in my arms. I've longed for her over the years. It's been a sorrow that we never saw her grow and become a woman of God. One day we'll see her sweet face, and all the sorrow of what we missed will be washed away." She hugged him with her head against his chest. She was listening to his most secret thoughts. How good it was of him to share what had been there all these many years.

He was silent for a long time and then said, "Sede, my love, Yahweh has told me something, and I think this is the time to tell you."

Something in her knew what he was about to say. She began to weep and said, "I know what you're going to say, and I don't know if I can bear to hear the words."

"Then Yahweh is preparing you, even now," he whispered. He hugged her gently and kissed the top of her head. "Yes, Sede, it is time for me to leave this life and enter the next. Yahweh came to me on the breeze and told me my days have been fulfilled."

She continued to weep. Her father had used the same words when he had tried to prepare her the day before he died. "We'll be united soon. Remember what Plaquanay told us: It will be but a short time."

Her heart felt such pain. Even the words of preparation from the Watcher, spoken so long ago, held no relief for her. "I don't know if I can bear a day without you, Shem. It's not that I will be alone but that I won't be at your side, experiencing each day with you. Our lives have been so braided together, just like our wedding rope, that without your strand woven through-out my day, I would be incomplete and undone."

He brought her hand to his lips and gently kissed her fingers. "I set my love upon you, my precious Sede. You are in my heart always." She lay against his chest for a long time, listening to his heartbeat and soaking in his words of love.

Sleep came, and she dreamed. It was the same dream she had dreamed long ago. She was in the tall grass...waiting for Shem's signal. She heard the sounds all around her: the olumba lowing as they grazed, the breeze gently moving the tall grass, and a hawk calling from high above. She felt the warmth of the sun as she closed her eyes and absorbed its rays. All around her was a sense of peace and wellbeing.

When she woke in the morning, she stirred and drew near that she might wake him with a kiss. His hand was warm, but he didn't stir. Within her heart she knew...and tears filled her eyes. She laid her head on his chest in loving adoration. Her beloved had bid farewell last night and fallen asleep, not to wake again. She drew his hand next to her heart. She would wait here with him until Shoda came. They would share these last moments together and alone.

Word was sent over all the lands. Father Shem had died. They came from far away to honor the one who had loved them, the one who had led them in righteousness and truth. Their son's children and grandchildren came, along with their wives and families. Japheth's sons and grandchildren came and from far away, Mizraim and Phut's few faithful, who wished to honor their righteous uncle, the son of their grandfather, Noah. When Melchisedec came with his prophets, great peace fell upon the lone mountain and the village that lay at its feet. Even Abram, now a grown man, came from Ur. All were there to honor the holy man of God.

Sede had lovingly placed the beautiful spices and leaves from the jeweled box on Shem's face and palms as she had Noah. By the glory that had been given Adam, he had prophetically seen Shem. The time had come for him to be given honor by "the first of creation." With her own hands she made the veil that now rested on his face. His face had shone upon their people, and with his hands, he had lovingly touched their lives. The remaining treasured spices and leaves she laid over his heart—hidden beneath his embroidered robe. Only she would know they were there. For it was with his tender heart he had loved her.

As her days quieted after the ceremonial custom to honor the dead, and the many visitors had come and gone, she spent peaceful hours with Sarai and Abram. They came often to visit. In the soft lamplight of her chamber, they sat at her bedside listening to her stories of her life with Shem and the great love they had known. Although she never told them, Sede began to discern that these two young people would someday know a love as great as she and Shem had known. She felt Yahweh prompting her to share her secret story of the seed of Eden and the many adventures she had experienced while it rested against her heart. It had accompanied her during three captivities, the ark; the long years as they saw their families established, and the great confrontation at the tower of Babel. It had been her constant companion almost her whole life—nearly 600 years.

As days blended into more days, she found herself wanting to rest more and more. She loved the quiet of her cave and found great comfort within its walls. She would lie upon her soft furs, facing the eastern sky, and watch the stars rise each night in the sky. Shem's last words were ever in her heart: 'I set my love upon you, my precious Sede. You are in my heart always.'

In the following weeks Sede knew her days had been fulfilled just as her father and Shem had known. And it was on one particular evening, as the sky cast a beautiful sunset that Shoda called all the women to come to Sede's chamber. Her time had come. As she lay upon her furs, her breath grew shallow and soft. Shoda drew near, tenderly listening and waiting for her last words. Sede's sons' daughters, their daughters, and their daughters were there. Shoda's young maidens, too, sat at her feet, filling the room in solemn respect. There before them lay the last of the "eight"—the last living person to have known the old world and the last link to the "days of old" and their ancestors.

Sede gathered her strength to speak. She wanted to leave them with the "Promise" she had been given. She looked around the room. All those beautiful faces looking upon her, all loving her. "My daughters, you were all born from the love between Shem and me. You are loved by me, your mother. I leave you with one last word: One of you will carry the promised seed into the next generation. Your seed will continue the lineage for the 'Promised One' to come. This is the very 'seed' promised to Eve, the one that will crush the serpent's head."

She searched their faces, looking for some sign from Yahweh. Her eyes fell upon young Sarai. As she intently searched her face, a light began to shine from her forehead. The symbol of "Tella-la-no-ah" formed in brilliant white. Sede's chest rose and fell in sudden excitement. It was Sarai who had been chosen! She was Yahweh's choice! Sede raised her feeble hand and bid her to come near.

Sarai drew close, tears filling her eyes. "Yes, mother Sede. I am here."

"Sarai, it is you who has been chosen. You will be 'the seed' in *your* generation. You will marry Abram and from your love will come a great people. Yahweh will choose a seed in each of their generations. Our people will rise to see a 'new day'—a day when the 'Promised One' will restore all that was lost to Adam and Eve, and us, their descendants."

Sede motioned for Shoda to bring her bundle. Laying it before her, Sede's hands began to gently shake as she tried to unfold the edges. Sarai patiently and tenderly helped her. Inside the fur were her treasures: the wedding rope, Playtheus' pearl box, her cape from Ba-nea, the carved box Shem had made her, her father's stone, the scroll diary from the ark, and Ne-el's tiny flute. "Open the wooden box, child," she said weakly.

Sarai's trembling hands opened the lid and withdrew the elegant blue fur. Unfolding the edges, she saw Eden's seed. "It's yours, child, to keep and give to the next generation that Yahweh will give you. He will explain its meaning to you as you walk with him. I wish for you to also have the ark scroll and my cloak. The rest of my treasures I wish to give to you, my beloved daughter Shoda." She lovingly smiled at Shoda, who struggled to hold back her tears.

Sede lifted the thin, delicate crown that rested on her gray hair. With her aged hands, she placed it on Sarai's bowed head. "You now are the mother of our people. I go, leaving this blessing with you Sarai." Sede struggled to sit, and Shoda gently helped her lean forward. Resting her forehead against Sarai's, she whispered her blessing: "May Yahweh bless you and keep you, Sarai. May Yahweh's face shine upon you and be gracious to you. May he lift up his countenance upon you and give you peace. Amen and amen." Sede lovingly kissed her cheek and then slowly leaned back against the furs. Smiling sweetly at Sarai one last time, she closed her eyes and softly exhaled her last breath.

Immediately, Sede felt herself drift through mist and time, peace enfolding her like loving arms. As the mist began to clear, she found herself suddenly crouched in tall grass. She somehow knew she was waiting for Shem's signal. She waited but felt somewhat confused. How could she suddenly be here…in the grass? She looked down. She was wearing her skins. Her bow was at her side, and her seed necklace hung at her chest. Her hands were young and smooth. The breeze softly rustled the grass, and she heard the gentle low of the herd nearby. Closing her eyes, she raised her face to the sun; its rays fell soft and warm on her face. Her ears strained to hear the faint call of a hawk from high above.

Then she saw him rise. It was Shem, standing in the soft swaying grass only a stone's throw away! "Come to me…come to me, Sede!"

It was just as her dream of long ago. She stood and stepped forward, filled with wonder. Shem was so young and strong, and she could see his love for her in his eyes. As she clasped his outstretched hands, joy burst within her, and she threw her head back, smiling and laughing for the joy that filled her. "Shem, oh, Shem!"

He lifted her and began to joyfully spin her around and around, happiness beaming from his face. Then she heard something. A little giggle…

Looking through the grass, she saw her. It was Ne-el! As she stepped out of the grass, she ran to her mother's open arms, her pigtails flopping against her leather skins. Tears of joy ran down Sede's face. "Oh, my 'little cricket.' It's you." She could hardly contain the joy rising within her. With her little hands, Ne-el stroked her mother's cheeks, her smile reflecting the love in her heart for the mother she'd been waiting for. It was a moment like no other! It was the moment Sede had longed for, to feel her 'little cricket' in her arms once more.

Standing to her feet, she began to see a multitude of people coming toward her from all directions. Slowly, she turned in a circle to see them all… coming to her. Her heart leapt as she saw her father. His hand was clasped with Lettah's, the mother she never knew. There were Shoda and Japheth, so young and full of life, smiles beaming from their faces. Noah and Ezmere came waving excitedly as they moved through the grass. And oh, there were

Playtheus and Marah, their eyes dancing with joy at the sight of her. Dollo lifted his hand in greeting while he held Zilla's with the other. She could faintly hear Dosta's great belly laugh while Adah and Hattil kept pace with her swift stride. Gruetat and Mersta, with Ne-el and little Adat, all hand in hand, parting through the tall grass. Zara seemed to be skipping as she came with her mother and father, Erud and Tallma. They **all** were coming—coming to their beloved Sede.

She saw a multitude behind them too: family she dearly loved: her sons Elam and Assur and Arphaxad; and her grandson Shelah and his grandson Peleg; along with all their wives. She saw elders from long ago, who had loved her and mentored her. Others, too, whom she had mentored during her lifetime: the Sethite warriors she had trained, who loved her dearly and had defended their family in battle, and the many maidens she had taught and encouraged during their "time of preparation." She had been their unseen standard of love and fidelity. Coming with them too, were the sweet children from the tower of Babel that she and Shem had loved and rescued; Fromos and A-thia; along with the dignified Sethite woman, who stood in line before her at the slave market in Atlantis. This great multitude had known the touch of Sede's loving and gracious heart.

And then at last she saw the Watcher, Plaquanay. He suddenly appeared with two people she instantly knew. They had come too. It was the father and mother of mankind: Adam and Eve. She had wished she had known them, and now…here they were.

As she stood still, watching them come, she heard Him. It was **Yahweh**. He was whispering on the breeze. "Look, Sede, they come to you. Your seeds!" She clasped her seed necklace that rested on her chest. "You've always wondered what my Watcher meant when he said, 'this is Eden's gift: seeds within a seed.' **Your life, Sede, is the seed. And these, your loved ones, are your seeds within your seed!**"

Awe filled her as His words settled in her heart. Now she finally knew the meaning of the Seed of Eden. Just then the hawk flew overhead, his call going over them all. She raised her head and watched as he majestically soared high above. Then she saw it in the far distance. The city of God, the New Jerusalem! The throne of God was on its mountain top-radiant in splendor, brilliant in glory! Even from the great distance she felt it, Yahweh's love, coming to her, embracing her, filling her with joy. Sede was home ... home in the arms of love.

About the Author

Kathleen Nennemann is the author of a new book series: the "Seed of Eden".
While in Bible College, she became fascinated with Biblical history and began
a quest researching ancient writings and manuscripts. From this research
came a desire to inspire readers with the women who lived then. After
receiving her degree in Biblical Studies, she now resides in Western Nebraska
where she continues to write, inspiring Christians to consider their rich,
spiritual heritage: 'From the roots, come the tree'.